DATE DUE

HARBORED SECRETS
BOOK ONE

LIVING LIES

NATALIE WALTERS

Revell

a division of Baker Publishing Group
Grand Rapids, Michigan

© 2019 by Natalie Walters

Published by Revell
a division of Baker Publishing Group
PO Box 6287, Grand Rapids, MI 49516-6287
www.revellbooks.com

Printed in the United States of America

Library of Congress Cataloging-in-Publication Data
Names: Walters, Natalie, 1978– author.
Title: Living lies / Natalie Walters.
Description: Grand Rapids, MI : Revell, [2019] | Series: Harbored secrets ; 1
Identifiers: LCCN 2018045190 | ISBN 9780800735326 (pbk. : alk. paper)
Subjects: | GSAFD: Suspense fiction.
Classification: LCC PS3623.A4487 L58 2019 | DDC 813/.6—dc23
LC record available athttps://lccn.loc.gov/2018045190

ISBN 978-0-8007-3632-3 (casebound)

19 20 21 22 23 24 25   7 6 5 4 3 2 1

To my Gigipa, the greatest storyteller I'll ever know.

To CeCe, you knew this day would come and I wish you were on this side of heaven to celebrate. I miss you, friend.

ONE

JUST LET GO.

The breeze lifted Lane Kent's auburn hair from the back of her neck. Her heels edged closer to the side of the bridge, sending loose rocks and dust spiraling into the Ogeechee River below. The dilapidated structure had long since rusted and was no longer up to code for vehicle use, but the litter of broken bottles thirty feet below meant its condition hadn't scared off bored teenagers. Or Lane.

Her fingers strained against the metal railing behind her as she leaned forward. A leaf rushed along with the current, careening through the water with no control over its destination. Like her.

Twenty-eight and a widow. Lane closed her eyes and thought of Noah. It wasn't fair that she'd stolen his daddy away from him. He deserved better. They both did.

Just let go. Lane fought to regain control over the darkness invading her mind. Noah. She had to live for Noah—even if it was all a lie. Pretending to be alright was part of the deal she had made when she had returned to Walton. But people who were alright didn't stand at the edge of a bridge wondering if relief waited for them among the jagged rocks.

A throat cleared behind her. "Excuse me, is everything okay?"

Lane's heart vaulted inside her chest. Her grip slipped, but strong hands clamped on to her wrists, securing her.

"Easy. You don't want to fall."

Lane's eyes met the deep blue ones of the man steadying her. A mountain bike lay on its side next to him. "Uh, you scared me."

"Did you drop something?"

Lane started to move, but the man's grip tightened. Pulse

pounding, she looked down at his white knuckles and then back up at him. "You can let go."

A muscle in his jaw popped. His eyes searched her face, and Lane swallowed under the scrutiny. She wriggled her wrists free, swung her leg between the railing, and pulled herself through so she was standing next to him. *Think of something, Lane.*

Letting a loose strand of hair fall across her face, Lane pretended to adjust her backpack. "Uh, no—"

"So, you just enjoy death-defying gravity tests?"

Lane's head jerked up. Their eyes met again and though it sounded like he was being humorous, the sentiment wasn't reflected in his gaze. There she saw—what was it? Concern? Fear? Did he think—

A drop of rain hit Lane's cheek. Dark storm clouds had rolled in, blanketing the blue sky in darkness. She waved a hand. "I was just getting ready to leave."

"Are you sure everything's okay?" His voice was deep, masculine. "I didn't mean to scare you."

"You didn't. I mean, you did." She didn't recognize the man and lots of people used the trails around the Ogeechee, but if he recognized her—knew who her father was—and thought she was going to jump . . . "I really need to go."

"Ma'am—"

But Lane didn't wait to hear what the stranger had to say. A crack of thunder echoed in the distance like a warning and Lane headed for the protection of the copse of live oaks guarding one side of the river. It wasn't the way she had come, but she knew the Coastal Highway ran parallel to the river. If she could get to the highway, she could follow it back to where her car was parked and avoid any further questions. Questions she couldn't answer.

Wasn't allowed to answer.

The dense woods grew darker the deeper she went, making the path difficult to see—if she was even on a path. Too dark to tell. Large roots climbed out of the ground and forced her to slow to avoid tripping over them. Humidity thickened the air and Lane's chest squeezed with each breath. As she passed beneath a low branch, a vile odor washed over her. She jolted to a stop.

What is that? The odorous assault made Lane's head swim and her stomach rebel. Was it a dead animal? She didn't want to find out. Forcing herself to breathe through her mouth, Lane searched for a way out of the overgrown brush surrounding her.

Where was she? She pressed forward, guessing the direction of escape. What if she was heading back to the river or deeper into the trees? A noise spooked her and she spun around. Her eyes searched the darkness for the source of the sound. A squirrel? A twig snapped and Lane's gaze swung to the right. Was the man from the bridge following her? *You're being paranoid.*

Rain began to penetrate the canopy of branches overhead and run into rivulets, churning the ground into sticky mud. Lane covered her mouth and nose with both hands and backed up, but something grabbed her foot and pitched her backward onto the ground.

Ouch. She scowled at the tangle of thick roots stretching from the massive tree next to her and adjusted the straps of her backpack, thankful she hadn't landed on it. Trying hard not to breathe in the toxic air, Lane used the tree to steady herself and free her foot but stopped when her hand landed on—a shoe? Lane froze. It was a tennis shoe. Laces untied. Attached to a foot and then a leg and then a body.

"Aghhhh!"

Blank eyes on a bluish-green face stared up at her. Lane scrambled, digging her fingers into the mud to get away from the body. A swarm of black flies buzzed around her head. Angry. Like she had interrupted their morbid feast. Bile choked Lane's ability to scream again.

Run. Move.

Lane clawed at the tree next to her, ignoring the way the bark cut into her palms as she yanked herself up. Finding her footing, she backed away from the lifeless body and ran. Branches slapped at her arms and face as fear chased her into the darkness.

⁂

The scream stopped Charlie Lynch in his tracks even as his pulse jackhammered in his ears. It came from his left. He dropped his bike and surged forward, ignoring the twigs catching on his skin.

That was distress. It didn't take six weeks at the police academy or six years as a Marine MP to recognize it. It was her—the woman from the bridge. Charlie had no problem recalling the features of her face, even as she tried to hide it behind a curtain of auburn hair. Green eyes awash with emotion so deep they revealed the answer to his question that she did not answer—what had brought her to the edge of that bridge?

Sad hazel eyes and a lopsided smile flashed in Charlie's mind. Tate Roberts. How many conversations had he shared with him in Afghanistan? And how many times had Tate stared at death as the only answer until he'd allowed it to swallow him? Was that what he saw in the woman's gaze? Defeat? The kind that stole life? Or was he jumping to conclusions? Charlie ground his molars and raced in the direction he thought he had heard the scream come from. He had to find her. Make sure she was okay.

He wouldn't fail. Not this time.

A movement to his left captured his attention and he instinctively reached for the weapon he no longer carried. Biting back a curse, he forced himself to take a breath. This wasn't a war zone. It was Walton, Georgia, and about as idyllic as a Norman Rockwell painting. And the peaceful charm was exactly why Charlie had chosen the small town to call home. This was not Afghanistan.

Charlie searched the thicket of trees for the source of the movement. Could be an animal. He hadn't even been in Walton a day before he saw his first alligator sunning near the bike trail. He'd avoided that route this time, which led him to the bridge—to her.

From the corner of his eye, a branch swayed, and before he could turn a force slammed into him.

<hr>

"Aghhhh!" Lane struggled to break free from—it was him. The guy from the bridge. "What are you doing? Let go."

"Wait." He looked down at her anxiously. "I heard you scream. What's wrong? Are you alright?"

"I . . . I . . ." *No.* Lane swallowed, but the odor still clung to her—the eyes still staring. "I'm going to be sick."

The man released her arms just in time for her to turn and expel the contents of her stomach.

"Ma'am, what's wrong?" A warm hand covered the skin on her bare shoulder in a gesture he probably thought was comforting but only made her feel worse as she continued to retch. "How can I help?"

"9-1-1," she gasped, wiping at her mouth with the back of her hand. "There's . . . a . . . g-girl."

"A girl? Where? Is she hurt?"

"D-dead." Nothing was left in Lane's stomach, but it didn't stop her body from purging again. She couldn't shake the glassy stare of the girl. Young. Too young.

"A dead girl?" Disbelief colored his words as his hand slipped from her back.

Lane fought through the retching long enough to peek up. The man rocked back on his heels and was scanning the area as his gaze darkened. Where was his bike? How did he get here? Why was he here? Pulse pounding in her ears, Lane took a step back. "Were you following me?"

The man's eyes rounded. His hands flew up in surrender like he knew what she was thinking. "No. I mean, yes, but only to be sure you were okay. I heard you scream. My name's Charlie Lynch. I'm a deputy for Walton—"

"Walton's not that big and I've never seen you before."

"I'm new. Start on Monday." His gaze held hers. Keeping one hand up, he reached into the pocket of his shorts and withdrew a cell phone. "I need to call Sheriff Huggins now and report this."

He knew the sheriff's name. That was reassuring, right? Lane eyed the wet shirt clinging to a physique that, at the very least, proved he was physically fit enough to be a cop.

"Here," the man said as he held the phone out to Lane. "The sheriff wants to talk to you."

"H-hello?"

A second of silence filled the phone. "Lane, is that you?"

The sound of Sheriff Huggins's voice eased Lane's worry almost as quickly as it caused her knees to feel like they were going to buckle. "Y-yes," she answered, her voice cracking.

"I'm on my way, honey." Sheriff Huggins's voice was tight. "You stay with Charlie, but I'm on my way."

Lane couldn't reply because of the lump in her throat. Sheriff Huggins was Ms. Byrdie's husband, and together they were the main reason Lane had had the courage to return to Walton. Lane passed the phone back to the deputy while her mind drifted back to the girl's body. Lifeless blue eyes staring.

A crack of thunder made Lane jump, bringing her back to the present. She wrapped her hands around her waist to stop the tremors that were wracking her body beneath the pelting rain.

"The sheriff is on his way." The deputy glanced up from his phone. "My GPS says the Coastal Highway is just over—hey, are you okay?"

Lane wanted to tell him she was, but as an angry strike of lightning lit up the sky, she could feel her legs begin to shake and all at once his arms were wrapped around her body.

"You're in shock."

"N-no. I'm f-fine," she said, pulling herself out of his hold. "Just wet and cold."

"There'll be blankets in the squad car. Do you think you can walk? I can carry your backpack."

"I've got it," she said through clenched teeth and took a step in the direction he pointed to prove she did.

By the time they reached the side of the Coastal Highway, sirens echoed in the distance and Lane could see flashing red and blue lights barreling toward them. The deputy led her to the sheriff's car but paused. He turned so their eyes met.

"Death is never easy." Rain trailed over the features of his face. Chiseled jaw with a day or two's growth. Deep blue eyes mining, it seemed, for information. "I'm really sorry you had to see that."

Lane swallowed and pushed her gaze over the deputy's shoulder to the squad car that pulled up, followed by two more that parked along the side of the road. "Y-yeah. Me too."

A tall, burly man with a shock of white hair emerged from the first car and rushed over. The deputy stood back as Sheriff Huggins wrapped his big arms around her, swallowing her in a hug. "Honey, are you okay?"

That question. Again. Lane understood why they were asking, but it didn't stop her eyes from cutting to the deputy hanging back. His comment about death not being easy seemed to come from a place of understanding—maybe even experience—but it was the look in his eyes that scared her more. The one that suggested he understood why she was at the bridge today.

"Lane?" The lines deepened around the sheriff's gray eyes.

"Y-yes. I'll be fine." Lane rubbed her arms. "Just need to warm up and dry off."

"Let's get you into the car." Sheriff Huggins walked her to his car with the deputy close on their heels. "There's a blanket in the trunk, Charlie."

Lane sat in the passenger seat of the squad car as Sheriff Huggins turned on the heat. A second later, the deputy returned with a blanket and the two men exchanged a glance before Sheriff Huggins tucked the fabric around her shoulders.

"Honey, can you tell me where you found the body?"

"I-I don't know exactly. I got scared and ran—"

"Sir, I can take you to where I found her"—the deputy tilted his head in Lane's direction—"it's not far from here. Maybe thirty or forty feet in."

"Let me grab Deputies Wilson and Hodges. They'll go with you." Sheriff Huggins gave Lane's knee a quick pat before he jogged over to the other squad cars, leaving Lane alone with the deputy.

"Are you warm enough?"

Lane glanced up at the deputy. His T-shirt and shorts clung, soggy, to his body. He wiped at the wet hair covering his forehead. "Yes. But it looks like you need a blanket too."

"I'm alright."

"Charlie, take them to where you found Lane," Sheriff Huggins said as he walked back with the other two deputies. "Spread out and search the area. Be mindful not to disturb too much."

"Yes, sir." He straightened and took a step toward Sheriff Huggins and the waiting deputies but hesitated. He turned to Lane, his eyes asking her if she would be alright.

Adrenaline or something else stole Lane's voice. She nodded and watched as Charlie led the deputies into the woods. She should go with them. Help them find the girl's body. The thought sent her pulse pounding in her ears and her stomach churning.

"I've got a paramedic coming to check you out—"

"No." Her adamant tone stopped Sheriff Huggins. "I mean, I'm fine."

"You're in shock, honey." Sheriff Huggins's thick, silver eyebrows drew in close. His serious expression said he wouldn't be satisfied until she was checked out. "The ambulance is already on its way."

Lane pulled the blanket tighter around her shoulders and tried to smile, but her face wasn't cooperating. She'd experienced shock before and this wasn't it. And the last thing she needed was someone asking a bunch of questions about her medical history. "Really, I'm okay. Just a bit startled."

Another set of sirens echoed behind her, growing louder with each passing second. The ambulance.

Sheriff Huggins's radio crackled. He gave Lane's hand a squeeze before excusing himself to step away.

". . . female . . . possible suicide . . ."

Suicide? Lane's breath quickened, sending her pulse pounding in her ears. She curled her fingers into tight fists, letting her nails dig into her palms to stop her hands from shaking.

Lane blew out a frustrated breath as the ambulance pulled up and the medics hopped out and hustled over to her. They took her vitals while Sheriff Huggins lingered nearby, watching. It took the medics several minutes to convince the sheriff she was okay.

At that moment a thickset deputy with smooth, dark skin and a muscular build emerged from the tree line, along with a much smaller deputy. Lane recognized them but couldn't remember their names. It didn't matter. Her gaze was drawn to Deputy Charlie Lynch.

Square jaw, straight nose. Even soaking wet he exuded that rugged look all the girls seemed to fall for. He wore the same concerned expression as the sheriff and it reached an ache she held deep inside. One she thought she'd long since tucked away.

Lane rubbed her arms to cut the chill seeping in despite the muggy temperature as the deputies walked toward her.

"Lane, I'm going to have Deputy Lynch take you home."

"Oh, no. I can drive myself, Sheriff." She glanced down at herself, feeling entirely too aware of her muddied clothes and limp hair hanging over her shoulders. "EMTs said I'm good."

Sheriff Huggins looked like he was trying to decide if she was telling him the truth. "You have my number. You call me or Byrdie if you need *anything.*"

"I will." She grabbed her backpack from the back of the ambulance. "I promise."

Lane could read the hesitation in the sheriff's face, but after a minute he let out a breath. "Okay, but I want Deputy Lynch to take one of the squad cars and drive you to your car."

Even without the finality in Sheriff Huggins's tone, Lane wasn't going to argue. She was wet, cold, and not about to walk through the trees to get to her car. "Deal."

Sheriff Huggins pulled her into another one of his hugs and kissed her forehead. "I'll check on you tomorrow."

Blinking back the emotion, Lane gave a tight-lipped smile and followed Deputy Lynch to a squad car.

"Where are you parked?" he asked after she had climbed into the passenger seat.

"The Ogeechee Park lot. West side of the river."

"I know it." He nodded as he started the car. "I usually park down the river, but today I parked farther up. Found the trail that led me to the bridge."

Lane's insides cringed. *Change the subject.* "Storm's passing."

"That's the thing about storms, right? Come in quick and then leave just as quickly."

"Not all storms." Lane watched a drop of rain trickle down the window. "Sometimes they stick around and make life miserable."

"I'm sorry I scared you."

Lane turned in her seat. The deputy's eyes were focused on the road. "What?"

"Back in the woods. I didn't mean to scare you." His hands tightened around the steering wheel. "Or at the bridge."

It was like a weight had settled over the car and silent seconds filled the space between them. Lane unbuckled her seat belt and opened the door as soon as Deputy Lynch pulled into the parking lot. "Thanks for the ride." She picked up her backpack and started to climb out but stopped. She held her bag up. "I take pictures. That's why I was out there today."

Deputy Lynch's jaw flinched before his lips pulled into an easy smile. "Sure."

She closed the door and walked to her car. Did he believe her? If he did, it didn't show. It wasn't a complete lie. Lane didn't go to the bridge very often. Just when she needed to think. To breathe.

From the corner of her eye, she caught the deputy still watching her. *Just smile*, the voice in her head reminded her. *Pretend everything is fine. That you're fine.*

What were the odds that Deputy Charlie Lynch would catch her at a moment of weakness? And what if he told Sheriff Huggins? The sheriff was like a father to her, but what if the truth of why she was out there got back to her actual father?

Lane pressed her lips together, her fists tightening over the straps of her backpack. No. That couldn't happen. Wouldn't. Whatever opinion the new deputy formed about her she'd prove wrong. She had to—she had *everything* to lose.

TWO

CHARLIE TUGGED AT HIS COLLAR, much preferring his soggy T-shirt and shorts from earlier to the stiff polyester uniform. The vinyl raincoat trapped the humidity against his body like Mother Nature had decided Walton, Georgia, was her own personal sweat lodge. How thoughtful of her.

After he had dropped off Ms. Kent at her car, the sheriff had instructed him to swing by the station and change into a uniform. Today would now be his first official day on the job. By the time he returned to the crime scene, the perimeter around the body had already been taped off.

"Lynch." Mud-spattered boots stepped out of the tree line. Deputy Ben Wilson. The man himself could easily have been confused with a tree trunk. "Sheriff needs a second man in charge."

Was it a request? An order? Wilson was the most senior deputy and at least ten years older than Charlie. Wilson's square jaw shifted as his brown eyes squinted into tight lines. He was a man of few words, but being the size of a side-by-side fridge allowed him that privilege.

"Yes, sir." The ingrained response fell from Charlie's lips. Second man in charge? Charlie tugged on his collar a second time. The heat was suffocating. Or was it the pressure?

With a grunt and a nod, Deputy Wilson marched off.

Charlie wiped the sweat from his brow and readjusted his hat.

"Lynch." Sheriff Huggins waved him over.

"Yes, sir." Charlie followed the sheriff back into the wooded thicket, grateful his uncle had stopped calling him by his first name. He saw the way the other deputies eyed him. It was impossible to keep his relationship to their boss a secret, but Charlie didn't want any of them thinking he wasn't on the force by his own merit.

19

He'd proven himself as an MP; he'd do it here too and prove his father wrong in the process.

A putrid smell punched him the face. He swallowed the urge to gag. He'd never get used to the smell of death.

The thought reminded him of Ms. Kent—Lane. When he offered the advice, he noticed that she didn't react. In fact, the only discernible emotion on Lane's face came through her green eyes. Their color was so rich it reminded Charlie of the emeralds mined in the Panjshir Valley of Afghanistan.

"I've got something that can help with the smell if you'd like."

Charlie shook his head. He was the new guy, but this wasn't his first dead body. He tempered his breathing. Studied the grayish pallor of the victim's face. She was young. A raindrop trickled down her cheek.

Deputy Hodges and Deputy Wilson were erecting a tarp over the body to prevent evidence degradation.

"You have the digital camera?"

"Yes, sir." Charlie held up the camera.

"Start at the edge of the perimeter and work your way in."

"Anything specific I should be looking for?"

Sheriff Huggins rubbed the back of his neck. "Until we can confirm how this young lady died, we're looking for anything and everything."

Charlie spent the next hour methodically taking pictures. It all looked the same. Mud. Branches. Leaves. Three hundred photos of sloppy, wet earth. Any chance they'd find evidence had washed away with the rain. When he was certain he had enough photos, he returned to the body.

"Max, this is Deputy Lynch." Sheriff Huggins made the introduction. "He's going to be working the investigation with me. Fill him in."

The Savannah County medical examiner kneeling next to the body gave a subtle nod as he handed off a small plastic baggie to an assistant.

"Female; young—maybe late teens to early twenties; abrasions across both hands and the right side of the face." The ME pointed to the reddish blotch on the girl's face. "Her left leg is also broken. But that's not what has me intrigued."

With the help of his assistant, the ME turned the girl facedown. He lifted her muddy shirt, exposing her back. Varied shades of purple and black bruising hedged one-inch gashes tracking her upper torso.

Charlie took a step back. Images of soldiers torn apart by roadside bombs, limbs shattered or missing, filled his vision. Three tours to the war zone, witnessing destruction and death, and it never got easier.

"You okay?" Sheriff Huggins's voice was low.

"Yes, sir." Charlie remembered the other deputy's first impression of the scene. "It's not suicide then."

The ME looked up at them. "Most people who want to kill themselves don't break their own legs or stab themselves in the back."

Charlie pushed out a breath. Seeing her lying there, exposed—she was so young. Defenseless. Anger churned his gut.

"My initial assessment"—the ME stood, his pants caked in mud—"you have your first murder. Congratulations." The smirk on his face was wiped clean by Sheriff Huggins's disapproving glare.

The ME returned to his work as the sheriff dragged a hand down his face. Even beneath the shadows of the tall oaks, the effects of the caustic comment were visible. Charlie knew his uncle took great pride in protecting his city—a small town with a reputation as one of America's safest cities to raise a family—and someone had violated his mission.

"If the victim's ready, I can begin photographing the entry and exit wounds." It seemed important for Charlie to stay sensitive to the situation. "I'll help bag her body for transport."

"Thank you." Appreciation glistened in the sheriff's eyes. "Deputies Hodges and Wilson will be here to assist."

"I'll take care of it, sir."

Sheriff Huggins took a long look at the young woman lying in the dirt. "Someone somewhere has a daughter who didn't come home."

⁂

The sky was black when Charlie and the other deputies walked into the station damp, muddy, and in his opinion, smelly. Clearing the scene had taken more out of him than he had expected—both physically and mentally.

Bagging a soldier was different from bagging a civilian. In war, the playing field was even, or it was supposed to be. Soldiers train to fight their enemy. But who was Jane Doe's enemy?

"Everything okay?"

Charlie's focus returned to the present. His gaze collided with Deputy Wilson's. "Yes, sir. About to drop the crime scene log on the sheriff's desk before heading home."

"Don't forget, we'll need a statement from Lane Kent. The sooner the better."

"Yes, sir." He didn't think this day could feel any longer, but the idea of talking with her seemed to ease the tension in his shoulders a little. "I can stop by her house and check on her. Set up a time for her to come in."

A curious look passed over the big man's face. "A phone call will accomplish the same result. Number's on the sheet in your hand."

"Yes, sir." Charlie dropped off the report before picking up the phone and dialing Lane Kent's number. He let out a sigh. Why was he feeling nervous? This was his job. Procedure. His breathing became easier with each unanswered ring until at last a machine picked up. A robotic voice asked for his number and message.

"Ms. Kent, uh, this is Charlie—I mean Deputy Charlie Lynch with the Walton County Sheriff's Department." Charlie cringed. Where else would he be calling from? "I'm sorry to bother you this evening, but we need to get a statement from you about today." He could still see the way her body trembled. Cold. Wet. In shock. "I know it's a difficult thing to think about, but it's important we get the information while it's still fresh in your mind. You can come in or I can come to you. Um, or another deputy can come to your home and get your statement tomorrow. Okay, well, please call us at your earliest convenience. Thank you."

Charlie hung up the phone and pinched the bridge of his nose. The call couldn't have gone worse, nor could he have been more unprofessional if he had tried. He grabbed his gym bag, which contained that morning's soggy workout clothes, and let the night shift know he was heading home.

He didn't even have a foot out of his truck and could already hear the yapping coming from inside his house. He unlocked the front door and was met with a spring-loaded terrier, bouncing almost as high as his waist.

"Bane, sit," Charlie commanded.

Like a magnet, the dog's hindquarters found the ground. Bane stared up, waiting for the next command. The small cottage-style home off Ford Avenue was the perfect size for Charlie, but he wasn't so sure it would be able to handle Bane's energy. Thankfully there was a nice-size yard behind the home and a huge park a block over where he could run his dog's energy to a livable level. He hoped.

"Stay." Charlie inched toward a basket near the door, keeping his eye on the terrier. The dog's tail swept the floor like a propeller ready to wind up for takeoff. Charlie cupped a green tennis ball in his hand.

"Stay." Charlie edged to the back door and opened it. A floodlight illuminated the yard. Charlie threw the ball so that it landed in the farthest corner of the fenced yard and looked back at his dog. Bane's entire body shook now, his eyes fixated on Charlie's hand. He knew the drill and what came next but was unwilling to disobey his master even if it meant his body was convulsing. "Go get it, boy!"

Like a rocket, Bane shot past Charlie with speed unnatural for his short legs and bounded through the yard in search of the ball. Charlie ticked off the seconds in his head. When Bane's head popped up with the green ball tucked securely in his jaw, Charlie shook his head.

"Almost forty seconds. You're slacking." The dog dropped the ball at his feet for round two. "It'll have to wait, buddy. You're not the only one with pent-up energy."

Charlie had spent the last several weeks at the academy with his nose in police procedure manuals, and being the new man on the force meant he was going to be pulling the night and weekend shifts for the foreseeable future—especially now.

"Long day?" A familiar southern drawl steered Charlie's attention to the white fence in his backyard. His Aunt Byrdie emerged out of the darkness, stepping through the gate with a covered dish in her hands. Bane yipped, his nails scratching at the laminate flooring as he raced to meet their guest. Aunt Byrdie rolled her eyes. "I still can't believe you kept this dog."

Neither could he, but Charlie grinned when his aunt pulled a dog bone from her pocket and tossed it to Bane. The dog attacked the treat and trotted off a safe distance to enjoy it.

"I brought you dinner." His aunt handed him the plate. "Meatloaf, garlic mashed potatoes, and sautéed green beans."

Charlie peeked beneath the foil and an aroma met his nose, sending his stomach roaring. He was famished. "It smells delicious. Thank you."

"I figured you'd appreciate a home-cooked meal after the day you've had." His aunt looked up at him and gave a wistful smile. "It's pretty convenient that you moved in behind the Way Station Café."

"Convenience had nothing to do with it." Charlie lifted the plate of food. "Strategic reconnaissance."

His aunt smiled again, and this time it stretched to her eyes. "Well, whatever it is, I'm glad you're here, and I hope you plan on staying a while."

Charlie started to answer, but his cell phone rang.

"I won't keep you." His aunt waved her hands in the air and turned to leave before pausing. "When you finish your dinner, you can stop by and grab a bowl of peach cobbler."

"Yes, ma'am." Charlie picked up his cell phone and shook his head. His mom. It'd only been, what—an hour since her last call? He'd let them all roll over to voicemail, but if he didn't answer soon she would probably be calling the sheriff.

"Hey, Mom." Bane, finished with his treat, followed Charlie inside the house and immediately found his green ball and nosed it toward Charlie's foot. Charlie kicked it and watched the dog slip across the wood floor as he chased it under a table.

"Finally. I was about to call your uncle."

Charlie snorted. "I was working."

"All day? It's almost ten o'clock. I was hoping you were out . . . with friends."

His mother did nothing to hide the concern in her tone. Bane found the ball and dropped it. He waited for Charlie to continue the game. He decided it probably wasn't best to inform her that his only friend at the moment was a stray dog. Charlie kicked the ball down the hallway this time.

"Mom, I just moved here." Charlie looked at the boxes stacked around him. The small kitchen opened up to a decent-size living room and the mismatched furniture revealed his bachelor status. "I'll find time to make friends."

"And settle down? That's why you moved there, right? To settle down?"

Charlie ran his fingers through his hair. It felt different having some length to it. His days of high and tights were over, along with his military career. But he was good with that decision. It was the right decision.

Even if his father didn't agree.

"Are you happy, Charlie?"

He recognized the worry in her voice. He'd seen it in her eyes every time he deployed. And again the night he stormed off after he told his father he was leaving the Marines. "I got your card in the mail. It was the first piece of mail at my new address."

"I know it's early, and you don't need any money, but you're impossible to buy for. You can use it to buy food or curtains. You do have curtains, right?"

"Blinds."

"And you're eating?"

Charlie looked at the dinner his aunt had brought over. "Yes, Mom. I'm eating."

"I'm just making sure. I don't need my brother-in-law finding your skeletal remains in the middle of the swamp."

"You remember you grew up here with Aunt Byrdie, right?"

"I know. But I also know there's not much to do in Walton. Your aunt and I would drive out to Tybee Island every chance we got. Have you been there yet?"

"Not yet."

"Oh, honey, your dad just got home. Hold on, I'll get him—"

"It's okay, Mom. It's late and I need to take the dog out." Charlie frowned. Where was his furry excuse?

"Are you sure? He'd probably like to talk to you."

Yeah, and tell me what a mistake it was for me to leave the Marines or what a disappointment I am to his legacy. No, thanks. "I'll talk to him later."

"On your birthday, then."

"Sure." Charlie's birthday was still a couple of weeks away. Should be enough time to prepare for another lecture on duty and obligation. A speech Charlie didn't feel his father was qualified to give. "Tell him I said hello, and thanks for the card."

"I love you, Charlie."

"Love you too, Mom."

Ending the call, Charlie rubbed the back of his neck. Frustration twisted his insides, diminishing his appetite. Charlie scooped Bane's kibble into his bowl and walked down the hall and into a pile of white fluff. His voice came out in a low growl. "Bane."

Movement came from beneath a layer of shredded fabric and pillowy cotton.

"Bane."

His dog's head popped through the mess, guilt written all over his panting face. Was the dog smiling at him?

"What did you do?" Charlie stared at the remains of the pillow as frustration at his dog's antics knotted the muscles in his shoulders. "I thought you liked it here. Do you want to go back to scavenging food from trash cans? Don't I feed you well?"

The dog dropped his head to his paws and rolled over.

"You really think you deserve a belly rub after this mess?"

The dog barked.

"Fine." Charlie reached down and gave Bane a quick rub. "You're lucky you're the only friend I've got. Otherwise, I'd give you the boot. And not to chew."

THREE

JUST KEEP SMILING. Lane Kent pressed her lips into what she hoped looked like a smile more than it did the grimace she was holding back. The two older women standing at the counter in front of her stared at her expectantly.

"Well?" Mrs. Babcock asked. "What do you think?"

What had they been talking about? Lane had stopped listening—truthfully hadn't really been listening in the first place. Her thoughts were back in the woods with the body.

"It's too much. Too soon. Right?" Mrs. Kingsley slipped in front of her friend, pressing her arthritic hands onto the Formica. "I don't blame you, dear. Who wants to be the one piece of caramel popcorn dropped into a bed of ants? Now, my grandson, Henry—"

"Gladys, what in the world does that even mean?" Mrs. Babcock elbowed her friend. "Lane should have options. Besides, *my* grandson—"

"Ladies." Ms. Byrdie emerged from the kitchen with a towel over her shoulder and two foam takeout containers. "You've been such a great help this evening, but I think Lane and I can finish up the rest of the cleaning. I've packed up some peach cobbler for y'all to take home to your husbands."

Whew. Lane cast an appreciative glance in Ms. Byrdie's direction. Shielded—was that even what it was?—once again by the same woman who'd protected her countless times in high school. She might have been the school librarian, but she acted more like a guardian.

"Are you sure?" Mrs. Babcock looked around. "We could wipe down the tables when everyone leaves."

"We don't mind staying to help," Mrs. Kingsley added.

"You ladies have been incredibly helpful. Right, Lane?"

It took a subtle bump to Lane's side by Ms. Byrdie to jar the words from Lane's mouth. "Yes. You ladies have made tonight a real success. Thank you."

Mrs. Kingsley and Mrs. Babcock exchanged proud smiles before they began to untie their aprons. Lane scanned the remaining few still filling the seats of her café. On Friday nights, the Way Station Café closed early to regular customers, but it didn't mean the café would be empty. Tonight the seats had been filled with Walton residents who needed a warm meal. Ms. Byrdie started the Friday Night Club ten years ago when she retired from the high school. Bored and still feeling like she had something to contribute, she offered to come in and make home-cooked meals free of compensation to serve the community.

"Lane, dear."

Fighting hard not to cringe, Lane turned to find Mrs. Babcock and Mrs. Kingsley smiling at her. "Yes, ma'am?"

Mrs. Kingsley's eyes brightened a second before her face took on a serious expression. "Marge and I are worried we might have upset you."

"You're young, darlin'," Mrs. Babcock added. "No reason a pretty girl like yourself needs to be lonely."

"Hush, Marge," Mrs. Kingsley hissed. "We are sorry for your loss, dear."

Where was Ms. Byrdie now? *Just keep smiling*, Lane reminded herself. But she couldn't. The best she could muster was a tight-lipped nod.

"It won't be long until you're ready again."

Mrs. Babcock patted Lane's arm encouragingly, but numbness had set in, blocking Lane's senses to the point that she could no longer hear the words still being spoken to her. *Pretend.* Lane nodded and pushed the words out of her mouth. "Yes, ma'am."

The two women each gave a sympathetic nod before making

their way toward the exit. Mrs. Kingsley looked over her shoulder and gave a tiny wave. *Pretend*. Lane waved as the two women stepped out of the café. When the door closed behind them, a whoosh of breath escaped her rattling chest. *Ready again?* Was it really so simple to recover from having one's heart ripped from their chest? Their lives, future, hope—demolished in the blink of an eye?

No. Life wasn't that simple. Or easy. But all Lane could do was go on pretending like it was.

It was the only way she knew how to survive.

"The peach cobbler and ice cream were a great idea, Lane." Ms. Byrdie returned with the creamer refilled and set it on the counter. She paused. "Honey, don't you pay any mind to those old biddies. Their hearts are in the right place even if their good sense hasn't caught up."

"It's okay."

Ms. Byrdie wrapped an arm around Lane's waist and leaned in. "No, it's not."

Lane swallowed against the lump forming in her throat. No, it wasn't and she didn't need to lie to Ms. Byrdie. The woman always seemed to know or see the truth anyway. Inhaling deeply and then letting it go, Lane lifted her head and met Ms. Byrdie's gaze.

"Apparently, there's going to be a singles' mixer an hour before the seafood festival. Mrs. Babcock wanted to know if she could add me to the list."

"Honey, Mrs. Babcock has been trying to marry off her grandson since he was in diapers." Ms. Byrdie laughed, sending soft tufts of white hair dancing across her brow. "I think Dane actually enjoys teasing his grandmother by purposely staying single."

Lane rubbed her thumb over her wedding band and glanced at the photo propped against the chalkboard menu. A happy family—a little boy, a husband, and a wife—smiled at her. They looked . . . *perfect*.

"It's been a long day." Ms. Byrdie's violet eyes held compassion.

"Why don't you go on upstairs? I'll finish up down here and close up."

Ms. Byrdie's worried glances hadn't stopped coming in Lane's direction since she had returned from the river, soaked and emotionally numb. Lane guessed the sheriff had spoken with his wife before her arrival. Ms. Byrdie didn't ask a single question as she ushered Lane upstairs and into a hot shower, which was good because even now Lane couldn't shake the image of the dead girl from her mind and the thought of retelling the experience made her sick. *Suicide*. It was too close to home. Literally and figuratively.

"I'm fine." Lane picked up two bowls of cobbler and ice cream. "It helps to stay busy."

Lane ignored the knowing look on Ms. Byrdie's face as she walked toward a small table tucked into the corner of the Way Station Café. A pair of craggy old men with long whiskers sat there with anticipation on their faces and spoons at the ready in their hands.

"Peach cobbler a la mode." Clarence wore a tattered veterans cap, while Wilbur wore his military service tattooed all over his arms. Lane handed them their desserts. "You boys doing alright?"

"Even better now." Clarence winked before digging into his dish.

"How was your visit with your grandkids?" Lane asked Wilbur.

"Taught 'em how to fish. The oldest, Eric, he caught a big one." Wilbur held his hands apart about seven inches. "First time. He was so proud."

From the glow on Wilbur's weathered face, Lane could see the pride that reached across generations. Clarence and Wilbur began talking fish and Lane excused herself to a third man chatting up Ms. Byrdie at the counter.

"And what about you, Ducky?" Not his given name but a title earned by the number of fowl casualties he amassed with his boat, or so the rumors said. "Can I get you a refill on the coffee? More peach cobbler?"

"Nah." Ducky's shoulders hunched at an angle and his right eye drifted. "I've had three bowls already. I'm just sitting here taking in the view."

Lane frowned and then followed Ducky's gaze over to Ms. Byrdie, who was putting the rest of the cobbler into a plastic storage container. "Ya know, if the sheriff catches you eyeing his wife, you'll find yourself on the wrong side of the law."

"But the right side of love." He smiled, exposing a toothless mouth before erupting into a fit of laughter, which sounded more like he was choking.

For a moment Lane was able to forget the morbid events of the day. She glanced around the room. Once upon a time the old home was built as a kindergarten, some said at the direction of Henry Ford. The first floor was spacious for desks and a sizable kitchen to feed the children. Upstairs, an apartment was kept for the teacher and was where Lane and Noah called home. But most days, the Way Station Café was Lane's excuse to ignore reality.

Lane tossed a glance out the tall windows of the Georgian home turned café. "Have you seen Miguel?"

Ms. Byrdie's gaze swept the room. "Actually, I haven't."

"He's never missed Friday Night Club." Lane looked at her watch. "We'll be closing soon."

"I wouldn't worry about it, dear." Ms. Byrdie grabbed a towel and wiped the counter. "I think the only reason he comes in is to see you."

"It's 'cuz she's pretty," Ducky barked.

"Partly, yes." Ms. Byrdie winked at Lane. "But I think it's because of the way you treat him."

Lane balked. "I think it's for your home cooking."

"Honey, I've been running the FNC for several years, and if Miguel stopped by it was by chance. But that first night he came by and you were here—" Ms. Byrdie paused. There was a sheen in her eyes.

"Miguel's never talked to a soul," Wilbur said, holding his empty bowl. "Not even me and we were in basic together."

"Nam was hard." Ducky lifted his cup of coffee to Wilbur and Clarence. The three men shared the same solemn expression.

"I better take the trash out to the dumpster," Lane said over the tightness in her throat.

It was devastating to think about how many American veterans were like Miguel. They came home from a war, forever changed. Even now, she had heard the reports of soldiers returning from overseas and the effects of what they witnessed chasing them until they could take it no more. Lane bit down on her lip. What was her excuse?

"Lane." Ms. Byrdie caught her as she was about to walk out. "You have a good heart, sweetie. Compassionate and kind. One of these days I hope you can see how much you affect those around you—and not in the way you believe—but in the way I do. The way God does."

Lane dropped her gaze to the trash bag. "I'll just take this out now." She slipped out the back door, avoiding Ms. Byrdie's gaze and the pressure of having to respond.

What could she say? There was no response worthy of the woman who continually offered little pieces of hope that Lane carried through the roughest years of her life—or so she thought.

"Are you still open?"

"Wha—" Lane spun, shock stealing her breath at the sight of the man standing in the shadows.

"Sorry." He stepped into the light. He had tan skin and black hair pinned against his head with enough oil that Paula Deen would be jealous. He rolled a toothpick between his teeth and smiled at Lane. "I didn't mean to scare you."

Something in his smile belied the sincerity of his words. "I'm sorry, but we're closed for the night."

"That's too bad." His lip curled and he removed the toothpick. Lane couldn't help but notice the tattoos on his fingers. He took another step toward her. "I'm not from around here. Was hoping to get a home-cooked meal before I hit the road."

His dark eyes held on to her gaze far longer than she felt was comfortable and a chill skated down her spine. "Besides fast food, I'm afraid most of the home-cooked places in Walton have shut down for the night."

A sharp bark echoed in the darkness as a little white dog bounded through the bushes at the back of her property. The dog raced toward Lane, sending the strange man stepping back.

"Bane!" A deep baritone voice called out.

The little dog sniffed the trash bag at Lane's feet before sitting. He tilted his head like he was waiting for scraps. Lane turned in the direction of feet pounding the pavement and her heart stalled.

"Bane! I'm sorry. He just took off—Ms. Kent?"

Halting to a stop next to her was the tall, handsome deputy who had found her at the bridge. Wait—handsome? Where had that come from? Well, he *was* handsome, but where had he come from? She bent to pet the dog between his ears. "Yours?"

"Yeah, sorry." The deputy bent over and picked up the dog. "He's not trained very well."

Lane rose and noticed that the man with the toothpick was gone. She glanced around. Weird. No, creepy. Definitely creepy. Or maybe it was just odd and she was putting a creepy spin on it because of what had happened earlier?

"Everything okay?"

The question drew Lane's eyes up to his. The deputy's puzzled expression triggered something inside of her. "Yes . . . it's just— never mind." *Way to make the deputy believe you're normal.* "It's nothing."

"Need help?"

"I got it." Lane hurled the bag into the dumpster before wiping her hands together. "Thanks, though."

"So, you work here?"

Lane looked up at the home turned business. "Actually, I own it."

A strange look crossed the deputy's face. "Interesting."

Interesting? Lane shrugged. "Maybe stop by sometime and grab a bite. Ms. Byrdie is the cook/baker extraordinaire, and you won't find a better meal in all of Walton."

"I believe that." His lip tugged up at the corner and sent Lane's pulse thrumming.

"Lane, honey, everything okay?" Ms. Byrdie's voice called from the back porch.

"Yes, ma'am."

"Evening, Aunt Byrdie."

Lane's stomach somersaulted. "Wait. Did you just call her *Aunt* Byrdie?"

The deputy's shoulders raised a fraction. "Surprise?"

\\\\\\\\\\\\\\\\\\\\\\

"Well, now that you've met your neighbor, don't just stand there. Come on in and get the last piece of cobbler before it's too late." Aunt Byrdie spun around and let the screen door slam shut behind her.

Charlie waited, trying to discern the surprise—no, shock—covering Ms. Kent's face. If she didn't know—

"That means Sheriff Huggins is your—"

"Uncle," Charlie finished her thought as Bane squirmed in his grip. He clipped the leash on the dog and set him down. "Aunt Byrdie is my mother's sister."

Ms. Kent's face paled. Why?

"This might be a wild guess, but from your expression I'm guessing Aunt B didn't mention anything about me?" Charlie couldn't deny the sting of that thought. He'd asked his aunt and uncle to keep his moving to Walton quiet to avoid any rumors of nepotism—at least until he had a chance to prove his value to the force.

"Actually, she did mention her nephew, but I was expecting"—her brows pinched—"well, I don't know what I was expecting. And you're my neighbor?"

Natalie Walters

"Yes, ma'am." Charlie tilted his head toward a row of bushes with large white flowers. "Just on the other side of that picket fence."

The screen door swung open and his aunt appeared. "I can't fight these boys off forever, y'all."

"She's not lying either," Lane added.

Charlie grinned and followed Ms. Kent up the steps of the two-story house with the wraparound porch.

"Ms. Kent, is it okay if I tie him up out here?"

"Yeah, sure, but please call me Lane. We're, uh . . . neighbors after all. I think Ms. Byr—I mean your aunt keeps some doggie treats around for some of the customers."

"The last thing this little tyrant needs is a reward for his mischief." Charlie tied Bane's leash to the railing and gave the dog a warning look to behave before stepping through the back door of the Way Station Café.

The sweet aroma of cinnamon and freshly brewed coffee made his mouth water. Hearty laughter echoed against the pine-paneled walls of the large room with an eclectic collection of round and square tables. The room was mostly empty except for a group of men huddled near the counter where his aunt stood.

At Charlie's entrance, the room went silent.

Lane looked over her shoulder and then back at the remaining customers. "Have y'all met Ms. Byrdie's nephew?"

A tall man with a bristly beard of gray smirked. "Haven't had the pleasure, but thanks to the Rubies I've *heard* all about you."

"The Duke, huh?" The other man neared Charlie so close their toes almost touched. "Esther needs to get her eyes checked. Wayne's taller. More meat to his bones."

Rubies? Duke? Charlie grew hot under the collar and he was wearing a T-shirt. What were these guys talking about? He looked to his aunt for clarification, but she busied herself filling a bowl with cobbler.

"If I had a wife, I'd probably hear all about you too," the third

37

man perched on the stool chimed in. "And I wouldn't like ya neither."

Charlie swallowed and sidestepped the man still sizing him up. He might've been half a century older than Charlie, but there was enough muscle tone in the man's arms to demonstrate he wasn't enjoying the passive life of retirement just yet. "Um, it's nice to meet you."

"Wilbur, Clarence, and the ornery one on the stool is Ducky." Lane patted the back of the one nearest Charlie—Wilbur? "And they were just saying good night."

Aunt B set a bowl of cobbler on the counter. "Charlie's here to keep you fellas in line."

Charlie's eyes grew round. "What? No—"

"Uh-oh." The one called Ducky snorted and gave a gummy smile.

What was his aunt doing? Charlie didn't want any trouble—though he did have age to his advantage, and he was pretty certain he could outrun Wilbur and Clarence. But Ducky, he looked scrappy. From the corner of his eye, he saw Lane with her arms folded, amusement lighting her eyes.

"Harrumph." Wilbur scratched his beard. "Guess the Rubies are right."

Clarence sidled up to his friend and squinted in Charlie's direction. "It's gotta be the eyes."

"No, I think it's the baby beard he's trying to grow." Wilbur nodded. "Don't girls like that Grizzly Adams look?"

"He ain't no Grizz—"

"Okay, boys, that's enough hazing for now." Aunt B giggled and put a hand on Ducky's arm. "Let my nephew eat his cobbler while it's warm."

"Until next time." Wilbur held out his hand.

Charlie shook it, and then Clarence's. He still had no idea what was happening. *Hazing?*

A round of goodbyes sent the three men out the door, with

Ducky giving Charlie one final withering look before Lane locked the door behind them.

"What was *that*?" Charlie exhaled. "The Rubies? Duke?"

"Don't forget Grizzly Adams," Lane added.

Was she smirking?

"Would you like some coffee?" Aunt B asked. "Or milk?"

"Milk, please." Charlie slid onto the vacated stool in front of his aunt and picked up a spoon. "Can someone please explain what just happened."

"I'll get it," Lane offered, reaching for a glass. Her blouse skimmed the waistline of her jeans just enough so that some skin peeked—

"The *Duke*"—Charlie's aunt stepped in front of him, cutting off his view, while heat filled his face at the sight of her inquisitive expression—"is John Wayne. The Rubies are a group of seniors, women, at the church. And Grizzly Adams—"

"I know who Grizzly Adams is." Charlie ate a bite of the cobbler—it was delicious. And so was the second and the third.

"Still want milk with your"—Lane leaned across the counter and peeked into Charlie's bowl, bringing with her a sweet, soapy fragrance—"last bite?"

He smiled. "Please."

Lane pulled back and offered him the glass of milk, which he finished in one gulp.

"You *are* eating, right?" Aunt B raised her eyebrows. "I told your mom you were, but the way you scarfed that cobbler—"

"I'm eating. I finished that meatloaf, which was delicious by the way." Charlie leaned back. "But I limit my intake of butter and sugar."

"There's peaches in there too." Aunt B swatted a hand at him. She let out a sigh and leaned against the counter. "It's good to have you here, Charlie."

"Um, I'm gonna go start the dough for tomorrow." Lane hitched her thumb in the direction of the kitchen.

"Oh, no, dear." Aunt B moved toward the kitchen. "I need to do it because I, um"—her gaze crossed to Charlie and then back to Lane—"I have this special thing I saw on TV that I want to try."

Lane frowned and whispered something to his aunt, who then whispered something back. They did know he was sitting right there, right? A second later, Lane's shoulders drooped and his aunt marched into the kitchen—triumphant.

"More milk?" Lane picked up his glass and the empty bowl.

"I'm okay, thank you." Charlie studied her as she placed the dirty dishes in a plastic bin when his eyes caught a glimpse of the gold ring she wore on the third finger of her left hand. Married. How had he missed that detail earlier? The cobbler felt heavy in his stomach. "It's late. I should probably go."

"Okay." When Lane turned, he saw the photo on the counter. A family of three—Lane, a man, and a little boy who was the perfect combination of the smiling faces holding him. Lane glanced back at the photo and then up to him. "I, um, got your message from earlier. About the statement."

Charlie straightened. He moved here to prove himself and he had a job to do. Lane was reminding him of that. "Right. Yes, ma'am. About the events from today."

Lane flinched. "Lane, please."

"I know it must be difficult to think about, but we really need the facts to be fresh in your mind. Is it okay if I stop by tomorrow?"

"Um, yeah, sure." Lane bit her bottom lip. "I do have an event tomorrow afternoon, but you can stop by in the morning."

"Tomorrow then." Charlie stood. "I'll just tell my aunt good night."

"Right."

"Have a good night, Mrs. Kent."

FOUR

CHARLIE TAPPED THE MICROPHONE and listened as a thud broke the hushed air outside the sheriff's station. He stepped back and gave a nod to Sheriff Huggins. "It's ready."

"Yesterday afternoon a body was discovered near the Ogeechee River—"

"Have you identified the body?" a nice-looking reporter with long blonde hair cut in. Her gaze was sharp and focused on Sheriff Huggins.

"That's what we're hoping the citizens of Walton can help us with." Sheriff Huggins gripped the podium with both hands. Alone, his presence demanded attention, but coupled with the dreadful truth he was sharing, there was little chance anyone would turn away. "Right now, we're looking for help in identifying the victim—"

"Has this been declared a homicide investigation?" The question came from an older man in a white linen suit reminiscent of something he imagined Mark Twain would wear. An affiliate lanyard for the *Walton Gazette* hung around his neck.

"We're still investigating initial reports from the medical examiner, but it appears we're dealing with a homicide," Sheriff Huggins confirmed, heaviness in his tone.

"Do you have any suspects or does the killer still remain at large?" This question came from a beefy man in a mustard-yellow sport coat that should've disappeared with disco decades ago.

"A killer?" An older woman gasped, clutching her hands to her chest. A wave of murmuring rippled through the crowd.

Last night the deputies waited for someone to call in a missing persons report, but almost twenty hours later the body was still a

Jane Doe. Sheriff Huggins hoped a small press conference would give them a lead, but it only seemed to be stirring up questions they couldn't answer.

Charlie shifted under the unpleasant morning humidity and the expressions of those standing in front of him. They were expressing more than shock—it was almost disbelief that something like this could happen in their town. Even the church bells ringing in the distance seemed to be crying foul.

That's the way it is in small towns, isn't it? Everyone knows everyone or at least has heard of someone. People greet you on the street, offer you directions freely, and if you were inclined to sit a few minutes, they'd share some of the town gossip. Was that why they were here? Or maybe it was the harsh reality that in a tight-knit community like Walton, the young girl left to die in the muddy marsh could've been their daughter, sister, or friend.

Was that what stole the color from Lane Kent's soft features? Charlie's nerves buzzed at the notion he'd be getting those answers from her later today. He ground his molars. He'd do good to remember the woman—the witness—was married.

Married. The word—the thought—had chased Charlie out of the Way Station Café last night but lingered at the back of his mind into the early morning hours. If Lane was married, then where was her husband? Would he know that his young, beautiful wife stood at the brink of despair . . . no. Charlie wrestled the thoughts out of his mind. He had no right to let those kinds of questions consume his thoughts. Assumptions. That's what they were. He didn't know anything about *Mrs.* Lane Kent or the man she was married to. And no matter what he thought he recognized in her eyes, his attention needed to be on the investigation.

Charlie scanned the crowd. It didn't take a criminal mind to wonder if the killer was among them. His eyes landed on one of the men he had met at the Way Station Café the night before. Wilbur. His arm was wrapped around the shoulder of a silver-haired woman he tucked protectively into his side. The simple gesture opened up something inside Charlie's chest.

"Can you tell us who discovered the body?"

The reporter's question brought Charlie's attention back to his job. Where it should be. Expectant eyes waited for an answer.

"That information will not be released." Sheriff Huggins tucked his thumbs into his gun belt and rocked back on his heels. The extra skin around his jaw flexed in frustration. "Folks, we're going to make this investigation as transparent as possible, but remember that tragedies like this can rip apart communities. Please respect the process, and as soon as we have new information we'll let you know."

Charlie fell in step next to Sheriff Huggins. The reporters' shouts for more answers landed on deaf ears as the two men walked into the station.

The distress outside permeated the brick building. The silence of the station was somber and reflected the devastation each person was facing over the news. They had a body. Jane Doe. And from first appearances, her death appeared to be a homicide. Her gruesome wounds told the painful story of her last minutes on earth. If the reactions of Charlie's peers were any indication of how the town would react, he knew this murder had the power to change Walton forever.

"We will handle this case professionally and expediently." Sheriff Huggins paused and turned to address the grim atmosphere in his station. "Deputy Lynch and Deputy Frost will be working on this case directly, but I expect each of you to work diligently in light of the long road ahead of us."

Charlie straightened as he stole a glance around the room. If anyone disapproved of his being assigned to the case, the faces of those in the room didn't show it. Even Deputy Wilson gave a chin tilt—was it approval?

"For those unaware, Deputy Lynch is a former Marine MP. He brings a wealth of information and, more importantly, distance.

43

An asset I'm sure y'all will find necessary." Sheriff Huggins's gray eyes took on a steely gaze as he looked each person in the eyes. His features hardened. The lines set deeper. His tone became more assertive. "What happened to that little girl"—he cleared his throat—"it's personal. That truth is going to send a shock wave through our community."

It had been thirty years since Walton had a murder. How would the town react to the death of one of their children? What kind of person was the young woman found in the mud? The town's sweetheart or a rabble-rouser? Did it matter? No one deserved to die the way she had.

Sheriff Huggins finished giving instructions to the deputies and requested that those able to work overtime sign up with Deputy Hodges. The only sound in the room was the deputies returning to their work. Chair legs scraping against the oak floors, the shuffling of papers—normal sounds no longer reflecting normalcy.

"Sir?" Deputy Benningfield, an older lady with short salt-and-pepper hair who Charlie recognized as the one who had helped him with his paperwork, tapped Sheriff Huggins on the shoulder. Her expression was transparent. "We just got a call about a missing girl."

"Who?"

"Trevor and Amanda Donovan." The deputy tucked her chin. "Their daughter, Sydney."

⁂

A few hours later, Charlie massaged his temples as he looked over his notes one final time to make sure he hadn't missed a single detail from his and Sheriff Huggins's conversation with the Donovans. Right now, the sheriff was escorting the distraught parents to the Savannah County Morgue to identify the body of Jane Doe.

Charlie's gut clenched. As a Marine, he knew when to trust his intuition and right now it told him Jane Doe would soon have a name. Sydney Donovan. He stared at a picture of a young girl with fiery red hair and bright blue eyes. Seventeen. Ambitious. Bright. And also, according to her parents, was supposed to return home today from a sleepover with her best friend—Charlie checked the list of names he had collected—Jolene Carson. However, according to a neighbor, Jolene Carson and her mother had left town early this morning for a college tour up in South Carolina and so far hadn't answered any of Charlie's calls.

The phone on his desk rang. "Deputy Lynch."

"Lynch, it's Sheriff Huggins. Have you been by to get that statement from Lane Kent?"

"Not yet, sir." Charlie worked to keep his tone neutral. He didn't care for the way hearing her name sent a surge of adrenaline coursing through his veins—the same way it had when he found out she lived and worked in the café behind his home. *She's married.* Charlie gritted his teeth. Why did he have to keep reminding himself? "I'm meeting her today."

"Make sure you ask about her camera. She usually takes it with her when she hikes. Get a copy of the pictures. Maybe she caught something on them." The sheriff sounded rattled. Why wouldn't he be? He held himself as Walton's guardian. Did he believe this murder was *his* failure? "Oh, and find out if she saw anything or anyone out there."

"Yes, sir," he said, ignoring the uptick in his pulse. Isn't that what she had told him she was doing? Taking pictures? But Lane wasn't holding her camera when he saw her on the bridge. She was barely holding on to the railing. Charlie's fears had gone into overdrive when he had approached her, afraid he'd scare her and she'd let go. The thought unsettled him almost as much as finding out what had really sent Lane to the ledge of the bridge yesterday.

And what would've happened if he hadn't found her?

"Charlie." Sheriff Huggins's voice drew Charlie back to their conversation. "Son, I don't know the reasons you left the Marines, but you'll tell me if you . . . are having issues?"

"I can take a statement, sir." Charlie shifted in his seat, his ears burning. Was this his boss talking or his uncle? The weighted concern felt foreign and it scared him. Did the sheriff have doubts about his ability? Or the choice Charlie had made to leave the Marines and move to Walton? His own father certainly had doubts about his decision. "I've handled criminal investigations, including a couple of murder cases, but if you'd feel more comfortable with Deputy Wilson taking the case, I have no problem stepping aside."

"That's not what I want. I need someone who can handle the uncertainty. I believe you're that person, but you need to be honest with me." Sheriff Huggins spoke with the authority of a military general prepared for battle. "I don't want any mistakes."

"You have my word, sir. No mistakes." A foreboding feeling grew in the pit of Charlie's stomach even as the promise left his lips. He had let his father down. And Tate. Leaving the Marines was supposed to be a decision that brought him peace, but what if his dad was right? He couldn't let his uncle down, or the citizens of Walton. The pretty face of one in particular came to mind. No. Charlie would do whatever it took to prove he was not the man his father believed him to be—there would be no mistakes.

"Maybe my sister should be the one running for political office." Lane blew her bangs off her forehead, maneuvering another rectangular box into a corner. "If I knew how much space these things were going to take up, I'd never have agreed to hold it all."

"Meagan does have a way of getting what she wants." Ms. Byrdie winked. "I can make some room in the pantry closet. We could move some of the smaller ones into there."

"That's okay." Lane held an oblong box and studied her stack, finding a small space to stick it. "Meagan's supposed to come by so we can go through and catalog the items for the auction."

"Speaking of which, if you and Noah don't get cleaned up now, you'll be late." Ms. Byrdie used the hem of her apron to wipe flour dust from Noah's face. He giggled. "I'll finish cleaning down here and lock up."

Today, Lane's father, Judge Raymond Sullivan, and his family would be dedicating the new community center to the city of Walton and it was imperative, her father said, that the *whole* family be there. Exposure was everything during election season. *The right exposure equals votes. The wrong exposure loses them.* Lane had heard her father's mantra her entire life. And nothing won more votes than a strong family. Too bad they were *nothing* like a strong family.

That last thought drew Deputy Charlie Lynch's face to mind. "Why didn't you tell me about your nephew?"

Ms. Byrdie stopped wiping Noah's chin. "I did, honey. A couple of times, actually."

"No, I mean you *told* me that your nephew was coming, but you didn't *tell* me about him." Lane picked at the corner of a shipping label with her thumbnail. "Not, like, details."

"What, that he was handsome?"

"I didn't say that." Lane's gaze swung up to Ms. Byrdie's. "He's older than I expected. Surprised me."

"Charlie looks like my daddy. Tall, strong jawline, and the kind of eyes that seem to see right through you."

A zing zipped through Lane. She knew exactly what Ms. Byrdie was referring to because she'd seen it firsthand yesterday at the bridge. "Come on, Noah, let's get ready."

A pout found its way to Noah's little lips. "But I want to mash the rest of the nannas."

"You don't want to poke the Bear, do you?"

Noah's eyes grew wide as he swung his head back and forth emphatically, even as a grin tugged at his chubby cheeks. "No way."

"Good. Me neither." And that was the truth, though it wasn't for the same reasons as her son. After another restless night, the last thing Lane wanted to do was put on a plastic smile in front of the town, but if they were late she'd get a lecture about timeliness.

47

Who was she kidding? There would probably be a lecture no matter what. Lane hung up her apron before she bent down and planted a kiss on Noah's cheek. "Let's go get dressed."

Twenty minutes later, Lane gave up on trying to do anything with her mess of hair and Noah was MIA. Carefully dodging the LEGO land mines, she made her way down the hall.

"Noah, we're going to be la—" Lane stopped at the sight of Noah huddled on the ground, shoulders shaking, his face buried in his hands. Sweeping into the room, Lane dropped to her knees and pulled her little boy into her lap. "Noah, what's wrong? What's happened?"

"I lost my tags." He sniffled. "You told me to be careful and I lost my tags."

"Oh, honey." Lane pushed the hair from his forehead. "No, you didn't. They're on the dresser. See?"

Noah's gaze followed hers to the dresser. He slid out of Lane's hold and scooped up the military dog tags she'd found under his bed and placed on the dresser the night before. Noah admired the pieces of metal like they were gold. He looked up, his eyes still wet. "I'm sorry, Momma."

"Your daddy"—Lane gently took the tags and put them over his head—"he would be so proud of how big and responsible you're getting." She wiped the tears from the little boy's eyes. Noah was the only piece of Mathias she had left.

A knock on the front door pulled Lane from the bittersweet nostalgia. She wrinkled her nose. Ms. Byrdie didn't normally come to their upstairs apartment, but when she did she didn't need to knock. Who was it? Her parents? Ensuring Lane and Noah made it to the dedication on time—or at all? She groaned.

Another knock on the door, this one persistent, hurried Lane into the living room, making her forget about the colorful tiny blocks on the floor until her bare foot found one. She bit down on her lip to avoid the scream that wanted to escape. Rubbing her foot, she took a few seconds to regain her composure.

"Momma," Noah said, wrapping his fist tight around the dog tags. "Someone's here."

"Mrs. Kent, it's Deputy Charlie Lynch"—the strong baritone voice carried from the other side of the door—"with the Walton County Sheriff Department."

Lane's heart seized. Dread crept up from the pit of her stomach and reached around her torso, squeezing her breaths out in short, shallow gasps. Her mind flashed back to the moment two years ago when North Carolina troopers stood on her porch. Mathias was gone.

"Momma?"

Noah's voice chased away the haunting memories and brought her focus back to the deputy standing on the other side of her door. Catching her breath, Lane opened the door. And there he was. Deputy Charlie Lynch. Unlike yesterday, he wasn't wearing shorts and a T-shirt. Today his broad shoulders filled out the tan uniform, making him appear taller. Stalwart.

"Afternoon, ma'am. Aunt B said I'd find you up here. I hope you don't mind—" The door pulled wide and Noah appeared at her side. The deputy's gaze cut to Noah and softened.

"Hey, you're a policeman." Noah pointed at the deputy's badge. "My daddy was an Army soldier. Momma says when you wear a uniform, you are a hero. See these." Noah pulled on the dog tags around his neck. "These are my dad's tags, but they're mine now."

What was that look? Something tugged at the deputy's expression. Confusion? Whatever it was, she didn't have time to figure it out. Leave it to a four-year-old to tell a complete stranger their life story.

"Sorry, one sec." Lane looked down at her son. "Go grab three toys to bring with us to Bear and Gigi's."

Noah's lips twisted. "Can I bring four?" He lifted up four chubby fingers.

"Yes." She would've let him bring five toys just to put a stop to his show-and-tell episode. Lane waited until Noah disappeared down the hall before turning to the deputy standing at her door.

"Bear?" A soft smile curved his lips and Lane couldn't help noticing the two dimples wedged into his cheeks. Or the uneasy way her heart was racing.

"My father. A nickname." *And personality.* Most people in town knew her father's moniker, which confirmed this deputy was very new—and very unaware of Bear's wrath if she and Noah were late. "Will this take long, Deputy Lynch?"

"I promise not to keep you longer than necessary." The deputy shifted, looking around. "Would you feel more comfortable talking up here . . . or downstairs?"

Lane glanced over her shoulder at the tornado of toys amassed on the floor and the pile of dirty laundry still waiting to be washed. The last thing she needed was a stranger getting a first-person account of her real-life chaos. "Downstairs."

The deputy followed her down to the café's sitting area. After settling Noah with a basket full of plastic dinosaurs to choose from, Lane found the deputy studying the photos and art along the wall where a large fireplace anchored the room.

"These are great. Are they all yours?"

"Some." A tickle of insecurity pushed her forward. "Some are pieces created by students at the community center. I don't mean to rush you, but I really do have somewhere to be, Deputy Lynch—"

"This town isn't that big and since we're practically neighbors"—Deputy Lynch turned from the wall of photos, the edge of his lips curling— "you can call me Charlie. I'd actually prefer it over what the rest of the town is calling me."

Lane frowned. "Which is?"

"The new guy. Newbie. Deputy New." Charlie's tanned cheeks turned a subtle shade of pink. "And some others not worth mentioning."

A smile came so easily to Lane's lips that it startled her. Where had that come from? Her eyes found Charlie's and it was hard not to be drawn into the richness of his gaze or imagine the kind of names the handsome new deputy might be adorned with.

Lane shook the thought away and let the smile slip back to where it belonged. "Would you like some fresh banana bread? Ms. B—I mean, your aunt and I just made it. It's her recipe and very good." Amusement lanced Charlie's features, causing Lane to drop her gaze. "Of course, I'm sure you already know that." Why was she so nervous? Taking a breath to get control of her nerves, she met his stare. "I'm sorry, Deputy"—his chin tilted—"Charlie, but I'm really going to be late if we don't get started."

"Yes, ma'am." Charlie sat at the edge of an overstuffed club chair and pulled a notebook from his pocket.

"If I'm calling you Charlie, I must insist you call me Lane. Not ma'am or Mrs. Kent. Please." She sank onto the cushion at the farthest end of the couch, opposite him and the woodsy scent of his aftershave. "Being called ma'am makes me feel old." It was also a painful reminder that Lane needed to dismiss the thoughts she was having regarding the deputy who was there to do his job.

"I apologize. Habit." Charlie settled into the chair and opened the notebook. "Sheriff Huggins said you like to hike around the river. Take pictures?"

"Yes."

"And that's what you were doing out there yesterday?"

"Y-yes." Anxiety knotted in Lane's chest. He'd seen her at the bridge—standing at the edge. Was this a test? Seeing if she'd tell the truth? Or was it something more? She licked her lips and drew her shoulders back. "Yes, I went out there to get some pictures, but it started to rain before I could take any."

Charlie considered her answer before dropping his gaze to his notebook. After a second he looked up. "How long were you out there?"

"About two hours, I think."

"What time did you arrive?"

"I don't remember the exact time. Maybe one o'clock or so."

"How often are you in that area?"

"Once or twice a week, maybe." Lane swallowed. Or more,

depending on whether she allowed the darkness to take root. Some days it was harder to ignore. Harder to pretend.

"By yourself?"

"Yes."

"When you're out there, do you normally see other people?"

"Not usually. Sometimes I'll see someone on the river. Kayaking or fishing."

"And yesterday?"

Lane studied the deputy. His light brown hair was shorn close to his head. Typical of law enforcement . . . and the military. Where had Charlie come from? What was his background? Why did she care? And why was he staring—oh, staring. He asked her a question. What?

"Did you see anyone new or unusual out there yesterday?" Charlie repeated his question without a hint of annoyance. "Or any time before?"

"Before?" Lane grew uneasy. "Um, I overheard the other deputy say they thought it was suicide." The word was like acid on her tongue.

Charlie's square jaw flexed. His eyes probing. "You haven't heard? The death is being investigated as a homicide."

Homicide? Murder? In an instant, the girl's ashen face flashed in Lane's mind. Did she know her? The girl had to be someone from town, right? Lane's fingers tightened over the arm of the couch as chills marched down her spine.

"Mrs. Kent." A hint of softness returned to his eyes. "Are you okay?"

"Yes." Her lips were dry. "Who-who's the girl?"

"We can't release that information yet."

"But you think someone killed her? You think whoever did it might've been out there yesterday . . ." The noise. When she found the body, Lane discounted it as an animal, but what if . . . "There was a noise. When I found the body." Lane's heart was hammering inside her chest as her thoughts flashed to the strange man last night. Noah's tiny voice in the next room congealed her fear. "Should I be worried?"

Understanding reached Charlie's blue eyes as they locked on to hers. "No one knows you found the girl. And no one needs to know."

Lane swallowed against her fear. There was nothing investigative about the way Charlie was looking at her now. There was promise—like an unspoken oath to keep her and Noah safe. The sentiment stirred something deep inside. When was the last time she felt safe? That someone made her *feel* safe?

"Momma." Noah's voice chased away the warmth blossoming in her chest. There was no room in her life for those kind of thoughts . . . or feelings. Her son appeared at the edge of the room, a dinosaur in one hand and her ringing cell phone in the other.

Lane scooped up Noah and took the phone just as it stopped ringing. Caller ID said it was her sister, Meagan. She was probably freaking out that they weren't at the community center yet. "I really—"

"I think I have everything I need." Charlie stood, tucking his notebook into his pocket. "But Sheriff Huggins asked if we could get a copy of the photos you've taken at the river recently."

"Sure, I guess." Lane shifted Noah to her other hip and found her camera bag sitting on one of the boxes she had stacked earlier. She dug for her camera and withdrew the memory card. "Everything from the last couple of weeks is on there. Is there something you're looking for?"

"Part of the investigation, but because of the remote location we believe the killer had to be familiar with the area."

Lane instinctively pulled Noah closer. Was it possible someone in Walton was capable of killing? She swallowed. Lane already knew the answer to that question even if no one else did. A radiating alarm echoed from her cell phone. Officially late.

"I appreciate your time and I'll get this memory card back to you quickly, but if you need anything . . . well, we're neighbors."

A shy smile tugged at Charlie's lips as he looked around the café. "I'm sure I'll be around."

"Monday." Surprise sucked the moisture right out of Lane's mouth. "I mean, Mondays are when Ms. Byrdie, I mean your aunt, makes her famous banana pudding. Sells out. It's a good day to come. For food. Or coffee." *Stop talking.*

"Sounds perfect," Charlie said as he turned and walked down the front steps of the café's wraparound porch. He paused and waved to Noah before tipping his hat in her direction and then disappeared down her walkway.

"He's a big policeman, Momma." Noah stared after the man with admiration. Her son loved anyone in uniform but especially soldiers and police officers. "Can we see him again?"

Setting Noah down, Lane started massaging the knot forming in her shoulder. It was hard to share Noah's affection when those in uniform only reminded her of pain. And death. That last thought drew Lane back into the woods. Who killed that girl? And why?

Lane's cell phone rang. Her mother. They were late and her family would be angry. That should've been what scared her most—but it wasn't. Ignoring the call, Lane stepped into her house and, for the first time since she could remember, bolted the lock.

FIVE

LANE PAUSED ON THE VERANDA of her parents' sprawling estate in Walton East. The black iron of the gas lamps contrasted sharply with the white siding. Blooming lobelias draped from baskets hanging off the eaves and gave the palatial home a genteel impression, but to Lane the home she grew up in was merely proof the Sullivans were a family of distinction first; gentility came later—if at all.

The smell of something sweet greeted Lane and Noah once they stepped inside the home. No one came to greet her at the door. Why would they? She wasn't a guest; she was family. Lane swallowed. *Why didn't it feel that way?*

"Gigi!" Noah squealed, running into the grand foyer.

"Noah!" Lane called after him. "Your shoes."

Noah skidded to a stop and ran back. He plopped himself on the ground and pulled off his shoes and socks. "Now?"

"Kiss." Lane pointed to her cheek. He obliged and sprinted down the polished hardwood hall at full speed, dinosaurs in tow. She touched her cheek, wishing she shared Noah's enthusiasm to charge forward, fearless.

"I didn't think you were going to show up," Lane's mother, Elise Sullivan, said as soon as Lane made her way into the kitchen.

"Sorry I missed the ceremony." After Charlie left, Noah insisted he had to have a glass of apple juice, which he spilled all over his clothes and hers. By the time she cleaned themselves up and wiped the floor, the ceremony was over. Lane held up a basket filled with loaves of banana bread. Baking had become her go-to when sleep evaded her, and by the time Ms. Byrdie had opened up the shop this morning, almost two dozen loaves were cooling on racks. "I made these for everyone."

The timer on the oven went off and her mother grabbed a pair of oven mitts and pulled out a fresh cobbler. After setting it down on the giant granite island, she tapped her finger gently against the golden crust. It looked perfect, but Lane knew it could never compare to Ms. Byrdie's.

"Smells good," Lane tried again.

"Go tell everyone lunch is ready."

Lane sighed as she took in her mother. Her sable, shoulder-length hair was pulled into a low ponytail. Makeup perfectly applied. A colorful apron covered a vibrant coral blouse and white linen pants. She was the epitome of a southern debutante. And a debutante never engaged in quarreling, though they made sure to express their displeasure in other ways, verbal or not.

Inside her father's den, Lane found her brother, Wes, reading a newspaper on the leather couch. Meagan's son, Owen, was on the ground playing with the toy dinosaurs Noah had brought from home.

"Where's everybody else?" Lane kissed Owen on the head. He was the spitting image of Wes, complete with thick, dark hair that curled at the top and boyish good looks.

"Dad's in his office and Meagan's giving Paige a bath." Wes didn't even look over his newspaper.

"Didn't y'all just come from the community center?"

"Something about paint on a pinafore." Wes shrugged.

"Well, lunch is ready."

Wes grunted and she rolled her eyes. Her brother and Owen were probably the same age in maturity too.

"I smell fresh meat!" Lane's father barged into the room from his adjoining office.

"Bear!" The little boys screamed and scrambled off the ground to get to their grandpa. With his arms open, he curled his hands up like claws and growled. The boys stopped short and ran screaming in the opposite direction. In two large steps, Bear swept them into his arms and began tickling them until ear-piercing hysteria ensued.

Lane loved seeing this part of her father. The child inside who readily emerged around his grandchildren. The side of him that wasn't poised, serious, or controlling. A side absent to her when she was growing up.

"The food is getting cold," Lane's mother said, raising her voice to be heard over the kids. The laughing commotion ceased as though a drill sergeant had called his troops to attention.

Bear released the boys and saluted Lane's mom. Noah and Owen did the same, which made all of them smile, even Lane. Maybe lunch wouldn't be so bad after all.

"Lane." The muscles in her neck tightened and her last thought instantly evaporated at the sound of her father's voice.

Wes arched his eyebrows at Lane like when they were children and he knew she was going to get in trouble. "Come on, boys, let's go get some lunch so we can have dessert."

Lane turned to face her father as Wes prodded Noah and Owen into the dining room. Gone was the playfulness. She was now looking into the familiar hard lines of the father she had grown up with. He'd always been strict. Disciplined. And unapologetic about his ways. But part of her longed for her father to look at her the way he looked at her son—delighted—not the way he looked at her now.

"I'm sorry—"

"I don't need apologies, Lane. I want compliance. Now that you are home, you and Noah are expected to attend all family events." Her father's stern gaze bore into her, making her feel small. "Your mother and sister worked hard on the community center and your absence was noticed."

"I doubt anyone besides you, Mom, and Meagan noticed we weren't there." Lane fought for a more confident posture to look her father in the eyes, but she couldn't. Never could.

"It. Was. Noticed." His sharp tone vibrated around the room and into Lane's chest, removing any hope of being able to stand up to her father. "Our family is always being watched. It's part of the price we pay."

Lane dropped her chin to her chest. "It's not my debt to pay."

"Maybe not. But the day I faced a judge on your behalf is the day you forfeited your rights to object to my direction."

The comment found its mark and seared the truth into her heart. She had promised to do whatever her father asked—at the time. A nonnegotiable agreement she had made in a moment of weakness. But she'd had no other choice. She'd already lost Mathias, and her father was threatening to take away Noah. Her eyes stung, but she managed to nod her head. She wouldn't engage in this battle. She would never win.

"I'm sorry I missed the dedication. It won't happen again."

There was a reason her father was nicknamed Bear. His reputation in the courtroom was legendary throughout Georgia and even in other parts of the US. If you wanted to argue with Judge Raymond Sullivan, you'd better be prepared and you'd better be ready to lose.

"Ray, Lane, we're waiting," her mother called from the dining room.

"Remember, I was there for you. My request is that you be here when our family needs you."

Allowing her father to lead the way, Lane fell in step behind him. Since when did being there for your children become a condition to negotiate?

Meagan was already at the table, which was filled with fried chicken, potato salad, rolls, and a garden salad. It looked like a picnic lunch. A very fancy picnic lunch with linen napkins and her mother's china. Lane found her spot next to Noah and ran her fingers through his hair—a reminder of what was at stake if her father didn't get his way.

Paige, a five-year-old blonde version of Meagan, sat next to her. Paige gave Lane a weak smile from beneath a big pink bow holding back damp hair.

"Don't mind her." Meagan waved as she passed a full plate to Lane. "She's in a bad mood because she got paint all over her dress. Old Mrs. Davis thought it would keep the kids' attention if she gave them paint markers."

"Let's be thankful it happened after the dedication and photos were taken." Lane's mother cast a glance in her direction.

"Where's Ian?" Lane asked, noticing the absence of Meagan's husband.

"He's finishing up a deal in Savannah. He's been gone just about every night this week."

Lane pressed her lips together. She doubted Ian would face the same reprimanding for his absence that she was getting, but had she noted a tinge of sadness in Meagan's voice? Her sister's face remained stoic. Meagan was the younger reflection of their mother. Dark chestnut hair coiled around her shoulders, makeup perfectly in place. Her dress, probably designer, had no wrinkles. Nothing to indicate all was not well . . . or perfect. People always commented that Meagan and their mom could be sisters. Their mom basked in the compliment—Meagan not so much.

The gilded mirror on the wall reflected how different two sisters could be. If Lane stared long enough, she'd see the small lines around her mouth and at the sides of her green eyes. Meagan's tamed hair, styled and perfectly in place, contrasted with Lane's long, wavy tresses tucked into a bun at the base of her neck. She didn't wear makeup and according to Meagan needed to see someone about her eyebrows. But who had time for that?

Meagan.

Meagan had time for that. Not only was she a doting wife, member of the Junior League, part of the PTA, and mom of two kids, but she somehow made time to take care of herself. To be presentable. Staring back at her own reflection, Lane almost laughed at herself. There was no need to worry about the deputy seeing LEGOs or laundry piled up—she was all the mess necessary to warn him off.

Lane tucked a loose strand of hair behind her ear. What made her think the handsome deputy would give her a passing glance?

After seeing Meagan and her mom, it was apparent what a good night's sleep could do for one's skin. Dark circles beneath her own eyes revealed long nights, but getting more rest would do nothing to erase the etchings of her past. That would take a lifetime of sleep and Lane didn't have time for that either—or foolish thoughts about a man.

"Someone said a body was found near the Ogeechee."

Lane swung her gaze to her brother as the muscles in her stomach contracted. Had enough time passed for the morbid news to spread through their small town already?

"Think it might be suicide." Wes took a big bite of chicken as if finding a dead body in Walton was commonplace.

"Seriously, Wes?" Meagan asked. "In front of the kids?"

"What? It's what I heard," Wes said. He was already scooping a spoonful of potato salad onto his plate. "Waiting to notify next of kin."

"Is that true?" Her mother peeked over her glass of white wine, eyes wide.

"I don't understand what could drive a person to do that. Life can't be that hard," Wes said between bites.

A slap in the face couldn't have hurt worse. Her cheeks burned. What did her brother know about life being hard?

"Wes, that's not a discussion to have at the table. We had such a wonderful day. Let's not spoil it any further."

Lane's gaze was drawn to her mother. Ever the Southern socialite, sweeping everything under the rug, pretending life was perfect. Did it eat at her like it did Lane? Or was it easier to live the lie rather than face the truth?

"It wasn't suicide."

Lane looked up at her father. His dark brown eyes locked on to hers.

"I was just on the phone with Sheriff Huggins and it's not a suicide." Her father ate a bite of potato salad. His gaze was still fixated on her.

"Are you sure?" Lane's mother gave an off-putting laugh. "This is *Walton*."

If Charlie hadn't told her himself, Lane would be wondering the same thing, but she knew the truth. The thought of him churned an unusual desire to see him again. Why? *Because he makes you feel safe—even for just a moment. He makes you feel worth protecting.* That truth pierced something she'd been trying to deny since the second Charlie exited her home, leaving a tangible void in his wake.

Reminding her just how alone she was.

"So, it's . . ." Meagan leaned forward, her eyes round. "M-u-r-d-e-r?"

"No. It's hom-oh-cide," Wes said around a mouthful of food. "Man, I wish I was a trial lawyer."

"Can we please stop talking about this?" Lane was used to her brother's indifference, but he was taking it to a whole new level. "Someone was killed, Wes. Do you get that?"

"What? It's not like they went off and killed themselves."

"Wes!" Her mother's voice was sharp and snatched the attention of everyone at the table. "We will not continue this discussion any further. It is over."

Lane pushed her plate away. "I'm not feeling that well. I think we should go."

"We're not finished." Lane's mother rose from the table. "We haven't had dessert."

"I'm just messing around, Lane." Wes twirled his fork between his fingers.

"Come on, Noah. It's time to go home." Dessert was the last thing she wanted to stomach. She appreciated her mother's attempt to bring order back to the meal, but it was too late. Her appetite was gone and she was done being reminded of her past.

"But, Mommy, I didn't get any peach cobbler."

She kissed his forehead. "We'll get something at home."

"You know, they say laughter is the best medicine." But the

humor in her brother's voice from a second ago was gone. He ran a hand through his hair, letting it rest on the back of his neck. His eyes met hers. "Lane, I'm sorry."

Lane bit down on the inside of her cheek, unable to speak. Not that it mattered even if she could. Her mother's outburst was a clear reminder that there were some things the Sullivans did not discuss. And Lane had no answers to satisfy their questions. Why would she do what she did? Didn't she think about what it would do to her family? She had nothing to say. No way to explain why death had seemed like an answer that day. Or how the effects of that single decision had tormented her every single day since.

Her father remained seated and continued to eat. Wes sipped his tea. Meagan kept quiet and their mother stood motionless as she stared at her own plate. No one was going to stop her.

And no one did. They were content to let her go. A lump of emotion filled her throat. As much as her dad claimed hero status for coming to her rescue, Lane knew the only person who had ever fought for her—who had truly tried to rescue her—was buried in the ground.

―――――――――

The mood inside the sheriff's station was as stifling as the late-afternoon heat and the heavy revelation of Sheriff Huggins's words still echoing in Charlie's ear: "Jane Doe has been identified." Amanda and Trevor had confirmed the victim as their seventeen-year-old daughter, Sydney.

The buzz of the air conditioner on full blast did little to deflect from the shared despair of the deputies around him. How many of them knew the young lady? Were they friends with her family? Did she babysit their children? Maybe living in a small town was as much a blessing as it was a curse? If they were this close to the victim, could they be close to the killer too?

Sheriff Huggins entered the station and drew the gaze of every deputy, including Charlie. He paused for a moment and looked ready to say something but stopped. He pulled out a white handkerchief and wiped his face. To remove the afternoon's kiss of sweat or to wipe away any evidence of moisture in his gray eyes, Charlie wasn't sure.

"The Donovans"—Sheriff Huggins cleared his throat and tucked the handkerchief into his pocket—"are expecting our best. I'm expecting your best. As the community learns the truth, I want us to be prepared. I know some of you knew Sydney and her family, so if you need some time to . . ." His voice caught. "Grief counselors will be available, but I'm hoping that once you've had your moment—your time—you will focus that grief into finding the person or persons responsible. That's our job. To bring justice and some sort of peace back not only to Sydney's family but to our town as well."

The collective nodding of those around Charlie confirmed they were all on board. With straightened postures and sharp expressions, they were ready to put aside their emotions to focus on the case—the mission. It reminded him of the early moments with the command team before they embarked on a new operation. Their uncertainty about what may lie ahead was overruled by their focus on doing the job and doing it right. Charlie hoped the Walton deputies were ready.

"Lynch, Frost, I'd like to see you in my office."

Deputy Frost nimbly crossed in front of Charlie. Freckles covered the bridge of the young man's nose and matched his unruly reddish-blond hair. His uniform hung on a tall frame that his bony shoulders hadn't quite grown into yet. Charlie noticed the extra notch cut into Frost's gun belt. He smiled. The officer reminded him of a nerdier version of that prince in England, the younger one, trying to grow into a role that demanded respect.

"Get the door, Lynch." Sheriff Huggins tugged on his own gun belt, which wasn't too loose or too snug. Charlie was rather impressed by the agility the sheriff possessed for a man approaching his seventies.

When the door shut, Charlie stood with his hands clasped behind his back and his legs just wider than shoulder distance as he waited for his orders. Deputy Frost pushed up his thick black-framed glasses a second before his magnified gaze met Charlie's. Frost straightened his shoulders and turned to face Sheriff Huggins, mimicking Charlie's at ease position.

Sheriff Huggins sat at the edge of his desk and looked at Frost, then at Charlie. A smile pulled at his lips, but he recovered. "Have you found Sydney's cell phone?"

"No, sir," Charlie answered. "Deputy Wilson took a team out there this morning and they combed the area, but nothing was found."

Disappointment flickered in Sheriff Huggins's eyes. "Frost, I need you to go to the Donovans' and pick up Sydney's laptop. I want you to do a thorough search of her social media presence. Facebook, Twitter, Instagram. All of . . ." Sheriff Huggins's bristly white eyebrows came together. "What is it, Frost?"

"I'm sorry, sir." Frost's thin frame tensed. "Just surprised you know about social media."

"I'm not in the grave yet. Now, wipe that smirk off your face. You don't see Lynch itching in his britches, do you?"

Frost shot a sideways glance at Charlie. "No, sir."

"Someone's daughter was killed, Frost. For Pete's sake, she could have been in high school with your sister."

That fact hit home and Frost straightened. "Yes, sir."

"Lynch, were you able to get a statement from Lane Kent?"

"Yes, sir. Earlier this afternoon."

Worry pinched Sheriff Huggins's features. "How's she doing?"

Charlie recognized the sheriff's look of concern. It was the same one he wore when he held Lane in his arms near the river yesterday. Paternal. Protective. Like he knew the real reason behind the anguish Charlie had seen pooling in Lane's green eyes.

"Lynch?"

"Sorry, sir." Charlie needed to rein in his thoughts, which lingered on Lane. What was wrong with him? She was married—off-limits. But why hadn't he seen any proof of her husband? He hated to admit it, but he had looked that morning in the Way Station Café. For a pair of shoes, the lingering scent of aftershave, something that said a man lived there. Sheriff Huggins cleared his throat. "She was in a bit of a rush. Had an event or something she was running late to, but I was able to get a quick statement and the memory card from her camera. Lane—Ms. Kent said she didn't take any pictures yesterday and the ones on the card are about a week old."

"Right. The campaign." Sheriff Huggins folded his arms across his chest. "That's going to make our job more challenging."

"Campaign?"

"Lane's father is Judge Raymond Sullivan and he's currently the front-runner for a senate bid." The sheriff released a sigh before moving behind his desk. "It means there are a lot more unfamiliar faces in Walton."

Realization spread through Charlie. "Which means less chance of a stranger standing out."

"Frost"—Sheriff Huggins pulled a business card from his desk and held it out—"I have a friend, David Padello, in the FBI out of Savannah. That's his card. He's agreed to help us if we need it. And we may need it."

The FBI allowed city, county, and state officials to operate their own investigations unless called upon, but Charlie also understood the feds liked to extend their assistance to the point of overstaying their welcome. He couldn't imagine what Walton would look like overrun by suits and sedans.

"I also want you to make copies of the memory card from Lane's camera. Maybe we'll get lucky." Conviction was missing from the sheriff's tone and expression in that last statement.

"I'm on it." Frost hurried out of Sheriff Huggins's office.

"Do you think Frost can handle this investigation?" Sheriff Huggins stared past Charlie. "He's a genius when it comes to computers and technology but a little vague when it comes to common sense."

"He seems eager." Charlie had detected an energy buzzing through the younger deputy. Maybe that's why Sheriff Huggins stuck him in a small room, away from the others, where he could unleash his enthusiasm to attack the case without coming off as unsympathetic.

"Tell me, Lynch, how many baby-faced Marines fresh out of boot camp are ready to face war?"

"Sir?"

"They're all eager. Trained. Armed. And then what? They get out there and face demons they never knew existed outside of a comic book or video game." Sheriff Huggins's eyes went to the window in his office that faced out to the rest of the station. "All of them are about to face a battle I'm not sure they're prepared for."

It was true. Charlie had seen and breathed death and destruction at the hands of the enemy. Young Marines came in all *oorah!* only to watch a bullet take out their buddy right in front of them. Sobered them up real quick. Put purpose in their mission and faith in their soul.

"This murder is personal."

"That's right." Sheriff Huggins leaned forward. "Which is exactly why I want you taking the lead. You have no ties to this town, or the people in it."

Was that supposed to make Charlie feel better? Unattached and impartial to death? Or was that the expectation because he used to be a Marine? That he should be immune to the effects of death.

"A little separation is healthy for everyone." Sheriff Huggins said it as though he were answering Charlie's thoughts. "Brings perspective."

"Is that what you're asking for? Perspective?"

"I'm asking you to be the man I know you are. The person who I watched as a little boy see things others missed. Use those skills that made you invaluable in the Corps to help us . . . help me bring peace back to Walton."

Charlie digested the words, allowing them to bring him back to reality. To his purpose. He was there to do a job and the sheriff was reminding him of that. "Do you believe the killer is local?"

"Agent Padello is running a search through the federal database to see if there are any similarities with the victim or the crime." Sheriff Huggins shook his head and stared out the large window. "I don't want to think someone here is capable of doing to Sydney what they did. No child, woman, or man should ever meet their Maker like that."

On that, Charlie could agree. She wasn't just a victim. She was Sydney Donovan, proverbial daughter to all who called Walton home—or so it seemed. It was up to him to find out if a killer was lurking among those mourning the young lady left to die in a swampy grave.

SIX

THE RANK HUMIDITY had turned the mud hole into a sauna. Miguel took a long drag on a cigarette. His lungs burned. He was alive. For now. If he made it home, he'd remember to thank God. It was still too early to celebrate.

Bringing the cigarette to his lips took several attempts. His hands hadn't stopped shaking since the chopper had let 'em down—what was it? A month? Two months ago? The days blurred into one long, hellish nightmare with no end.

A mosquito landed on his arm. Bloodsucker. He slapped at it but missed. He'd never survive with that kind of aim. Draft didn't care about precision. Point and shoot. He'd follow orders. Always did.

Until now.

An explosive crack seized his attention and his breathing. He dropped the half-smoked cigarette and reached for his weapon, but his nails dug into thick mud. His weapon was gone. His eyes darted around the hole. Where was it?

Panic claimed his breath as the familiar squishing of boots against soft earth grew closer. They were coming and they would kill him. He couldn't tell who the enemy was any longer.

Biting down on his lip to stop it from quivering, he tasted blood. Proof of life, but for how long? He didn't want to die. He wanted to go home. His frantic search landed on the bayonet. Miguel lunged for it and wrapped his clammy hand around the thick handle. He struggled out of the muddy pit, afraid it would become his tomb.

The swamp became his foe, slowing his escape. His boots slipped in the muck that threatened to hold him until he could be killed. He couldn't slow down and he couldn't hide—they'd find him.

Screaming startled him. He swung around and found her standing there. She stumbled backward into a tree. Her lips formed a small o as tears fell from frightened eyes.

The footsteps sounded behind him. They were coming. Miguel tightened his grip. They were coming to kill her. He couldn't stop them. Salty tears stung his eyes, barely blurring her terrified expression.

It was too late.

Miguel took a step toward her and she screamed. He wanted to tell her to stop, but he knew if he opened his mouth his screams would match hers. He closed his eyes and swung his arm, bringing the bayonet down—

"Stop! Please stop screaming!" Miguel Roa's eyes snapped open, her screams echoing in his ears. Why couldn't he stop it? He should've protected them.

The throbbing in his head sent sharp pains to the back of his eyeballs. He groaned, closing his eyes. How long had it been since his last blackout? With more effort than it was worth, he pushed his eyelids open. The dark surroundings of his home spun around him. Miguel rolled to his side and let the cool cement floor bring him back to his senses.

When he was certain his world wouldn't shift, he lifted his head. Slow and steady he pushed himself up to a sitting position on the floor. His legs stretched before him, Miguel stared at the boots still laced on his feet. His clothes were wrinkled and dirty. What day was it?

Every muscle ached. Miguel couldn't remember his blackouts being this bad before. But then he could hardly remember anything about the dark lapses in time. No recollection of the minutes or hours when he slipped into the recesses of darkness. Or what caused them.

Well, that wasn't true. His nightmare was proof of that. Atonement for his sin.

Using the edge of an end table for support, Miguel winced as raw pain lit a fire in the palms of his hands. Withdrawing them left a smear of blood on the wood in their place. His vision blurred at the sight of crimson fissures carved into his skin.

A metallic taste filled his mouth. Miguel focused on the sink. If he could just get there and run cold water over the cuts . . . splash his face . . . return to reality. The shattering of glass made him jerk around, sending his vision and the room careening. Miguel reached for something to hold him upright but found nothing except for air. He crashed to his knees, the pain jolting through his arthritic joints.

A shadow crossed in front of the window. Heavy footsteps slowed at his front door. Time seemed to still before his door swung wide open.

"Get out of here." Miguel's words came out thick. "I've got nothing to steal."

"I'm not here to steal, amigo." The man stepped into the home and into the moon's waning glow. The light was just bright enough to expose the visitor's ill intentions. "Where's the painting?"

"Wh-what painting?"

The blow came quickly and sent Miguel's brain rattling inside his skull. He slumped the rest of the way to the floor as warmth slid across his forehead.

"I won't ask again."

"Who"—the pressure behind Miguel's eyes grew—"are you?"

The heat of the intruder's breath curled around Miguel's ear. "A collector. Where's the painting Sydney stole?"

"Sydney." Her name scratched against his throat. A glimpse of her face. Her blue eyes flashed in his memory.

The wide strokes of blue and green crashing over each other on the canvas. *Tumultuous Ocean.* Sydney had brought the painting to him. When? Last night? It felt so long ago. He squeezed his eyes tight. What happened? All he could remember were her eyes. Shocked. No, scared . . . she was scared.

And he was too late. Again.

SEVEN

THERE WAS A RUN in the carpet near the edge of the wall in Dr. Eddie Wong's office. Lane had been focused on it since her appointment began almost an hour ago. Focusing on the pulled thread of the gray carpet was easier than focusing on Dr. Wong's questions.

Always the same. *Do you feel like dying? How many times have you thought about suicide? Do you feel like a burden to those around you?* And all her answers were on the little card she filled out at the beginning of every session. The one he glanced at after each question as though he was trying to catch her in a lie. The only lie between them was how *this* continuous conversation about her depression was supposed to make her feel better when it only reminded her of her guilt—and the fact that she was broken.

"If we're going to make progress with your treatment, you're going to have to let me know what you're thinking."

Lane stared at her psychiatrist. Wasn't that his job? To tell *her* what she was thinking and why she was thinking it? And more importantly, what was wrong with her? Why she was this way and how she could fix it? *Yes, Dr. Wong. Please tell me why I feel broken and not worth the breaths I take every single day. Oh, and if you have an answer for the guilt* . . . She smirked. Those questions had gone unanswered all her life. Not even God heard her prayers. Or if he did, he chose to ignore them . . .

"What about activities? Are you doing anything fun?" Dr. Wong ran his fingers across a thin mustache and down the sides of his mouth to the goatee on his chin. He had more hair on his face than on his head, and it was graying, which was the only part of the man that made him look like a head doctor. The black T-shirt, dark jeans, and Converse high-tops gave the impression he was more of a hipster. Was the comfortable look supposed to make him easier to talk to?

"Lane?"

Fun? When was the last time she had fun? Laughed? *Charlie.* Lane shifted in the leather chair. He'd brought a smile to her face— a rarity the last two years. In fact, she smiled, laughed even, every time she thought about the way Wilbur, Clarence, and Ducky had harassed him inside the Way Station Café. What did that mean? Acknowledging the feelings Charlie stirred up within her felt like a betrayal. It unnerved her.

"Life's busy." Safe answer.

Dr. Wong tapped his pen against the notebook in his lap. If he was annoyed by her answer, she couldn't tell. He seemed to always be studying her. Maybe, like her, he was trying to figure out why she was so defective. "What about your family? This is a big time in your lives."

"*Their* lives."

"You don't think your father's campaign affects your life?"

Lane thought about the words her father had spoken to her— his demands for her presence. The inherent threat if she failed to do her part. And pretend. She shrugged.

"Depression doesn't only affect one person." Dr. Wong chewed on the end of his pen. "You know that."

She did. Every day, Lane was reminded of the effect her depression had on those around her. Mathias was gone. Noah didn't have his daddy. Her mother wouldn't discuss it. Her father used it to manipulate her. Her brother thought it was a joke. Darkness crept at the edge of her mind. The walls of Dr. Wong's office felt like they were closing in on her. Wasn't her session over yet? Her leg began to bounce as the urge to run set in.

"I'd like you to invite your parents to our next session."

The oxygen was sucked right out of the room. Lane shrank back. Did she hear him correctly? "Yeah right. Are you serious?"

"I am. Sometimes those who don't understand the illness don't know how to show their support. I think it would be good for them to hear how you feel."

The man was delusional. "My father is running his biggest campaign yet. He wouldn't be caught dead coming into a psychiatrist's office—no offense."

"Lane, these appointments are for your benefit and part of the hospital's condition of release."

Condition of release? "I'm doing everything you've asked. I take my medicine regularly. Get exercise. Sunshine." Never mind all the conditions her father had placed on her. Dr. Wong didn't know that part. Everything she agreed to was to regain some normalcy to her life.

No.

Every deal Lane made was to keep Noah in her life.

"I've come to terms with my illness. I've accepted it and everything that comes with it."

"Meaning?"

"Meaning it's my burden to bear."

"We're not meant to shoulder the burden of life on our own all the time. To be successful we need support from those who love us and believe in us."

Lane wanted to argue with him. A therapy session with her parents wasn't going to change their ignorance. They avoided the topic because they were ashamed. And she was left paying the consequences. Her moment of weakness—that cry for help—killed the only person who truly ever saw past her flaws. The alarm on Dr. Wong's phone beeped, indicating their session was over. Finally.

"One month." Dr. Wong stood. "This is for your health and for Noah."

Lane scowled. He was using Noah as leverage. Like her father. She hurried out of the building, ignoring the receptionist who was calling after her to make a follow-up appointment, and didn't see the man holding the tray of drinks until it was too late.

Liquid and ice splashed all over the ground.

"I'm sorry." Lane tried scooping up a cup before the remainder of its contents emptied out, but it was useless. The day couldn't get any worse.

"Lane?"

She squeezed her eyes shut. Was it possible to already recognize the absence of a drawl in his voice? What kind of God would allow this level of embarrassment? One, it seemed, intent on using Charlie Lynch to disrupt her life.

"Hey there, Deputy." Where did this guy keep coming from? "I'm so sorry."

"It's Charlie, remember? Are you okay?"

A wet stain was spreading across his uniform. Still holding two white paper bags in one hand, he reached out to her with the other. Humor filled his eyes, making it nearly impossible to avoid matching the smile lighting his handsome face.

"Yes, I'm fine." Ooh, taking his hand was a mistake. The touch of his skin set off an internal alarm. Too soon. She pulled her hand back. "I didn't see you."

The glass door to Dr. Wong's office swung open. "Ms. Kent. Your appointment card." The receptionist handed Lane the card as her eyes darted from Charlie to the mess then to Lane, before she turned around and returned to the building. Why couldn't the ground just swallow Lane up like it did the ice?

"Money." Lane grabbed her wallet. "Let me pay for the drinks and your dry cleaning."

"Don't worry about it. It was an accident. Unless"—Charlie narrowed his eyes—"you meant to douse a member of law enforcement in high fructose carbonated syrup?"

He was joking. He didn't flinch. Lane fidgeted. He *was* joking, wasn't he?

"I'm kidding." Charlie lifted the white bags in his hand. "I saved what really matters. Lunch."

"On a hot day like today, you might've been safer saving the drinks."

Charlie's lips curled and those dimples returned. He could easily be the poster boy for law enforcement. She was finding it harder to heed the caution bells ringing in her ears over the flutter of butterflies awakening from a prolonged dormancy inside her chest. Pay him and get out of there.

"Do you think this will cover it?" Lane pulled out a ten-dollar bill.

"It was an accident and taking money from a citizen while in uniform is a crime."

Truth? Or more of his easy humor?

"Deputy Lynch."

Charlie and Lane turned to see a woman crossing the parking lot in a skirt so tight her knees turned. Lane didn't recognize her, but apparently Charlie did, based on the groan he released at the woman's approach.

"Deputy Lynch, don't you always pick up lunch a little closer to the station?"

"A change in scenery, Ms. DeMarco."

The woman's gaze cut to Lane, giving her a less-than-subtle once-over before her heavily coated eyelashes batted back in Charlie's direction. "I've been looking for you. I was hoping I could ask you a few questions regarding the Sydney Donovan murder."

"I've already told you and the rest of the reporters that if we get any new information, we will let you know."

"So, no new leads? What about the person who found the body? Maybe they remember something. I can be very persuasive." DeMarco's voice dripped like syrup. "We can work together."

The heat returned to Lane's cheeks as she watched Ms. DeMarco sidle up to Charlie. The woman had a sort of citified poise about her that probably did make her very persuasive to the opposite sex, but she reminded Lane of a snake coiling for the strike.

"I think you should leave the police work to the professionals." Charlie took a purposeful step out of Ms. DeMarco's path and winked at Lane.

What was that? Flirting? A flood of emotions sent Lane's pulse spiking to a dangerous level.

"What about new suspects? Evidence? Or the family?" Ms. DeMarco wasn't going to be easily dissuaded. "Don't you have anything to say about Walton's reputation being ruined by this murder?"

That last comment was just loud enough that it drew the attention of a few people nearby. Charlie's jaw flexed, his brows knotting as he took in her question.

"Ms. DeMarco, I've told you everything I can about our investigation and I expect you to do your job as a reporter. Report the truth. If you want to judge this beautiful city, that's welcomed you by the way, on this one horrific event rather than on its character . . . well, all I can say is that would be a shame."

"Wha—I . . ." Ms. DeMarco huffed and gave Lane a disdainful look before storming off in the direction she had come from.

"I don't think speechlessness is a good trait for a reporter." Lane smirked.

"She's new. Works for some paper out of DC and is trying to make a name for herself by writing a story about Walton's first murder in thirty years."

There wasn't any malice in his tone. Just . . . understanding? The good-looking deputy was catching her off guard in more ways than one. Did he really believe what he said? That something could be defined by more than one horrific event? Or *someone*?

"I'm sorry I didn't make it in on Monday." Charlie looked sheepish. "This case makes me lose track of time—"

"Oh, no, I get it. Ms. Byrdie said Sheriff Huggins is sucking down antacids like they're Tic Tacs." Lane played nonchalant. Or at least she hoped she was. Disappointment was what she really felt when Charlie didn't show up at the Way Station Café and she wasn't ready to admit that—or the possibility of what it meant. She eyed the stain on his uniform. "I feel really bad about your uniform. Are you sure I can't pay for the dry cleaning at least?"

Charlie waved his hand. "It's almost dry. Sticky but dry."

"Okay, but promise me you'll stop by the café and I'll make it up to you." The words slipped out of her mouth before she put thought to what she was asking. "I mean, for breakfast, or coffee. We have these cinnamon rolls that the whole town loves and I'm sure y'all could use some coffee, right? On the house—to make up for the mess I've caused. I insist."

"Okay, but only because everyone at the station will appreciate it. I'm glad we ran into each other."

"It was mostly me running into you." She blushed.

"Most excitement I've had all day. Well, except for hiding from Ms. DeMarco."

"Have a good day, Charlie."

"You too, Lane."

Lane turned and strode to her car before Charlie could steal another one of her breaths. Could he hear the anticipation in her voice to see him again? Why was his presence in her life so disarming? And what was she going to do about it?

<hr />

Charlie dropped his hat on his desk and wiped the sweat from his brow. He didn't think he'd ever get used to the humidity, but the pressure outside was nothing compared to the pressure mounting inside the station. Deputies hunched over their desks, pounding back their third or fourth cups of coffee as they answered the assault of phone calls.

Everyone had a tip. Heard a strange noise. Or wanted details. The peaceful community Sheriff Huggins worked so hard to maintain had been shaken. Now the citizens of Walton wanted answers. And based on the messages sitting on Charlie's desk, so did the reporters. Just like Ms. DeMarco—they'd have to wait.

Charlie changed out of his sticky uniform and into a fresh one before heading back to the small room reserved for him and Deputy Frost to use while the investigation remained active. The flurry of activity he passed reminded him of the chaos in the Tactical Operations Command when a unit was under assault.

When the scrap hit the fan, the TOC became a lifeline, sending in reinforcement or air support to those fighting the enemy. But this was different. They didn't even know who the enemy was. Yet.

The drone of chaos quieted as he made his way to the small office at the back of the building. After a quick stop at a vending machine, Charlie entered the room with humming fluorescent lights and no windows.

"Sorry it's late." Charlie lifted the bag holding their lunch. "And probably cold. I owe you."

And it was a debt well worth it. Running into Lane, literally, had been the highlight of an already long day. And it might have been the exhaustion he felt, but Charlie swore he saw a spark light her eyes when she insisted he stop by for breakfast. Or did he *want* to see that? Lane Kent was married. And the breakfast offer wasn't just for him. It was for the entire station. He blew out a breath. Definitely exhaustion.

"No biggie." Pushing up his glasses, Deputy Frost looked away from the computer screen. "I think I found something."

"Oh yeah?" Charlie took a seat in front of the desktop computer, their sandwiches forgotten.

Frost's thin fingers moved nimbly over the keyboard before a Facebook page filled the screen. "Check it out."

Charlie leaned forward. The name on the account was *Saint Denis*. The cover photo was of a redbrick wall lined with paintings in bold strokes of greens and blues. In the corner was a smaller black-and-white image of a woman who was not Sydney Donovan but the iconic Audrey Hepburn. "Who is Saint Denis?"

"Not just a *who*"—Frost adjusted his glasses again as he resumed typing—"but also a location."

"A location?"

"A cathedral in Paris, France." Frost pulled up a screen filled with information and photos of an old gothic church. "Saint Denis was decapitated. There's a story that he picked his head up and carried it six miles. Look."

Sure enough, there was a photo of a stone statue with wings holding a head in its hands. "Does this have something to do with Sydney?"

"I've traced the account back to her."

"Legally?"

"Mostly." Frost returned to the Facebook page. "It's a private account, so I can't show you anything more than what's been made public until I talk with the FBI. There's an album here, but it's mostly photos of art. Paintings."

Charlie watched Frost scroll through the album. Each click displayed the bold colors of painting after painting. Why would Sydney Donovan have a private Facebook account full of pictures of art? Was she an artist? He didn't remember seeing anything in her room to indicate a love of art. No painting supplies. No books on art. No posters of abstract paintings beside the photos of Hollywood hunks taped over her bed.

"Who's the artist?"

"I tried enlarging the photos, but as far as I can tell there's no signature. At least not that I can see," Frost said.

Charlie blew out a frustrated breath. An account tracing back to Sydney Donovan with pictures of art meant what? She was a budding artist? A hidden artist? Did her parents know?

"Wait, stop. Go back." Charlie squinted at the screen. "Click on that."

"You want to like the picture?" Frost's glasses slipped down his nose as he frowned.

"No. I want to see *who* liked it."

When Frost clicked the button, only one name appeared and caused him to snort. "Art D. Healer."

"Click on the name."

Frost obeyed and another screen opened up. "It's private."

"And you can't see who it belongs to?"

"I can try." Frost grabbed a second laptop from the desk next to him. Stickers covered the back of it. He typed a bunch of ones and zeroes Charlie couldn't follow. A few minutes later Frost pulled his hands back from the keyboard. "The only name that comes up is Art D. Healer. I've got some friends who—"

"No." Charlie roughed his chin. "We have to do this legally. We'll call Agent Padello. He might be able to help."

"The FBI will have to help, because I doubt Art D. Healer is a real person. I mean, come on. How lame is that?" Frost leaned back in his chair. "No imagination."

"May I?"

Frost slid his chair back and grabbed a sandwich out of the bag.

While Frost munched on his cold lunch, Charlie clicked through the photos again.

"Heard the autopsy report was gruesome," Frost said through a mouthful of food.

"I guess that depends on what one considers gruesome."

Frost's chewing stopped.

"It wasn't pleasant." And it wasn't, but Charlie's opinion of gruesome had been formed on the battlefield.

"You probably saw a lot of death in the war."

"More than I'd like." Charlie paused on a picture. It was different from the rest. Not a close-up of a painting like the others. This one was taken outside, looking into the storefront of a gallery. He looked closer. "Ever hear of Ainsley's Antiques?"

"No."

"Google it. Find out where it's located."

"Are you looking for antiques?" Frost licked his fingers and was about to wipe his mouth across the back of his sleeve when he looked up and saw Charlie watching him.

"No, but we might be closer to finding out why Sydney has a Facebook page of art."

Frost grabbed a napkin before leaning in. "What? How?"

"Look at the reflection in the window." Charlie focused on

the lettering above Sydney's head. "The gallery in this picture is nearby Ainsley's Antiques and maybe someone at that gallery knows about Sydney's secret love of art."

"Oh, man. I can't believe you caught that." Frost pushed up his glasses. After a quick computer search, a smile appeared on his face. "Bohemian Signature Gallery is located by Ainsley's. It's in Savannah."

"What's in Savannah?" Sheriff Huggins stepped into the room, his large frame dominating what remained of the cramped space.

"Deputy Frost found a private Facebook account linked to Sydney Donovan." Charlie lifted his eyebrows so Frost could continue. "He's got some serious computer skills."

"That he does." Sheriff Huggins patted the young deputy on the back. "Show me what you got."

The new lead sent a glimmer of hope pulsing throughout the station. Charlie planned to drive into Savannah tomorrow to meet with Annika Benedict, the owner of the Bohemian Signature Gallery.

"I have a sleeping bag in my trunk."

Charlie looked up from his notes to find Deputy Cecilia Benningfield staring down at him. "What?"

"Your shift ended two hours ago. I have my grandson's sleeping bag in my car if you're planning on being here all night."

Benningfield was kindly regarded as the den mother of the station. She came in early to make sure coffee was made and kept it hot all day long, and she never forgot a birthday.

"No, that's okay. I didn't realize the time."

"Sheriff is a stickler about overtime . . ." Benningfield's benevolent face creased in thought. "I suppose he'd allow it now, under the circumstances."

"Oh, I don't need the overtime." He glanced down at his notes again. "Just making sure I'm not missing anything."

"Don't worry. In all my years here, I don't think I've ever seen a new deputy as eager as you."

"What about Frost?"

"Ha!" Benningfield's laughter echoed in the quiet station. "That boy's eager all right, but it's just youthful pride. You're out to prove something. But remember, this is a job like any other. At the end of the day, you gotta go home to somebody. Hopefully, in your case, a nice young lady."

Charlie couldn't stop his thoughts from going to Lane. What it would be like to go home to her and Noah after a long night. Benningfield was smiling at him like she could read his thoughts. He cleared his throat. "No. No girl. Just an insane dog who probably thinks I'm AWOL and has taken over the house."

"A dog is as good a reason as any to call it a day, but I hope you'll find as great a purpose to invest your time in out there as you do in here."

\\\\\\\\\\\\\\\\\\

Deputy Benningfield's remarks followed Charlie from the office. Inhaling a deep breath of the country air, he watched streaks of orange melt into soft peach across the sky as the sun began to set. *A greater purpose?* That's what he'd come to Walton to find, right? And what greater purpose was there than finding out who killed Sydney Donovan? Even his dad would have to agree that bringing a killer to justice was a purpose worthy of leaving the Marines.

But first he needed to rescue his home from the Terror Terrier.

Charlie found Bane rebounding between the front and back doors. By the time Charlie changed out of his uniform, the dog was certifiably manic. "Okay, bud. Leash first."

Bane's harness did nothing to stop him from dashing between Charlie's legs and lunging out the door as soon as it opened. "Bane!"

The dog jerked to a stop, tightening the entangled leash wrapped around Charlie's lower extremities and pitching him forward. Letting go of the leash was the only way he could prevent the inevitable, and like Houdini, Bane whipped around, pulling the loosened leash until it was free and he was gone.

Ugh. That dog. Charlie heaved out a sigh and started for the street in search of his headache.

"I believe he belongs to you?"

Charlie turned to find Lane walking toward him, Noah smiling at her side. Bane was in her hands, tail wagging, tongue dripping. Charlie swore the dog was smiling at him.

"Not unless you want him?"

"Momma—"

"No." Lane shot Charlie a look that could only be understood to mean *don't you dare*. "This is Charlie's dog and he'd be very sad without him."

"Right." Charlie took Bane and made sure he had a grip on his leash before setting him down. "I was just taking him for a walk . . . would you want to join me?"

"Actually, we—"

"We're getting ice cream. Do you like ice cream?"

"Ice cream is my favorite." Charlie smiled at the exuberant little boy pulling his mother's hand.

"Mine too! You can come with us."

"Noah." Lane's voice rose.

"That's okay." Charlie read her reaction loud and clear. He should go. A tickle of attraction was beginning to cloud his judgment. Or maybe it was a lust for some human companionship? Didn't matter. He needed to go home. Study the case. He didn't have time for ice cream. "I should really take Bane on his walk."

"He can go with us," Noah pleaded. And like Bane understood the little boy's plight, the dog sat obediently next to him and lifted a paw.

"Well, with those faces, how can we resist?" Lane's shoulders relaxed a fraction and she ruffled Noah's hair. "We're walking to Sandie's. A couple of blocks away."

Soft auburn hair fell over her forehead, but he could still see her eyes. They seemed to be searching. Maybe for a way out of the uncertain invitation.

"Are you sure?"

"Yes!" Noah answered. Lane nodded.

Two blocks, two cups of butter pecan, and a cone of rocky road later, the three of them sat around a small iron table in front of Sandie's Ice Cream Shoppe. The day's heat hung around, even with the sun gone, and was doing a number to Noah's frozen treat. Most of it was dripping down the side of his hand.

"You should've let me pay for the ice cream. Make up for what I did to your uniform."

"And miss out on the cinnamon roll offer?" Charlie raised his eyebrows. "There'd be riots if I didn't show up with those cinnamon rolls."

"Did you know my daddy was an Army soldier?" Noah said as he licked the melting ice cream.

"Noah, it's not polite to talk while your mouth is full."

"My mouth's not full, Momma. My hands are." He held up a sticky hand covered in ice cream.

Charlie couldn't help laughing and for a fraction of a second he noticed the curves of a smile lift the edges of Lane's lips, but before he could linger on them too long she turned and grabbed for some napkins.

"Your husband, is he deployed?"

The second the words fell from his mouth, he regretted them. Darkness seemed to shroud her features for a moment until the emotion vanished almost as quickly as the ice cream was melting. Deployment was hard on families. He knew better.

"No. He died two years ago." Lane finished wiping Noah's hands.

He'd been a fool not to figure it out before. Noah wore his father's dog tags and referred to him in the past tense, and she always changed the subject to avoid talking about him. An ache settled in Charlie's chest. Another casualty. Another family left behind.

"I'm sorry."

"Don't be." She frowned, tucking a loose strand of hair behind her ear. "It wasn't your fault."

That was an odd response. "No, but we should all bear the burden of responsibility for the sacrifice made by your husband. For that I'm grateful, and I'm sorry for your and Noah's loss."

Lane's eyes flashed under thick, dark lashes. "I think that's enough ice cream for the night. Can you tell the deputy thank you for joining us?"

"What's a deputy?" Noah tilted his head.

"It's a police officer." Lane took the soupy mess from Noah's hands and pitched it into the nearest trash can.

The little boy wrinkled his nose and brought his finger up to his chin in deep concentration. His eyes grew wide. "But you're not wearing your policeman uniform."

"I'm not working right now." Charlie smiled at the little boy, admiring him. "But I have this." He reached into his back pocket and pulled out his wallet and showed Noah his badge.

"Don't touch that," Lane said as Noah reached for it. "I don't think the deputy wants sticky ice cream fingers all over his shiny badge."

"Charlie."

Confusion pinched the smooth skin between her eyebrows.

"He can call me Charlie."

"If I wash my hands, then can I touch it?"

"Noah, it's getting late." Lane glanced at her son.

"Can I walk Bane back to our house?"

Lane seemed tense. Maybe she really didn't want to be here with him? His stomach knotted. He finished the last of his ice cream and tossed his trash. "It's alright with me. Bane actually seems calmer around Noah, but I'll hold the leash too."

"Please, Momma."

If Lane could resist Noah's pleading eyes, she was a lot stronger than he'd ever be. A single outing for ice cream and Charlie was already willing to give Noah anything and everything the little boy wanted.

Lane chewed on her bottom lip for a second before answering, "Okay, sure."

Charlie couldn't tell who was more excited—Bane or Noah.

"He's licking my fingers." Noah giggled.

"I think he likes you." Charlie watched his dog's pace slow to match the little boy walking him. Kid's best friend. Maybe he could convince Lane to let Noah help him walk Bane every day. Or at least play with him. A good excuse to see more of them.

The chirping of crickets serenaded them home and Charlie couldn't deny the desire burning in his heart for more of this. This is what he longed for. Summer nights walking with a beautiful woman and their kids. And dog. The thought made him smile and he stole a glance at Lane. She was watching Noah and Bane. Charlie would do anything to know what she was thinking, but the walk to his house came to an end too quickly.

Lane took the leash from Noah's hand. "Thanks for the ice cream."

"Thanks for inviting me." Charlie searched her face for any indication that her emotions matched his, but nightfall obscured the answer. "I can walk you to your house—"

"We'll be alright. Good night, Charlie."

"Good night, Charlie." Noah echoed. "Good night, Bane."

Charlie watched mom and son walk until they rounded the corner heading to their street. Bane barked after them.

"Yeah, I know, Bane."

What *did* he know? Lane was a widow. She was protective of Noah. He also knew that ignoring the way his heart pounded in his chest for the woman who still wore a piece of her heart on her finger was going to be impossible.

EIGHT

LANE ICED THE TENTH BATCH of cinnamon rolls. Setting down the spatula dripping with cream cheese frosting, she picked up her third cup of coffee. Sleep had evaded her again last night, but this time it was because of her neighbor whose name she couldn't seem to get off the tip of her tongue. *Charlie.*

Ms. Byrdie popped her head around the corner. "Gail Evans just called and asked if it was too late to order a dozen rolls for the PTA meeting."

"On top of the three she already ordered?"

"Mm-hmm. She said those women practically licked their plates."

Lane wiped the back of her hand against her brow. "Yeah, I'll box this batch for her and I've got another two dozen in the oven that should hopefully cover us for the rest of the morning."

"I think you could sell these rolls and nothing else and live happily ever after."

Happily ever after. The words stung even though the woman delivering them hadn't meant them to be hurtful. Purchasing the Way Station Café had been Ms. Byrdie's idea—a way Lane could make use of her sleepless nights. When Ms. Byrdie explained the way she'd been serving the community through Friday Night Club, Lane found it to be an easy decision. And the café kept her busy. And busy meant Lane didn't have to think about her past. Or her guilt. Or her broken happily ever after.

Lane grabbed the bag of sugar. "I think this town has an insatiable sweet tooth."

"It is the South, shugah." Ms. Byrdie winked and then disappeared back to the front.

An hour and a half later, Lane placed the last pinwheels of

dough and cinnamon sugar onto a tray before pulling a hot batch of cinnamon rolls out of the oven and setting them on a rack to cool. She cleaned up the bowls, put away the remaining ingredients, marked down what they'd need from their supplier, and was about to head upstairs when she heard his voice. The cadence of his words set her heart marching in her chest.

"I could smell these two blocks away."

Lane edged her way down the hallway and peeked around the corner of the kitchen. The man could wear a uniform, that was for sure. She sighed and his name escaped her lips. "Charlie."

"Morning, Lane." His lips slipped into a smile. "Someone said these cinnamon rolls are the best thing in Walton."

"Charlie's here to pick up the last batch of cinnamon rolls. We're officially sold out." Ms. Byrdie looked at her watch. "Less than two hours. I think that's a record. Right, Lane?"

Had he heard her whisper his name? She stepped out of the hallway and toward the counter, hoping it looked like she meant to come this way and wasn't just called out for hiding. He was watching her with those eyes, those big blue eyes that felt like an ocean she could easily drift away in. Lane shook her head. "Uh, yeah, I think so. I'm just going to go start icing those."

She was about to turn when the toe of her shoe caught the edge of an auction item box, sending it and her careening forward. Lane cringed knowing she was going down, when a pair of strong arms slipped under her right before impact.

"Gotta watch out for boxes," Charlie teased. "They'll jump out and grab you."

Lane's cheeks burned with embarrassment. *Seriously?* At this point it probably looked like she was throwing herself at him. She disentangled herself from his grip, struggling to ignore the woodsy scent of his skin and the way the entire scenario made her feel less stable now than she had when she was falling.

Charlie bent down and picked up the box from the floor. He gave it a little shake. "I don't think anything's broken."

"I hope not." Lane took it from him. "My sister would kill me if something happened to the art pieces."

"Art?" Charlie quirked an eyebrow.

"I'll go get started on icing those rolls." Ms. Byrdie gave a less-than-subtle wink in Lane's direction before ducking into the kitchen.

"Coffee. You need coffee with those cinnamon rolls." Lane moved toward the counter, taking extra care to watch her footing. Really—what was wrong with her lately? It was like some cliché Hallmark movie scene where the lovestruck girl falls into the arms of the handsome boy. Sheesh. Charlie was definitely handsome, but she wasn't lovestruck—was she?

When she was safely behind the counter, Lane began filling a travel coffee urn. "I'm a little low on decaf, but if you have time I can brew another pot."

"I bring decaf back and it's likely I'll never have a weekend off." Charlie was still next to the boxes. He lifted one and read the mailing label. "You collect art?"

"No." Lane withdrew a bag and began filling it with creamers and packets of sugar. "Those are donations for an upcoming fund-raiser."

"Any of it local?"

"I'm not sure. Maybe. You like art?"

Charlie returned to the counter and shrugged. "Just curious, I guess."

Lane needed to check on the cinnamon rolls, but Ms. Byrdie was already stepping out of the kitchen with two boxes in her hands.

"These should bring some joy to the station."

"I know *my* morning's already better." Charlie passed a quick glance in Lane's direction. "But I better get these back there before any riots break out."

"Have a good day, honey." Ms. Byrdie nodded. "Tell Huggy he's not allowed to eat any of those."

"Yes, ma'am."

Lane busied herself with a towel, but from the corner of her eye she watched Charlie get into his truck and drive away.

Ms. Byrdie's violet eyes sparkled. "Seems you two keep bumping into each other—literally."

Lane groaned. "He told you about the drinks?"

"He might've mentioned that little incident." Ms. Byrdie's gentle laughter filled the space between them. "You've made quite an impression on him."

"I can only imagine the impression I've left on him." Her thoughts went back to those seconds on the bridge. "He hasn't exactly caught me at my best."

"Honey, we can only be who God created us to be. Mess and all."

If anyone else brought up God, Lane dismissed them, but Ms. Byrdie never pushed the subject. Her faith came out in gentle displays of kindness and love. She had taken care of Lane and all the other kids at school who needed a loving mentor. How many kids had she saved?

A tinge of jealousy lapped at Lane's heart. Why couldn't she have a faith like Ms. Byrdie's? Would it have helped save Mathias? Would it have prevented depression from rotting her from the inside out? Lane sucked in a sharp breath. There were so many days when she wanted to give up. Believed the fight wasn't worth it.

"I'm so grateful for you and Sheriff Huggins. I wouldn't be here—" Lane choked on the lump in her throat.

"Honey, it's hard. I know." Ms. Byrdie pulled her into a strong embrace. "You know you're not meant to go it alone. Huggy and I are on your side. God too."

Lane bit her lip. She didn't need to hide anything from Ms. Byrdie. The woman already knew her secrets and loved her despite them. Was that a shared family trait too?

After a few seconds, Ms. Byrdie released Lane but held her gaze. "If there's one thing I know about God—he's a God of second chances. And sometimes second chances come tall and in a uniform."

A second chance? With Charlie? What would that look like—or

feel like? Was it possible? A spark of hope lit inside her chest but was smothered instantly as one thought played through Lane's mind. Charlie didn't know the truth and if he did . . . would he believe she was worthy of a second chance?

〰〰〰〰〰〰〰

"You ready?" Charlie looked in on Deputy Frost. The young man's shoulders were hunched over the keyboard in front of him. His skin looked pastier than usual and he'd lost a bit of the charge he'd first had at the beginning of the investigation. Charlie figured a field trip might bring some color and life back to Frost's bearing.

"Yes." Frost pushed out of his chair so fast it slid into the table behind him. "Do I need my jacket? Oh, I have to get my hat." He patted the holster on his hip and looked like he was running through a checklist in his mind.

"It's a thousand degrees outside, so you won't need your jacket, but you will need your hat." There's the pep. Charlie smiled. Sheriff Huggins had offered to go with him to talk with the gallery owner in Savannah, but Charlie had suggested it would be a good chance for Frost to gain some experience . . . and some sun.

It took Frost a full five minutes to stop squinting once they stepped out of the station. His posture straightened the farther they drove toward Savannah, but a little twitch in his hand made Charlie pause. Was he nervous or excited?

"What made you become a deputy, Frost?"

The young man shrugged. "Chicks dig a man in uniform."

Charlie gawked until Frost crumbled into a fit of hysterics for so long that he couldn't help but join. "For the chicks, huh?"

"Well, it worked for you." Frost's eyebrows danced above his glasses. "You've been in town what, a few weeks, and already half the town is all googly-eyed for you. Even my sister."

Charlie rolled his eyes. "Please tell me she's not the one who keeps calling the office and then hanging up when I pick up the phone?" Frost laughed and shook his head. Charlie relaxed a little.

The only person he hoped was googly-eyed for him was Lane Kent, and she seemed content to make him guess what those green eyes of hers were saying—or hiding. "How'd you get into computers?"

"I wasn't a popular kid. Got picked on. Mom bought me a computer from a pawnshop and I spent a lot of time in my room. Taught myself how to use it. I figured I'd always be able to find a job if I could master the computer."

Frost was humble and proving himself to be a man, albeit a young man, of character.

"When I was in high school, your aunt told me there are universities where I could study computer science, so I researched it." Frost snorted. "MIT. Stanford. I'd have a better chance of getting Jennifer Aniston to be my girlfriend than getting into one of those schools." Another snort.

Jennifer Aniston? Charlie imagined a poster from *Friends* tacked up on Frost's bedroom wall. He seriously needed to update his crushes.

"Anyway, I kept searching and found a site. DEFCON Hacking Conference." Frost's lips slipped into a sly grin. "Pretty cool name, huh?"

"Very cool." And highly suspicious.

"They hold a competition every year in Las Vegas. Well, I couldn't afford to go, but I . . ." Frost shifted in his seat. "I sort of cheated my way into the contest."

"How'd you do that?"

"I started following this guy on Facebook. He was going and we started chatting. I end up hacking into his computer and then mirrored his system so I could see exactly what he was seeing."

"You mirrored his system?" It was like Frost was the Bobby Fischer of computer hacking.

"Yeah, remotely. Anyway, it caused a huge problem. The judges caught the anomaly and thought *he* was cheating. He wasn't. I was just overriding his system."

"What happened?"

"I got caught." Frost shrugged. "A couple of government agencies came to town. They really do drive sedans with tinted windows. Just like in the movies."

The whole thing sounded like it could've been in a movie. "Did you get in trouble?"

"No. That's the best part. They wanted *me* to come work for them after I graduated high school. CIA wanted me to go to college first. They offered to pay, but the schools were out of state. I couldn't leave my mom and sister."

"So, you stayed here and became a deputy?"

"Yep. Went to college at Anderson and Sheriff Huggins said a few years working here would give me the experience I'd need to work for the Feds." Frost wiggled his fingers like he was typing on the air. "Magic fingers."

"Does anyone else know you're a genius?"

Deep red melted Frost's freckles into a blotchy blush. He pushed up his glasses. "Besides the sheriff, you're the only person to ever ask."

Charlie took the exit to Savannah. Long moss dripped from the limbs of the large oak trees shading the old streets. People crowded the sidewalks outside boutiques or gathered on benches in the small parks tucked between Georgian style homes with their tall chimneys standing sentry.

"You ready to use that brain for some police work?" Charlie pulled into a tight spot in front of the Bohemian Signature Gallery.

"Oh yeah."

After they climbed out of the car, Frost hitched his thumbs into his gun belt and appeared to be assessing the storefront. The building had large colonnades of aged redbrick that framed wide windows displaying several painted canvases in gold-gilded frames.

"Oh, that's the antique store from the photo." Frost's exuberance grabbed a few curious stares.

"That magic brain of yours know anything about art?"

"Nope."

"Me either." Charlie opened the door and a bell jingled, announcing their entrance. "I'm going to ask the owner some questions. If you think of anything or if I forget something, I want you to speak up. Got it?"

Frost nodded and strolled into the gallery like an Earp brother would stroll into Tombstone. Hiding his grin, Charlie followed him in.

The interior of the gallery was larger than it appeared from the outside. Temporary walls positioned in the middle of the room held art of varying sizes. Some had wild strokes of bright colors while others depicted scenery or portraits.

A young man with a small goatee was eyeing them instead of the framed prints he was pretending to look at. Charlie walked over. The wall was covered with black-and-white photos of people sitting on stoops, buildings falling apart, and live oaks bending beneath dark clouds. It reminded him of Lane's photos.

"Did you take any of these?"

Goatee man shook his head. "Nah, man. I'm into oils and acrylics. Metal too if the urge is there."

"Cool." Charlie raised his eyebrows. He had no idea what goatee man meant, so he left him to his musings.

"Can I help you?" Black heels clicked against the polished wood floor. A tall woman with black hair cut to match the angle of her thin jawline approached.

"Hello, ma'am. I'm Deputy Lynch and this is Deputy Frost. Do you work here?"

"I'm Annika Benedict, the owner." It took a second for her dark eyes to do a sweep of them. "How can I help you?"

"Ms. Benedict, we're from Walton and would like to ask you a few questions about a case we're investigating."

"An investigation?"

A bell jingled and two young women entered, causing Frost's posture to straighten. A flash of something Charlie couldn't identify passed over Ms. Benedict's face.

"We need help identifying an artist." Charlie pulled out his phone. He'd taken a screenshot of the Facebook page. "These paintings in"—he held up the phone—"this picture were taken outside your gallery."

Ms. Benedict pulled on the bright red glasses dangling from her neck and studied the pictures on the phone. "And why do you need to know who the artist is?"

"Like I said, ma'am, it's part of an investigation."

Frost's gaze followed the two girls wandering through the gallery. One had hot pink hair and a nose ring. The other carried a large black tube slung across her back and wore a shirt with the initials SCAD on the front. They didn't look much older than Sydney. Would they have known her?

"I wish I could help you, but unless I have permission from the artist I'm not at liberty to tell you who they are," Ms. Benedict answered, removing her glasses.

"Why not?" Charlie lifted one eyebrow.

A thin laugh pushed through equally thin lips. "Some artists want to be known. Others wish to live in obscurity, allowing their art to have the spotlight."

"I don't think this artist is going to be worried about the spotlight anymore." Charlie locked eyes with the dismissive owner. "We believe this artist was murdered."

"What?" Ms. Benedict clapped her hand over her mouth. "Killed? How terrible."

"So, you know the artist?"

"I do." She nodded.

"Can you confirm the name of the artist?"

"Sydney. Sydney Donovan." She clutched her throat. "I . . . I really just can't believe it."

"How long have you known Sydney?" Charlie pulled out his notebook and pen.

"Oh, I wouldn't say I really knew her. I know her art, of course, but I didn't have much contact with her."

"And you're sure these are her paintings?"

"Yes. Follow me." Ms. Benedict turned on her heel and walked to the back of the gallery. She stopped in front of a display with varying sizes of painted art pieces. "This"—she pointed to a medium-size picture off to one side—"is one of Sydney's pieces."

Deep reds faded up into lighter shades. The piece was named *Burning Dawn*.

Frost pushed up his glasses and leaned close to the painting. Then he pulled back, removed his glasses, and looked again. "There's no signature."

"Not all artists sign their names in the way we expect." Ms. Benedict stepped forward and drew a line with her finger along a bright red stroke. "If you look closely, you can see her signature."

Charlie followed the deep red brushstroke and saw a small curve and then another. Sydney Donovan incorporated her signature into her art. Was it hidden for a reason?

"It's quite brilliant, if you ask me. Most want their names recognized, but not Sydney."

"Sydney's parents didn't know about her painting. According to her school, she's never taken an art class. Do you know why she would have kept her talent a secret?"

"I didn't know Sydney very well. Perhaps she was afraid."

"Of what?" Frost spoke up.

Ms. Benedict frowned. "I don't know. Most artists are introverts. Displaying their work takes courage. Maybe she couldn't handle criticism, so she kept her work hidden."

"And yet you found it." Charlie didn't like the feeling growing in his gut. Ms. Benedict was being helpful without helping. "How did you come to acquire her art?"

"I don't recall how I came to acquire Sydney's art. I must've seen something in it that I liked. Still do." Ms. Benedict ran her hand along the edge of the painted canvas. "It's a shame this is all I have left."

"But you don't know where you met her?"

"Deputy, I own an art gallery, a reputable one. I get hundreds of inquiries a week from starving artists wanting a chance to display their work. I might have met her once or twice. But clearly those moments don't stand out."

"If you don't deal directly with the artist when bringing in new pieces, who does?"

"It depends. I do try to handle all inquiries, but I'm busy. Often I'll agree to bring in a piece and allow it to be displayed to see what kind of response I get."

"How much does a piece like this sell for?" Frost tapped Sydney's painting.

"Why? Are you interested?" A thin smile spread across Ms. Benedict's face. "The asking price for this piece is twelve hundred dollars."

Frost snorted. "You're serious?"

Charlie cast a look at Frost that silenced his snickering.

Ms. Benedict's eyes narrowed. "Very."

"Is that customary for a piece like this?" Charlie asked.

"No. Sydney's work was the exception."

The painting was nice but $1,200? Art was definitely in the eye of the beholder and in the hands of someone with a lot of money to spare.

"How many pieces of her art have you—"

"Excuse me." Ms. Benedict moved past them as the bell above the door jingled.

A well-dressed man entered and Ms. Benedict greeted him with a kiss on both cheeks. She spoke to him a few seconds before pointing toward a small hallway at the back of the gallery. The man held Charlie's gaze as he walked by, leaving a familiar scent behind.

"I'm sorry, gentlemen, but I have an appointment I must keep." Ms. Benedict raised her hand toward the door.

"We still have a few more questions." Charlie wasn't even close to finished.

"I want to help, but this is my business and, well, I'm busy." Ms.

Benedict reached across the desk and pulled a business card from the stack. "Here's my number. Call and set up an appointment."

"Yes, ma'am." Charlie took the card. In Afghanistan, if someone had information they'd be kept until it was wrung out of them.

"Have a good day, gentlemen."

Ms. Benedict disappeared down the same hall the man went down and left Charlie and Frost staring after her.

"I get the feeling she's not telling us the whole truth."

"My thoughts exactly." Charlie pushed out a frustrated sigh. There was nothing they could do about it now. He stuck the card in his pocket. He'd be calling for that appointment. A lot sooner than Ms. Benedict would probably like.

The two girls who'd come in earlier were sitting on a bench near the door, filling out paperwork. Frost paused. "What does your shirt mean?"

Both girls looked up, startled at the man in uniform staring over them. "What? My shirt?"

Charlie cringed. He'd need to help the kid with his pickup lines.

"Savannah College of Art and Design," the girl with pink hair answered.

"Are you artists?"

"Um, yeah." Again, the pink-haired girl answered. Her friend in the SCAD T-shirt elbowed her.

"Deputy Frost?"

Frost held up his hand for Charlie to wait. "Is your art here in the gallery?"

"I wish," the SCAD T-shirt girl answered. "That's why we're filling out this paperwork." She lifted the papers in her hand. "Ms. Benedict is looking for new artists."

"Does Ms. Benedict do this often?" Now Charlie was intrigued. Maybe this was how Sydney's art was acquired?

"This is the only gallery in Savannah that'll give art students a chance to display their art. A few of the students even get lucky enough to sell their work." SCAD girl let out a heavy sigh. "If I could sell just a couple of my paintings, I'd be able to graduate with no debt."

"Well, good luck." Frost tipped his hat just like John Wayne.

"Thanks," SCAD girl said.

The gallery door closed with a whoosh behind them as they headed for the patrol car. Charlie cranked the air-conditioning to full blast in an attempt to rid the stifling Savannah heat that had turned the car into a sauna.

"So, we know Sydney was an artist and this is where she sold her art."

"And that's about it." Charlie rubbed the back of his neck. This was their strongest lead and yet it led them nowhere. He'd be returning to Sheriff Huggins with nothing.

"No. We've got more than that."

"What am I missing?"

"Two things." Frost held up two fingers. "First, someone's paying a lot of money for a painting done by a teenager. I'm no specialist, but I can guess that work is overpriced—even for Savannah. We need to find out who's buying her work. And second, Sydney doesn't have a car." Frost sat back with a satisfied grin.

"And that's important why?"

"If homegirl didn't have a car, how'd she get her art to the gallery?"

"Okay, two things." Charlie started the car. "First, don't ever say homegirl again, especially when referring to our victim. And second, where's a good place for me to buy your genius brain lunch?"

The kid still had a lot to learn, but he was right. This trip finally gave them the leads they needed, and for the first time since leaving the Marines, Charlie was beginning to see the future he longed for.

NINE

"ANY MORE BOXES and you'll have more art than food."

Lane looked at the small room she used to store food items at the back of the Way Station Café. At the moment, Ms. Byrdie was right. Most of the boxes stacked against the wall belonged to her sister, Meagan.

"A few more weeks and it'll all be gone." Lane signed for the delivery of more auction items and sighed. "I hope."

"Do you want me to help you move this one?" Ms. Byrdie gave an appraising look at the tall, thin box.

"Ms. Lane, I can get that for you."

This evening two regulars were visiting the café. Dottie and Harley Jones. A couple with personalities as unforgettable as their appearances. Tonight, the bottled blonde wore glittery blue eye shadow that matched her blouse, shorts, and nail polish on her toes. In contrast to all Dottie's femininity, her husband, Harley, was the opposite. His long black hair interspersed with gray was pulled back into a ponytail. Black shirt, black pants, motorcycle boots. It was the same wardrobe every time Lane saw him. The only color he wore came in the form of tiny beads in a rainbow of colors strung together on a shoelace tied around his neck. A gift from a tribe in northern Sudan that Harley received while serving there on a missionary trip.

"It's not too heavy." Lane slid-pushed the box into the dining area and settled it against the wall behind the sofa.

"Momma, do I have to eat these green beans?"

Lane swung her gaze over her shoulder to Noah, who was sitting at the counter pushing his food around with his fork. "Yes."

"How 'bout if I eat these green beans can I play with my Sarco-suchus for"—he tilted his head, thinking—"for fifteen minutes?" Noah held up his hand, palm flat, fingers splayed.

Lane bit her lip. Her willpower seemed to melt when it came to Noah. "Fifteen minutes—if you eat all your green beans and two more bites of your mashed potatoes."

Noah sighed and then looked at his plate. With a determined expression, he scooped up the first bite and ate it.

"I'd have negotiated for twenty minutes."

"Hush now, Harley." Dottie grinned before giving Lane a playful wink.

"Can I get you two more sweet tea?" Lane went to the counter and lifted a pitcher.

"We're good. This was delicious as always, Lane." Harley lifted his fork and pointed it at Noah. "And if he doesn't want his, I'll take it."

"Oh, he'll eat his if he wants to play with his—" *What was the name of that dinosaur?* "Well, he'll eat if he wants to play with his toys. Nonnegotiable—"

The screen door at the back of the café slapped open, silencing the room and jerking everyone's attention to the lone figure that entered. Miguel.

"Hi, Miguel!" Lane started for him but stopped short at the sight of his hands.

"Miguel, what happened?" Lane reached for his hands. Deep red gashes were etched into his palms. Most of them were scabbed over, but a few oozed bright red. He drew them back. "You're hurt."

Ms. Byrdie appeared from the kitchen, concern in her eyes.

Miguel's dark eyes darted around the room. "I-I just . . ."

"Momma?" Noah's voice sounded tiny.

Lane was unable to take her eyes off the slices in his palms. "You need to go to the hospital, Miguel."

"Momma, is he hurt?"

"No. I sh-should go." His voice was scratchy and low. "Shouldn't . . . shouldn't have come h-here."

"Wait." Lane rested her hand on his shoulder, but Miguel jerked away from her touch. "Let me get you something to eat before you go."

"Noah, why don't you come help me make a plate for Mister Miguel?" Ms. Byrdie took Noah's hand and led him to the counter.

Miguel shifted but remained silent. Lane hustled back to the counter. Where had he been? What had happened to his hands? They needed to be cleaned with antibiotics, maybe even stitched up, but if a meal was all he'd wait for, then that's what she'd offer him. She grabbed a Styrofoam cup and filled it with ice and tea.

"Is he okay?" Ms. Byrdie looked up from the to-go container she was filling with food. Noah was sitting at a stool near the counter, concentrating on a coloring book of dinosaurs.

Lane put a lid on the cup. "His hands look like they've been put through a slicer."

"Where'd he go?" Dottie asked.

The hallway where Miguel had stood seconds ago was empty. Harley stood and walked down the hall toward the back door.

"Wha—he was just here." What was going on? "His hands. He needs to go to the hospital."

"He's gone." Harley came back inside, carrying a flat, rectangular box in his hand. "This was near the steps though. Delivery guy must've forgotten to bring it in."

"Just set it on top of the others," Lane said. "Should we go after him?"

"Miguel carves wood. Sculpts." Harley lifted his napkin from the floor and set it on his empty plate. "Did it a lot when he first came home from Nam. Painful hobby, but it seemed to help him cope with his monsters."

Lane bit her lip. She understood monsters. "Something's not right. This is the first time we've seen him in what, a couple of weeks? And then when he does show up, his hands are a bloody mess."

"He only sculpts when it's bad." Harley scratched the stubble on his cheek. "He might not have died in those rice paddies, but his soul sure did."

"Honey"—Ms. Byrdie squeezed Lane's shoulder—"Miguel's having a bad day. He'll be back."

"But what if he doesn't come back? He looked . . . scared."

"It wasn't too long ago that men like Ducky or Miguel wouldn't be seen coming into town. Too many men came home from Vietnam different from the boys they were when they left, and I'm sad to say too many people in this town have been content to let them disappear into themselves. But not you. You brought him back with good food and a kind heart."

"Ms. Byrdie's right. Hard to say which is the worse fate." Harley grabbed Dottie's hand. "There was a time when Miguel was convinced no one would notice if he was gone. He doesn't say much, but don't think your kindness goes unnoticed. He'll be back."

The front door of the café opened and a man entered. Lane didn't give him a second glance. Her heart ached. How many times had she had that same thought? Believing no one would notice if she just slipped away. For good. Is that why she was drawn to him? She understood what it was like to cope with monsters.

And to do it alone.

Ms. Byrdie's words echoed in her ear, *"You're not meant to do this alone."* Well, if that was true for her, then it was true for Miguel too.

An hour later a group of teens left fully caffeinated and Lane wrapped up the last of the food and put it away in the refrigerator. A quick survey of leftovers revealed she might be able to offer vegetable soup as the next day's lunch special.

"I finished the list of items we need to reorder from Gus," Ms. Byrdie said around a yawn. "There's one customer left, but he's paid and just finishing his coffee."

"Sounds good. Why don't you head on home. I can finish cleaning and lock up."

"You sure, honey? I don't mind sticking around." But Ms. Byrdie was already untying her apron.

"I'm sure."

After hanging up the apron on a hook near the convection oven, Ms. Byrdie gave Lane a hug before disappearing down the hall and out the back door. Lane grabbed a towel and headed into the dining area.

"These pictures are nice."

The deep voice scared Lane right out of her skin. She spun around and saw the man standing near the wall where a dozen or so photographs and paintings hung. Hadn't Ms. Byrdie said all the customers were gone? No, she said there was one more—a man—finishing up his coffee.

"Are they yours?" The man's back was turned to her as he studied each picture. Finished coffee or not, he didn't seem to be in a hurry to leave.

Lane smoothed her apron before checking her watch. It was only a few minutes past closing. And it wasn't in her to shove anyone out of her café . . . but she *was* tired. Maybe if she kept the chitchat to a minimum and started to clean up, the guy would get the hint.

"Some. Some are local artists." Lane began straightening chairs. Ms. Byrdie had done a good job cleaning up. Too good. There wasn't much left for Lane to do. She took a step toward the front door. "I hope you enjoyed your meal tonight. Ms. Byrdie is making her famous fried chicken tomorrow night—"

"Your mother?" The man returned his attention to the paintings on the wall. "She lives here too?"

Oh-kay. Hint not taken. Lane studied the man closer. Hands shoved inside his pockets, he wore a long-sleeve shirt, the collar pulled close to his neck but not so close that she couldn't see the edge of a tattoo peeking out. A baseball cap shaded his face, but she caught something familiar there. Did she know him?

Didn't matter. He needed to leave. The sooner, the better.

"Your husband was in the Army?"

The room seemed to shift for a second. What? Clearly, she hadn't heard the man correctly. She blinked a couple of times before her gaze landed on his dark one staring back at her. The sense of familiarity lingered, but Lane was certain the man wasn't local to Walton and therefore wouldn't—shouldn't—know anything about Mathias.

"Your niño looks like you though."

Lane's gaze whipped in the direction of the family photo she kept up near the cash register. One of the last ones taken of Mathias, Noah, and her. The only one she kept downstairs. Next to it was the baby monitor she still used when she worked downstairs while Noah was upstairs—where he was now. Sleeping.

"I'm sorry to push you out, but we're closed now and I need to begin preparations for tomorrow." This time Lane walked straight to the front door and opened it, leaving no mistake that it was time for him to go.

The man's eyes narrowed a second before the smallest sliver of a smile pulled at the right side of his lips. He withdrew his hands from his pockets and Lane's heart seized. Tattoos. On his fingers. She *did* know the man. He was the one from the shadows outside the café. The one asking about a place to eat.

He stuck a toothpick in the side of his mouth before peeling several dollar bills from a money clip. After dropping them in the tip jar, he started for the door before pausing. "Maybe I'll stop by for that fried chicken."

The second he walked out, Lane locked the door behind him and hoped he didn't. In fact, she'd be content never to see the strange man again.

TEN

SHERIFF HUGGINS RAN HIS FINGERS through his hair before lacing them behind his neck. Charlie watched as the sheriff's weathered features firmed and then slacked as he stared out the window. Thinking. Trying to put the pieces together that had Charlie and the rest of the deputies puzzled.

"Why was she hiding her art?"

"I don't know, sir. Kids hide things from their parents."

"But she wasn't hiding a life of drugs or alcohol," Sheriff Huggins reasoned, leaning forward in his chair. "She was hiding her talent. Why?"

"Our meeting with the gallery owner didn't offer us any answers on that front. Ms. Benedict—"

"Benedict?" Sheriff Huggins's gaze swung to Charlie. "Annika Benedict?"

"You know her, sir?"

Sheriff Huggins gazed out the window again. "Her father. Noble Benedict. The infamous Savannah district attorney and philanthropist. Although his generous spirit never reached inside the courtroom. A bit of a wolf in sheep's clothing."

Charlie thought about his meeting with Annika. That description seemed to fit her too, but why, he didn't quite know yet. "Ms. Benedict wasn't very *generous* in her information regarding Sydney. Claimed she didn't remember how she acquired Sydney's art or where she met her."

"You think she's lying?"

"I'm not sure it's the whole truth." Charlie shrugged. "First impressions of the woman don't have me pegging her as the charitable type."

"No, I don't think she shares her father's passion for helping others, but she does donate supplies for the veterans' art program and our community center still receives a healthy donation annually. A new veterans home is being built near the river by Ford Plantation. Noble always had a softness for veterans. He had a heart condition"—Sheriff Huggins tapped his chest—"that kept him from being drafted. Went to college while his friends were being killed or coming home wounded."

Charlie shuffled the contents of the file in his lap. His father joined the Marines at the end of the Vietnam War but wasn't drafted. He volunteered . . . and Charlie never asked him why. Maybe like Noble Benedict he felt a sense of duty? Obligation?

"What else do we have on Sydney's background?"

The question returned Charlie's focus. "Her parents and teachers paint her as the all-American kid—no pun intended. Honor student. Was accepted to Anderson University on a partial scholarship. Volunteered locally. No history of drug or alcohol abuse. Not allowed to date—"

"No boyfriend?"

"No, sir. Not according to her father."

Sheriff Huggins drummed his fingers on the desk but said nothing more.

"Best friends are Jolene Carson and Annabeth Mendoza—"

"Jolene Carson is the one Sydney was supposed to spend the weekend with, right?"

"Yes, sir. They've been friends since kindergarten." Charlie flipped through his notes. "Jolene Carson is coming in shortly. Deputy Wilson spoke with Annabeth Mendoza yesterday."

"Any other friends?"

"I had Deputy Wilson talk with the principal at the school, along with Sydney's teachers, to see if there's anyone else we should interview. We got a few names. Deputy Wilson's going through that list now."

"Based on what you just told me, does she seem like the kind of girl who would have a private Facebook account?"

"No, but maybe she was hiding something else." Charlie thought about his meeting with Annika Benedict. That reminded him. "Sir, we've checked all the evidence and Sydney's cell phone was not recovered at the scene."

"Teenagers, especially girls, don't leave home without their phones, do they, Lynch?"

"No, sir. Her parents gave me a description and the serial number, but if the phone is turned off or dead it will be impossible to track."

"Contact their provider. They might be able to tell us the last location picked up by satellite."

"Yes, sir." Charlie flexed his jaw at the oversight. Why hadn't he thought of that? How many times had they found terrorists hiding in holes because of the cyber crumb trail they left behind?

"And you're making good use of Agent Padello?"

"Yes, sir." Charlie appreciated Sheriff Huggins's humility and willingness to reach out for help. Even if it meant reaching out to another agency. Far too many times Charlie had seen pride destroy lives because one alpha team had to outdo another alpha team, only to have the enemy humble everyone with an overlooked IED. "The FBI agent has been working with Frost on Sydney's computer. We're hoping we find something there."

"Deputy Lynch." Deputy Benningfield knocked on the doorframe of Sheriff Huggins's office. "You have a visitor. Lane Kent."

"Thank you." A zing zipped through Charlie's heart before his gaze landed on the sheriff. Gray eyes held concern. "She's probably here for her memory card. Deputy Frost is finished with it."

"Go take care of it."

As Charlie stood and moved to the door, he could feel the sheriff's stare boring holes into him. Why did it feel like he'd been caught with the man's daughter? He stopped by his desk and grabbed her memory card. His heart thumped in his chest. Whether it was because of the troubled look on the sheriff's face or because Lane was waiting for him, he wasn't sure.

In the front of the station, he found Lane chatting with Deputy Benningfield. Lane's long hair was pulled into a ponytail, revealing the delicate features of her face. Their eyes met and she smiled, a small one, but it was powerful enough to send his pulse thrumming.

"Lane just made herself the best friend of every officer in the station." Deputy Benningfield's eyes sparkled as she looked in Charlie's direction, giving him a wink before heading back to her desk.

"I just brought in some cookies. And these." Lane picked up a tray of drinks and brought them to the counter. "To make up for the ones I spilled the other day." She bit her lip as she glanced down at his uniform. "And I'd still like to pay for your dry cleaning."

"The coffee and cinnamon rolls more than made up for the drinks. And I learned a long time ago how to get stains out of my clothing."

Her dark lashes fluttered. "That's a good skill to have."

"A virtue instilled in me during basic training." And a father who required order down to the folds of his underwear.

Her face shifted. Pain pinched the edges of her eyes. "You were in the military?"

"Yes. Marines."

Lane seemed to consider his answer before speaking. "I don't want to keep you—"

"Wait." Charlie looked down at the memory card in his hand. "We're done with this."

"Oh, thanks." Lane took the card from him and put it in her pocket. "Did it help?"

"We're looking through the photos. You're good. I mean, the pictures. They're really good."

"Thank you." A pink hue colored her cheeks. "I should go."

"Um, right. I'll, uh, just walk you out." Charlie came around the counter. What was he doing? He could already feel the stares piercing his back—not enough body armor to defend him from the teasing that would assault him when he returned to his desk. He didn't care. He held the glass door open for her. "Dinner." He blurted the word out like he'd just learned how to talk.

"What?"

Charlie let the glass door close behind them, giving them a little privacy. "Would you like to have dinner with me sometime?"

Lane swallowed. Her gaze fell to her hand, the one with the golden reminder on it. Charlie's heart sank.

"Maybe."

Her voice was so quiet that he thought he had misheard her. "Maybe?"

She lifted her chin, her green eyes meeting his. "I like dinner."

"Me too." Charlie smiled. It felt goofy, probably looked that way too, but he couldn't help it. The zing from earlier morphed into electrical pulses that were impossible to ignore. "There's a restaurant I've heard is pretty good—"

"The church benefit," Lane said, her eyes flicking over his shoulder. "Tomorrow night."

It took a second before Charlie remembered the benefit for Sydney Donovan's family. Amid the rumors and uncertainty, Amanda and Trevor Donovan refused to allow Sydney's murder to define her, and together with the church they were having a benefit to raise money in their daughter's honor to support the arts program at the community center in Walton.

"Are you sure?"

"Yes." And then she nodded, almost like she was reassuring herself it was the right answer. "Pick me up at my place."

Lane hurried down the steps and Charlie stepped back into the station—smiling.

"Deputy Lynch."

Sheriff Huggins's gruff voice grabbed Charlie's attention. He spun around and found the man watching him, along with a few of the deputies who wore amused expressions. "Jolene Carson is waiting in the conference room."

"Yes, sir." Heat radiated from the center of Charlie's chest, up his neck, and across his face.

Charlie looked down at the tray and smiled again. He had a date.

~~~~~~~~~~~~~~

Jolene Carson hugged her arms close to her body. She shivered and Charlie dropped his gaze to the notes in front of him. Was she cold or nervous? The muggy warmth of the early summer day seemed to seep through his uniform despite the thrumming air conditioner blowing full blast.

"Would you like me to turn the air down?"

The girl shook her head, letting her long blonde curls fall over her shoulders like a blanket.

Charlie studied her clothing. Tiny shorts and revealing tops were the fashion, but they didn't appear to do anything for comfort. Jolene kept adjusting the straps falling off her shoulder or tugging at the barely there denim shorts every few minutes. His eyes shifted to Ms. Carson. Her attire wasn't much better. Nothing left to the imagination.

"Deputy Lynch." Ms. Carson's voice dripped with annoyance. "How much longer? I don't want Jolene to miss too much school." With a manicured finger, she tapped the chunky rhinestone watch on her thin wrist.

"Just a few more questions." It had taken Jolene and her mother three weeks to fit this interview into their busy schedules. A little too long, in his opinion, for someone whose best friend was killed the night they were supposed to be together. He went over the notes. "I want to make sure I've got everything so you don't have to come in again. Don't want you to miss any more school."

"It's my senior year." Jolene lifted her wide blue eyes up to meet his. She gave a tiny smile.

Jolene had reminded him of that fact several times throughout the interview. He watched her knee bounce. She was nervous.

114

He'd seen similar behavior when a soldier was called into the commander's office.

"Sydney was supposed to come to your house after school on Thursday?"

"Yes, but she didn't show up. I figured she'd changed her mind. She did that sometimes."

"What do you mean?" He leaned forward.

"Well, for a while there were times when we'd invite Sydney to hang out. She'd agree and then cancel."

"Do you know why?"

"She never told us why. We guessed it was a boy."

"Sydney had a boyfriend?"

"Oh, no." Jolene's eyes went round. "I'm not saying that. I don't think she did. Sydney never told me if she did. She wasn't allowed to date, but why else would she back out of plans? We've been friends forever."

Good point. Love had a way of interfering in someone's routine. His thoughts wandered to Lane. She would be a good interference in his day.

Ms. Carson tapped her fingers on the table, bringing Charlie's attention back to the room. "And Sydney never showed up at your house?"

"No." Jolene's lip trembled and she covered her mouth as tears spilled down her cheeks.

There was something about this Cinderella-esque girl that made him wary. Jolene was popular, smart, and probably the source of many boys' daydreams. But she was nervous. Those big blue eyes were unable to hold his gaze for long. Maybe she was just scared. After all, her best friend was murdered. Charlie pushed a box of tissues toward her.

"I'm sorry." Jolene wiped her face, and like a faucet the water-works were done. She began picking at her silver nail polish. Her leg resumed its bounce. "It's been hard without Sydney."

"Please, Deputy Lynch." Ms. Carson reached her hand over

to his. "We've been here long enough. Jolene's tired, and she lost her best friend."

"Just one more question." He looked at his notes. "Did Sydney like to paint?"

"Paint?" Jolene laughed. "Like an artist? No. Definitely not."

"She never took an art class at school?"

"No way." Jolene leaned in. "The art students are a little weird. She'd never hang out with that group."

"Is that all?" Her mother rose but stopped when Jolene remained in her chair.

"Is there anything else you'd like to tell me?"

Jolene fidgeted.

"Anything that might help."

"I don't want to get Sydney in trouble." Jolene's eyes darted between her mother's bewildered face and him.

It was silly for Jolene to think she could get her dead friend in trouble, but she was just a kid—a nervous kid with something to say.

"It's okay. If you can help us find the person who hurt Sydney, you'll be helping and honoring your friend's memory."

Jolene swallowed. "It's just that I think she did have a boyfriend."

Charlie nodded for her to continue.

"Brady Matthews. You should talk to Brady Matthews."

A new name. A new lead? After confirming Jolene wasn't holding anything else back, Charlie thanked them for their time. He escorted them to the exit and reiterated that if Jolene thought of anything else, she should call him. Ms. Carson took his business card and stuck it in her purse before winking at him.

Sheriff Huggins met Charlie at his desk. "What'd you get from Ms. Carson?"

"A wink." Charlie smirked at Sheriff Huggins's confused expression. "But the younger Ms. Carson told me Sydney might've had a boyfriend."

"A boyfriend?"

Natalie Walters

"Brady Matthews."

"That's interesting." Sheriff Huggins tilted his head. "He's on the football team. Pretty good too. Was he interviewed?"

"No." Charlie ran a hand through his hair. "His name wasn't even brought up by teachers."

"You seem bothered by that."

"Kids post everything about their lives on social media. If Sydney had a boyfriend, she did a good job hiding it from her friends and teachers."

"She hid a Facebook account."

"That's true." Charlie exhaled. "There was just something about Jolene. She was jittery. Nervous."

"Jolene seems like a good girl, even if her mother's a bit flirty. But don't let that wink tease you. Ms. Carson prefers men with established bank accounts."

"Not sure if I should be offended by that, sir."

"Take it as a warning." Sheriff Huggins sighed. "Let's talk in my office."

"Yes, sir." Why did it feel like he was being summoned to the principal's office? Once inside, Charlie remained standing after he closed the door behind him.

"Have a seat." Charlie sat and so did Sheriff Huggins. "You're doing a good job, Charlie."

"Thank you, sir." Hearing his first name set the tone for this conversation. It was personal.

"I heard you're having dinner with Lane tomorrow night?"

Charlie's cheeks grew warm. Definitely personal. "Yes, sir."

"What are your intentions with her?"

"Intentions?"

"When I learned about your move to Walton, I was under the impression that you intended to stay temporarily. Your military record is clean. Recommended promotion within the ranks. Even a medal or two. Could've had a long and successful career in the military—like your father"—Sheriff Huggins's skin tightened around his eyes—"but you left."

Charlie flexed his jaw but kept silent. The rundown of his achievements meant they weren't up for question. There was a point and he would wait until it was made.

"Makes me wonder if maybe you aren't running from something."

Was that the point? Did his uncle think he would run away if things got serious with Lane? Charlie shifted under the assumption. He wasn't running away from the Marines. He had fulfilled his obligation. Honorably. If he were running, it was toward a life that didn't reflect his father's. He wanted a life that put family before career.

"Sir, I have no intentions of hurting Lane. Or Noah. The emotion lingering in her eyes is as real as the ring still on her finger." Charlie swallowed. "My intention is to get to know her. Have dinner. I'd like to take her some flowers, maybe even chocolate—if people still do that kind of thing—and if given the chance, make her smile. Because, sir, she has a smile that'd make troops sign up for boot camp a hundred times over."

The sheriff's deep gray eyes appraised him. "Lane's been through more than her fair share of grief and I don't want to see her get hurt, but your aunt says she's been different since you've come around."

Charlie's pulse surged. "Good different?"

Sheriff Huggins peered at him beneath a blaze of white hair. "Son, I don't reckon she'd have agreed to a date with you if it was bad."

The affirmation was like a balm Charlie didn't know his soul needed.

"Be careful. That's all I'm asking."

"Yes, sir." Charlie hesitated a second, wondering if the parental speech was over. When Sheriff Huggins reached for a file, Charlie took a chance and stood. "Is there anything else you need?"

"Lane prefers potted flowers over bouquets"—Sheriff Huggins picked up a file and thumbed through it—"and salted caramel chocolate is her favorite."

Charlie grinned. "Yes, sir."

ELEVEN

HAD SHE REALLY DONE THAT? Agreed to a date with Charlie? Lane chewed the inside of her lip. A smile begged to be released. A date? No, it wasn't a date. Not really. It was the church benefit. Casual. Right. Then why hadn't her heart regained a normal rhythm since leaving the sheriff's station?

"Are we at Daddy's garden?"

Noah's tiny voice brought sobriety to her thoughts. "Yes, buddy. Do you have your picture?"

Noah held up a coloring-book page he had finished while her grandfather, Pops, had watched him. Lane helped Noah out of the car and together they walked through a path of oak trees until they reached the large granite slabs. Noah went straight to the section in the back where Mathias's name was carved and sat down in the shade of a magnolia tree. His lips moved and Lane kept her distance, knowing this time between her son and his daddy was precious and private.

Lane sank onto a nearby marble bench and inhaled a deep, cleansing breath, letting her eyes close. The bells from the church rang out a melody. A hymn? It sounded familiar, a whisper of her past when she was naïve enough to believe there was something bigger watching out for her . . . caring about her.

The day's heat was beginning to melt with the setting sun and Lane let the lingering warmth and the chiming tolls of the bells resonate within her soul. *God, are you there?* When was the last time she prayed? A chill skirted her arms. The night Mathias died, when she asked God to spare him and take her . . .

Lane's eyes flashed open at the sound of footsteps behind her.

"Sorry." Charlie stopped. "I didn't mean to scare you. I thought it was you from behind . . . I mean, uh, because of your hair. I recognized your hair."

Lane fought to control her racing heart at Charlie's unexpected appearance. For whatever reason, she had expected to see the creepy man from a few weeks ago popping out behind her. His slick smile had appeared in her dreams the last couple of nights and Lane swore she'd seen him in town, but when she looked a second time no one was there—and that only made her feel foolish. "Um, hi. No, it's okay. You just surprised me."

"That seems to be our thing."

Our thing. Those two words sent her heart on another lap and squashed the fear permeating her soul. She studied him waiting at the perimeter of the garden. Out of his uniform, Charlie wore casual well.

"What are you doing here?" Lane struggled to keep her voice steady.

"I just got off work. Needed to think. This is a quiet place to do that."

"Who are you talking to, Momma?" Noah skipped over. "Hey, I know you." He pointed at Charlie.

"Hi, Noah." Charlie smiled. His dimples made their appearance beneath a shadow of stubble shading his jawline and Lane's heart beat faster.

"We're visiting my dad." Noah climbed onto the bench next to Lane and swung his legs. "It's your turn, Momma."

"I'm sorry." A muscle in Charlie's jaw pulsed and he took a step back. "I didn't mean to interrupt."

"No. Please stay." Lane bit her lip, surprised at her desire to keep him there. "I mean, you're already here."

"Are you sure?"

No. *Yes.* It was the second time he'd asked her if she was sure and, truthfully, she didn't know. All this felt new and foreign and . . . sort of right—like he was supposed to be there.

"You can sit here next to me." Noah patted the empty space next to him on the bench.

Charlie smiled but waited, like he was giving her a chance to back out of her spontaneous invitation. Instead of making it easier, the generosity in his gesture made it hard to resist.

Made *him* hard to resist.

"There's plenty of space on the bench." Lane scooted over. "And this really is the best place to think in all of Walton."

Charlie hesitated a second longer before sitting down. Lane relaxed when he chose to sit on the side of the bench that kept Noah between them.

Noah glanced up. He lifted the edge of Charlie's sleeve and pointed at a tattoo. "What's that?"

"Noah, that's not polite." She pulled Noah's hand back. Her knuckles grazed Charlie's skin, sending a tingling up her arm. "Sorry."

"That's okay." Charlie lifted his sleeve farther to reveal the Marine emblem tattooed on his chiseled arm.

"Is that an eagle?" Noah twisted around so he was sitting on his knees, studying Charlie's arm.

"Yes."

"Did you know the bald eagle is our national bird?" Noah, done with his inspection of Charlie's arm, slid off the bench. "And it's in danger."

"Endangered," Lane said.

"Yep," Noah agreed. "Momma said she'll take me to see one at the zoo."

"Eagles are very cool." Charlie let the sleeve fall back over his tattoo.

"Yeah. It's cool." Noah nodded. "Momma, can I play?"

Lane pressed her lips together. It was funny hearing Noah say the word *cool*, but the admiration in her little boy's face for the man next to her was unsettling. Lane didn't date. Hadn't even thought about dating, so there was never an opportunity for a man to be introduced to her son and this was why. Noah was clearly taken by the new guy who kept appearing in their lives.

"If you're quiet and you stay close." Lane looked around the empty garden. "Remember, if you can't see me, then I can't see you and that's a . . .?"

"No-go," Noah answered.

"Right."

Lane waited until Noah settled himself beneath a tree with a pile of rocks before sliding a look at the man sitting next to her. Quiet stretched from seconds into minutes. Maybe inviting him to sit wasn't a good idea.

"This place is beautiful," Charlie said finally.

Looking around, she agreed. "There's a lot of military history here in Walton. This memorial holds the names of the men and women who served since the First World War."

"Which one is your husband?"

Lane pointed out Mathias's name and her throat grew thick. Two years hadn't erased the guilt, and now she was sitting here having feelings that confused her. She peeked over at Noah. He was still there. Playing. Maybe she should call him over—let him be the distraction her heart needed.

"Army, huh?" There was a tease in his voice.

"So, Marines?"

"Semper Fi."

"How long were you in?"

"Six years." The smile slid from his face.

"Enjoyed it that much?"

"My father is, or was, a colonel in the Marines. He's retired now, but growing up I ate, slept, and breathed the motto." Charlie's eyebrows tugged together for a moment. "There was never a question in my father's eyes that I was going to be anything but a Marine."

Oh, man, she could relate. "But you wanted something else."

"My life was good, but my dad was never really there for me. Not in the way I wanted. Being a Marine took priority and that left me trying to figure out life pretty much on my own. I taught myself how to play baseball. My friend's father taught me how to drive. It practically took an act of Congress to bring my dad home for my high school graduation."

"And yet you became a Marine?"

Charlie let out a chuckle void of humor. "Ironic, right? Became the very thing I swore I wouldn't. I just hoped . . . maybe *that* would be enough."

It was like he was reading into her soul. Not being enough had felt like her life's motto until she'd met Mathias. A breeze picked up a faint trace of Charlie's cologne and Lane swallowed hard. An emotion she wasn't ready for was warring for her attention.

"Momma, I need to go potty."

"Okay." She'd never been more thankful for Noah's small bladder. "We should probably go."

"No, sure. When you have to go, you have to go." Charlie rose. "It was nice running into you again—even without the tray of ice-cold drinks."

"Very funny." Noah was doing the familiar dance that told her there was no time to waste flirting—was that what they were doing?

"Tomorrow night, then?" Charlie winked and offered Lane a smile complete with deep dimples that kept drawing her in.

"Tomorrow night." Butterflies took flight in her stomach and didn't settle during the half-block walk back to her house. He was easy to talk to and charming and kind. Add his rugged good looks and her doubts seemed silly.

"I hope we see Charlie again," Noah said when she lifted him out of the car.

"You do?"

"Yeah, he makes you smile."

Lane reached up and touched her face. It'd been a long time since her emotions on the outside matched what she felt on the inside. The smile graced her face only a second before it fell. As she crossed the street, she saw somebody peeking into one of the side windows of her café. Her *closed* café.

"Hey, can I help you?"

The shadows of dusk made it impossible to see the person's face. Guessing by their build and height, she assumed the person was a man. Lane stopped in the middle of the street and tightened her grip on Noah's hand. Was it him?

Whoever it was didn't waste a second before they took off in the opposite direction of Lane and Noah.

"Hey!" Lane yelled, the echo of her voice filling the street. A man carrying a bag of groceries farther down the street stopped and turned. A mom driving a minivan full of kids turned the corner, pausing when she saw Lane and Noah still standing in the middle of the road.

Lane gave an apologetic wave and pulled Noah the rest of the way toward the café. What was that person doing? Was it the same man as before? Or someone else?

"Who was that, Momma?"

"I don't know, buddy." Lane unlocked the door of her café and flipped on the lights. Everything was as quiet as it was when she left it earlier. The only thing unsettled was her nerves—and the cure lived in the house behind hers.

TWELVE

"SO, THAT'S ATLANTA FALCON CLUB SEATS. Golf package at Turtle Cove in Hilton Head. And what's in that box?"

Lane heard her sister's voice, but it was muted. Fuzzy. Like it was when they were little girls and they tied paper cups to a string so they could talk to each other at night. But today it wasn't a playful memory blurring the words or Lane's thoughts. It was the man.

The stranger she had seen outside her café last night brought back the face of the man who'd been asking her about Mathias and Noah, haunting her fits of sleep. Was it the same person? Or maybe it was just someone looking to see if the café was open? A stranger, yes, but maybe not the man from before. The town was seeing an uptick in new faces as the investigation into Sydney's death continued. She was just being paranoid, right? Or maybe she was looking for a reason to invite Charlie over. His presence seemed to be a balm to her soul, restoring peace to her life.

"Helloooo, Lane." Meagan snapped her fingers in front of Lane's face. "I'd really like to get these items recorded before the kids get out of school."

"Sorry." Lane dropped her gaze to the thin cardboard box in her lap. "This one doesn't have a label."

"Let me see it." Meagan leaned over and picked up the box to inspect it. "If I didn't know better I'd say it's a man that's got you all dreamy-eyed."

"What?" Lane pressed a hand to her face. Was she smiling again? She'd caught herself more than once thinking about Charlie, and if her four-year-old was keen enough to see a change in his momma's face, no doubt Meagan would zero in on it too.

Meagan's hazel eyes met hers and then a coy smile spread across her lips before a squeal emerged. "It *is* a man?"

Lane squeezed her eyes shut and pressed the heel of her hand to her forehead. Sleep deprivation and her sister's excitement weren't a good combination.

Ms. Byrdie peeked her head out of the kitchen. "Everything alright in here?"

"Lane was just getting ready to tell me about the man she's daydreaming about."

"I am not." Lane's cheeks grew hot. Her eyes bounced to Ms. Byrdie and Meagan's gaze followed.

"You know him?" Meagan's pitch rose. "Who? How come I don't know this?"

"How are those cheddar biscuits coming?" Lane raised her eyebrows in Ms. Byrdie's direction, hoping she'd get the message. "And *we* need to finish itemizing these donations so you can get them out of my café. These boxes are a fire hazard."

"The biscuits are finished," Ms. Byrdie said, flashing a playful smile in Meagan's direction. "And I'm heading to the church to help there. I'll be back later to pick up the biscuits."

"I'm disappointed in the town gossips," Meagan murmured as she lifted the unlabeled box. From the corner of her eye, Lane could see her sister pretending to be interested in the box, but her lip was twitching. Was she going to ask more questions or race after Ms. Byrdie and pry the information from her? But what would she get? Lane and Charlie could hardly be considered an item. They hadn't even gone out on a date.

Yet.

Was going to the benefit with Charlie such a good idea? After tonight, there'd be no shortage of whispers—maybe she should cancel. Stay in.

Meagan opened her mouth to speak when Noah's animated voice echoed up the back porch. Lane breathed a heavy sigh of relief. Saved.

The screen door swung open and Noah tromped inside in Pops's brown military dress hat with the familiar Marine emblem on it and green paint smeared across his cheeks. Pops followed, his white hair mussed, sweat pressing it to his head, and the same paint spread on his wrinkled but smiling face.

"Has the war been won?" Lane tilted Noah's cap up and planted a kiss on his damp forehead. Sticky proof of an afternoon of fun with her grandfather.

"Mommy, soldiers don't get kisses at war. They get kisses when they come home from war." Noah wiped his forehead with the back of his hand and scrunched his eyebrows together in a tight scowl.

Lane's throat grew thick. Noah was two when Mathias returned home from war the second time. Too young to really remember, but he'd seen the pictures she had at the house. The two of them holding balloons and a homemade sign in hand as they waved their hero home.

"Soldiers and *Marines*"—Pops tapped the hat on Noah's head—"should get kisses any time they can."

Noah twisted his lips to the side and squinted his eyes. A look he got when judging whether he was being told the truth. The same look as his daddy. Lane swallowed in an attempt to clear the lump from her throat.

"What about tickles from aunties?" Meagan reached around Noah's waist and tickled him until he collapsed in a fit of giggles between her arms. "Hey, Pops." Meagan leaned in to hug the man but paused. "You need soap."

"They both do," Lane said. "Wash up and I'll get you boys some lemonade."

"And cookies." Meagan winked. "These soldiers need nourishment."

Pops straightened, his shoulders pulled back. Noah imitated him. Irresistible. "Fine."

A few minutes later, Pops and Noah emerged from the bathroom with clean faces. Lane plated the fresh batch of cookies and poured them all a glass of lemonade.

"Now, those are faces I can kiss." Meagan planted a kiss on Pops's cheek and then Noah's, which made him draw a face. "You need to come swim with Paige and Owen soon."

"Can I, Momma?"

Lane rubbed her neck. "Noah doesn't really know how to swim."

"That's okay." Meagan waved her hand. "I'll be there and the country club has lifeguards."

"Please, Momma." Noah pouted.

"Yeah, please, Momma." Meagan stuck her lip out and batted her eyelashes.

"Fine."

"Yeah!" Noah and Meagan slapped hands.

Pops pulled out a chair and sat. "Where are the kids?"

"School." Meagan turned her wrist to check the time. "But not for long. I'm glad you're here though—saves me a trip. Can I stop at your house later to look at Gram's rosebushes?"

"Sure, honey."

"What for?" Lane asked.

"For the barbecue." Meagan smoothed a piece of hair back as she opened the rectangular box and slid out a painting. "Mom didn't like any of the choices the florist offered her."

"You're going to cut Gram's flowers?"

Gram had been dead only three years, and Lane knew Pops missed her. The vibrant rose garden in his front yard was a testimony of his love. He planted a rosebush every year for their anniversary and now there were sixty-two of them.

"Not all the flowers. Just a few for the centerpieces. Mom wants this year's event to reflect a homey feel. Southern hospitality."

Lane's insides slithered around like jelly. Every year for as long as she could remember, her parents hosted a barbecue and charity event at their home. It quickly became an annual tradition, which, according to her mother, was "a sweet way to bring local Southerners together in the name of a good cause."

Really, it was an excuse for Georgia's rich, famous, and politically aligned to get together to drink, eat, and see who could outbid whom, all in the name of charity. Luckily for the charities involved, the more the guests drank the more they raised at the auction. And Lane's mother kept the bar fully stocked.

Pops helped himself to a second cookie. "That time of year already?"

"It does seem to come faster each year, doesn't it? But this year is really important. Dad heard a rumor Judge Atkins is trying to throw a party on the same day as the barbecue." Meagan shook her head. "The lengths people will go to win an election."

"I might skip the barbecue this year."

Meagan's wide eyes looked up from the painting in her hand. A mixed expression of disbelief and fear painted her face. "You can't not go. Everyone will expect you there. It's a campaign year."

Her father's words—no, threat—rang through her mind. Lane's gaze flicked to Noah who was finishing his cookie. "It's just that I know how late these events run and when people drink . . . I don't think I want Noah around that."

Meagan came over and put her hand on Lane's shoulder. "Mom would really like the whole family there, together."

Was this kind gesture genuine or was Meagan delivering her parents' message? After last time, would they assume she'd try to get out of going?

"What if I offered you a way out of the spotlight?" Meagan asked.

Lane raised her eyebrows.

"We haven't found someone to take photos this year. Maybe you can hide behind your camera?"

Pops drained the last of his lemonade. "Or you could take the deputy with you."

"The *deputy*?" Shock registered on Meagan's face. "Not the young, scrappy one who looks like Prince Harry? He's too young."

Lane shot a look at her grandfather, who raised a shoulder and gave a mirthful chuckle. She never should've told him about Charlie—who was definitely not scrappy.

"Is that a smile?" Meagan's voice rose in a singsong tone. "Wait—not the new deputy? The one all the PTA moms are talking about?" Her eyes darted back and forth from Pops to Lane.

"Yes." Lane wrinkled her nose, feeling like a schoolgirl admitting a crush to her best friend. Was that what this was? "Charlie's a friend."

"I know Charlie." Noah raised his hand and gave a toothy grin.

"Why don't you go put your toys away?" Lane pointed at Noah's backpack on the floor near the screen door.

Tilting his head to the side, Noah waited for Pops. The wink came and Noah smiled. "Okay." He slid out of his chair and collected his bag.

Noah's foot barely hit the first step of the stairs when Meagan said, "Spill it."

"There's nothing to spill." Lane picked up the clipboard and pointed a pencil at the painting. "What do I put down for that painting?"

Meagan waited a second longer and then gave up. They may have shared secrets when they were Noah's age, but those days of sisterly conspiracy had ended when Meagan met and exceeded their parents' expectations of the ideal daughter.

"This painting doesn't have a tag." Meagan turned the painting over. "I don't know where it came from."

"It's nice." Lane peeked over her sister's shoulder at the ocean piece. A bright yellow orb kissed the horizon, sending out bold rays of red, orange, and peach that stretched into a sky fading in twilight. "Who's the artist?"

"I don't see a name. Anything on the packaging?"

Lane looked at the box. "Nope." Hmm, that's weird. "There's not even a shipping label or stamp."

"Someone must've delivered it then. Local place, I'm sure. I'll just add it to the rest." The alarm on Meagan's cell phone beeped.

"Perfect timing. I'll send Ian to pick these up after he drops the kids off at their art class. Can I put you down as a plus-one?"

"I already told you I'm not sure if I'm coming. Besides, what makes you think he'd want to come with me?"

"Ask him tonight on your date."

"Pops!"

"You're going on a date?" Meagan squeaked.

Lane groaned. "No. We're going to the benefit for Sydney's family tonight."

"Is he picking you up?" Meagan quirked an eyebrow.

"It's across the street at the park. We're walking there."

"But together."

"If you don't leave, you'll be the mom who forgot to pick up her kids from school." As far as Lane was concerned, the conversation was over. It was bad enough she still hadn't sorted through her feelings for the handsome deputy who "all the PTA moms are talking about," but the idea that Meagan's inquisition might be only the beginning of the chatter that her and Charlie's presence together would cause made her head hurt.

"So, I'll let Mom and Dad know you'll be a plus-one for the barbecue."

"What?" Lane's gaze spun to her sister, who was smiling.

"Thought that'd bring you back." Meagan grabbed her purse. "In all seriousness, we could really use a photographer for the event and it'll be a good excuse to stay busy without Mom and Dad, you know, being Mom and Dad."

Lane didn't quite know how to respond to Meagan's sudden understanding. The perfect wife, mother, and daughter lived a scheduled life, and helping Lane out wasn't usually penciled in. But as her sister stood in the doorway watching her, Lane believed Meagan was being genuine.

"I'll think about it."

"Perfect." Meagan flashed her perfect smile. "And if you want . . . bring a date."

///////////////////////

Charlie ended the call with Trevor Donovan. Sydney's father sounded like he no longer had any life left in him.

He didn't know how the Donovans were going to make it through the benefit. The town wanted to show their support for the family, but maybe it was too soon. And with no strong leads in the case, Charlie felt the burden of finding Sydney's killer grow with each passing day.

He was letting them down.

Deputy Wilson charged out of the interview room like a bull seeing red.

"How's it going with Brady Matthews?" Charlie asked.

"It's no wonder young athletes today think they're superstars." Wilson stretched his arms in front of him, flexing his fingers until the joints cracked. "Believe nothing can touch them. Told the kid that colleges didn't look too kindly on their athletes having police records."

"Wasn't too long ago you were that superstar." Sheriff Huggins appeared from his office with an empty coffee cup in his hand.

"*That* was almost twenty years ago." Wilson seemed to sink into a memory. "Playing ball meant getting an education, not signing a multi-million-dollar contract."

"Was he dating Sydney?" Charlie was slowly learning about the people he worked with and it came as no surprise that Wilson's hulking frame meant he once had a future on the football field. So, what happened?

"No. Matthews said they were just friends."

Disappointment shouted in the silence. Another lead with no results.

"There has to be something we can press him on. Or Jolene? Why would she give up Brady's name if he wasn't anything more than a friend?"

Sheriff Huggins lifted his cup before heading to the coffeemaker. Charlie clenched his fists and let a frustrated sigh slip from his lips.

Deputy Frost plopped down in the chair next to Charlie's desk.

"Any luck on Sydney's phone?" Charlie asked.

"Nothing. It's probably dead." Frost's face froze. His eyes darted back and forth behind his thick glasses. "Sorry. The phone can't be tracked unless it's on. The last time she used her phone was Thursday night at her house."

"And there's no record of her contacting the art gallery?"

"No."

"So, we're still stuck with how she was getting her art to the gallery." Charlie ran both hands down his face. "Her parents only have one car and Sydney didn't have a driver's license yet."

"Unless she's a Trekkie and can beam herself around town, she'd need a car."

"You're a genius, Frost."

Wilson snorted.

"What? What'd I say?" Frost pushed his glasses up.

"If Sydney canceled her sleepover with Jolene, then someone had to have picked her up. Someone with a car." Charlie went through his notes again. He wasn't sure what he was searching for, but he was certain he'd know it when he found it.

Wilson grunted from his desk. "Maybe she walked."

"Wilson, you interviewed the neighbors and none of them saw Sydney leave that night?"

"Right."

"We, or I, assumed she was taking her work to the gallery. What if someone was picking it up for her?" Charlie pulled up an aerial map of Sydney's neighborhood. He honed in on the four long rows of buildings on the east side of the neighborhood. They were self-storage units he'd seen the day he and Sheriff Huggins spoke with the Donovans. He zoomed in. "Has anyone contacted the self-storage company?"

Both men looked at each other before shaking their heads.

"Call them. They probably have cameras all over the place. Maybe one of them caught Sydney leaving that night."

Frost jumped out of his seat and hurried down the hall to his office.

"If I had half his energy . . . or his brains." Wilson shook his head.

"How's your wife?"

"She's on bed rest. My mama is here helping." Wilson's long fingers rubbed his knuckles.

"Do you have a name picked out yet?"

"Benjamin Samuel." Pride accented each syllable.

Charlie imagined Wilson would be a good dad. Teaching his son the value that an education carried more merit than the skill of throwing a football. Would Charlie take as much pride in teaching his child the fundamentals of life? He hoped so. At least he knew his son would never have to worry about his dad not being there for him.

Charlie would never choose his career over those he loved.

A torrent of fresh emotions filled his chest as the faces of Lane and Noah filled his mind. Who would teach Noah how to throw a ball? A pang of longing filled him. Could he be there for Noah? The little boy was already charming his way into Charlie's heart, and his mom . . . well, he couldn't deny the way being next to her made him feel. His heart clenched at the possibility. Was there any room in Lane's and Noah's lives for him?

Deputy Frost rushed down the hall. His dark glasses slid down his nose. He pushed them up. "Diane from U-Store We-Store is sending us the video footage from the day Sydney died."

"Sending it? When?"

"Shouldn't take long. Her son is going to upload the footage and send it." Frost's smile consumed his face. "There's more. After I saw how much Sydney's paintings were selling for, I did a little research."

Wilson and Charlie exchanged a look.

"What did you find?" Charlie prayed the research was legal.

"Nothing. Well, nothing and then something."

"Come on, Frost," Wilson grumbled.

"Okay, okay. See, if I was making bank—that's what they call making a lot of money—and it was supposed to be on the down-low—you guys know—"

"Yes, Frost, both Wilson and I know what that means. Please continue."

"Right, so if I was keeping my art a secret, I'd probably be keeping my money a secret too, right? I mean, a painting for $1,200?"

"Sydney had a private bank account?" Wilson asked.

"Yes. But that's not what's important." Frost pushed up his glasses again. "It's where her money was coming from."

Wilson cocked an eyebrow. The young deputy had their attention now. And from the smug look plastered on his face, he was enjoying the moment.

"You going to keep us waiting, Frost?" Wilson stood.

"Uh, no. Sorry. Here." Frost held out a piece of paper. "This is Sydney's account."

Charlie took the sheet and scanned the numbers until his eyes hit the bottom figure. "Twelve thousand dollars?"

"That one sheet is the total account history." Frost took off his glasses and wiped them with his tie. "You can see she opened up the account a year ago and since then has made a number of deposits. A couple hundred dollars at a time."

"Please tell me you got this legally." Charlie stared at the paper in his hand.

"Agent Padello helped me." Frost slid his glasses back on. "That's how we found out the money was coming from—"

"Something tells me I need to hear what's going on over here." Sheriff Huggins returned with a full cup of coffee. "What's happened?"

Charlie tilted his head toward Frost. "Sir, I think Frost missed his calling."

"Is that so?" Sheriff Huggins took a seat on the corner of Charlie's desk.

"The kid's got talent." Charlie handed the sheriff the bank statement. "If you're not careful, the FBI's going to push a little harder to recruit him."

The compliment hit its mark and Frost's smile spread from ear to ear. The spattering of freckles gave the impression Frost was young, but Charlie knew better. They were lucky to have him on their team. It would be bittersweet if he ever took the Feds up on their offer.

"It's true. Agent Padello told me I had potential." Frost smirked. "Told me if I got bored of Walton I could head up to Virginia for some real action."

Wilson grumbled something incoherent in their direction and Charlie tucked his chin to hide the smile playing on his lips.

"Before you sign up for the academy, why don't you tell me what you found." Sheriff Huggins settled into an empty chair and sipped his coffee.

Charlie let Frost fill the sheriff in about what they had found. Sheriff Huggins listened and only interrupted twice to slow Frost down. As his excitement grew, so did the speed with which he spoke.

"You're saying Sydney was getting paid for her paintings, but the money wasn't coming from the gallery?" Sheriff Huggins looked puzzled.

"That's what I was just about to tell Deputies Lynch and Wilson. Remember I said that I found nothing and something at the same time?" Frost's head bobbed back and forth between the three of them. "What I didn't find was anything about Sydney's paintings. Nothing."

"So?" Wilson craned his neck. "She's a local painter."

"Yes, but her art, which in my opinion is eh"—Frost waved his hand side to side—"is selling for more money than just a local painter."

"And that means something?" Sheriff Huggins scratched his chin.

"Yes. It means someone really wants her paintings. Agent Padello thought it was suspicious too, so he looked into her account and saw that all the deposits were being made electronically." Frost pointed to the paper sitting in front of Sheriff Huggins. "From accounts outside the country."

Wilson whistled and Charlie moved to Sheriff Huggins's side so he could see the bank statement again.

"That means Sydney's killer could be someone outside the US." Charlie stepped back and allowed the information to settle. The investigation had just taken a giant leap into the abyss. Finding a killer locally was proving to be difficult, but if the killer lived outside the United States . . . that was a whole other ball game.

Deputy Benningfield walked over. "Sheriff Huggins, you have a phone call on line two."

Charlie's computer chirped just as he pushed his phone over for the sheriff to use. It was an email from the storage company. With Sheriff Huggins on the phone and Wilson and Frost looking over his shoulder, Charlie watched the video.

It was grainy. He played it a couple of times. Then paused it. His pulse accelerated. The long red hair gave her away. They had her last moments on tape. "That's her. Sydney Donovan."

"The video is time-stamped 4:58 p.m." Frost pointed to the corner of the screen. "What is that, like five or six hours before she was killed? Do you think the driver is her killer?"

"There's a glare blocking the driver and part of the license plate. It looks like a sedan."

Sheriff Huggins hung up the phone and squinted at the monitor. "How do you know?"

"When Sydney first approached the car, she put something into it." Charlie hit the rewind button and played the video again. "I'm assuming it was through the back seat window, because why wouldn't she have held it as she got in?"

"Good eyes." Sheriff Huggins rubbed his eyes. "Mine aren't what they used to be."

"If Agent Padello can do something about the video image, we might be able to get those plate numbers," Frost added.

"Good job, genius." Wilson's wide hand slapped Frost on the shoulder, sending Frost tumbling forward. The two men laughed.

The burden felt slightly lighter and Charlie was happy to see some playfulness in the office. His cell phone vibrated. It was an email message from his father.

With Frost and Wilson joking in the background, Charlie opened it up and saw an attachment to a news article. Charlie's old unit had taken out another terrorist leader. He wondered which team members had the honor. Were any of them hurt?

Like a seesaw, the feeling of wanting to be with his team rose and fell with the questions of whether he belonged there or here. At the bottom was a note from Charlie's father.

Your old unit is doing pretty amazing things over there. Thought you should know.

—Dad

The muscles in Charlie's shoulders knotted. His father just couldn't let it go. Couldn't accept that life outside the corps might be worthwhile. He deleted the email. What was so wrong with wanting a life off the battlefield? Wasn't being a father and husband just as important as serving and protecting the country? His dad would never understand that not all heroes carry a gun and fight on foreign soil. Some heroes throw a football with their sons and lead ordinary lives. Having ice cream on a hot afternoon with a beautiful woman and her son was more important than any medal clipped to his chest ever would be. But in his father's eyes—that would never be enough.

THIRTEEN

LANE PACED. What was she doing? Going to the benefit with Charlie was a date whether or not she admitted it. Was she ready? She wanted to say no, but the light of hope flickering within her fueled a tucked-away desire to believe that maybe Ms. Byrdie and Pops were right.

Did she deserve a second chance?

Passing a mirror, Lane paused. A T-shirt with navy and white stripes paired with white linen shorts. Lane bit the inside of her cheek. *Too casual?* Streaks of sunlight spilled into the room and glinted against her wedding band. She rubbed it with her thumb.

Maybe Charlie would be a jerk. It'd be easy to turn down a jerk. Lane stared at her reflection. She was talking to herself or, rather, negotiating with herself. Charlie wasn't a jerk—at least he hadn't been so far. She'd put on some mascara and a little blush. Pouting her lips, she decided to add some lip gloss. Not colored but clear.

Casual.

After she applied the lip gloss and added some gold earrings, she surveyed her house. Picked up. Mostly clean. Normal. A knock sounded down below and Lane jumped. This was it. Her first date since Mathias. Another knock.

"Coming." Lane rounded the bannister and made her way down the stairs, the whole time listening to the voice inside her head tell her, *This is crazy.*

Whatever trepidation Lane felt melted the second her eyes latched on to the man standing on her porch. The blue polo shirt highlighted his tan and was fitted enough that she could make out the muscled definition beneath.

"You look amazing," he said when she opened the door.

Lane blushed. "You're exaggerating."

"No, I'm not." He spoke with conviction, and the way his eyes sparked made her believe the compliment wasn't superficial. "I brought you flowers." Charlie lifted a pot of white gardenias in one hand and held a candy bar in the other. "And chocolate."

"They're beautiful." The sweet fragrance filled her house. "They smell so good. I know the perfect spot for them outside my window."

The strong angles of Charlie's jaw shifted with a smile. "Is Noah here? I brought him a gift too." He lifted up a plastic dinosaur. "I hope he doesn't have an . . . Archaeopteryx."

Lane couldn't help but giggle at his practiced pronunciation of the winged dinosaur's name.

"It kind of looks like an eagle, don't you think?"

"It does and he'll love it."

"Is he ready?"

"He's already there with my sister and Pops."

Charlie hooked his elbow and lifted his arm. "Shall we join them?"

Hesitating a second, Lane set down the flowers and chocolate and looked at Charlie with his arm raised. Her heart raced, as she was very aware of the attraction growing inside her. Was this how dates started? It was so long ago . . . and the people of this town thrived on juicy gossip. Being escorted by the handsome new deputy was sure to get their mouths watering.

"My mom taught me all the ways to be a gentleman around girls." Charlie lowered his arm and for a second his lips dipped down at the edges, but a second later the dimples returned. "But more importantly, she taught me that respect goes a lot further than chivalry."

A whoosh of air left her lungs. Without her saying a word, Charlie seemed to pick up on her inhibition to take his arm. To announce to the town of Walton that the young widow was on her first date. "You have a sweet momma."

"She's wise too." Charlie winked.

Together Charlie and Lane walked across the street to the park. A bluegrass band was set up at the edge of the grassy field near the old brick church. Families set up lawn chairs and laid out quilted blankets across the grounds as children skittered between them chasing each other. Lane searched for her sister and Noah, trying in vain to ignore the way the breeze picked up the spicy scent of Charlie's skin or the way curious eyes seemed to follow them.

"Lane!" Meagan called over to them from a playset.

"Hey. Where's Noah?"

"Getting his face painted with Paige." Meagan pointed to a table nearby but kept her eyes on Charlie. "They've already been in the bounce house, eaten a snow cone, and jumped through rounds of potato sack races. And we just got here."

"Mommaaaaahh!"

Lane spun around and Noah crashed into her legs. His face was covered in green paint with black lines across it. "What are you supposed to be?"

"An alligator!" he squealed.

Meagan smiled and held out her hand to Charlie. "I'm sorry, but it seems like my sister has forgotten her manners. I'm Meagan Sullivan-Gallagher."

"Charlie." He smiled warmly as he took her sister's hand and shook it. "A friend of Lane's and Noah's."

Friend. Lane forced herself to breathe. Friend was good. Friend was casual. Friend stung a little bit.

"Just friends, huh?" Meagan winked at Lane.

"Have you seen Noah?" Charlie teased, looking around. "I wanted to give him a message from Bane, but—"

Noah raised his hand. "I'm right here."

"What?" Charlie mocked surprise. "No way! You're an alligator."

Noah burst into giggles. Charlie was winning Noah's affection and an alarm sounded in her mind. Her son had already lost one man in his life—the last thing she needed was for Noah to grow attached to a man who might not stick around.

"Where's Pops?" Lane asked.

"Grabbing some chairs." Meagan helped Owen off the slide. "Next to the tables."

"I'll help." Charlie jogged over to Pops and grabbed an armful of folding chairs.

"Me too!" Noah chased after him.

Meagan elbowed Lane in the ribs. "The PTA moms were right. He's cute."

Lane's cheeks warmed. "He told you we're just friends."

"But your face says you want more."

Uneasiness spread through her. "I don't know. I think it's too early. I'm not sure I'm ready. And I don't want Noah to be hurt."

Lane watched Charlie scoop Noah up and spin him overhead. Pops stood by, smiling. Paige and Owen lifted their hands up for their turns. Charlie obliged. He was winning them all over. And hope weaved itself around her heart.

A second chance.

"Look at him." Meagan put her hands on Lane's shoulders. "Does he look like someone who wants to hurt you?"

Lane wanted to warn her sister about looks being deceiving, but she couldn't bring herself to say it because Meagan was right. Charlie didn't look like the kind of guy who would hurt her or Noah. And that made her feelings all the more complicated. Was she ready?

"Friend, or whatever you want to call him, I'm just happy to see the life back in your eyes."

"What do you mean?"

"There's something different about you." Meagan shrugged. "You seem happier. And if *he's* what's making you happy, then I'd like him to stick around. Even if it's just as *friends*."

They walked over to the tables covered in butcher paper. "You keep saying that like you don't believe we're just friends."

"Some of the best relationships start out as people simply being friends." Meagan stopped. "But promise me one thing." She waited until Lane nodded. "Just breathe. Stop listening to the doubts inside that pretty little head of yours and live in the moment. And enjoy it. Life's too . . ."

Lane didn't need Meagan to finish her thought. Life was fragile and unpredictable and, yes, very much too short. But was there really a change in her? If there was, it wasn't just with her.

Meagan seemed different too. They had never been close. The only things they shared were the same last name, same parents, and same address. Meagan was Miss Popularity growing up. President of everything, queen of everything, part of everything, while Lane just tried to survive. It didn't feel much different now. Her sister was still very social and she . . . well, she was still trying to survive.

"You might want to slow down on the spinning. These kids ate blue snow cones," Meagan warned Charlie as they approached.

Charlie wrinkled his nose at Lane and sat down. *Just* breathe. She could do that. Relax and have fun. It's supposed to be fun, right? First dates—and that's all this was—are supposed to be fun. Lane took Noah from Charlie and placed him in the chair between her and Charlie. A buffer to remind her that not all first dates ended with the promise of a second date and she needed to keep her growing hope in check.

"Momma, I want to sit next to Owen."

"He's sitting next to his daddy. There's no room."

"I can move over one." Charlie stood and exchanged seats, allowing Noah to take his.

Meagan flashed her a knowing look only sisters understood.

"Folks," Pastor Tarpley spoke into the band's microphone. "Before they bring out the food, I wanted to say a few words on behalf of Trevor and Amanda Donovan."

Behind him, Sydney's parents held hands and offered tight-lipped smiles as some clapped and others shouted words of encouragement. "They're so grateful to everyone who has come to honor their daughter, Sydney. Unknown to them and probably to most of you, their precious daughter was a talented artist."

Lane felt Charlie's body stiffen.

"God has given each of us a gift, a talent, a purpose, and he expects us to pursue life. That's just what Sydney did, and now Trevor and Amanda hope to raise enough money to start a scholarship for young people who want to pursue their God-given purpose. For God does not call us to merely survive this life we've been given but to thrive in it. Thank you all for coming out and supporting the legacy Sydney Donovan has left behind. Let us pray."

Pastor Tarpley's words stayed on her mind after the "amen." It felt like they mirrored what Meagan had told her earlier. Surviving had become her way. It didn't feel like there was any other option. How was she supposed to pursue life when she had no idea what purpose God had for her?

"What exactly are we going to eat?" Charlie leaned close to her ear. His breath tickled the hair at the back of her neck.

"You haven't been to a shrimp boil yet?" Lane pulled out her deepest southern drawl.

"No."

Before she could explain, men in white aprons carrying tall stockpots walked to the table, drawing a roar of applause and whistles from the hungry crowd. They turned over the pots, dumping shrimp, sausage, red potatoes, and cobs of corn down the middle of the tables.

"Grab some and start eating." Lane picked up a few pieces of shrimp and some potatoes.

"With our hands?" Charlie's smile traveled to his eyes. He turned to Noah, who was already working on a piece of corn. "We eat with our hands?"

"Yes, silly." Noah gave him a corny smile.

Charlie didn't wait to dig in. He grabbed some of everything as ladies from the church dispersed rolls of paper towels along the tables. Lane waved to Ms. Byrdie, who was delivering baskets of their homemade cheddar biscuits.

"This might be my favorite thing about Georgia," Charlie said between bites.

"Your *favorite* thing?" she teased. Or was she flirting? Whatever it was left her feeling awkward. Lane caught Meagan's curious glance and then Lane choked on her bite as she saw her father and mother approaching. They were waving and shaking hands as though they were in a parade.

"Just breathe," her sister mouthed.

"Now, this is a good-looking family." Her father's eyes zeroed in on Charlie. "I don't think we've met, son. You're the new deputy."

"Yes, sir." Charlie wiped his hands and then stood to shake hands with her father. "Pleasure to meet you."

"Likewise, I'm sure. And this is my wife, Elise." Charlie shook hands with Lane's mother. "I trust my daughters are representing Walton's hospitality properly."

Charlie's eyes met Lane's. "They are, sir."

"Daddy, go find a seat and get something to eat," Meagan said as she wiped her mouth. "Before it's all gone."

"Now, that would be a serious crime." Lane's father laughed, along with several of those sitting around them, before someone called him and her mother away.

Lane released a long breath. Now it was her turn. "Thank you," she said to her sister.

Meagan smiled. In the waning sunlight, her sister's face took on a glow that made her look very much like their mother. "So, Charlie, is Walton growing on you?"

"Yes." He cast a sideways glance at Lane. "Growing up, I lived a lot of different places, but this is the smallest city I've ever lived in. I like the way the community comes together to support one another in their time of need. And the people are really nice."

As the food disappeared and twilight ushered in a starry canvas, Lane finally felt herself relax. Charlie and Meagan's husband discussed football. Behind her, Noah and his cousins chased after fireflies. Meagan attempted to begin a conversation with Lane but kept getting interrupted by members of the Junior League who were either praising her sister for something or seeking advice about upcoming events.

Was this what *normal* was? As the band played, couples swayed in rhythm to the steady beat, the trickle of laughter drifting all around her. Lane thought she even caught a small smile gracing the lips of Sydney Donovan's parents for just a second. Their lives would never be normal, but someday a new normal might begin. And what about her and Noah? What would be their new normal?

Lane allowed her gaze to settle on Charlie. It felt like butterflies had taken up permanent residence within her chest whenever she thought about him. And that was happening more frequently than she cared to admit. What would normal look like with Charlie included?

What would Charlie say or do if he knew about her depression and what it had cost her—what it had cost Noah? What he had said about his father choosing career over family . . . is that what she did that night? Chose to succumb to her weakness rather than choosing Mathias and Noah?

A chill skirted her arms and, instantly, the darkness was there. Ready to remind her she wasn't worthy of a second chance. Lane called to Noah. It was time to go.

"Are we leaving, Momma?"

"Yes, buddy," Lane answered as Charlie shifted closer to her. "It's getting late and you need a bath."

"I can take him home, Lane," Meagan offered. Her gaze moved toward Charlie. "In case y'all want to stay a little longer."

"Um, I don't . . ." Lane turned to meet Charlie's blue eyes. "Unless you want to stay."

"Actually, I have a dog at home who will live up to his name if I don't get back soon."

Lane expected to hear disappointment in his voice. Something to tell her he'd wanted her to stay a little longer. Maybe share a dance. This was, after all, their date. Sort of. If sharing a family style dinner with her four-year-old son and the rest of Walton could be considered a date. But as Charlie stood, their eyes locked and meaning passed through them—what it was, she didn't know—but it felt like he understood her unease.

"It was really nice meeting everyone."

"You too, Charlie." Meagan smiled. "Did Lane invite you to our father's barbecue fund-raiser next weekend?"

Lane stiffened. She hadn't fully decided if she was going, much less inviting the man whose perceptive ability had her on alert. Charlie's arm brushed up against her shoulder, but rather than pull back, he stilled. The warmth of his nearness spread through her.

"Actually, I'm already scheduled to be there."

"You are?" she asked, looking up at him.

Charlie's gaze reached Lane. "We're handling security for the event."

"Security?" In all the years, there'd never been security. "Because of the election?"

"Partly, yes." Meagan sighed. Her face seemed paler than usual beneath the moon's glow. Exhausted even. "A lot of people have been pressuring Daddy. They want to feel safe. You know, with the whole investigation."

"It's always good to err on the safe side," Charlie added, and this time Lane heard the disappointment in his voice. She didn't know a lot about him, but from the long hours he'd been putting in at the station with Sheriff Huggins and the other deputies, Lane guessed the pressure of not finding Sydney's killer was getting to him.

"See, now you have an ally—"

"Ready, Noah?" Lane cut her sister off before shooting her a look, only to receive an amused grin in return. "Charlie's dog is waiting for him."

Noah grabbed a piece of sausage and wrapped it in a dirty paper towel. "Give this to him for me. We're best friends."

"Best friends for life if you keep spoiling him." Charlie accepted the gift as the three of them left the park, the prying eyes, and her sister's enjoyment at making Lane uncomfortable. That, in itself, was odd. Why the sudden camaraderie between them? Something had shifted in their relationship and Lane hated the skepticism lurking in the corner of her mind.

Noah paused at the edge of the park. "Momma, my legs are tired."

The days of carrying her son were quickly diminishing, as much as it pained her. "Buddy, we just have to cross the street and walk another block."

Charlie held out his hands. "Come here, bud."

Noah lifted his arms into the air and before Lane could protest, her son was wrapped around Charlie's chest. Mixed emotions rattled within her as a whole game of what-ifs plagued her thoughts. What if they became more than friends? What if she just lived in the moment and saw where things went with Charlie? What if he found out the truth? Lane looked at her son's head snuggled into the crook of Charlie's neck. It wouldn't just be her heart breaking—Noah would probably be devastated too.

The walk back to her place didn't take long, but it was long enough for Noah to drift off to sleep on Charlie's shoulder.

"He's dead weight when he's asleep," Charlie said as Lane unlocked her front door.

"He is." Lane set her keys down and flipped on a light. "I can take him now."

"Let me carry him upstairs."

Charlie was already starting for the stairs, so Lane followed, knowing she'd have to wake up Noah or risk breaking her back to get him upstairs. After putting Noah in bed, Lane and Charlie walked back downstairs.

"Tonight was nice," Charlie said when Lane stepped onto the porch.

A slight breeze had picked up, cooling the air and carrying with it the music from the park. It was a perfect summer night. "Did you have fun?"

"I did." He looked up at the stars. "Sometimes I forget how important it is to step away from the job and catch my breath. It was like that in Afghanistan. I'd get caught up in the monotony of our mission and forget to look around at the beauty of the world around me."

"Beauty in war?" Lane bit her tongue at the hint of sarcasm in her tone. "Sorry, but it's hard to imagine seeing beauty in that kind of darkness."

"It wasn't always easy, but if you look for it beauty can be seen even in the ugliness of war."

Charlie's words reminded Lane of Ms. Byrdie's. About God being able to love someone despite their flaws. If Charlie was able to find beauty on a battlefield, would he be able to see beyond her ugly past?

The slow melody of another song filled the air and Charlie turned so he was facing her—close enough that she breathed in his scent. Her heart pounded. Certainly he could hear it. She stepped back, but Charlie closed the space between them.

"Lane, I want you to know that I'm not here to hurt you or Noah." His fingers traced the outer edge of her hand, sending a surge of nervous energy pulsing through her. "When I left the Marines and moved to Walton, I knew what I wanted." He wrapped her hand in his, cocooning it in gentle strength. "I know you've lost love and I know I will never replace that, but I'm asking if there's a chance that I can be the one to offer it to you again."

Melting. It was the only way Lane could describe what was going on inside her. Charlie was melting her defenses with his kindness and compassion, and it didn't hurt that on this lazy summer night the heartbeat of attraction was pounding louder than her inhibitions. Louder than her fear.

"All I'm asking is that you think about it. There's no rush and I'm not going anywhere." Charlie brushed a piece of hair from her face. He drew her closer to him. "Now, Ms. Lane Kent, may I have this dance?"

Lane swallowed, trying to bring some moisture back to her mouth to answer. She couldn't, so she nodded. Charlie's hand found the curve of her back and her breath caught in her throat as his strong arms guided their bodies to the slow rhythm of the music. It took a few seconds before she allowed herself to relax.

Live in the moment.

It all came back to her. The flood of emotions and feelings she had long since shoved away returned with a force so strong it weakened her knees. She missed this. Being in someone's arms. Feeling special. Wanted. The world around them disappeared and for the first time in too long, Lane felt peace.

FOURTEEN

THE POUNDING ON THE DOOR rattled Miguel from sleep. He blinked a few times to gather his bearings. The dome of light from his bathroom cast a yellow glow into the living room. It was still dark. Maybe the pounding was a dream.

"Miguel!" a voice from outside called.

He cringed as he pushed himself off the couch. A few of the scabs on his hand split open. He grabbed a rag from the floor and wrapped his wound.

"Miguel!" The pounding continued. Leaving the lights off, Miguel twisted the bolt and opened the door.

"It took you long enough." Dark eyes glared at him. "I've been standing out here with the cockroaches for twenty minutes."

The woman was cast beneath the shadows and Miguel could only make out the sharp features of her face. A fearful recognition brought a chill to his skin. "It's late."

"Of course it's late." She peered into the house. "Why are the lights off?"

"I wasn't expecting company."

"Well, I wasn't expecting to drive all the way down here. Where is the light switch?"

Miguel's guest pushed past him and fumbled along the wall to find the switch. A second later his living room was bathed in a brightness that made him wince. When his eyes adjusted, they focused on Annika's thin body and the expression on her face. She looked upset.

"Why are you here?" She never came to his house. Too much trouble. *Trouble*. The word pricked his consciousness, but the reason evaded him.

151

Annika stared at him. Her eyes narrowed for a few seconds. "How long have you been *out*?"

Miguel's head started to throb. He pressed the heel of his hand to his forehead. He couldn't remember. Only that the hours he was awake had grown longer.

"What happened to your hands?" Annika started for him and Miguel stepped back until his back hit the door. Her cold fingers wrapped around his wrists, lifting them so she could see his hands.

"I cut them."

"I can see that, but how?" She moved the wrap covering his wound, her fingers pressing into the sliced skin. Red blood oozed from another broken scab.

"Work." He twisted his hands away from her.

"You're sculpting again?"

It had been months since he'd picked up his tools, but the urge to cut into the flesh of the tree had overwhelmed him. He'd needed a release. A way to escape the monster haunting him.

"Can you still paint?"

"Is that why you're here?" He adjusted the rag over his hand. His head started to throb . . . like it did when he needed to slip away.

Annika's face grew indiscernible, or maybe it was his mind beginning to fade. "Why did Sydney call you?"

Fear slid down his throat as images flashed in his mind. Short bursts of a nightmare that kept him shrouded in darkness. "What?"

"You know what's happened, don't you? Sydney's dead, Miguel. After she called you."

Miguel took an involuntary step back, dropping the bloodied rag in his hand. Sydney's pale blue eyes flashed in his mind. "I-I didn't do anything."

"What did you do to her, Miguel?" Annika's voice softened. "Why did she come to you?"

What happened? He squeezed his eyes tight. Sydney had been trying to tell him something. She didn't want to paint anymore. Was scared. Of him? He wouldn't have hurt Sydney. She was just

152

a girl. A young girl. She had come to him for help. Needed help, but for what? He couldn't remember. Why couldn't he remember? His gaze drifted over to a painting against the wall.

"Ah, yes." Annika followed the direction of his gaze to the painting. "You remember, don't you? Sydney gave you a painting . . . or did you kill her and then steal it—"

"No!" he barked. Miguel looked at his hands. The slivers of gouged skin made him dizzy. He stumbled to his couch.

"Why were you in the woods that night, Miguel?"

He felt like he'd swallowed a mouthful of cement. His tongue wouldn't work. Miguel clenched his hands. His nails dug into the torn flesh of his palms. He couldn't remember. He had woken up with dirt on his clothes.

His eyes found the spot on the floor where his muddy footprints had been. He swayed.

"She was a nice girl. You liked her." Annika touched his shoulder and he flinched. "You didn't mean to kill her."

"No, I didn't kill her," he said, his voice a hoarse whisper as he brought his fists to his head. He began hitting his skull, trying to fight through the blackness and remember. What had he done?

"Stop! Miguel, stop!"

Annika's hands wrestled his fists away from his head, stopping the blows he was inflicting on himself. Her strength surprised him. Fresh blood was smeared over his hands. But there was no pain. Only numbness.

"You have to calm down. I can help you. But you need to trust me." Her voice soothed the throbbing in his head. "I'm going to let go of your hands. Promise me you won't start hitting yourself again."

"I didn't . . ." He groaned as his eyes filled with tears. "She was young. Innocent. She didn't deserve to die."

"Listen to me." Annika released his wrists. "My father spent his whole life helping people like you. Gave away all his money so veterans could have a fair chance. But no one is going to give you a fair chance, Miguel. The people in this town already believe you're crazy. They'll kill you if they find out the truth." She began to pace. "They won't understand you couldn't help yourself."

"I'm sick." That's what they had told him when he had come back from war. He was sick. Needed help. But he had been afraid. They'd kept talking about what had happened and all he'd wanted to do was forget it. Now, the nightmare had come back to haunt him in real life. "I deserve to die."

"Maybe, but not right now." Annika stopped in front of him. "Now, tell me about the painting."

Like a projector with missing slides, Miguel couldn't put the pieces of his memory together. His eyes darted around the room. Frantic. The painting . . . Sydney . . . blood . . . *"Miss Lane."*

"What was that?" Annika snapped. "Is that the name of your friend at the café? Is that who you gave the painting to?"

Miguel's mouth went dry. He swallowed against a new fear rising within him. "She's j-just a friend."

"A friend you trust?"

Pity. That's what he saw in Annika's eyes. A look half the town gave him while the other half avoided looking at him altogether. Except *her*. Miss Lane. Bile climbed up his throat. He shuddered and pressed his hands to his temples.

"Don't worry. I'll protect you." Her voice dragged against his nerves. "Take these." She held out her hand, her eyes flashing down to his bloody wounds. "You're going to need something for the beating you gave yourself."

Miguel held out his hand and she dropped two small pills in his palm. They were white against the crimson blood dried on his hands. Annika left the room only to return seconds later with a glass of water.

"What are you waiting for?"

He chased the pills down with a gulp of water.

"Good." Annika walked to the door and stopped. She leveled a cold glare at him. "I think it'd be wise for you to stay away from your friend. I'd hate to imagine her ending up like Sydney."

What had he done? Annika's words stoked the fire of doubt in his mind. He killed Sydney? How? Why? His head felt heavy. His body too. The room went black. The burden of what he did sunk him into the depths of darkness. He didn't fight it. Miguel allowed the abyss to swallow him.

Sweat dripped into his eyes. It stung. His clothes clung to his body, damp with moisture. The bayonet slipped in his hand. If he dropped it, he was a dead man. It was the only weapon he had to defend himself. He heard shouting. He pressed his face deeper into the mud. Muck filled his nostrils. He would suffocate out here. He turned his face for a breath and saw her. Piercing blue eyes. Unusual. Striking. Sydney.

She cowered. Pressed herself deep into the hollow of the tree behind her. It almost hid her. Almost. The shouting grew louder and he knew if he didn't move soon, they would kill her. He couldn't understand why.

He clawed his way through the marsh, and with each move her blue eyes grew wider, wild with fear. He was coming for her and she knew it. He was only a few feet away now. He'd try to make it quick . . . wait. What was she holding? Was it a blanket? The long piece of fabric moved. He saw a hand. It was little. No. It couldn't be. The little boy's face looked up at him. How?

No! It wasn't Sydney. It was Lane. Holding her son in her arms. She smiled. Miguel had to warn her. They couldn't be here. They were in danger. Opening his mouth, he tried to yell but nothing came out. He looked behind him. They were coming. He inched closer. How could he protect her? She was innocent. They were innocent. If they found her . . . He tightened his grip on the bayonet and lunged for her. Her smile melted into terror. She screamed.

FIFTEEN

NEWS VANS WERE PARKED OUTSIDE the courthouse. Lane passed through the metal detector. She could do this. Wanted to do this. For her and Noah. For a future. She turned down the marble hallway and faced a crowd of reporters filling the wide hall. Thankfully, their attention and their microphones were focused on her father.

"Justice will be served." Judge Sullivan's voice echoed against the cold stone. "Walton's finest are doing everything they can to find out who killed that sweet girl."

Hearing her father call someone sweet sounded odd. Out of character—especially within the confines of the courthouse. This was *Bear's* den, where he lived up to the moniker and delivered justice swiftly and firmly. Sometimes she was comforted to know that the lack of empathy he displayed at home he also shared with the defendants brought before him. Some people were critical of his severity, but they couldn't deny that Walton was exceptionally safe considering its proximity to Savannah. And her father held no qualms about taking credit for his part.

Until now.

Lane slipped into the judge's chambers and was glad to find it empty of his secretary. This conversation would be better received without anyone else present. At least that's what Lane hoped.

It had taken her a week after hearing Charlie speak those words to her on the front porch of her house to get the courage to face her parents. Before their bodies swayed as one, Charlie had sought permission to offer her a chance at love and she hadn't been able to stop hearing those words. The hope they ignited within her soul had kept the monsters of her depression at bay and only when she thought about what she was about to do did their roars become louder than the thundering within her chest.

"Lane?" Her mother stepped through the arched doorway separating the sitting area of the judge's chambers from her father's private office. "I didn't expect to see you here."

"I thought this would be over by now."

Lane glanced up at the flat-screen television mounted in the corner of the room that displayed a live feed of her father's press conference.

"It should've been." Her mother sighed. "Judge Atkins is using the murder as a means to question your father's ability to deliver justice. And the media is eating it up."

In a sharp black suit and red tie, her father leveled a serious stare at the reporters. "There is no question that I will make sure whoever killed Sydney Donovan pays for his or her crime. Leniency in this case will not be an option."

"He's not going to be happy when this is over." Her mother checked her lipstick in the gilded mirror next to an antique desk. "But your support will mean a lot."

Her support? Lane was here hoping to get *their* support, but maybe this could work to her advantage. If her father believed she was here to support his bid for Senate, then maybe it would make what she was about to tell him easier. If he could see she was trying, then just maybe—

"I picked up some barbecue sandwiches from the Smoking Hog. There'll be enough to share."

Lane followed her mother back into her father's office. A mahogany desk sat in the center and gold baroque curtains framed the large picture window overlooking Walton's park and memorial garden. A wall of shelves lined with law books filled the other half of the room, along with a long conference table. Her mother began unpacking the foam to-go containers, releasing the smoked aroma of barbecue into the room.

Helping her mother put the food onto plates and set the table,

Lane heard her father's voice answer the last question from the reporters. The press conference was over and Lane's stomach twisted into a knot of dread. Could she do this?

The door behind Lane closed and it felt like the air in the room evaporated along with her courage.

"Honey, you did great." Her mother's voice was soothing. "Right, Lane?"

Lane spun to face her father. His eyes settled on her. She nodded. Hesitantly at first and then a little more assuredly, hoping it conveyed her agreement and not so much her fear of upsetting him. This wasn't a good idea.

"Remind me to call Huggins." Her father strode across his office, loosening his tie. "If I'm feeling the pressure, he's going to feel it too."

A trace of indignation spurred Lane's gut. Did her father really believe the sheriff and his deputies weren't feeling the pressure of the case? Lane wasn't the only one who had noticed that the sheriff's normally jovial expression was quickly replaced with deep lines of exhaustion. Customers often asked Ms. Byrdie how her husband was doing, not always out of concern for the case but because they cared. And Lane was only slightly embarrassed that she had found herself searching Charlie's driveway for his truck the last several days only to find it empty from the break of dawn until she turned her lights off at night.

"I think they're feeling the pressure more than most."

Her father's forehead wrinkled at Lane's harsh tone. "Pressure produces results."

"Who's hungry?" Lane's mother pulled out a chair at the conference table and sat, expectation on her face for Lane and her father to do the same.

Lane had no appetite but sat anyway. Her father removed his suit jacket and sat in the chair at the head of the table.

"It was nice of Lane to show up, wasn't it?"

"Yes, it was."

Her father's words said he agreed, but his eyes held hers as though he knew her unexpected appearance at the courthouse held motive. She swallowed. She might as well get it over with. The spark Charlie had lit in her soul was spreading, and before it fanned into something she didn't dare dream possible, Lane knew this moment had to happen first.

"You remember Charlie Lynch? He's the new deputy. The one I was with at the church benefit for Sydney."

"I remember him." Lane's mother set down her fork and wiped her lips. "I didn't realize he was *with* you."

Heat flooded Lane's cheeks. "It was kind of a . . . date."

"A date?" Her mother reached across the table toward Lane's hand, but her father quickly interrupted the gesture by grabbing her mother's hand and holding tight.

Lane tucked her hands into fists beneath the table. "It's been, uh . . . well, he's nice and he likes Noah. And Ms. Byrdie thinks maybe I could start, well . . . I don't know, but—"

"Lane, what is it you want?" Her father's deep voice sent a tremor through Lane's chest. "Why are you here?"

"Dr. Wong wants you and Mom to join me at a session," Lane blurted out. And before the last ounce of what remained of her courage—or stupidity, she wasn't sure which it was yet—left, she said, "And I'd like to tell Charlie the truth."

The lines around her father's eyes tightened. "For what purpose?"

Lane wasn't sure which part he was referring to and whether it mattered. From his expression, she could already see him forming his answers, but her mom . . . well, something was there. Something Lane had been noticing in the way Meagan looked at her recently as well.

"Charlie's a nice man. He's sweet to me and, more importantly, to Noah. I don't want to start a relationship without him knowing about my past . . . or what I'm going through now."

"So, you're still having issues?"

Lane stiffened. "Dad, it's depression. It doesn't just go away."

"But isn't that why you're seeing Dr. Wong?" her mother asked. "To help you get better?"

"I am getting better, Mom, but it doesn't mean my condition is going to change or ever fully go away. It doesn't work that way, and if you and Dad came to an appointment—"

"That's not going to happen."

"What?" Lane faced her father. "Why not?"

"You realize I'm running for the United States Senate? Judge Atkins wants the position bad enough that he has my life under a microscope, trying to find something to nail me on."

Lane blinked. "And you think he'd use me to do that?"

"This is politics," her father said. "Nothing is off-limits." Her father released her mother's hand and sat back in his chair, studying Lane for a moment. "What do you think people will say when they find out our daughter has depression? Was suicidal? Actually attempted to take her own life with zero regard for her two-year-old son?"

"They can't." Lane curled her fists tighter so that her nails were digging into her palms. "It's confidential."

"You think that will stop someone from digging? And what do you think those reporters"—he jabbed a finger in the direction of the courthouse hallway—"will ask?" He leaned back farther in his chair and crossed his arms. "They'll ask what was so bad in Judge Raymond Sullivan's home that their daughter has depression and wanted to kill herself. They'll blame us."

"It isn't about you." Lane hated that her voice shook. Was his reputation all her father cared about? Could he not even see past an election to realize that he had as little control over her depression as she did? "It's never been about you."

"Oh, but it is." Her father leaned forward, elbows on the table. "It's been my job to protect you—even from yourself. And Noah if I have to."

"Ray," her mother said.

"No, Elise. She needs to hear this." Her father kept his gaze trained on Lane. "You think my concern is selfish, but I'm looking out for you. Those reporters won't stop with me—they'll go after you too. And Noah. You might be ready to tell that deputy your secrets, but are you ready for everyone else to find out? Ready for the way your customers will look at you? Or have people question whether Noah should even be with you?"

Lane looked down at the untouched plate of food in front of her. Her head swam as the threat of her father's words extinguished the flicker of hope she'd been holding on to. She felt sick. She needed to leave.

"I should go." Lane pushed out of her seat and ignored her mother calling after her, but when she heard her father say her name, she stopped and turned to look over her shoulder.

"We'll see you and Noah at the barbecue next weekend."

Was Noah safe with her? Is that what people would wonder when they knew the truth? Lane couldn't risk losing him. The lump in her throat was almost as large as the one in her stomach. The back of her eyes stung, but she wouldn't cry. Not here. And not in front of him. So, she nodded, accepting the command.

Lane hugged the walls of the hallway, keeping her eyes on the doors in front of her. She bit down on the inside of her cheek to keep the tears at bay. A blast of heat met her when she pushed through the tinted glass doors of the courthouse. Her cheeks grew hot as she took the steps down two at a time. She moved her feet faster to get away from the monolithic building.

Reporters were still lingering outside and her father's words loomed around her, making her feel conspicuous. He was right. Lane didn't have a television or need one to know the level to which people would stoop to win an election, and the last thing she wanted was for Noah to be drawn into that ugly world. It was bad enough she'd had to deal with it—and that was before opinions flew in every direction on social media. Noah was old enough to listen and understand. She needed to protect him.

Eyes on the ground, Lane missed the uniformed man stopped in front of her until she smacked into him and stumbled back. She squinted against the sun. Charlie.

"Lane, are you alright?" Charlie's gentle hand reached around hers and steadied her. "What's wrong?"

Lane swallowed the emotion that was ready to spill in Charlie's presence. Why was he always around when she was at her worst? And why—even at her worst and after everything her father had said—did she want to be wrapped in his arms?

"Talk to me, Lane." Charlie searched the area like he was looking for whoever was responsible for her state. With a firm and gentle grip, he pulled her next to him and assumed a protective position over her. "What's happened?"

Lane's chest constricted, forcing her to drag in a long, steady breath. She averted her eyes and pulled away from his touch. "It's nothing. I'm fine."

Charlie studied her face. "You don't look fine—I mean, you look good but . . . just upset. Like something's wrong."

"I'm okay." She took a deep breath and couldn't meet his gaze. His ability to read her, to know . . . "I'm just, uh, running late."

She could tell by the way his eyebrows pinched together that he didn't believe her, but the corner of his lip turned up and a sparkle filled his blue eyes. "I guess it's good you ran into me. I wanted to ask—"

A man with a camera anchored over his shoulder brushed past them and Lane remembered . . . this couldn't happen. Whatever Charlie was going to ask, she couldn't do it.

"I need to go. I'm sorry, Charlie." Lane knew the apology wasn't enough, but it was impossible to say anything else over the sob trying to scratch its way out of her throat. Before Charlie could react, Lane started for the street and crossed it, leaving not only her father and the ugly truth of her past behind but also Charlie.

Charlie's muscles tightened. He ran his hand over his head again. Running into Lane in her distraught state had him on edge. Her lack of explanation and quick escape consumed his thoughts most of the afternoon.

Until now.

An eerie quiet settled over the sheriff's office. It was bad enough a murder had taken place in their town, but it was unthinkable to realize a neighbor or best friend might be involved.

"The license plate number on the car in the video is registered to Jolene's father, but the car is insured under Jolene's name." Charlie handed Sheriff Huggins a file.

"What are these?"

"Screenshots of Twitter posts made by Jolene and her friend Annabeth Mendoza the week before Sydney's disappearance and death. The last sheets are the postings the two girls made after the discovery of Sydney's body."

Sheriff Huggins's face grew grimmer the further he read. "'I thought we were best friends, but you go behind my back. How dare you. Betrayal is worse than a stab in the back. Favorite Shakespeare play Julius Caesar. Time doesn't heal all wounds.'" Sheriff Huggins adjusted the reading glasses on his nose. "Jolene Carson posted these?"

"Yes, you can see her name in the corner of each post, along with a time and date stamp. They were all posted before Sydney was killed, but there's one posted the day before Lane discovered her body."

"'You can never take it back.'" Sheriff Huggins turned to the last sheet. "'Rest in peace, Sydney. My heart is broken, but I know our friendship will last forever. Worst day ever.' These ones are recent."

"Sir." Deputy Wilson tapped on the door. "Jolene Carson and her mother are here."

"Escort them to the interrogation room." Sheriff Huggins's gray eyes clouded into a murky mess of determination, dread, and disbelief. "Are you ready?"

"Yes, sir," Charlie said.

"Let's find out the truth."

Would Jolene tell the truth this time? The young girl, wearing a T-shirt and sweatpants, walked stiffly down the hall. More clothes than the last time. Her mother, however, looked like she was ready for a date in her tight blazer, skinny jeans, and very tall heels.

"I hope there's a good reason why I had to take Jo out of school in the middle of the day. I thought he"—Jolene's mom lifted her chin toward Charlie—"already asked all the questions."

"Some new information has surfaced and Deputy Lynch would like to ask a few more questions." Sheriff Huggins stood in the doorway, his eyes fixed on Jolene, who kept rubbing her arm. "Would you like an attorney present?"

"We didn't need one the last time," Jolene's mom scoffed. "As long as we hurry this up. I've got a nail appointment at four."

A few more seconds ticked by before Sheriff Huggins excused himself, along with Deputy Wilson. They would be in the next room watching the interview through the two-way mirror.

"Just like before, our conversation will be recorded." Charlie sat and placed his notebook and file on the table before pointing to the camera perched in the corner of the room. "Any objections?"

Jolene shook her head. Her mother said no.

"How are you doing, Jolene?"

"I'm okay," she answered slowly.

"Good. Like Sheriff Huggins said, we've come across some new information we'd like to ask you about." He opened the file and pulled out the same paper the sheriff had read from just minutes earlier. "Is this your Twitter account?"

Jolene leaned across the table. "Yes."

"Do you remember posting these comments?"

"Yes." Jolene leaned back and crossed her arms. "Why?"

"What about these?" He laid out still shots of the self-storage video surveillance side by side. "Do you recognize anything?"

Her blue eyes flicked down at the images for a second. Her

mother leaned over and picked up one photo, then another. She gasped. "That's Sydney."

Charlie lifted his eyebrows, waiting for Jolene's answer.

"It's Sydney," she agreed.

"Do you recognize anything else?"

"I don't think so."

"What about now?" Charlie pulled another set of photos. He placed the enhanced images of the car and license plate number on top of the others.

Ms. Carson smirked. "That's your car." Suddenly, a frown displaced the smirk. "Wait. That's your car?"

Jolene bit her lip.

"Is that your car?" He stared at the teenage girl trying to sink into the chair. Her eyes flashed to her mother and back to him. "Jolene?"

"Yes, I'm sorry. I should've told you, but I was scared. It was supposed to be a joke. We never thought she'd get hurt, but—"

"We?"

"Annabeth and I." Jolene glanced at her mom, who was stockstill. "It was a joke. Sydney was blowing us off. Keeping secrets. We would never have left her if we knew she . . ."

"Tell me what happened," Charlie said.

"We thought she'd call her mom or dad or whoever she'd been spending so much time with. It was a joke."

"You were with Sydney the night she disappeared."

"Yes." Jolene swallowed.

"Was Annabeth with you?"

"No. I was supposed to pick her up, but then she called and said her parents were being jerks and wouldn't let her hang out."

"But you said Annabeth was with you and Sydney?"

"Yeah." Jolene rubbed her arm, glancing at her mom from the corner of her eye. "Annabeth snuck out of the house later. I picked her up."

"What time?"

"It was dark. I don't know, maybe ten or eleven." Jolene fidgeted in the chair.

Getting her to talk was like pulling teeth, which usually meant there was more to the story. Jolene was holding back. "What happened next?"

"We wanted to know where Sydney was going and who she was hanging out with. Why she kept ditching us. She wouldn't tell us, so we sort of, um, we told her if she didn't we'd leave her out there."

"You did what?" Ms. Carson emerged from her stupor.

"Out where?" Charlie continued. He didn't want Jolene to get distracted or change her story for fear of getting in trouble with her mom.

"There's an old gas station on Coastal Highway. A lot of kids go there and get high or drunk."

"Was anyone else there?"

"No. We were by ourselves."

"What were you doing?"

"Drinking." Jolene bit her lip and glanced at her mom.

Ms. Carson fell back against her chair in dramatic flair. "I assure you, Deputy, this is not how I raised her."

Jolene narrowed her eyes at her mom.

"Just drinking?" Charlie asked.

"Smoking too."

"Drugs or tobacco?"

"Marijuana."

Another dramatic exhale came from Ms. Carson's direction. Charlie slid forward in his chair. Finally, they were getting somewhere. "What happened next?"

"When Sydney wouldn't tell us her secret, Annabeth and I decided to play the joke. We ran to the car and locked the doors. Told Sydney if she didn't tell us the truth, we'd leave her there. She refused, so we left. But we came back," Jolene quickly added. "We just wanted to teach her a lesson, but she was gone. We figured she'd called someone to come get her."

"How long were you gone?"

"I don't remember. We drove down the road a little bit and finished the beers." Jolene chewed on her thumbnail.

Charlie studied the girl sitting in front of him. Something had been off in her first interview, but he wasn't expecting this.

"Is Jolene going to get in trouble for this?" Ms. Carson laughed. "I mean, it was a joke. The girls couldn't have known what was going to happen."

"Did you drive yourself here, Jolene?"

"Yes."

"Would you mind if I had a deputy look at your car?"

"Why?" Ms. Carson's gaze turned suspicious.

"We'd like to search the car for Sydney's cell phone. It's missing. We're hoping there might be a name or number in it that could lead us to the person Sydney had been talking with."

"Okay." Ms. Carson's shoulders relaxed. "But Jolene gets credit for helping you, right? Now you know where Sydney was before she was, um, killed."

Charlie set his jaw. "Is there anything I can get you? Some water? Coffee or a soda?"

"Do you have cappuccino?" Ms. Carson pulled a lipstick tube and mirror from her purse, seemingly undisturbed by the fact he hadn't answered her question.

"Just black. Sugar and cream is available."

"Water is fine." Jolene glared at her mother.

"Yes, water is fine." Ms. Carson pressed her lips together.

Charlie rose from the table and opened the door to find Sheriff Huggins and Deputy Wilson waiting outside the room. Wilson held a forensics kit and two bottles of water. Jolene and her mother rose from their seats and followed the team of deputies to the parking lot. Sheriff Huggins fell in step at the rear. They stopped in front of the white Camry from the video. Jolene unlocked the door and shrank back behind her mom.

"Deputy Lynch." Wilson motioned him over to the front of the car.

The right headlight was broken and a huge dent marred the right front bumper and part of the hood. Charlie kneeled down to get a closer look. There were a few brown spots.

"Blood?" Wilson said under his breath as he opened the kit. "Autopsy report said Sydney was hit by something before being stabbed. Maybe a car."

"Test it."

Another deputy searched the inside of the car while Wilson rubbed a cotton swab along one of the brown spots.

"What's he doing?" Jolene unfolded herself out of her mother's shadow. "What's he putting on my car?"

"What happened to your car?" Charlie exchanged a pointed look with Sheriff Huggins, who joined Wilson at the front of the vehicle.

"What?" Jolene's eyes flashed. "I, uh, I hit a deer."

"When?"

"Um, a couple of weeks ago. Is he taking pictures of my car? I thought you were looking for Sydney's phone," Jolene said, her voice squeaking.

"Did you report the accident to your insurance company?"

"Why?" Jolene wrinkled her brow.

"We need to verify the date of the accident."

"It was a couple of weeks ago." Ms. Carson shaded her eyes with her hand. "I can't remember the exact day, but she came home very upset. The car was a gift from her father. We only have liability coverage."

Wilson whispered something to Sheriff Huggins. The steadfast lawman gave an almost imperceptible nod and stepped forward.

"Ms. Carson, we tested a spot on the car and it came back positive for blood—"

"She just told you she hit a deer." Ms. Carson stalked to the front of the car. "It's probably deer blood."

"We need to impound the car and have our experts run tests on it."

"What? No! I need my car." Jolene paced in front of her car. "It's my blood. After I hit the deer, I checked to see the damage and cut my finger on the broken glass."

"Is that really necessary?" Ms. Carson put her hand on Jolene's trembling shoulder. "She told you the truth. She had nothing to do with that girl's death."

Charlie's ears piqued at Ms. Carson's choice of words. Her daughter's best friend was now "that girl." Interesting.

"Why can't you just do the test here?" Jolene whined. "I'll even give you a sample of my blood."

"Stop talking." Ms. Carson opened her purse and pulled out a cell phone. "I'm calling my lawyer."

Jolene stamped her foot. "I have to get my stuff—" Wilson stood in her way. "What are you doing? Move!"

"Nothing can be moved from the vehicle." Wilson's voice was low. He was not impressed with the teenager's tantrum.

Tears fell over her cheeks. Were they real? During their first interview, Jolene was able to control the waterworks at the blink of an eye.

"We'll take an inventory of the items this afternoon and call you to come pick up your belongings after that," Sheriff Huggins said.

"What about her schoolbooks?"

"We'll get those back to you as well. Now, let's go inside and fill out the paperwork." Sheriff Huggins held his hand up toward the station.

"Come on, Jolene. I can't believe we came here to help and now we're being treated like criminals."

They ushered a distraught and red-faced Jolene back into the station, along with her mother who was making sure her side of the conversation with her lawyer could be heard by all.

Sheriff Huggins excused Charlie to fill out the paperwork while he handled Ms. Carson and Jolene. The gesture would've been appreciated more if Charlie's mind wasn't distracted with worry over Lane. What had her so upset outside the courthouse earlier? And the way she looked at him . . . almost mournfully. That bothered him the most. He told her she had time to think—maybe that was it? Maybe a future with him wasn't in Lane's future? Charlie swallowed. That wasn't the outcome he wanted or had hoped for. But could he accept it?

Charlie stared at the mountain of paperwork stacked in front of him. It was Friday, but he knew he'd be pulling another late night. He tapped his fingers on the desk. If he hustled, he might be able to get the majority of it done and still catch Lane before she closed up after Friday Night Club. But what if he was too late? The thought sent his heart plummeting. Pushing back from his desk, he grabbed his hat. He'd stay up as late as necessary to finish the job, but right now his first priority was Lane.

SIXTEEN

LANE OPENED UP another package of buns and counted the last few patrons of the Friday Night Club who were waiting for their plates.

"I think our little club is getting more and more popular." Ms. Byrdie scooped up potato salad and put it on a plate before using another spoon for the macaroni and cheese. "All these folks needing a home-cooked meal for the soul."

A little girl, the youngest of the group, with stringy blonde hair and deep brown eyes edged toward the pans of Ms. Byrdie's banana pudding.

"Would you like some more dessert?" Lane asked.

"Samantha." A woman with the same dark eyes came to the counter, her cheeks pink. "I'm sorry, ma'am. She's already had her serving." The mother tried to take her daughter's hand, but the little girl's pleading eyes looked up at Lane.

"We have plenty. If she wants more of anything, y'all are welcome to it." Lane looked to Ms. Byrdie, who nodded. "In fact, I think we may have enough extras for you to take some home with you."

A sheen covered the woman's eyes before she gave a tight smile and then took the bowl of pudding Ms. Byrdie held out to her. The woman and her daughter returned to their table, where a man scooped up the little girl into his lap.

"I don't recognize them," Lane whispered.

"They're from Blythe County," Dottie said as she walked up behind Lane, carrying a pitcher of freshly brewed tea. "That's Billy, his wife, Chrissy, and their little girl, Samantha. They're having a rough time of it and Harley invited them—hope that was okay."

Lane nodded. "Of course." She studied the family. Nothing on the outside to indicate they were having "a rough time of it," but the mother had a distant look in her eyes that Lane recognized. A look that said there was so much more to the façade.

"You alright, honey?" Ms. Byrdie asked. "You've been awful quiet since you got back this afternoon."

"Hmm?" Blinking, Lane saw that both Dottie and Ms. Byrdie were watching her. "What?"

"Everything okay, sugar?"

"Oh, yes." Lane sighed. "Miguel's a no-show again."

Ms. Byrdie looked around. "Yeah, I noticed that too."

"And where's Harley?" Lane wiped some stray macaroni from the counter. "I want to thank him for smoking all of this pork."

"Girls, I didn't tell you? Harley's at the hospital."

"What?" Lane stopped.

"Decided to fillet his hand instead of the fish."

"Is he alright?"

"Fifty-five stitches. He said one for each year of life he saw flash before his eyes."

"That's terrible, Dottie. I'm so sorry." Lane looked down at the tray of smoked meat. "How did he—"

Dottie shook her head. "He put the meat in early this morning before his fishing trip. He kept calling me from the hospital. I think most of County General knows how to smoke a pig now."

"Well, it's delicious. You did a great job."

"Don't you go telling Harley that. He'll have his feelings hurt."

Dottie, Ms. Byrdie, and Lane shared a laugh as they served second helpings until everyone was satisfied. Lane had just begun to clean up when the door to the Way Station Café opened, letting in a blast of the day's high temperatures and a familiar face that turned her insides warm and disoriented her thoughts.

"Well, there's my good-looking nephew." Ms. Byrdie went around the counter and embraced Charlie. "Perfect timing. We have enough to make you a plate. Have a seat at the counter."

His eyes were locked on her as he strolled up to the counter and sat on a stool. "Hey, Lane."

It felt like she had swallowed a mouthful of sawdust. She was unable to offer even a simple greeting in return. In his uniform, Charlie was drawing a mix of curious and anxious looks from the others in the café.

"Lane, do we have any more napkins in the back?"

Dottie's question snapped Lane out of her trance. "Um, yes. I'll just go get them."

"I got it." Dottie leaned close to Lane's ear. "Go help that hunk of handsome before I forget I got a man of my own."

Ducky's grating laughter pulled Lane's attention to where the scrappy senior citizen sat next to Charlie, slapping his shoulder like they were old friends.

"You need anything else, Ducky? A refill on dessert or iced tea?"

"Just telling this city boy who's been eyeing you that you're already spoken for."

Lane rolled her eyes, to which Charlie smiled, dimples and all. "Don't mind him. He's ornery."

"I don't know." Charlie rotated on the stool. "I think the man's pretty astute to recognize a beautiful lady when he sees one."

"Doncha' try and use that city talk on me, son. I know astute when I see one, and you ain't gonna pull one over on ol' Ducky." Ducky winked with his good eye and pointed a finger at Charlie. "I'm watching you, young fella."

Charlie's eyes were wide as Ducky found an empty chair at a table with Wilbur and Clarence. "Seems like I've got some competition."

Lane blushed, unable to meet his eyes. There was no competition if the heat rising in her chest was any indication of what her heart felt. "Um, can I get you something to drink?"

"I know these aren't regular business hours"—Charlie reached across the counter and let his fingers play across hers, making it hard for Lane to breathe—"but I needed to be sure you were okay. You know, from earlier."

Lane started to respond when another puff of warm, muggy air breached the air-conditioned atmosphere of her café. Lane looked over Charlie's shoulders at the man who had entered. She blinked twice to convince herself the disheveled man in a dirty shirt and torn jeans with dark hair pointing in every direction was Miguel.

"I'll be right back." Lane came around the counter, but Dottie stepped in front of her.

"I'll take this one, honey. You go take care of Mr. Good-Looking."

Miguel's eyes had a wild look about them as he searched the place. With heavy, unsteady steps, he moved toward the table where Samantha's family was and her father put a protective hand on his daughter's back.

Lane started for Miguel.

Dottie reached for Lane's arm and redirected her steps. "I've got him, hon. You take care of your deputy friend," she whispered in Lane's ear.

The look in Miguel's eyes set off an alarm inside her. He was in trouble. Lane wanted to protest, but Dottie used her eyes to send a message to Lane. Lane looked to Charlie, who was standing, his gaze fixed on Miguel and hand flexed near his gun belt. The corners of his eyes creased. Alert and ready.

"Do you need help?" Charlie tipped his head toward Miguel.

"No, no. It's fine." Now she knew why Dottie was intervening. "Dottie will take care of him."

Charlie returned to his stool, his eyes dancing between her and Miguel when a chair screeched along the wooden floor and grabbed their attention.

"Where is it?" Miguel pushed the table back with a growl. Dottie placed her arm on Miguel's shoulder, but he shrugged it off with enough force that it sent her stumbling backward. A few customers stepped away from the commotion. Charlie stood, but before he could join the others Lane was already pushing her way toward Miguel.

"Miguel." Lane reached for his arm. He shook her hand off like he had done to Dottie. It was like he didn't recognize her. "Miguel."

"Honey, I don't think it's safe to be around him right now." Dottie pulled on Lane's hand.

"It's okay. Give me a second." Lane stepped closer and noticed the layer of powder-like sawdust covering his gray shirt and the pungent smell of something she recognized but couldn't put her finger on. It wasn't alcohol . . . was it? "Miguel, it's Lane. Do you want to go for a walk?"

"Where is it?"

Dottie ushered the customers back to their tables. Some left, including Samantha's family. From the corner of her eye, Lane saw Charlie coming toward them. She didn't know how Miguel would react to him.

"Miguel, I don't know what you're looking for," she said, keeping her voice low. "But let's go for a walk and see if we can find it."

"Where is it?" Miguel snarled and whipped his arm back in a wide arc, catching Lane in the cheek with his elbow. The force sent her crashing into an empty chair behind her as sharp pain filled her face. Lane put a hand to her cheek and ran her tongue over her teeth, surprised they all felt in place.

"Lane!" Ms. Byrdie's and Charlie's voices collided.

The rest of the room was stunned silent. Several men, including Ducky, had their hands wrapped around Miguel. Charlie, his face lit with rage, stormed toward the belligerent man.

"I should go." Miguel's voice was calm. Quiet. His wild eyes seemed to have found somewhere to focus and they were on Lane. "I came to say goodbye."

"I'll take it from here." Charlie reached for Miguel's elbow and a flicker of something crossed in the veteran's eyes. Fear.

"No." Ouch. Her jaw ached and it felt like her face was already beginning to swell. "I've got it."

"Lane, he hit you."

Charlie's eyes found the spot on her cheek that was throbbing. It probably didn't look good, judging from his pained expression, but it didn't matter. This wasn't like Miguel. Something was wrong.

"It was an accident." Pushing away the fear, Lane moved slowly toward Miguel. She laced her arm gently around his elbow and started for the door. "We're just going to be outside."

"Lane." Charlie stepped in front of her.

"It's okay. Give me a few minutes."

Ms. Byrdie reached for Charlie's shoulder and gave a quick nod. Charlie returned his attention to Lane before reluctantly stepping back. Lane steered Miguel out the back of her home toward her garden. Beneath the trellis was an old bench glider that had belonged to her grandmother.

"Why don't we sit here?" She loosened her grip on Miguel's arm and let him slide down onto the bench before taking a seat next to him. His head hung so low that his chin touched his chest. His hands shook. He looked broken. Pained.

The melody of night life was filled with chirping crickets, a hooting owl, and the occasional trickle of laughter from somewhere nearby. Lane breathed in the fragrant air of the still-blooming purple hyacinths. Maybe he just needed a moment to breathe. She watched him rub the fingernail on his right thumb. It was black and cracked. The rest of the cuts were scabbed over. They looked rough. Untouchable. Lane's heart ached. How often had she felt untouchable?

"Harley says you like to sculpt. Have you been sculpting?"

Miguel barely moved his head.

"I've missed seeing you here."

"Are you afraid to die?" Miguel's raspy voice was barely audible over the anthem of chirping around them.

His question punched the air right out of her. "Are you okay, Miguel?"

He didn't move.

"Sometimes there are days when I think death is an answer." She'd never said those words aloud to anyone, but she felt a connection to the subdued man sitting next to her. This veteran who kept to himself had no idea how much alike they were.

"Why are you nice to me?"

Lane's heart ached. "Because you're my friend, Miguel. When a friend is hurting or in trouble, you help them. You take care of them."

"I'm a bad person. I've done bad things."

She swallowed. "Miguel, we've all done bad things, but—"

Two bright lights lit up the dark night around them. A truck stopped and the driver got out.

"Lane? Miguel?"

Lane shielded her eyes from the headlights. It was Harley.

"Dottie called." Harley's left hand was wrapped in white bandages. "Said I should come take Miguel home."

"Did you just get out of the hospital? You should be resting."

"It's no big deal. Besides, Dot said there's a very anxious deputy waiting inside for you."

Charlie, right. It was probably better for Harley to take Miguel home to avoid any further confrontations. She helped Miguel to the truck.

Harley tilted his head. "He did that to you?"

Lane's hand instinctively went to the sore on her cheek. "It was an accident."

"Hmm." Harley's expression matched the feeling in her gut. Something wasn't right with their friend. "I'll get him home."

"Thanks, Harley."

"Sure thing, doll." Harley glanced past her. Charlie stood on the porch. Watching. "Now, why don't you go reassure that anxious fella?"

Lane reached into the truck and put a hand on Miguel's shoulder. He didn't flinch this time. He looked at her with clarity in his eyes that wasn't there before. Then a flicker of pain or guilt passed through them before his lip quivered slightly.

"I'm sorry."

"Miguel, you have nothing to apologize for. It was an accident." Miguel dropped his gaze to his hands and said nothing. "Tomorrow I'm going to bring you some muffins or cookies, okay?"

There was no response. Miguel had retreated back into himself. Lane said goodbye to him and thanked Harley again before watching them pull out of the parking lot.

Charlie came up behind her holding an ice pack. "I brought ice. Are you okay?"

"Me? Yeah, I'm okay." She stared after the cloud of dust from Harley's truck. "I just hope he is."

"Does he come in here a lot?"

"Miguel's a regular." She tried to read Charlie's tone. Was it curious or concerned? "He's not normally like that."

"Seems like he's having a rough night."

Heat radiated from her cheek. "He's not the only one."

"Let me see." Charlie moved in front of her. She breathed in his scent, a mixture of musk and woods and sweat, uniquely him, that sent her heart beating in time with the throbbing in her cheek. He brushed his thumb lightly against the tender spot and she winced. "The ice will help."

Lane reached up and took his hand away from her face, exchanging the warmth of his touch for the sting of the ice pack. Good. She needed to steel herself for what she had to do. "Can we talk?"

"Sure."

Her nerves were an energized tangle. Charlie followed her back to the same glider she and Miguel had just been sitting on. What would she tell him? It felt lame to say she couldn't date him because her father said so—she was way past that. She could say she wasn't ready, but her heart knew that wasn't true and she had a feeling Charlie would see through it. He had that way about him. Since running into him, Lane had been trying to come up with a dozen different reasons why this couldn't work—why they couldn't work—but one thing stood out above all of them. He didn't know the truth about her.

And maybe telling him the truth would make him realize she wasn't right for him—or anyone.

"Your garden rivals my aunt's."

"Pops helps me with it."

Slow seconds of silence ticked between them as the evening's first stars began to twinkle above. Their shoulders touched and Lane realized for a quick second how nice this moment was. She wanted to remember it. Hold it close so on those nights when darkness loomed she'd remember what hope felt like. She breathed deep and began.

"Charlie, I have depression." Saying the words didn't give her instant relief, and now that they were out she desperately wanted to take them back.

"Lane, you lost your husband. That's completely understandable."

"No, you don't understand. I've had depression all my life. I still have it."

She watched his expression. Waited for him to recoil, but the only thing reflected in his face was compassion.

"I'm sorry . . ."

There it was. He was sorry she was messed up. Sorry about getting involved with a mentally disturbed person. Sorry—

"What can I do to help?"

"What?" The question had caught her so off guard that she hadn't realized he'd taken hold of her hand. His thumb rubbed her knuckles.

"How can I help? I've read exercise is good. I've been running in the morning with Bane because my work hours are so long, but maybe you could join me. Or we could paddleboard on the river—"

"Charlie, I'm never going to get better." She withdrew her hand. "This is who I am."

He frowned. "I feel like I'm missing something?"

"I can't be in a relationship. I'm not—"

"Ready? If you're not ready, that's okay." Charlie moved closer to her. "I told you I'd wait. I'm not looking for a romantic fling, Lane. I want someone forever—"

"That's not me." She closed her eyes. "I'm not forever material."

"I don't understand."

"There are side effects to my illness." Her thoughts tumbled to the day on the bridge. "It's not fair to you. I'm not worth the risk."

"I've faced a lot of risk in my life." He tucked a piece of hair behind her ear. "But I can't believe you're not worth it."

The soft touch of his skin against hers sent her heart soaring. He was making this harder for her. She pulled away even though everything inside her wanted him to take her into his arms and protect her. Possibly love her.

"I've tried to kill myself." Her admission came out as a whisper, barely audible over the strained beating of her heart echoing in her ears.

Charlie pressed his lips together and searched the skies . . . for what? An answer? He wouldn't find one there. She'd looked. Prayed. Searched for an answer to why God would make her broken.

"I lost a good friend in Afghanistan. We were battle buddies. Met on the flight over. Both scared out of our minds. But we had each other's backs. Trusted that if one of us ran into something, the other would fight with everything they had to get us out of it." His voice was low, and just like Pops, she could see that Charlie's mind had transitioned back to the battlefield. "There was an ambush. The attack was brutal and most of my team didn't think we were going to make it out of there. My buddy, Tate, was already whispering prayers and giving me his list of farewells. He was inside a building when a rocket-propelled grenade was launched at it. I thought we had lost him, but as a team we fought our way in and pulled him out."

Charlie turned to face her and she could see the moisture in his eyes. "When he woke up in the hospital, he was ready to get back to the field, but it didn't take long for us to realize something was different. Nightmares. Aggression. He went home a different man. Two months after our tour ended, I got the call that Tate had killed himself."

"I'm sorry," Lane said over the lump in her throat.

"If we had known about Tate, if I had known what he was going through, I would've helped him. I would have done whatever I could have because the world was a better place with him in it." Charlie picked up her hands and held them firmly between his. "Depression I can accept. Not having you in my life or having the possibility of you being in my life—that's harder to accept."

Charlie's words soothed her soul and seemed to erase the concerns her father had raised earlier. Charlie wouldn't hurt her or Noah. He wasn't that kind of man. But was she ready to defy her father's wishes? And at what cost?

"Lane, I'm not going anywhere. There's no rush for you to make a decision." He lifted her hands up so his lips just grazed her knuckles, causing her insides to tremble. "I'm only asking for the chance to get to know you better. All of you."

Lane wanted that too. Deep in her core the longing to be loved fully and completely awakened. Could Charlie really see past her depression or was this commitment to her a type of penance for him not being there for his friend?

"Hi, Charlie." Lane jumped at Noah's voice coming through the flowers. "Did you bring Bane?"

Charlie squeezed Lane's hand before standing. "Sorry, buddy, not this time."

"Oh, excuse us." Pops emerged behind Noah. "I hope we aren't interrupting anything."

"No, Pops." Lane swept Noah into her arms and kissed his neck. Charlie and Pops exchanged a handshake.

"Momma, stop." Noah giggled and then looked at her cheek. "What happened to your face, Momma?"

She'd almost forgotten. "Mommy got an owie."

"Does it hurt?"

Lane looked to Charlie. "Not so much anymore."

Noah's attention returned to Charlie. "Can I play with Bane tomorrow?"

"Tomorrow we have Bear's party, remember?"

"Is it a birthday party?" Noah scrunched his nose. "For Bear?"

"No, it's not."

"But birthdays are important, right, Momma?"

Lane kissed Noah's cheek, catching Pops's eye. Her grandfather sent her a card not only on her actual birthday of August third but also on April eleventh. The day she got out of the hospital and chose life. That was her living birthday. "Yes, they are."

"I'm going to take this one inside and get him ready for bed." Pops took Noah from her arms and started for the house. "Nice seeing you again, Charlie."

"You too, sir." When the screen door shut, Charlie smiled. "I guess I'll be seeing you tomorrow night too."

Even in the dimness of the night, Charlie's eyes shined bright. "Oh, right, because you're working the barbecue."

Charlie's gaze lingered long enough that she could feel the heat rise in her cheeks.

"I meant everything I said, Lane. I'm here for you, whatever you need."

There was so much reassurance in his words that Lane couldn't respond. Not since Mathias had she felt so protected. As Charlie backed away and headed toward the squad car, Lane stopped at the gardenias Charlie had given her, which she had planted near her window. Every morning she noticed new blooms uncurling in the promise of a new day. Maybe her father was wrong. Maybe Charlie was Lane's chance at a new day. A new hope. A new future.

SEVENTEEN

THE SCREECHING ALARM propelled Lane down the oak stairway of her home and into the café. Her nose instinctively sought the acrid smell of smoke . . . but there was none. As her eyes adjusted to the pre-dawn light filling the room, it took only a second for her to realize all was normal. Not normal. It wasn't the fire alarm blaring but the security alarm.

Lane's heart began an erratic pounding that only slightly distracted her from the alarm warning her that all was not normal. Her eyes tracked the first floor. Windows were still closed. Locked. The doors too. "Momma!" Noah came to her side, both hands covering his ears. "It's hurting my ears."

"I know, buddy." Lane tucked Noah to her side. Why was her alarm going off? The memory of the man she had seen lurking on the side of her house came barreling back. Had he returned?

Glancing around once more to ensure nobody was hiding in the diminishing shadows, Lane went to the panel near the back door and entered the code. The previous owner had installed the alarm system, but Lane had never seen a need for it in sleepy-town Walton until the other night when she'd found the man peeking into her home. *Odd.* The alarm continued to blare.

Lane punched in the numbers again. In defiance, the alarm seemed to scream louder, growing more obnoxious with every passing second. Why wasn't the code working? She was putting in the right code, wasn't she?

"Momma!"

"I know, Noah." Lane bit back her frustration. Why wasn't this thing shutting up?

The phone in the kitchen rang. Great. Probably the neighbors

185

complaining about the noise. Neighbors? Charlie. Would he know how to shut this thing off?

"Hello?"

"Lane, honey, is everything okay? I got a call from the alarm company—is that the alarm?"

"Yes, Ms. Byrdie." Lane covered her other ear with her hand. She forgot she never updated the security company to call her instead of Ms. Byrdie. "It went off a few minutes ago, but I can't get it to shut off."

"I'm on Highway 17, I'll be there in a few minutes."

Lane hung up and tried the code again. Her head started to throb. Noah was rolling on the ground with his blankie wrapped around his head.

Brap-rap-rap-rap. Lane screamed and jerked around to find a face staring at her through the window of the back door. It took her several breaths to realize it was a familiar face—one that made her heart skip and gave her inexplicable reassurance. Charlie.

Lane unlocked the door and opened it. "You nearly gave me a heart—"

"Are you and Noah okay?" Charlie's chest heaved. His chest. Bare chest. Muscles flexing with each shallow breath. "Lane?"

Oh my, she was staring. But how could she not? A half-naked man—never mind that he was attractive—was standing in her home . . . with a gun. *A gun.* "What are you doing with that?" she hissed, taking a step toward him to block the weapon from Noah's line of sight.

"I heard the alarm." Charlie looked around, his eyes searching. "I ran over."

He ran over? For *her*? Lane's heart jackhammered beneath her ribs and it wasn't from the chaos of the morning. "I, uh. It's okay. The alarm is spazzing out. Ms. B—"

"Is here, dear."

Lane jumped. Ms. Byrdie was standing behind her, keys in hand

186

and an impish smile playing on her lips as her eyes bounced between Charlie and Lane.

"This isn't . . ." Lane looked down at her pajamas covered with tiny T. rexes eating donuts before turning to Charlie for help, but the shadowed expression he wore a second ago had relaxed into a playful smirk. His gun was no longer visible. "He was just . . ." It was now Lane's gaze passing between Charlie and Ms. Byrdie. It was as if the two shared a secret . . . "Y'all really need to stop popping up behind me. Especially with this alarm going off."

Ms. Byrdie cast one more conspiratorial look in Charlie's direction before moving past them to the wall panel. She punched in the code, but it didn't silence the alarm. She tried again to no avail.

"Maybe it's the wiring." Ms. Byrdie pulled out her cell phone. "Lane, why don't you go show Charlie where the old electrical box is."

Lane hesitated. She peeked across the room and saw Noah with his head still covered, only now instead of rolling on the ground he was walking around with his arms stretched out in front of him like a mummy. She rolled her eyes.

"Hurry, Lane, or you're going to have the whole town here, and Joe hasn't delivered the coffee beans yet."

Charlie stepped aside and waited for her to lead the way. Outside, the short, high-pitched wail of the alarm ripped into the peaceful morning. Lane walked gingerly across the gravel to the other side of the house. "I'm sorry the noise woke you up."

"I was up. Getting ready for a run."

"You run with your gun?" Lane stole a glance at his body, wondering where he kept it. "Seems dangerous."

Charlie cocked his head and offered a sly smile. "Only for the bad guy I'm chasing."

As she rounded the corner of the house, Lane let out a hushed cry. "Wha—" She knelt to the ground and looked at her gardenias.

The ones Charlie had given her. The white petals were scattered across the ground.

"Did an animal do that?" Charlie knelt down and fingered the splintered branches.

"A deer could, but they tend to stick to the tree line outside of town."

Lane didn't know why the sight of her flowers torn from their stems and pressed into the soil upset her so much. It was silly. They were just flowers. But they weren't. Not to her. Unintentionally, Lane had assigned symbolism to these simple white blooms when she planted them. Hope. Promise. Expectation. It was irrational, she could see that now, but it felt purposeful at the time.

"I'll get you a new one." Charlie's hand went to the small of her back. "To replace it."

"No. There are still some buds on this one. It'll survive." Lane rose and pointed to a metal box attached to the house. "That's the panel. Though, I'll be honest, I don't really know what I should be looking for."

"We just need to find the wire to the security system. It should be marked." Charlie opened the box. "Yep, right here. Hmm."

"What is it?" Lane stepped closer. Warmth radiated from his skin and Lane forgot about her flowers. The beat of her heart filled her ears so loudly she was certain Charlie could hear it. She started to step back when something in the corner of the metal box caught her attention. Triggered something.

Charlie played with some wires and the house went silent. "You've got some frayed wires. Like something started chewing through it. I can't imagine what since the box was closed but"—he looked up at her, the edges of his blue eyes crinkled—"what?"

Lane licked her lips, wrenching her eyes away from the tooth-pick. It wasn't a coincidence, was it? The man who had come into her café was chewing on a toothpick. Had it been him the other evening too? Why had he returned?

"You look like you've seen a ghost." Charlie's fingers brushed a piece of hair from her face, careful to avoid her bruised cheek. "What is it?"

Fighting to ignore the way his touch rattled her nerves, Lane shook her head. "Nothing. Probably nothing." The words came out like they were stuck. "It's . . . it's a toothpick."

Confusion drew Charlie's brows together.

"That night, after finding"—she hated saying the words— "Sydney, there was this man. I'd never seen him before, but he was out here. He asked about a place to eat, but we were closed. A few days later, he came back. He asked about Noah and my husband—I guess he saw the picture near the cash register. He sorta gave me the creeps and I asked him to leave. I didn't think I would see him again . . ."

"But . . ."

Lane heaved in a breath. "The other night after we talked in the memorial garden, there was someone standing outside the café, looking into the windows."

Charlie's expression tightened. "Was it the same guy?"

"I don't know." Lane rubbed her arms. "Whoever it was took off before I could get a good look at them."

"And you haven't seen him again?"

Lane bit her lip.

"You've seen him again?"

"Not exactly. At least I don't think so. It might've been my imagination playing tricks on me. His questions about Noah and Mathias freaked me out so much that I thought I was seeing him around town, but whenever I'd try to get a second look he was gone . . . if he was even there to begin with."

"And the toothpick?"

If Charlie had any doubts about her sanity, this would be the clincher. "The man was chewing on a toothpick."

"Come on." Taking her hand, Charlie pulled her in next to him as they made their way back to the porch. His eyes alert, body rigid—poised and ready to protect.

Lane wondered if her instincts were correct. Had the man returned? If so, why? Back inside, they found Ms. Byrdie filling a bowl with cereal for Noah.

"Charlie!" Noah scrambled off the stool and lunged at Charlie, who immediately scooped up the child into his arms like he'd been doing it all his life. "Where's Bane?"

"At home, buddy."

Hearing Charlie call Noah by his nickname stole Lane's breath. That and the man was still shirtless—hiding a gun somewhere on his body. Lane needed a distraction. Quick. "Noah, you need to eat breakfast if you want to go to Pops's."

Ms. Byrdie smiled and handed Noah a spoon. "Did you figure out what the problem was?"

"Something might've chewed through the wire," Lane said, grabbing the attention of both Charlie and Ms. Byrdie with her eyes. They weren't going to discuss strange men lurking outside their home in front of Noah.

Charlie crossed through the kitchen and into the main room, with Lane and Ms. Byrdie following. "It *might* have been an animal or it could have been something else."

"Something else?" Concern drew Ms. Byrdie's lips into a frown. "Like what?"

"The other day there was someone peering into the windows of the café when it was closed," Lane said.

Charlie went to each window and inspected the locks. "You have anything of value here? Money in a safe?"

"No, not really. I mean, we have a normal amount of money on hand, but a courier from the bank comes by and picks it up each night before we close. It's nothing to break in for. Besides, this is Walton."

Ms. Byrdie pressed her lips together a second as though that kind of reasoning was no longer applicable. "What about the donations?"

Charlie's gaze swung in Lane's direction. "The donations for your father's barbecue fund-raiser?"

190

"Yes." Lane looked at the empty spot near the back of her café where the donations once took up space. "Those got picked up. But how would anyone even know they're worth stealing?"

"Honey, this isn't your father's first fund-raiser," Ms. Byrdie said. "And Meagan's solicited some rather impressive donations. I'd wager there's more money sitting in those boxes than the Savings & Loan has in its vault on most days."

Lane couldn't argue with that. "Do you really think someone would break in and try to steal the donations?"

"Maybe, if there was something someone wanted badly enough." Charlie scratched the back of his neck. "Do you remember any of the items?"

"Not everything." Lane rubbed her forehead. "There's artwork, football tickets. I think there might've been a vacation voucher. But none of it matters since it's not even here."

"But who else would know that?"

Lane didn't have an answer. Charlie's tone and the way his jaw muscle flexed . . . his whole demeanor shifted from friendly neighbor helping out to suspicious police officer asking questions that unsettled her.

Charlie ran his hand through his disheveled hair. "I'd like you to come by the station later and give me a description of the man you saw."

"I think that's a good idea," Ms. Byrdie said. "Can't be too careful these days."

"You don't think I'm being paranoid? I mean, he could've been someone just looking to see if we were open." But even as the words left her lips, Lane knew it wasn't as innocent as that. Sydney's killer was still out there. "Well, this day is just starting out fabulous, isn't it?"

The front door to the Way Station Café jingled open.

"Good morning!" The chipper voice belonged to Mrs. Kingsley, one of the ladies who, what felt like a lifetime ago, had tried to arrange a date for Lane with her grandson. Her eyes fixed suddenly on Charlie's still-bare chest and the most ridiculous smile plastered her face.

"Oh, Gladys, I'm sorry." Ms. Byrdie hurried behind the counter and flipped on the coffee machine. "We had a little alarm mishap this morning, but I'll have your coffee ready in a second. Muffins won't take but a few seconds to warm up."

"Take your time, Byrdie. I'll just enjoy the view."

Charlie's eyes grew as wide as his smile, which sent Mrs. Kingsley into a fit of adolescent giggles that seemed to eviscerate the tension that had only seconds ago filled the café. Charlie skirted behind Lane, his cheeks as red as Mrs. Kingsley's lipstick.

"Deputy Lynch was just leaving." Lane pressed a hand to his chest to nudge him in the direction of the back door—big mistake. Gladys let out a *whoop* and whistled. "You're distracting our customers."

"So, we're back to deputy now?" Charlie put his hand atop hers, their fingers interlacing just long enough for her to feel the beat of his heart. "Don't be jealous."

Lane pulled her hand out from under his—thankful this intimate moment happened in the privacy of her kitchen. "I appreciate you coming over to check on me."

"Anytime." Charlie tilted his chin. He swallowed and for a second Lane thought he was going to kiss her—maybe hoped he would—but instead two dimples framed his perfect lips as he smiled before pushing through the back door and taking the steps down her porch two at a time. At the bottom he turned and started walking backward toward the fence that separated their yards. "Wanna bet my dog has probably eaten my pillows for breakfast?"

Lane shook her head as her lower lip slipped between her front teeth. She smiled at the thought of Charlie walking into a house full of feathers, his wiry dog perched innocently in the middle of it all. She started to laugh. A giggle at first, but then the feathery scene that began to unfold in her mind sent her into a fit of hysterics that left her holding her side and tears sliding down her cheeks.

Ms. Byrdie and Mrs. Kingsley stepped into the hallway, concern creased on their faces, but Lane couldn't stop. Could barely breathe. And she didn't want to stop. Or explain. Didn't want to think about alarms blaring or the reason why. She only wanted to relish this moment of emotional freedom.

To laugh. To feel. To live.

Her laugh. Charlie hadn't imagined it as he left the Way Station Café and made his way home after the alarm fiasco. Lane laughed. He couldn't explain why that simple act or the way the sound of her happiness—even at his expense—kick-started his spirit, but it had. Charlie was willing to do many things for Lane Kent, and making her laugh was near the top.

"Brought you some muffins from the Way Station." Charlie set the bag of pastries his aunt had brought over just before he left for work in front of Frost. "They're fresh and warm."

The small office down the hall had turned into a headquarters of sorts. Files of reports, tips, and interviews were stacked in boxes and on the table. Photos of evidence were taped up. Sydney's innocent smile the only bright spot on the wall of death and mystery.

"Hey, thanks." Frost slipped one out of the bag. "You want the good news or the bad news?"

Charlie groaned. "Isn't it too early for bad news?"

"Test results came back on Jolene Carson's vehicle. Brown spots were blood, but not human. Jolene was telling the truth."

"I can't say that I'm disappointed." Charlie dropped into the chair next to Frost. "I didn't really want to believe Jolene was capable of killing her best friend."

"Yeah, but she sure didn't hesitate to tease her," Frost said around a bite. He pushed up his glasses. "After we found the blood on her car, Deputy Wilson and I made some calls to some of Sydney's friends and teachers. Jolene might be popular, but it's because most students are afraid of her. Some even said she's a bully."

"Maybe that's why Sydney hid her art."

Sheriff Huggins stepped into the office, dwarfing the room. "In my day, if you didn't like someone you said it to their face. You might have scuffled in the schoolyard, but then it was over. These days kids bully from the safety of a computer."

Frost nodded with an expression of someone who knew first-hand. "How about some good news?"

Charlie looked at his watch. "How long you been at this, Frost? Our shift only started a half hour ago."

"Came in a little early." His gaze promptly swung to the sheriff. "I'm saving up the overtime to help my sister with college."

Sheriff Huggins placed a hand on Frost's back and, oddly, he didn't look as scrawny as he had before . . . of course, he was already working on his second muffin. "Son, whatever it takes to end this investigation." The sheriff reached in front of Frost and grabbed a muffin before looking at Charlie and sitting down next to them. "Don't you tell your aunt about this."

"No, sir." Charlie wouldn't tell him that Aunt Byrdie had purposely put low-fat muffins in the bag. "Alright, Frost, what do you have?"

Frost started typing and a second later the three screens on the desk came alive. "Agent Padello was able to get me the video feed of the surveillance cameras outside Ms. Benedict's gallery—"

"Annika Benedict gave us access to her security footage?" Charlie could see the sour look on the sheriff's face. He was probably thinking the same thing—Frost went through one of his *special* ways.

Frost let out a "yeah right" laugh. "No. But we didn't need her permission because this footage came from a nearby business and the city cameras." He looked at Charlie and the sheriff, a smile playing at his lips. "Smart, right?"

"Very smart," Sheriff Huggins said before he swallowed the last bite of his muffin. "Now that my blood pressure is good and high, why don't you tell us what you found?"

"Right." Frost pushed up his glasses. "So, I thought since we found something in the video at the storage unit, maybe I'd find something outside the gallery. Here's footage taken on Wednesday afternoon from the alleyway behind the gallery."

After a few keystrokes, one of the screens played a video of Sydney rushing out of the alleyway, carrying a rectangular object. Her movements hurried, she looked over her shoulder before walking into the street and out of range of the video.

"Do we have more? Where does she go?" Charlie sat at the edge of his seat. Seeing the teenager living, breathing . . . did she know that less than twenty-four hours later she'd be dead? "What was she carrying? A painting?"

"Do any of the videos show where she goes next?"

Frost rotated in his chair and shook his head. "Once she crosses Bull Street and heads into the park, the sun's glare blocks her movements."

Charlie pressed back into his chair. Frustrated. Tired. Angry. He pinched the bridge of his nose. If this was good news, it was going to be a very long day.

"Is there footage of Sydney leaving the gallery?" Sheriff Huggins asked.

"Not directly, sir. The cameras in that alleyway were positioned to catch footage of the businesses who owned them, but based off what she was wearing we can see she's coming from that direction."

"So, she was probably carrying a painting."

"That's the good news." Frost's voice picked up. "After Lynch spotted the name of the gallery in that photo, I thought maybe if I"—Frost hit a few keys to manipulate the image on the screen until it grew larger and larger—"focused on what we could see, we'd find a clue."

"An address." It was blurry, but Charlie could make out what appeared to be an address label on the package Sydney was holding.

Before either Charlie or Sheriff Huggins could ask, Frost was already typing again. "Tax records show the home belongs to Seth and Callista Hollins of Chicago, Illinois. A second home currently occupied by their only son, Savannah socialite and playboy extraordinaire, Floyd Hollins."

"You got *that* from the tax records?"

"Social media, my dear Watson. I thought by now you'd understand the method to my madness." Frost's voice became nasally. "His profile on the LINKUP website says he likes rugby, polo, and women who are hot. Spelled h-a-u-t-e." Frost turned to Charlie. "But pronounced hote. It means 'fashionably elegant' or 'high class.'"

Sheriff Huggins and Charlie exchanged amused expressions before the sheriff asked, "And LINKUP is?"

"Dating website, and no, I don't have a profile," Frost added quickly.

Charlie believed him. "Does Floyd's profile say anything about him being an art connoisseur?"

"No." Frost scratched at the cowlick in his hair. "Unless you consider posters with women who—"

"That's not what he means." Sheriff Huggins adjusted his gun belt.

Frost typed and a second later a profile page for Floyd Hollins popped up on one of the screens.

His wavy blond hair curled over a tanned forehead and his teeth were unnaturally white. The kid stood in front of a massive boat—no, yacht—wearing a polo shirt with the collar popped and plaid shorts. Frost didn't seem far off on his assumption of status. The profile picture stunk of money and privilege.

"Frost, I want you to contact Agent Padello and see if you can get the financial records of Mr. Floyd Hollins, particularly those connected to art purchases." Sheriff Huggins stood. "If he's pur-

chased Sydney's art before, maybe Ms. Benedict will be more helpful since she won't be divulging any private client information."

"Yes, sir."

"Lynch, how about you and I take a drive into Savannah and
see if Mr. Hollins can teach us a thing or two about art."

Charlie nodded as he rose from the chair. "Great job, Frost."
He gripped the young man's shoulders like an older brother and
felt some meat on his bones. "You've been working out?"

Frost's face turned the color of ketchup. "A little."

"If you ever need a workout buddy, let me know."

"Really?"

"Sure. But for now, you just keep giving that brain of yours a
workout."

In the hall, Sheriff Huggins was waiting for Charlie. "You know,
that kid looks up to you."

"He's a good deputy, sir. Truth be told, we'd be a lot further
behind in this investigation without him . . . or his brain."

The sheriff let out a low laugh as they walked through the station. Charlie could see Lane wasn't the only one his uncle poured
out fatherly affection on. He gave it freely to anyone who needed
it and doled it out in whatever form necessary. For Frost, it was
mentorship and guidance. For Lane . . . protection.

Who was the man who had come into the café and asked about
Lane's husband and Noah? Charlie didn't doubt Lane had seen
him in town, but why was he here? Surely, Lane would've recognized him if he was a local. Was he the same man she had seen
outside her home? Charlie's gut said he probably was, but were
the man's intentions criminal? And what was the focus—the value
of those donations or was it something more?

The image of Miguel striking Lane—even though he did it
accidentally—flashed in his mind. Why was she so protective of
the disheveled man? How well did Lane really know him?

"Do you know a man named Miguel?"

"Miguel?" Sheriff Huggins slowed. "Why?"

Had his aunt not told him what happened? "Last night he showed up at the Way Station Café. He was agitated . . . he hit Lane."

Sheriff Huggins's jaw flexed. "Byrdie told me it was an accident."

"Lane said it was, but does that matter? He might've been drunk or on drugs or—"

"He's a veteran." Sheriff Huggins let that sit between them a few seconds. "He's a few years younger than I am. Went to Vietnam with the rest of us and came back like most of them. He's got issues the military understands a lot better now than they did then, but he's mostly harmless."

Harmless? "The bruise on Lane's cheek might say otherwise. I can't tell you how many investigations I had to look into where PTSD mixed with alcohol or drugs created the perfect storm. I'm concerned Miguel could hurt someone else."

Sheriff Huggins stopped outside the steps of the sheriff's station. "We live in a small town, Charlie. Under most circumstances, that's a good thing. Neighbors look out for one another, but you know that old saying 'sticks and stones'? Well, words can be deadly." Sheriff Huggins heaved a sigh. "Miguel's been sober for more than two decades, but I'll stop by his place and check on him."

"Thank you, sir, but . . ." Charlie stared in the direction of the Way Station. His eyes lingered on the men passing by as though he could guess if they were the one bringing fear into Lane's life. "Someone has been harassing Lane. Showing up at the Way Station after hours. Peeking into her windows. Her alarm went off this morning, and I'm just concerned—"

"Your aunt called me this morning and told me." Sheriff Huggins wiped at his forehead, which was already glistening with sweat. "Lane's coming in later to give you a description of the man, right?"

"Yes, sir."

"Good. Let's get that and go from there."

The conversation was over. Whatever the sheriff was thinking behind his crystal-clear eyes, he was keeping it hidden from Charlie. His uncle warned him not to hurt Lane, and Charlie wasn't going to allow anyone else to hurt her either. Whatever it took—he'd protect her.

EIGHTEEN

"MOMMA, WHO ARE we taking muffins to?"

"A friend, buddy." Lane helped Noah out of the car and grabbed the basket of fresh muffins. She caught a glimpse of her bruised and swollen cheek in the mirror. A tingle danced its way down her spine. It *was* an accident, but it also wasn't like Miguel. His absence and odd behavior had her worried. "Ready?"

"Does he like muffins?" Noah's cherub face looked up at her.

"I hope so."

"I like muffins." Noah's eyes grew wide. "Does he like dinosaurs?"

She looked down at the drawing Noah had made earlier. "I think he'll like yours," she said as she slipped the drawing into the basket.

Noah smiled proudly and looked up at the tall trees towering over them. "Does he live in the woods?"

"Sort of."

Lane had been lucky to find Miguel's home. Harley's directions were vague and the house had no discernible features that could be seen from the road. Not even a mailbox marked the property. If someone wasn't looking for the small inlet between mile markers 17 and 18, they'd miss it. Even she had passed it a couple of times. The copse of trees hid Miguel's home and any sign that life existed behind nature's wall.

The house's secluded location made her wonder how Miguel made it into town since she'd never seen him drive. Of course, they were only two miles or so outside of Walton, so it was possible he walked. And he was in good shape.

Noah slipped his hand into hers. Together they walked along the small manmade path of crushed leaves and snapped twigs.

Birds, locusts, and the chattering of squirrels were the only noises penetrating the silence.

The memory of finding Sydney sent another chill running along her shoulders. She hadn't been this deep into the trees since that day. How far were they from where she found the body? Lane peeked down at her son. Maybe bringing Noah was a bad idea.

A few yards in, a large barn came into view. Then she saw a house. The rusted tin roof and lopsided patio covered in pine needles gave the impression no one lived there. Concern for Miguel pushed her forward. Or maybe it was because Noah was with her. She rolled her eyes at the irony. So much of her strength came from the almost five-year-old little boy walking next to her. It wasn't a fair burden.

"Mommy," Noah whispered as he maneuvered himself behind her leg and tightened his grip over her hand, "your friend's house is scary."

"It's just old, buddy." Lane forced herself to shrug off her own absurd fear. She stepped onto a rickety step and knocked on the door. A spiderweb swayed overhead.

"Is he here?" Noah's small voice squeaked.

"I don't know." The basket of fresh muffins wouldn't fare very well if she left it on the porch. Maybe he wasn't home. "Maybe he's sleeping."

"He's not sleeping." Noah wrinkled his nose and squinted. "The sun is out."

"I know, but sometimes people sleep during the day because they work at night."

"You work at night, huh, Momma?"

"Mm-hmm." Lane knocked again. There was a thump. She craned her neck to get closer to the door.

"Miguel, it's Lane from the Way Station Café. I brought you some muffins." She held her breath. There was another thump. She waited.

The knotted pinewood door creaked open and Miguel's dark

202

eyes loomed in the darkness. "Why are you here? You shouldn't be here."

"I, um." Lane licked her lips. The thought that coming out here with Noah wasn't a good idea crossed her mind again. She understood enough about PTSD to know it could lead to unpredictability, but was it enough to ignore the pain in Miguel's eyes? She lifted the basket. "I made these for you."

The door opened wider, revealing Miguel, and the pungent odor she smelled last night wafted over her. His hair was still wild and the jeans and gray shirt he wore were covered in dirt. "What is it?"

"Muffins. I hope you like blueberries." Lane held out the basket to him and he slowly took it from her. There was a tremor in his hands, which was almost unnoticeable because of the bloodied scabs covering the deep gashes across his palms. "After last night—"

"I did that." His eyes zeroed in on her face.

Lane had tried to use makeup to cover up the bruising, which made her look like she'd lost a round with Laila Ali, but the look of guilt on Miguel's face made her feel bad for showing up there. "It's okay, Miguel. It was an accident. I know you didn't mean to do it."

Miguel was silent for several seconds. "Who's that?"

Lane followed Miguel's gaze to Noah, who was peeking up from behind her. "This is my son, Noah. You've seen him at the café before, haven't you?"

The hard lines around Miguel's eyes softened. He stepped onto the porch and Noah pressed his body into her leg. Her son wasn't normally shy, but with the bristly faced man in dirty clothes moving toward him, she didn't blame Noah for cowering.

"Do you like alligators?" Miguel asked Noah.

Lane's eyes darted around. Miguel's property was close to the Ogeechee waterline, which meant it was probable alligators could be on the property.

"I like dinosaurs." Noah's voice was just above a whisper.

"Alligators are dinosaurs."

"I know that, silly." Noah stepped out from the protection of Lane's leg.

"I have alligators. Do you want to see them?"

Oh, dear Lord, please don't let Miguel have a pen of alligators around here. "I don't think that's a good idea."

"Are they scary?" Noah was now completely entranced in the conversation about the reptiles.

"No. Not these ones." Miguel shut his door and started walking into the wooded area with the basket of muffins still in his hand.

"Come on, Momma. Let's go see the alligators." Noah pulled her hand to follow Miguel.

If Lane had better judgment, she would politely decline Miguel's offer to lead her precious son to vicious swamp monsters. Then she would pick up her son and run. But Miguel wouldn't endanger her son, would he?

Leaving no time for her to have second thoughts, Noah pulled her around the side of Miguel's house. Lane's mouth fell open. Instead of a pen of hungry alligators, she was surprised to find another large barn-like building with a pitched roof and rectangular skylights cut into it. Open double-sliding doors revealed a half dozen or so sculptures carved out of huge chunks of wood.

"You have alligators in there?" Noah wrinkled his nose in disbelief.

Miguel pulled the door back farther and the same smell that lingered on him spilled out. A whirring noise echoed from the large fans mounted into the long wall at the back of the barn as they spun to purge the fumes of what Lane figured out was turpentine. Miguel pointed in the direction near the front. Dead branches sprouted from the trunk of an old tree. The exposed roots had been carved into blades of grass and the larger roots had been chiseled and shaped into alligators. The face of one peeked through the reeds. The tail of another wrapped around the base of the trunk and morphed into a full-size alligator.

"Alligators!" Noah darted toward the sculpture with the boldness only a dinosaur-loving four-year-old could possess.

"Look, but don't touch, Noah." Lane left her son admiring the alligators while she took in the creativity and skill displayed in the other sculptures.

In the base of another tree trunk, Miguel had sculpted a large wave cresting over a jetty of rocks. The age rings in the tree added to the appearance of depth. Next to it the trunk was left in a more natural state with its bark still intact. It held an eagle perched above its nest with her wings spread wide. All of it was carved from the same tree trunk. It was incredible.

"You made this?" She turned to find Miguel standing by the door, the basket of muffins at his feet. He gave her a small nod. "They're beautiful, Miguel. You're very talented."

"What's this?" Noah picked up a tool.

"Noah, don't touch." Lane took the tool with a sharp v-shaped edge from her son and placed it next to a stack of painted canvases leaning against a trestle table. "Do you paint too?"

"Not anymore." Miguel shifted back and forth and rubbed his arm. Then he stepped a few feet forward and repeated the pattern again. The third time he did it, Lane knew Miguel needed his space.

"Come on, Noah. It's time to go." Lane was grateful he didn't fuss about their sudden departure. She took hold of his hand and began escorting him out of the studio-barn. "Noah, what do you say?"

Noah turned to Miguel. "Thank you for showing me your alligators."

Miguel nodded. Shifted. And rubbed his arm.

"You're a beautiful craftsman. Thank you for showing us your sculptures."

"You have a good boy." Miguel rubbed his arm again and a trail of blood smeared down his arm from a broken scab. "Keep him close."

A breeze rustled the foliage and the ugly feeling Lane had the day she found Sydney's body returned. Her eyes skated the shadows beneath the trees. Was someone out there? Watching?

"Are you okay, Miguel?"

"You need to leave."

The hardness returned to Miguel's eyes. Lane wasn't sure, but she thought she saw Miguel's body stiffen as though he too sensed something. "Come on, Noah. Time to go home."

"Bye, friend Miguel." Noah waved.

Lane hurried Noah to her Jeep, unwilling to find out what had spooked Miguel so suddenly. Inside the safety of the SUV, she realized two things: it'd be a long time before she stepped foot in the woods near the Ogeechee River again, and something had Miguel terrified.

<hr />

"DEA?" Charlie slipped a sideways glance at Sheriff Huggins as he took the exit toward Savannah. The sheriff was only catching Charlie's side of the conversation he was having with Agent Padello, but he imagined they shared the same expression—shock.

"Yep. Deputy Frost sent me that address, and as soon as I hit enter on my keyboard my office phone rang with a curious DEA agent demanding information," Agent Padello said.

"What did you tell him?"

"Only what I know. Video shows your vic carrying a package with the address on it the day before she was killed."

"And what'd they say?"

"He, Agent Mitch Edmonds, is wondering if you'll let him observe your knock and talk?"

"Knock and talk?" Charlie scratched his cheek. This day . . . this case . . . was not what he was expecting. "Why? What's the DEA's interest in our case?"

"Wish I could tell you." Agent Padello's tone went rigid. "Unfortunately, not all agencies have an affinity for sharing information. All I can tell you is that they're interested and I'm not sure you have much of a choice in letting him *observe* you, if you catch my drift."

"Yeah, I got it."

"Oh, and I'm running the video footage we have of Sydney

leaving the gallery through facial recognition. Maybe we'll get a hit on someone in the area who's not supposed to be there."

"Like Pablo Escobar frequenting an art gallery in Savannah?" Charlie's mention of the infamous Mexican drug lord drew a short laugh from Agent Padello, but something else pricked his memory. "We appreciate your help more than you know."

Charlie filled in Sheriff Huggins on the rest of the information as they pulled in front of a clapboard house on West Hull Street. An ornate iron gate surrounded the home facing Orleans Square and looked postcard ready. The kind of home that would have lots of art hanging on the walls.

"These homes remind me of the ones in Annapolis." Charlie's phone beeped with an incoming text message. "Frost says the Hollinses have been out of the country since May and aren't scheduled to return until late August."

"Interesting." Sheriff Huggins stepped out of the car with Charlie. "So, it's unlikely they made any art purchases around the time of Sydney's murder."

A black Suburban with heavily tinted windows was parked in front of the Hollinses' home. The driver-side door opened and out stepped a sizeable man in an ebony suit, with skin that almost matched. A pair of aviators shielded his eyes as he looked in their direction and gave them a nod.

"What do we know about the DEA agent?" Sherriff Huggins asked.

"Not a whole lot except he wanted to be a part of the knock and talk."

The sheriff's forehead creased. "Knock and talk?"

"Afternoon, Sheriff, I'm Agent Mitch Edmonds." He held out his hand. They exchanged handshakes and introductions. "I appreciate you fellas letting me tag along."

Charlie almost smirked at the agent's attempt to make it sound like they had a choice.

"If it helps us come closer to catching a killer, I'm obliged to be cooperative." Sheriff Huggins straightened his shoulders, bringing him an inch taller than the DEA agent. "But I'm curious to know what the DEA's interest is in Mr. Floyd Hollins."

"I'm just here to observe." Agent Edmonds bowed his head slightly. "This investigation is yours, Sheriff, and I have no intention of interfering."

So, cooperation was going to be one-sided. At least they knew where they stood. Charlie led the way to the home. It was a corner property with a gated driveway at the side that was open. A silver Tesla was parked inside. Hopefully that meant its driver was home. They passed the Tesla and climbed the stairs decorated with planters of ferns and colorful flowers. It reminded him of Lane's garden.

Tonight was her father's barbecue fund-raiser. Though Charlie and a few of the other deputies were working security, Judge Sullivan wanted to make sure his guests weren't aware of their presence. They wouldn't be wearing uniforms and would be allowed to mingle with guests. The only person Charlie wanted to mingle with had fiery green eyes and auburn hair.

"We waiting for something?" Agent Edmonds asked.

Charlie brought his attention back to the mission at hand and pressed the doorbell. A couple minutes passed and he tried again. The door opened and Floyd Hollins stood there in boxer shorts and a T-shirt, rubbing his eyes like he'd just woken up.

"Mr. Hollins?"

"Who wants to know?" The man ran a hand through his disheveled hair. He didn't seem to be aware that he was in his underwear—or he didn't care.

"I'm Deputy Lynch and this is Sheriff Huggins. Would you mind if we talked to you for a few minutes?"

"Who's the suit?"

Charlie wasn't sure if there was a protocol for protecting a DEA agent's identity and he hadn't asked.

"I'm Agent Edmonds. Just here for observation."

"Uh, okay." Floyd disappeared down the hall.

"I guess we show ourselves in?" Charlie looked at Sheriff Huggins. He shrugged before nodding his head.

They entered the foyer and walked down the hall, past a living room with a television the size of one wall. Pizza boxes and empty cans and bottles littered the leather furniture. Charlie thought he heard Agent Edmonds mutter something about ungrateful kids, but he kept walking.

Floyd was in the kitchen scooping a spoonful of cereal into his mouth, his eyes on another flat-screen TV.

"Can you believe it? I lost five grand on those losers." Floyd threw a piece of cereal at the TV. "Braves decide to start winning."

"Mr. Hollins?" Charlie said, trying to get the kid's attention.

"That's my dad. You can call me Floyd or F-Dawg."

Agent Edmonds's cheek flinched as Charlie fought the urge to roll his eyes. What was wrong with kids these days?

"I'll stick with Floyd." Annoyance colored Charlie's words. "Does anyone else live here besides you?"

"My parents own the home if that's what you're asking, but they haven't lived here since I graduated from Tech." Floyd picked up the remote and turned up the volume. "And you can tell my neighbor that I have the same rights as he does to entertain friends."

Charlie flicked a look at Sheriff Huggins before asking, "Any of those friends in the house right now?"

"Nope."

"How long have you known Sydney Donovan?"

"Who?"

"Sydney Donovan," Charlie repeated, stepping in front of the television. "A high school student from Walton."

"I don't know any Sydney whatever you said her last name was." Floyd's head bobbed side to side as he tried to see the television over Charlie's shoulders. "I know better than to touch jailbait."

"How many times have you been to Bohemian Signature Gallery?"

"Do I look like someone who likes art?" Floyd spoke around

209

another mouthful. "Is that why you're here? To check out my decorating?"

"Actually, we're investigating a murder."

"And drugs," Agent Edmonds added.

Floyd choked, the color draining from his face. With wide eyes, he glanced at each of them. Charlie's eyes cut to the DEA agent. Was that the reaction Edmonds was expecting?

"Look, man, I don't know anything about a murder. I thought y'all were here because of the noise. My neighbors are always complaining, but I was here all night. Had some friends over. I'll give you their names. They'll tell you."

"Why don't we start with why Sydney Donovan was carrying a painting with your address on it a day before she was murdered?"

"I already told you I don't know any Sydney Donovan."

Charlie pulled up a picture of Sydney—the same as the one sitting on the Donovans' mantel—on his phone. He turned it so Floyd could see. "Tell me you don't know her."

Floyd looked at the phone before raising his hands up defensively. "I've never seen that chick in my life." Floyd's eyes flashed to Sheriff Huggins. "I swear, man."

"I didn't hear you say anything about the drugs," Charlie said, his instincts returning. What wasn't said usually spoke louder than what was.

"I-I don't know anything about that either."

"I'm not a betting man like you, F-Dawg, but if I were, I'd bet my entire salary that my associate in the suit over there is going to find drugs in your parents' home."

"Wha—no. Wait." A sheen of sweat broke out on Floyd's forehead, washing the rest of the color from his face. "You can't do that. Don't you need a search warrant or something like that?"

"You invited us into your home, Mr. Hollins," Sheriff Huggins spoke up. "If we see anything out in the open, say, in an ashtray in your living room, that looks like it might be drug paraphernalia, we'd have probable cause to search the rest of your home."

Charlie closed the space between him and Floyd. "My interest isn't in the drugs. It's in the murder of Sydney Donovan, who was holding a package with your address on it hours before she was hit by a car and then stabbed over and over—"

"Stop, please." A greenish hue put color back into Floyd's cheeks. "A package was delivered to my house a few days ago. I don't even know if it's a painting, man. I was just doing a favor."

Adrenaline surged through Charlie. "For who?"

"I don't know, man."

"You don't know?" Charlie leveled a cold stare at Floyd. "Maybe we should check the house for drugs. What do you say, Agent Edmonds?"

The man grunted and cracked his knuckles.

"No. Wait. I swear. I don't know anything about the package or what's in it. I was just following directions."

"Last time I'm going to ask—for who?"

"Look, man, I already told you I don't know." Floyd's voice rose an octave. "I swear." His eyes darted to Agent Edmonds. He lifted his hands, palms outward like he was trying to calm a bull from charging. "Just . . . just wait here."

When Floyd hurried out of the kitchen, Sheriff Huggins turned to Charlie and asked, "What makes you think there are drugs here?"

"Same reason you assumed those ashtrays in the front held more than cigarette butts. He's a frat boy with complaining neighbors."

"He's probably hiding his stash right now," Agent Edmonds mumbled. "The F-Dawg nickname almost makes me want to call in the dogs."

"My deputy here's done a good job soliciting information." Sheriff Huggins raised his eyebrows. "Maybe now you can share some information about why you're here."

"Have you ever heard of *El Chico*?"

Charlie and the sheriff shook their heads.

"Benito Rodriguez runs the largest Mexican cartel out of

Atlanta that specializes in meth. He's been smuggling throughout the Atlanta region for years, but it's slowed. What hasn't slowed is the money. We have an informant on the inside who says the money is still coming in—"

"Which means the drugs are still going out," Charlie said.

"Right." Agent Edmonds ran his hands over his bald head. "We've tracked payments to this address."

Sheriff Huggins, looking ashen, rocked back on his heels. "I can't picture Sydney being involved with drugs . . . or a cartel."

Neither could Charlie, if he was honest, but outward appearances could be deceiving. Unlike Miguel, most people didn't let their issues out in the open. They kept them hidden. Private. Protected. Like an ugly secret that made them feel ashamed. Charlie thought about Lane. And Tate. If his battle buddy hadn't kept his secret hidden, maybe he'd still be alive today. And Lane . . .

Floyd returned with a package wrapped in brown paper. He tossed it onto the counter. "Last time I checked, doing a favor wasn't a crime."

"If it's connected to a murder it is." Charlie watched Sheriff Huggins pull a pair of latex gloves from his belt. "Now, tell us who gave it to you."

"*Dude*, I don't know how many times I have to tell you that I don't know who it was."

Charlie's blood pressure was rising. He stepped around the kitchen island and closed in on Floyd. "Have you been to jail before, F-Dawg?"

"N-no."

"Well, it's a good thing you've got some money. See, it's dangerous for pretty boys like you to be mixed in with gen pop. Do you know what that is?" Floyd swallowed, barely moving his head. "General population. It's where the rapists, killers, mutilators, and the like hang out. They have their own code of justice—funny enough—and the murder of a beautiful young girl ranks pretty high on the list of crimes they don't tolerate. But I'm sure a wealthy boy like yourself can pay for a private cell while you wait for the judge to consider your innocence."

"Is that true?" Floyd looked like he was going to be sick.

"Nah." Agent Edmonds narrowed his eyes. "They don't believe in segregation in the prison system. Rich. Poor. They're all mixed up. Killers. Baby-faced art lovers doing favors for people they don't know."

"I swear, man." Floyd's voice became whiny as he edged farther away from the package like it was a contagion. "It was just a quick way to earn a few bucks since my parents have me on a stupid allowance until I get a job."

Sheriff Huggins pulled out a stool and put a hand on pretty boy's shoulder. "Why don't you sit down and tell us how this package came into your possession. From the beginning."

Floyd nodded and looked up at Sheriff Huggins with tenderness and appreciation. "I found an envelope on my doorstep. Inside was a letter and a wad of cash. The letter said there would be more. Next day a package gets delivered to my door and all I have to do is attach an address slip and mail it out. Then I get another five grand."

"That's it?" Agent Edmonds growled.

"And you have no idea who's paying you or what the packages are?" Charlie asked.

"Dude, they left a stack of bills on my porch. Why would I ask questions?"

Sheriff Huggins continued. "How many times have you done this?"

"Only a couple. Am I going to get in trouble for this? I don't want to go to jail. I didn't do anything wrong. Didn't kill anyone."

As much as the playboy annoyed him, the evidence just wasn't there to prove Floyd Hollins had anything to do with Sydney's murder. He looked down at the painting Sheriff Huggins had unwrapped. Charlie knew the broad strokes of this piece made it a contemporary abstract. Red and black. Charlie wasn't artistic in the least, but he could've probably created something similar. He searched the canvas for the artist's signature, conflicted about whether he wanted to see Sydney's name on it or not. But there was no signature. Weird.

"We're going to do you a favor, Mr. Hollins." Agent Edmonds grabbed some paper towels from the kitchen counter to handle the painting as he wrapped it back in the brown paper. "We believe the person who delivered this painting to your front steps is a member of a cartel. We need to take this painting to our labs to run some tests on it for fingerprints—"

"Wait. What if this cartel guy comes around looking for his painting?"

Charlie fixed his eyes on Floyd. "I guess you should've asked questions before you pocketed money from the devil."

"Man, I've seen what those guys do to people who double-cross them." Floyd's face went slack. "Leave them naked and headless in the middle of the street."

"Where's the shipping label?" Sheriff Huggins asked.

"I haven't received it yet." Floyd's voice wobbled. "Those guys are going to kill me."

"Does the label come by mail or is it dropped off on your porch?" Charlie asked.

Floyd looked up at Charlie, his face green again. "Dropped off."

"If you cooperate"—Agent Edmonds pulled out his cell phone—"we can offer you protection."

"Yes, sir. Whatever you need," Floyd answered, offering his first act of respect.

"But first, you need to go put on some pants and brush your teeth." Agent Edmonds sighed. "And call your parents."

"Yes, sir." Floyd disappeared to the upstairs.

Fear does that to a person. Makes them start listening to the one who can offer protection. It was hard to feel sorry for the kid. He didn't need the money and yet greed made him an unwitting participant in a scheme that could've cost him his life.

Sheriff Huggins's forehead creased. "You can trace money . . . you think you can trace a painting?"

"We'll run prints first, but yeah, I think we can put a tracer in it and find out where it leads. I don't know if it'll help out your investigation, but it might help ours." Agent Edmonds put his phone back in the clip on his belt. "Sent a message to my guys and they're going to work with Metro police to make sure Captain Oblivious here stays safe."

"What if we take the painting back to the gallery? Ms. Benedict lied to us. Sydney was there the day before she died." Charlie caught Agent Edmonds eyeing him, but he didn't care. This was a huge step forward in their case, and while they were currently on the same side, Charlie couldn't help but feel that the DEA's cooperation might conveniently cease the second the painting was in their hands. "Doesn't murder trump a drug bust?"

"Deputy Lynch, I don't mean to trivialize the murder of the young lady in your town, but drugs kill millions of people every year. If we can take another one of these dealers off the streets, that's thousands of lives we can save."

"I'm sure that'll make us *not* finding Sydney's killer justifiable to her parents," Charlie said through gritted teeth,

Sheriff Huggins leaned toward Charlie and whispered, "My gut tells me this painting is going to tell us a whole lot more if we let it go, but if you think this is something we need to fight back on, we can. This is your case. I trust you."

Trust. Charlie licked his lips. It felt like a recurring theme these last couple of weeks. Trusting he'd made the right decision to leave the Marines and move to Walton. Right now, Sheriff Huggins was trusting him to make the right decision for the case. To bring justice to Sydney's family. And what about Lane? She trusted Charlie enough to tell him about her depression.

"I believe this painting is going to lead us to Sydney's killer."

Sheriff Huggins set his jaw. "There's only one way to find out."

NINETEEN

THE DRIVE FROM FLOYD HOLLINS'S HOME to the art gallery was quick but not quick enough to prevent doubt from settling into the crevices of Charlie's mind. Letting Agent Edmonds take that painting removed that portion of their investigation from his hands. Would the DEA hold up their end of the bargain? Charlie was tired of the dead ends this case was leaving him with. And the doubt that maybe his father was right.

Charlie found a parking spot outside the gallery just as his phone rang. He glanced at the ID. "It's Frost."

Sheriff Huggins nodded. Charlie kept the car running and the AC on full blast. "Lynch."

"Hey, how did the interview with Hollins go?"

"Not as well as I'd hoped. It's in the DEA's hands now. What's up?"

"Yeah, Agent Padello said they're involved now, but we've got some leverage."

Charlie's ears perked. "What?"

"When we found out the DEA had sunk their fangs into the case, we ran the videos through facial recognition software and got a hit on a member of the cartel the DEA's investigating. Marco Solis. He's the second cousin of Benito Rodriguez by marriage. Among a long list of prior crimes, including assault, robbery, and drug charges, it appears Mr. Solis has a taste for fine art."

"How much of a taste?"

"We've got him on video visiting the gallery two times the week before Sydney was killed and once a few days after, but that's not what makes him interesting. He only goes through the back door and it's always after hours."

"Frost, I could kiss you right now."

"Whoa now, I'll just take more of your girlfriend's cinnamon rolls. No offense, but the muffins were a little bland."

Charlie laughed and thanked Frost, not bothering to correct him about Lane. After all, it's what he wanted. Cutting the engine, Charlie and Sheriff Huggins climbed out of the car. *Trust.* That's what the sheriff had told him about their investigation and now they had a new lead.

Sheriff Huggins adjusted the brim of his hat as they approached the gallery. "You ready?"

"Yes, sir." Charlie pulled open the glass door of the gallery. He recognized the girl with the hot pink hair standing on point in every direction and approached her. She was one of the art students he spoke to the last time he and Frost were there. "Is Ms. Benedict in?"

"Is she expecting you?" There was a fluster of pink tinting the student's cheeks that matched her hair.

"I doubt it," Charlie said.

"Let her know we're here to talk to her about the death of one of her artists."

If their uniforms weren't drawing enough unwanted attention, Sheriff Huggins's words hit their mark. Pink-hair girl's eyes bulged, making her look like a comic book character.

"I—uh. Let me call." Her fingers fumbled with the phone on the desk.

A few minutes passed before the cadence of heels clipping on the wood floor filled the gallery. Annika crossed toward them. Expression tight. Lips pursed. Annoyance undisguised. Charlie liked that, for whatever reason, their presence irked her.

"I've come out here as a courtesy, but unless you have an appointment I'm afraid your visit won't be long."

Sheriff Huggins removed his hat. "I apologize for our unannounced visit, but we have a few more questions we'd like to ask."

"I've already answered everything your deputies asked."

"We have a few more questions," Charlie added. His blood pressure hadn't leveled since their visit with Floyd. "Now, would you like to do this out here or in the privacy of your office?"

"I already told you that unless you have an appointment—"

"Why don't you tell us why you lied about seeing our murder victim the day before she was killed?" Charlie let his voice rise on the last part of his question just enough so that it had the effect he wanted. Several heads turned in their direction.

"I didn't lie," Annika hissed, her eyes searching the faces around them. "You have five minutes." She spun on her heel and started for the hallway that Charlie guessed led to her office.

Annika's office was larger than he'd imagined. An acrylic desk with two pedestals in the same red as her lips was positioned in the center of the room. A velvet couch was pushed against the wall where the building's original brick was left exposed. Charlie stared at the life-size painting of a man on a horse.

"Oglethorpe," Sheriff Huggins said, pausing next to Charlie. "Savannah's founding father."

"Four minutes, gentlemen." Annika perched herself against the corner of her desk.

Sheriff Huggins nodded to Charlie to take over. They were both hoping to catch the woman—who seemed to know the answers before the questions—off guard.

"How many times has Floyd Hollins purchased art from your gallery?"

"What?" Annika pushed herself off the desk. "I thought you came here to ask about Sydney?"

Deflection. "We're here to investigate Sydney's murder. So, you know Floyd Hollins?"

Annika's brows pinched. "No."

"Did you know that Sydney was seen coming out of your gallery the day before she was killed? She was carrying a package. It had Floyd Hollins's address on it. You don't know anything about that?"

219

"I had no idea Sydney was here. I was in a meeting."

"And you still claim you don't know Floyd Hollins? He's not a customer of yours?"

"As far as I know, I've never sold a painting to anyone named Floyd Hollins."

"And you can't think of a reason why Sydney Donovan would have a package with his address on it?"

"No."

"Did Floyd Hollins ever purchase any of Sydney's art?"

"I don't know."

"Can you give us the names of customers who've purchased Sydney's art?"

"Why do you need that information?" Annika eyed Sheriff Huggins.

"One of your artists was murdered. A day after she was seen leaving *your* gallery with a package addressed to Floyd Hollins." Charlie was growing impatient. "One of your buyers could be the killer."

"And you believe Floyd Hollins might be that killer?"

"Or Marco Solis," Sheriff Huggins offered quietly.

Annika's eyes narrowed but not before Charlie caught her eyes round slightly when Sheriff Huggins said the name. Annika knew him.

"Is that name supposed to mean something to me?" she asked.

"Does he purchase a lot of art?" Charlie watched Annika's fingers rub the beaded necklace on her neck. Nervous. "I imagine his love of art grew while he served his time at Coastal State Prison."

Annika glared at him. "Background checks are not a part of my business, Deputy. If someone wants to buy art, who am I to stop them?"

"All we want are the names of buyers who purchased Sydney's art."

"I'm not at liberty to give you that information."

"Why not?"

"Privacy, Deputy Lynch." Her tone dripped with condescension.

"We'd appreciate your cooperation, Ms. Benedict." Sheriff Huggins stepped forward and placed a hand on Charlie's shoulder.

"I've cooperated, Sheriff Huggins, but I must warn your deputy. My field of expertise is not limited to the art on this wall. I have another wall full of frames and those pieces of parchment beneath the glass will tell you I know a little about the law too. Unless you have a warrant, I'm afraid your five minutes are up and I need to get back to work. Please see yourselves out. And if you need anything else, I suggest making an appointment first."

Charlie stepped into the sweltering heat outside the gallery and let out a frustrated breath. That woman had his insides twisted into a knot. Sheriff Huggins said nothing as they walked to the squad car.

"Will you get a warrant?" Charlie asked when they got into the car.

"Somehow I think Ms. Benedict might already have a plan for that," Sheriff Huggins grumbled. "Before Annika Benedict entered the world of art, she followed in her daddy's footsteps."

"She's a lawyer?"

Sheriff Huggins pressed his lips into a tight line.

"Knows enough about warrants, then." Charlie sank into his seat and brooded over Annika's arrogance. "You think she's involved?"

"Yes. How, I'm still chewing on that." Sheriff Huggins steered their vehicle into traffic. "But you leave that to me for now. You need to get home and get ready."

"Ready?"

Sheriff Huggins gave him an amused look. "For the barbecue tonight at Judge Sullivan's estate. Your aunt said Lane's really looking forward to seeing you there, even if it's under an official capacity."

The memory of sitting in the sheriff's office and being warned that Lane was special, that she'd been through more than her fair share, reverberated through his mind. Especially after what she confided in him about her depression—almost as though she thought it would chase him away. He'd wanted more than anything in that shared moment to assure her that it'd take a lot more than that to drive him away.

"I . . . um." Charlie wiped his sweaty palms down the front of his uniform pants. He met the wizened eyes of his uncle. "I want you to know my intention . . ." Why were the words so difficult? Or was it the way his uncle stared at him—like he was torn? "I really like her. All of her. She's told me about things and I . . . I just want you to know that I would never do anything to hurt her. Or Noah."

"Charlie, I have no reason to believe you would. Since you came into Lane's life, your aunt and I have noticed a difference in her. A good difference. I don't know what the future holds for either of you, but I'm going to share a piece of advice I've lived by in my forty-eight years of marriage to your aunt." Sheriff Huggins's eyes locked on to Charlie. "Never stop being the man Lane deserves."

Chills had permanently staked out territory across Lane's skin as she drove down Old Ogeechee Road and away from Miguel's home. What had scared him? Had she set him off by showing up unexpectedly? Her gut told her it was something more, and for now she was thankful she and Noah were safely driving away from whatever was putting fear into Miguel's eyes.

"Momma, can I visit those alligators again?"

Lane looked over her shoulder at Noah sitting in his car seat. His eyes, no doubt, searching the muddy swampland they were passing for any sign of real alligators. "I'm not sure, buddy."

Would she take Noah back to Miguel's? When she had the idea to bring him muffins, it was really an excuse to check on him. Make sure he was alright even though she was the one who'd suffered a bruised cheek from his outburst. But what had caused his outburst? And why hadn't he been coming to the Friday Night Clubs lately? Lane tried to remember the last Friday he'd shown up. Her throat grew thick. She calculated the weeks again. Was that right? Was the last Friday Night Club Miguel showed up to really the week before Sydney died?

Suddenly it wasn't chills Lane was concerned with. Her stomach rolled at the dark thought. Not Miguel. He was not violent. Quiet, reserved, maybe a little nervous—but never violent. Lane caught her reflection in the rearview mirror and focused on the bruise marring her cheek. It was an acc—

Lane's attention shifted from her reflection to the two cars following her. They were a ways behind her, but from the way they seemed to be growing larger they were moving fast. Too fast. And one of the cars was on the wrong side of the road. Were they racing?

Old Ogeechee was a two-lane stretch of highway sandwiched between swampy marshland. There was nowhere for Lane to pull over to let the moronic drivers pass without her truck slipping off the road completely. Pulling her focus back to the road in front of her, Lane tapped her foot on the brake. Maybe they'd think there was a cop ahead of her and slow down, but a quick glance in the rearview mirror showed they either hadn't seen her warning or didn't care.

Keeping an eye on the road ahead and on the rearview mirror, Lane watched the cars race up behind her. A white sports car was driving in the lane next to her, going the opposite direction of traffic. A darker car, maybe it was blue, drove up right behind her. The driver flashed his lights at her like she was the one breaking the law.

Lane blew out a frustrated breath. What did he want her to do? There was nowhere for her to go. The driver of the white car pulled up next to her and mirrored her speed. Even if Lane dared

223

to peek out her window, she could see from the corner of her eye that the driver was hidden behind black tinted windows.

The white car surged forward and pulled in front of her. The dark car behind Lane's Jeep swerved into the lane on her left and shot forward, leaving her in its dust. Her hands were sweating and her heart was pounding. Why did people have to drive so recklessly? She peeked over her shoulder to find Noah had fallen asleep. *Thank—*

Lane slammed on her brakes, her seat belt crushing her against her seat. The white car and the dark one—blue—were stopped in both lanes in front of her. The smell of burnt rubber filled her car and Noah woke up.

"Momma, my chair is squishing me."

Before Lane could respond, both cars shot forward like the green flag had just been dropped. Lane swallowed the mouthful of words she wanted to spit at the drivers. It was a miracle there were no other drivers on the road with her or there would certainly be an accident. Maybe she should call it in to the sheriff . . . or Charlie.

The idea of hearing Charlie's voice immediately slowed Lane's racing pulse and she wasn't sure it was a safe thing for him to have such control—even if he didn't know it. Lane continued on the road and waited to be sure the racing cars were not coming back. After a few minutes, she picked up her phone and dialed the number to the sheriff's station, allowing a flame of hope to flicker inside her chest that Charlie would be the one to answer.

"Walton County Sheriff's Department, Deputy Benningfield speaking."

"Hi, Deputy Benningfield," Lane said, biting back the disappointment she felt. "This is Lane Kent. I'm driving south on Old Ogeechee Road and I wanted to report two cars that were racing and almost drove me off the road."

"Oh dear. You said on Old Ogeechee Road? Can you tell me what mile marker you're near?"

Lane looked around her but didn't see one. "I'm driving toward Ogeechee Highway . . . I can tell you in a second—oh no."

"Lane?"

But Lane didn't answer. Her eyes were glued to the white and blue cars approaching her head-on. The dark blue car was in her lane, its lights flashing a morbid rhythm while the white car sped next to it.

"Lane?"

"They're coming. Two cars. White. Dark blue. They're headed straight for me." Lane's voice cracked. "They're going to run into me."

"Lane, I'm sending patrol cars out to you right now. Can you safely pull off the road?"

Lane looked to both sides of the road. The shoulder was only a foot or two wide. Not big enough for three cars.

"Please"—the shrill in Lane's voice was enough to draw a whimper from Noah—"they're going to hit us." The memory of Mathias's death, the state troopers on her porch, filled her mind and tears began to cloud her vision.

"Momma?" Noah's voice trembled as though he could sense something wasn't right.

Lane blinked the tears away. "It's okay, baby." She kept her focus on the cars charging forward. She slowed down and moved as much as she could to the right side of the road, but rather than change lanes the cars kept coming at her. They were too close. Too close.

The sound of screeching tires forced Lane's eyes closed as she prepared for impact, but none came. She opened her eyes only to see a cloud of white smoke and both cars stopped inches from her truck's front bumper. Lane tried to see the faces of the drivers terrorizing her, but the windshields reflected black holes.

"Lane, are you alright?" Deputy Benningfield's voice interrupted the silence. "Lane?"

"Um, they're stopped in front of me." Lane tried to catch her breath. "What should I do?"

"Do not get out of your car—"

"I'm not." The smell of burned rubber filled her car as she

watched both cars reverse, their tires filling the air with smoke. A second later they stopped. "I-I think they're leaving."

"Okay, honey. Wait for them to leave, and then I want you to drive away as quickly and safely as possible."

License plate. Lane squinted through the haze, but the cars moved so quickly she was only able to read the last three numbers on the license plate of the dark blue car as it weaved in and out of the lane. 674.

"Are they gone?"

"They're driving away. North." Lane looked over her shoulder and tried to give Noah a reassuring smile. "You alright, buddy?"

"I want to go home, Momma."

"Me too, bud."

"Lane, can you give me a description?"

"I was only able to get the last three numbers on the dark blue vehicle. 674."

"That's good, honey. We've got a patrol car en route. Do you think you can continue on your way safely?"

"Yes, ma'am." Lane's legs felt like spaghetti as she pressed the gas. Her nerves were shot and she still had her father's barbecue to go to this evening. Maybe she could cancel.

A mile up the road, Lane passed an inlet and the sound of revving motors set her heart in a tailspin. *No!* Both cars had been waiting for her and pulled onto the road behind her. "They're back." She couldn't keep the panic from her voice.

"Honey, there's a squad car coming. He'll be there any second."

Deputy Benningfield's voice was controlled and she was trying to be soothing, but Lane could barely hear it over the thundering in her chest. These insane drivers were going to kill someone and she wasn't going to just sit there and let it be her and Noah. Lane pressed the accelerator and put some space between them. It was a mistake.

The cars took her advance as a challenge and met it. The white car came up to her side and started pacing her. The dark blue one stayed on her back bumper, making it impossible for Lane to slow down without fear of getting rear-ended.

"I need someone to help me!" Lane ground her teeth. "They're going to run us off the road."

Like an answered prayer, the sound of sirens rang out in the distance. Lane breathed a prayer and started to slow down but not before the white car whipped in front of her, clipping the front of her bumper. Her steering wheel jerked to the side. Lane hit her brakes, but it wasn't enough to stop the momentum of her Jeep from careening off the side of the road. They came to a jolting stop. Sirens and Noah's cries filled Lane's ears.

Before Lane could take another breath, the driver's door was ripped open. "Lane, are you okay? Are you hurt?"

It was Charlie. His handsome face a mask of fear and relief. All she could manage was a shaky nod before the tears started. She turned and looked over her shoulder to find Sheriff Huggins helping Noah out of his car seat.

"Lane, we've got an ambulance coming—"

"No." Lane wiped her face and took a breath as she tried to regain control over her adrenaline and emotions. She got out of the car and walked around the door toward the back seat. "We just drove off the road. If Noah's not hurt . . ." Lane reached for Noah, who was wiping his nose all over Sheriff Huggins's shoulder.

"I think he's just fine, darlin'." Sheriff Huggins passed Noah over to Lane.

"Are you okay, buddy?"

A sniffling nod was all she got before Noah buried his head in her shoulder.

"Are you sure you don't want the medics to check you both out?" Charlie helped Lane up the small embankment, which wasn't as steep as it looked or felt when she was driving off it. "I'd feel better if you did."

"No, I think we're mostly just shaken up." Lane looked back at her Jeep. "Is it drivable?"

"Probably, but I can drive you and Noah home. We'll need someone to tow the truck back up to the street and you'll definitely want someone to take a look at it to be on the safe side."

The drone of another siren filled the air. The ambulance pulled up and Lane blew out her breath. If she saw one more ambulance in her life, it'd be too soon. A look passed between Charlie and Sheriff Huggins. An unspoken message.

"Noah, do you want to check out what's inside the ambulance?" Charlie asked, holding out his hands.

Without a second's hesitation, Noah climbed into Charlie's arms and the two of them walked toward the waiting ambulance.

"Lane, can you tell me what happened?" Sheriff Huggins said as soon as Noah was out of range.

The ordeal felt like it had lasted forever, but in truth it probably lasted only as long as it took for her to describe it to Sheriff Huggins.

"Charlie gave me a brief rundown on the way over here about a man who's been nosing around your place. Asking questions. He said your alarm went off and you saw something that made you think that same man had returned."

Lane sucked in a breath. She wasn't angry with Charlie for sharing the information. Ms. Byrdie had already asked Lane to describe the man so she could be on the lookout for him. Part of Lane was grateful for so much concern, but another part of her felt silly. Like she was burdening them with one more reason to watch out for her.

"Lane, did you recognize the drivers?"

"No, the windows were too dark." Lane blinked. "Wait, you don't think the guy I caught at my shop was one of the drivers, do you?"

Sheriff Huggins ran a palm across the back of his neck. "Honey, I don't know, but in all my years I've never heard of such reckless driving on these roads. And you'll remember I lived through the whole *Rebel without a Cause* era."

Lane cracked a smile at the reference but couldn't ignore what Sheriff Huggins was suggesting. There were two drivers—not one. It couldn't have been the same guy. Because if it had been, did that mean he'd meant to terrorize her and Noah on the road? Had he wanted to hurt them? The uneasy feeling Lane had tried to leave behind at Miguel's returned.

"Deputy Benningfield said you got a partial plate number. We'll try to run it and see if we can't find out who owns the car and make sure they discover the benefits of public transportation."

Assurance resonated from Sheriff Huggins's voice, but her attention was on Noah. He was laughing as Charlie did some sort of duck dance while wearing an oxygen mask and a blue rubber glove on his head. When Charlie caught them staring in his direction, he slipped the oxygen mask off his face but the rubber glove gave a satisfying snap as he attempted to remove it, sending Noah into another round of laughter.

He was the perfect medicine—the perfect distraction from what Sheriff Huggins was implying. And a different kind of current charged through her body, easing some of the tension knotting her shoulders.

"He's a good guy, and I'm not just saying that because he's kin," Sheriff Huggins said. "And I think he's pretty taken with you."

"And Noah," Lane whispered.

"Well, you are sort of a package deal." Sheriff Huggins smiled. "The kind of package that comes once in a lifetime and is irreplaceable. I'm glad you're both safe."

Lane tried to speak, but her words had dried up with the emotion balled in her throat. Sheriff Huggins wrapped an arm around her shoulder and pulled her in for a hug. A second later, he released her and cleared his throat.

"Why don't we go rescue Noah from the man desperately trying to win your heart?"

Winning. Charlie was winning her heart. In every way he was proving he meant exactly what he said when she told him about her depression. He wasn't running off. No matter what her parents said, Charlie was redefining her idea of unconditional acceptance. And she was taken with him.

TWENTY

"WAKE UP!" A piercing voice echoed in Miguel's ears, slicing through the numbing nightmare. "Miguel, open your eyes!"

A sharp slap stung his cheek, sending his teeth clattering. The pressure in his head pushed at the back of his eyeballs. Miguel ground his teeth, allowing the pain to remind him he was alive. He buried his face in the crook of his arm. What time was it? How long had he been out?

Cold liquid shocked his system into awareness. His eyes snapped open and focused on Annika standing before him with a glass in her hand. "I said, wake up."

"Why . . ." Miguel forced his brain to work through the fog. The orange glow of the setting sun sent beams of light through his house. *Lane.* She was here. And Noah. The pressure behind Miguel's eyes began to build . . . the headache. "What-what was in that bottle?"

Annika set down the glass and bent forward so her face was next to his. Her breath was hot against his cheek and made the hair on the back of his neck stand up. "Only something to help you."

Miguel pressed himself up. Annika dragged a chair along the floor, its metal legs screeching. He winced as his head screamed. Why was she here? Again.

"What do you want?"

"I want to know why the sheriff and his deputy watchdog came by my gallery again today."

"I-I don't know." His eyes flickered to the table. The drawing. He quickly looked back, but it was too late. Annika was already on her feet.

"What's this?" She held up the crayon drawing of the dinosaur

231

little Noah had drawn for him. "How many times has she been here since I last saw you?"

He bit down on his tongue.

Annika's eyes narrowed. "What have you told her?"

"Nothing."

"You're lying to me!" Annika reached for the glass on the table next to him and hurled it against the wall, shattering it.

The noise set his teeth on edge. He wanted to close his eyes and bring some relief to the pounding in his head, but he didn't dare. Annika was dangerous—*she was dangerous*. Clarity started to melt the haze of murkiness clouding his mind, revealing something . . . something he needed to remember, but the pills Annika had given him acted like a thick veil, blinding him to whatever it was.

"Have you considered what will happen to you in prison?" A long eyebrow hitched high up her forehead.

He lifted his gaze to meet hers. "Where is he?"

"Who?"

The man didn't have a name, but his fists were like rocks. He came looking for the painting. Sydney's painting. "I don't know . . . I didn't think." Miguel clenched his teeth and tried to swallow the lump wedged in his throat. "I d-don't think I did it."

Annika crossed her arms. "You were the last one to see her."

The trembling in his hands crawled up his arms, through his torso, and down to his knees. Miguel squeezed his fingers into tight fists as he tried to ignore the image of Sydney's face staring at him. Annika was right. Sydney was dead and it was his fault. He couldn't protect her.

"My father spent his entire life, his fortune, helping people like you. The police won't understand. They won't be lenient. You'll go to jail for the rest of your life or they'll kill you."

Confusion settled over him. Miguel let his gaze fall to his scarred hands and swallowed hard against the bile rising in his throat. He didn't want to believe it. He couldn't believe it, but his mind had long since succumbed to its fate as a tortuous prison, blurring reality. If it were true—that he killed Sydney—then he was a monster.

One who deserved to die.

Death. He deserved it. For all of the suffering, the pain, the deaths he couldn't stop. Death would end his nightmares.

"Men like you don't survive in prison, Miguel." Annika's heels clicked across the floor. "Are you making toys now?"

Miguel looked up to find Annika holding a small piece of whittled wood. It was an alligator—or it would be when he was finished with it. But he kept his mouth shut.

Annika walked back. "Does she have the painting?"

"Leave her alone," he growled.

"Oh." Annika pressed in close to his face. "Does she know what you did to Sydney?"

Miguel's stomach clenched with nausea. "I-I didn't kill her."

"Really? Then tell me"—spittle landed on the side of his face—"who did?"

A flash of memory seared his mind, blinding him momentarily. Sydney. Panic. Car lights. Her voice . . . no, it was Annika's voice. *She's dangerous*. "You."

Annika cackled, spinning on her heel. "I'd be careful with accusations like that." She picked up something and tossed it at him. It landed next to him. "Call the police. Tell them I did it. I killed Sydney."

Miguel picked up the cell phone, the weight of it in his hand almost as heavy as the burden on his shoulders.

"They won't believe you." Annika ran a thumb over the toy alligator in her hand, then studied it. "You, a reclusive baby killer." She locked eyes with him. "That's what they call you Nam vets, isn't it? Do you really think they'll believe you . . . over me?"

"Please d-don't hurt her."

"I can't make any promises. Besides, you have only yourself to blame." Annika tossed the figurine onto his lap. "I only intend to get back what's mine."

Annika tromped out of his home, not bothering to shut the door or take her phone. The cold look in her eyes and the heartless tone in her voice chilled him like the splash of water from earlier. The convulsions took over, wracking his whole body as he released a sob from the depths of his soul. It fell from his lips like a howl. What had he done?

Miguel clutched the sculpture in his hands. He couldn't save anyone forty years ago . . . but the monster had returned and now Lane was in danger. He had to get to her before they did. They'd kill her. And Noah too.

TWENTY-ONE

A BUSTLE OF ACTIVITY was going on outside the Sullivan estate when Lane drove up. A valet hurried over to take her keys, but she waved him away and found a shady spot under a tree to park. She circled around the car to get Noah, thankful the tow-truck driver who hauled her Jeep back to the street was also a mechanic. He said the damage to her bumper was minor and the vehicle was in good enough condition to drive.

The day's events grew more distant with every passing minute that brought Lane closer to seeing Charlie again. It was impossible to hide the giddy smile that crept onto her lips every time she thought of him.

"You're pretty, Momma." Noah lifted the edge of her dress as they walked toward the house.

"Thank you, buddy." Lane had chosen a flowy lilac dress with a little flared hem. The color made her green eyes stand out and complemented her skin. The dress wasn't fancy, but it did make her feel a little bit beautiful. And beautiful was what she wanted to be tonight. She'd carefully applied her makeup and she couldn't thank Meagan enough for tips on covering up the bruise on her cheek.

Inside her parents' home, florists were putting final touches on the centerpieces of roses from Pops's garden. Servers in white shirts and black pants carried out trays of food.

"Lane, that color is stunning on you." Her mother came down the staircase, putting an earring in her ear. "I don't think I've seen you in it before."

Very observant of her mother. She purchased the dress a week before Mathias's death and had planned to wear it for the anniversary dinner they never made it to. Lane inhaled a slow breath,

235

pushing back the guilt and hoping Mathias would think it was time to wear it. Time to move on. "I've had it for a while."

"It's lovely and you look beautiful in it."

Lane breathed a sigh of relief. Receiving her mother's approval was half the battle. Maybe this night wouldn't be so bad after all.

"And Noah, you look mighty handsome tonight. Give Gigi a hug."

"I can't, Gigi." Noah wrinkled his face. "My feet are in a bad mood."

"Your feet are in a bad mood?" She looked up at Lane, confused. "How come?"

"He's outgrown his shoes, but I didn't know that until an hour ago."

"Who's outgrown their shoes?" Meagan came down the stairs, followed by her kids. Owen wore navy-blue shorts with a checkered shirt and bow tie. Paige wore an oversized navy-blue bow on her head and a dress that matched Owen's shirt. If ever there was a perfect family, it was Meagan's.

"Noah's feet hurt and Lane didn't know until just now."

Lane rolled her eyes. "He said they were okay at the house."

"Honestly, Lane." Her mother checked her makeup in the foyer mirror. "How long have you known about this event?"

Long enough to come up with an excuse not to attend. Not that she needed one. Sheriff Huggins asked her more than once if she wanted him to call her father and explain what happened, but Lane really didn't want to rehash a story that would lead to questions about what she was doing and where she was coming from before the incident.

"Noah, let's take your shoes and socks off." Meagan knelt next to him. She rolled up his pant leg and removed his small shoes and white socks before handing them to Lane.

Lane was grateful Meagan didn't comment about the length of Noah's pant legs being a little on the short side.

"He's not going to wear shoes all night?"

"It's a backyard party, Mom. It'll be alright. Besides, he looks cute." Meagan ruffled Noah's hair with her fingers.

"I don't want to wear shoes either," Owen whined.

"Me either," Paige added.

"If they don't wear shoes, then I don't wear shoes." Wes came out of the kitchen with a chocolate-covered pastry in his hand. He popped it into his mouth and started to untie his shoes.

"That's enough. Only the children may take their shoes off." Her mom shot an exasperated look at Wes. "Children under ten."

Wes stuck his lips out in a pout.

"We don't have to wear shoes?" Meagan's husband, Ian, came down the stairs with Lane's father.

"Enough with the shoes." Her mother's tone had grown impatient. "Guests are arriving, and I won't have my family greet them looking like cave people."

One look at their family and it was clear they would never be confused with cave people. Models for a J. Crew magazine shoot maybe, but definitely not cave people.

Lane's father gave her a cursory look. "You look nice."

"Thank you." Her cheeks warmed at the compliment. The second one in as little as five minutes felt unfamiliar and left her suspicious.

"Ray, the media has started to arrive," Jeffrey Adams, her father's campaign manager, said. "We'd like to get a couple shots of you greeting your guests and then we'll give them a quick interview before the event begins."

Ah. That was it. Eyes were watching and perfection was the name of the game. Nothing ever changed. In orderly fashion, Judge Sullivan and his wife would be escorted out of the home, followed by their children and grandchildren. They would receive their guests on the wraparound porch with a shake of the hand, kiss on the cheek, and a multitude of false sentiments.

And the media and voters would eat it up. Everyone loved a good fairy tale. Right?

"Are we ready?" Jeffrey clapped. He adjusted her father's tie and gave her a pointed look. "Just five minutes of smiles and we're done."

The man had a face like a bulldog and was just as stubborn. In her father's early years, Jeffrey would bribe her with everything from ice cream to new books to get her to smile for the cameras. Ice cream and books wouldn't work now. She grabbed her camera and the attention of her mother at the same time.

"What are you doing with that?"

"Lane's the official photographer of the event," Meagan said. "She's good and it keeps the costs down. More money for charity."

Their mother looked ready to protest but stopped. She pasted a smile on her lips and walked over to join the family, who was already on the porch. Meagan winked.

"Thanks." It felt nice having Meagan as her ally.

Jeffrey exhaled loudly. "Just five minutes, Lane."

"Three and a half."

He rolled his eyes and walked out the door.

"You should've asked for ice cream." Meagan laughed. "He'd probably give in."

After the guests were welcomed and the appropriate number of photos of her family had been taken, Lane made her way through the soft blades of manicured grass. Round tables with white linens were set up across the expansive lawn. The band played a peppy jazz number as guests greeted one another and found their way to the bar.

Lane snapped a few pictures but mostly let her eyes wander in the hopes of finding Charlie in the crowd. She recognized a few of the deputies in plain clothes as they attempted to blend in with the social elite, but eventually they paired off and kept to the perimeter of the party. Charlie wasn't one of them. Surely he would've come up to her and said hello, right? Lane bit the inside of her cheek, annoyed at her insecurity. This wasn't a date. Charlie was working. And so was she, sort of.

Lane lifted her camera and grabbed some candid shots of guests enjoying themselves. She paused at the sound of her father's voice speaking to a small group of reporters.

"I assure you, it's only a matter of time before we get him."

"It's been several weeks, Judge Sullivan. What makes you think you're any closer to finding the person or persons responsible for killing Sydney Donovan? And do you think this hurts your chance at winning the seat?"

Lane recognized the blonde reporter asking the questions. She was the one who had flirted with Charlie outside Dr. Wong's office. What was her name? De . . . something.

Jeffrey scoffed. "Judge Sullivan's leading in the polls. The people want someone like Ray bringing justice back to not only Georgia but, in my humble opinion, back to the United States. It's not too much of a stretch to imagine Judge Sullivan will one day be sitting on the bench of the US Supreme Court."

"Ms. DeMarco, you'll have to excuse my ambitious friend here, but to answer your question, I have it on pretty good authority that Sheriff Huggins and his team have made some significant progress recently—"

"What kind of progress?"

"All in good time." Lane's father clapped his hand on the shoulder of the man to his left. "Now, I think it's time we enjoy ourselves and the fabulous food."

Lane smiled on the inside at her father's dismissal of Ms. De-Marco. The reporter pursed her lips, undeterred, and moved on to a group of guests Lane didn't recognize.

The delicious smell of the caterer's menu of southern comfort food made her stomach grumble. Or was that the sky? A wall of gray loomed in the distance, ready to overtake the clear blue sky. A gust of wind swept in, causing an outburst of surprise as napkins flew off the tables.

"And y'all thought you wouldn't have to work for your meal this evening."

Laughter followed her father's charming response to the unpredictable weather. Her mother didn't look so relaxed. She kept gazing up at the sky and narrowing her eyes as if she could will away the impending storm.

As guests took their seats, Lane became aware of how lonely she was in the middle of all these people.

Where was Charlie?

"Momma, can I go inside?" Noah walked up, scratching at his cheek. "The squitoes are eating me alive."

Lane bent down and pulled her son into a hug and planted kisses on his face. He was her one constant in a life where her emotions shifted as quickly as the wind. "That's because you're so sweet."

"I'm going to take them inside and let them watch a movie." Meagan walked over, holding Paige's and Owen's hands. "Is that okay?"

"Charlie!"

Lane rose and took Charlie in as he strode across the lawn in a pair of pressed khaki pants and a teal-blue collared shirt, the sleeves rolled casually to his forearms. Butterflies danced inside Lane's chest.

"Hey, Noah." Charlie met Noah's excitement with a dimpled grin. He stuck out his hand palm side up. Noah smacked it with his hand. Charlie's electric-blue eyes met hers. "Sorry I'm late. I had some work to finish."

"Honey, with a smile like that, you can be late anytime you want." Meagan's drawl would've put Scarlett O'Hara to shame.

Lane forced her tongue to work. "You were going to take the kids inside for a movie, right?"

"Right. Come on, kiddos." Meagan guided the children in the direction of the house. "Maybe my sister will let me talk to you later?"

"Yes, ma'am."

"Sorry about that," Lane said to Charlie, ignoring Meagan's amused expression as she walked the kids to the house. "The work you had to finish?"

"We tried running the numbers you got from the license plate, but the search is too broad. Deputy Frost is working to narrow it down by the color and make of the car."

"Like a needle in a haystack then, huh?"

"Frost is a genius when it comes to finding needles."

Lane wasn't surprised. She'd spent the rest of the afternoon trying to convince herself the drivers of the cars were only stupid teenagers, but after Sheriff Huggins planted the idea in her mind that one of the drivers could be the man who had visited her café, she found it hard not to be jumpy.

Charlie leaned in. "You look amazing."

His whispered words tickled the hair on her neck. His hand brushed against hers until his fingers laced with hers, chasing away all the unwanted thoughts invading her mind. Lane's chest thundered at the intimacy of the moment, yet they were right there in the middle of the lawn where anyone could see them . . . like her father.

Lane's eyes scanned the crowd until she found her parents. Thankfully their attention was focused on the latest wife of a commissioner and not on her. "Um, you're just in time. They're getting ready to serve the food. Would you like a plate?"

"I'm not really that hungry." Charlie's words didn't match the hunger she could see in his eyes. His gaze fell to her lips for a long second before he looked away. "What's over there?"

Lane hadn't realized she'd been holding her breath. Did she want him to kiss her? She pulled her hand free and adjusted the camera sling on her neck. They needed a distraction. "The auction items. Do you want to see them?"

"Sure." They started toward the large white tent lit up with twinkling lights. "This is a little bigger than I expected."

"You mean you *don't* have catering, live music, and an auction at your barbecues?"

Charlie bumped her shoulder with his and flashed his megawatt smile. "No. We've got a grill, a cooler, and a radio."

Goodness, that smile did something to her. Lane ignored the heat blossoming in her cheeks and turned her focus on the long tables lined with gift certificates, pieces of jewelry, and art.

"Do you like football? There's a football signed by the Atlanta Falcons—all of them." Lane lifted her camera and snapped a few pictures of nearby guests reading the descriptions of the auction items. "Comes with season tickets, including the president's box on opening day."

"Mm-hmm." Charlie kept the distance between them tight as they walked. "What's over there?"

They passed a table full of jewelry. Lane turned to follow his gaze. A small group of people were crowded at the corner of the tent, but whatever had gathered the group's attention was blocked from her and Charlie's view.

Lane weaved her way closer, past the excited whispers, and then stilled when she saw what had triggered the oohs and ahhs. Her eyes traced the wild lines of the sculpture. A tree stump with its bark removed was carved into dozens of thin branches stretching from the base. At the end of each was a bird. Wings tucked at their sides as they perched or spread open as they swooped into flight. The roots were carved into knots crisscrossing each other in a strange but beautiful tangle of intricacy.

"It's breathtaking, isn't it?" Pride emanated from Meagan's face as she walked up to them. "People can't stop talking about it."

"Where did you get it?" The carving, the detail—it had to be Miguel's sculpture. Lane reached for the auction information card. The starting bid was twenty-five hundred dollars but bids had driven the price to almost ten thousand dollars. "There's no name."

"Some artists don't want to be known." A tall woman with short black hair approached and Charlie stiffened. "It's good to see you again, Deputy."

Meagan wrinkled her nose. "You two know each other?"

"The deputy has visited my gallery a couple of times." Annika Benedict lifted a thin eyebrow. "Seems his interest in art is spreading, considering the number of law enforcement officers continually interrupting my business."

"Why are you here?"

"Annika's been a long-time donor," Meagan answered Charlie. "And the proceeds from the auction tonight are supporting the Benedict House."

"I'm sorry I could only secure a single painting this time." Annika's eyes flashed to Charlie. "Don't worry, Deputy. That artist is anonymous as well."

Charlie's jaw clenched. "I'm surprised by how many of your artists wish to remain that way."

Lane and Meagan exchanged looks.

"If you ladies will excuse me"—Charlie took a step back—"I think I'm going to grab something to drink."

Meagan looked at her watch. "And I need to get ready for the auction. This piece is going to have people digging deep into their pockets," she said with a smile before she walked away in the same direction as Charlie.

A waiter held out a tray with two glasses. "Would you ladies care for a drink?"

"No, thank you." Lane's eyes were fixed on the sculpture, which was titled *Freedom*. She looked closely at the faces of the birds. Their eyes. The detail carved into each one. It had to be Miguel's, but how? Harley, Dottie, and Ms. Byrdie knew about Miguel's sculpting, probably Sheriff Huggins too, but one of them surely would've mentioned Miguel donating an item to her father's auction.

"I'd hate to offend our hosts." Annika picked up both glasses and offered one to Lane. "Let's toast this wonderful event and the money we hope to raise for our veterans."

Veterans. Lane absently took the glass and lifted it up to Annika's before setting it down on the table.

"You're looking at this sculpture as though you've seen it before," Annika said.

"I feel like I have."

"That would surprise me." Annika sipped from her glass of champagne. "This is the first time the artist's work has been displayed."

"You know the artist?"

"It's my job to know about local artists and the company they keep." Annika's tone shifted, along with the features on her face. "Nothing kills the career of artists quicker than their friends getting in the way."

Lane didn't have a clue what Annika meant, but she was growing uncomfortable beneath the woman's stare. "I should probably get ready for the auction."

"It was nice meeting you, Lane." Annika lifted Lane's still-full glass. "Don't forget your champagne."

Lane took the glass from Annika as an icy shiver slipped down her spine. Stepping far enough away so that Lane was sure Annika wouldn't see her, she tossed the contents of her glass into a flower bed before handing the glass to a passing waiter.

Lane scanned the yard for her sister or for Charlie. Someone to cut the chill from the weird conversation she'd had with Annika. A boisterous giggle drew Lane's attention to the spot where Vivian DeMarco stood, her arm laced through Charlie's. A spark of jealousy ignited in Lane's heart at the sight of them. When she had seen Vivian earlier in the sea of reporters, she hadn't caught the full effect of the woman's glamorous dress. A dress that made Lane feel plain.

And silly.

Lane's mood turned as dark as the sky. Who was she trying to fool? She could pretend a lot of things. Put on a smile for a camera. Pretend like she was fine. But believing she deserved someone like Charlie—that he could love someone like her—was just another lie she wasn't willing to live.

TWENTY-TWO

"COME ON, DEPUTY LYNCH, or can I call you Charlie?" Vivian DeMarco bit her lower lip as she gazed up at him beneath thick, black lashes. "My boss needs me to bring some life back to this story. You wouldn't want me to get in trouble or lose my job."

"Ms. DeMarco, that is the last thing I'd want for you." He withdrew his arm from hers. "But I have a job to do—"

Charlie caught Lane watching him. The sadness he saw in her eyes before she looked away pierced his heart. Something was wrong. She moved farther into the tent, where the auction was already in full swing.

"Are you saying Judge Sullivan was wrong when he said you made progress in the Donovan case?" DeMarco moved in front of Charlie. The strong scent of her perfume wrapped around him like a noose ready to choke out the truth. "I'd hate to bother the judge again to verify the information . . . but I can."

A threat? He had no idea what Judge Sullivan had said to set the obstinate reporter on his tail, but he had a job to do in keeping the event safe and couldn't do that with Ms. DeMarco in his shadow.

His cell phone rang with an unfamiliar number. Didn't matter. "I need to take this."

"Don't think you can get rid of me that easily, Deputy." De-Marco elongated the syllables in the last word. "I have my ways of making men like you talk."

He didn't doubt that. The flirting game—if that's what *that* was—had changed a lot in the years since his last girlfriend.

Charlie apologized as he excused himself to take the call. "Hello."

"Deputy Lynch?"

"Speaking."

"This is Agent Edmonds. I'm sorry to bother you, but I promised you an update and according to a Deputy Frost"—Edmonds released an audible sigh—"we probably owe you a favor."

Charlie didn't know what Frost had said or done, but tomorrow he'd be bringing him all the cinnamon rolls he could handle. Maybe a week's worth. "You have something on the painting?"

"We ran prints and got a hit. One guess and I'll buy you lunch."

"Marco Solis." Charlie walked to the edge of the yard and let his eyes roam. He found Lane taking pictures of a well-dressed couple holding the autographed football. Two men sipping drinks nearby stared at her with a hunger in their eyes that Charlie recognized in soldiers when they returned home from deployment. The lilac dress hugged her body in a way that made him possessive. He took a calming breath. Jealousy was never attractive.

"Yep. Metro has a BOLO out on him now. After Mr. Pretty Boy told us about the paintings, I had our informant in Atlanta check into any other similar packages going in and out of stash houses. He found a shipping receipt for a package we had agents intercept in Miami—"

"Miami? Who lives there?"

"It's a dummy address. Last known tenant moved out six months ago. Landlord said he's had to chase some squatters out of the place, but he and the neighbors haven't seen anyone inside the home in a couple of weeks."

Charlie flexed his hands. "Now what?"

"We put a tracer on that piece and left it at the address where we found it. We've got guys on the ground ready to follow it as well, but for now all we can do is wait."

"What about the shipping label?" Charlie paced. "Can we find out who's sending it or at least who paid for the postage?"

"Tried. Postage was purchased online using a dummy account— hey, hold on." Agent Edmonds's voice became muffled. "Sorry about that. Thanks to your video footage of Marco Solis, our cyber unit was able to track him through the city's camera system to a rental car that was seen at a gas station—El Cheapo, off Highway 17 about two miles west of Walton—the night you found your victim."

Charlie stopped pacing. The strange man Lane saw . . . A crack of thunder echoed overhead. Every eye turned upward, including Charlie's. A cold drop hit his face. Then another. Guests jumped from their chairs, but it was too late. The sky opened up and big, heavy drops poured down on them.

"Agent Edmonds, I have to go."

"Sure. I'll keep you posted if we get anything new."

Charlie ended the call and his concern shifted to the woman standing in the middle of the deluge with her camera in front of her face. Was she really taking pictures? The women around Lane squealed as they tried in vain to protect their heads from the pelting raindrops as they darted across the lawn, seeking shelter. Men tried their best to hold their hands or napkins over the women's heads, but it was useless.

Charlie, shielding his eyes from the pelting drops, jogged over to Lane. "Are you crazy?"

A flash of lightning lit up the sky, followed by an ear-splitting clap of thunder.

"Come on, we should go inside," Charlie said, putting his hand on her waist to guide her out of the rain.

Lane pulled away from his touch. Her hair fell across her forehead as she squinted against the rain. "It's fine. I'm leaving anyway." She removed the camera strap from her neck, shielding the camera against her body.

"Right now?" He looked around. The crowd around them had thinned as most had taken cover on the back porch or beneath the auction tent. Another peal of thunder echoed around them.

"Yes." She hurried toward the auction tent and pulled a camera bag up from under a table. She made quick work of drying the camera and then zipping it safely into the case before she gave him a look. "It's just a rainstorm," she said before marching away from the tent and house.

Charlie detected an edge to her words and followed her. "Is something wrong?"

Lane's pace picked up as she got closer to the outcropping of trees lining the border of her parents' manicured lawn. He kept up as she ducked between two large oaks and kept moving until she came upon a wooden structure on stilted legs and went inside. It looked like it might've been a child's playhouse at one time. But years of weather had taken its toll on the wood, leaving it rotten and the nails rusting.

"Will you talk to me?"

Lane spun around. Water streaked down her face . . . no, they were tears. She was crying. Something was definitely wrong.

"I just . . . I have all these feelings. Inside." She put a hand to her chest. "And it's because of you. You've given me something back that I haven't had since I was married to Mathias. And no matter how hard I try to fight it, I can't help the way I feel."

Charlie's heart pumped faster. "I have feelings for you too—"

"But it's not fair." Lane held up her hand. Her face twisted with words she wanted to speak but was fighting back. "You deserve better."

"I don't understand."

"I'm not whole, Charlie. I'm broken. My emotions are here one second"—Lane lifted her hand in the air and then dropped it—"and here the next. Seeing you with that reporter reminded me of what I'll never be, and I can't ask you to wait for me to change. This . . . who I am will never change."

What was she talking about? And then it hit him. Lane had witnessed DeMarco crawling all over him, looking for something she could headline for the ten o'clock news.

"That woman was begging for a story. There's nothing in her that I find desirable. You're the kind of woman I want in my life."

"You barely know me."

The tin roof above them dripped with the passing seconds.

"I know you cut your cinnamon roll in half and only eat the center. I know you always make double the amount of food you need for Friday Night Club so you can send extras home with families who need it." Lane lifted her gaze to meet his. He swallowed. "I know that when you look at Noah, you twist the wedding band on your finger."

Lane's breath hitched and the desire to wrap her in his arms and kiss her was almost more than he could bear.

"I know that when I got the call that you were in trouble today, my heart felt like it was going to explode out of my chest and I couldn't get to you and Noah fast enough. That if"—his voice cracked—"if anything happened to either of you . . . my life would never be the same."

"I don't want to hurt you." Lane moved in closer, placing her palms on his chest, sending a current of emotion rushing through his body.

Charlie leaned his forehead on hers and closed his eyes against the temptation warring inside him. *Lord, don't let me mess this up.* Opening his eyes, he found hers looking up at him expectantly. Every nerve was on fire. Taking her face in his hands, he lifted her chin, letting his thumb brush her cheek. Lane's lips parted and his heart thudded with each shallow breath he took until his lips met hers.

The kiss started soft. Lane's fingers curled into his shirt as he slid one hand to the nape of her neck. Lane's body melted into his and Charlie tucked her close, allowing the kiss to drown out the world around them.

It was over too quickly. Lane eased back but stayed in his arms, resting her cheek against his chest. "The rain stopped."

"I hadn't noticed," Charlie said, kissing the top of her head. "The fact that you did means I need to work on some things."

Lane glanced up—a sparkle was in her green eyes he hadn't seen before. "Practice makes perfect, right?"

Grinning, Charlie kissed her forehead and then let his lips move over her delicate features until they found her lips. This time he kissed her longer, allowing passion to guide the moment.

"Almost perfect," she said breathlessly once they parted.

Charlie tickled her, enjoying the sound of her laughter blending with the crickets serenading them as fog lifted off the grass and cast the property in an ethereal beauty.

"What is this place?"

"A secret hideout my Pops built for me when I was a little girl." Her slender fingers intertwined with his. "When I needed some time alone—to think or get away from the spotlight—I'd come here. It's where I felt safe."

The echo of a cell phone cut through the air. Charlie groaned. "Well, that killed the moment, didn't it?"

Lane stretched up on her toes and planted a kiss on his lips. "Promise we can make more moments?"

For the rest of my life. Charlie kept the thought to himself and simply returned the kiss before answering the phone.

"This is Lynch." Charlie let his tone reflect his annoyance at the interruption.

"Whoa—did I catch you at a bad time?"

"Sorry, Frost. No. What's going on?"

"Sydney's phone is back online."

"Repeat that."

"We're getting a signal from Sydney's phone," Frost said slowly.

"How?" Charlie's heart rate picked up. He'd all but written off Sydney's phone as another dead end. "When?"

"Agent Padello and I have been checking every day, hoping we'll get a hit. Someone must've found her phone and turned it on. Had to, otherwise we wouldn't have found it."

"So, someone has her phone. Do we know where?"

"Sydney's iPhone has a track feature," Frost said. "I'm dropping you a pin."

"Dropping me a pin?"

Frost chuckled. "Sorry, soldier. I'm sending you the coordinates. Sheriff Huggins wants you to meet him there."

Charlie glanced down at Lane. "Now?"

"Yeah."

There was something in Frost's voice. He was holding back. Why? "I'll head out now."

"Everything okay?" Lane asked when Charlie ended the call.

"Work."

"Probably need to head back to the house anyway."

Lane started toward the house, but Charlie pulled her back to him. He pressed his mouth to hers, wrapping his arms around her waist and lifting her off her feet. When he set her down, he noticed her cheeks were flushed.

"Yeah, we definitely need to get back to the house. Where there are people." She took an unsteady step back. "And people."

"If I'm not out too late, maybe I can stop by your place on my way home?"

Lane nodded. "Sure."

Charlie kissed her forehead and then hurried to his truck, anxious to get to work and then get back to Lane. As he followed the directions Frost had sent him, Charlie let the reality of what had just taken place settle in. He'd kissed her. And she'd kissed him back. He put his knuckle to his lips, a faint trace of Lane's perfume on his skin. This was where he was meant to be. Here with Lane. Proving himself—for as long as it took and as many kisses as it took—to be the man deserving of her trust and love.

TWENTY-THREE

CHARLIE PULLED HIS TRUCK off the side of Coastal Highway and parked behind a Walton squad car. Sheriff Huggins stepped out, the lines on his face tight and his eyes locked on Charlie. Charlie grabbed his service weapon and secured it in his pocket holster before clipping his badge to his belt and climbing out of his truck.

"This isn't too far from where Sydney's body was discovered." Charlie noticed a narrow dirt inlet and saw two more squad cars. Deputy Wilson was poised, alert and ready. "This isn't just some random location, is it?"

"That path leads to Miguel Roa's house." Sheriff Huggins pointed at the path to the left of the two squad cars parked on the highway shoulder.

Unless someone had taken an actual sledgehammer to Charlie's chest, the blow of the sheriff's words could not have been worse. Miguel. The same man Lane helped at her café. The one who hit her. Anger and nausea churned in his gut.

"This isn't going to be a normal situation, Charlie." Sheriff Huggins's radio cackled, but he turned it down. "I already told you Miguel has some issues, but I've never known him to be violent. Ever. Let's do our job professionally but with an extra level of compassion—until we know the truth."

"I understand, sir." And he did. Charlie knew plenty of wounded warriors who battled the psychological damage of war long after they left the battlefield. It didn't excuse them from their actions. Especially murder. "Do you think he's our killer?"

The sheriff looked troubled. Like a man who knew what had to be done but was burdened by the decision. "Only one way to find out."

The deputies spread out in a *v* shape. Their feet crunched over twigs and leaves as their flashlights lit the way down the path and through the outcropping of trees and bushes. It didn't appear as though anyone lived out there, but soon a dilapidated home covered in leaves and pine needles came into view.

The porch creaked under Charlie's boots. The loud boom of his knuckles against the rotting wood echoed. He kept his free hand on the gun at his hip. Miguel was a veteran, trained to kill, and when cornered . . . his reactions couldn't be predicted. There was no room for mistakes.

"Miguel Roa, this is Deputy Lynch and Sheriff Huggins. We'd like to talk to you." He listened for movement. Sheriff Huggins signaled some deputies to go around back. Charlie pulled open the screen door and paused. The front door was open. "Miguel Roa, this is Deputy Lynch."

There was no response. With the toe of his boot, Charlie pushed the door wide open and raised his gun. The house stunk of turpentine and varnish. He flipped on a light, illuminating the house. Dishes and some trash were scattered around. Sheriff Huggins stepped in behind him with his gun raised. They cleared the house in a few minutes.

"We got another building here in the back," Wilson said over the radio. "It's clear. No sign of Miguel."

As Charlie holstered his gun, his eyes were drawn to a pile of rags with brown blotches on them. Was it blood? "Does Miguel have a car?"

"I haven't known Miguel to drive in forty years."

"How does he get to town?"

"Walks."

"Lynch." A deputy was standing next to a couch and pointing at a cell phone with a hot-pink rhinestone case. "This what we're looking for?"

Charlie slipped on a pair of latex gloves as the sheriff's words tickled his ear, *"Only one way to find out."* He hit a button on the phone and Sydney's smiling face appeared with her two best friends next to her. "It's her phone."

Sheriff Huggins's shoulders dropped an inch. He looked as sick as Charlie felt. The whole time the killer had been sitting under their noses. And now he was gone. Charlie assigned two deputies to drive the area between the house and town. Walton didn't have a K-9 unit, but they could borrow one from Savannah Metro if necessary. They weren't going to lose him.

Deputy Wilson walked into the house, carrying a painting in his latex-gloved hands. "Sir, the building out back appears to be a workshop. We found this out there." He lifted the canvas.

Bright yellow streams of sunlight bathed large trees with thick green foliage. At the center was a sculpture carved out of a tree trunk, with birds flying upward from the base of it as though they had been set free.

"Did Sydney paint it?" Sheriff Huggins asked, looking over his shoulder.

Charlie took the canvas from the deputy and studied it. The scenery was peaceful, not like the other colorful abstract paintings. Like the others, there was no signature. Charlie ran a finger along the brush strokes. Yellow paint lifted. "It's not hers. Paint's still wet."

"Follow protocol. No mistakes. I'm going to put out a BOLO," Sheriff Huggins said as he stepped outside. Resignation was etched deep into the sheriff's face.

Did the sheriff believe Miguel was incapable of murder? Or was the weight of finding out someone you thought you knew was capable of killing finally getting to him?

"Lynch." Wilson held up a piece of paper with a crayon drawing of a dinosaur on it. Scribbled in the corner was Noah's name.

Charlie's jaw clenched as the acid rose up his throat. "I need to get back to Lane."

Lane felt like one of those Disney princesses who drifted on fluffy white clouds after an encounter with their Prince Charming. Or was Prince Charming just for Snow White? Lane couldn't remember and Noah wasn't too keen on watching movies with sappy singing princesses in pink.

"Either you snuck the last of the éclairs or you're falling in love." Meagan leaned her elbows on the railing of the back porch. "Soooo?"

"Those éclairs are magical, aren't they?" Lane tucked her chin, hiding the blush rushing to her cheeks. She picked up a soggy napkin and tossed it onto a pile with the others she had collected. Was she falling in love? The thought of using that word felt sudden and too intimate to share, but it also felt sort of right.

"Nice try." Meagan collected a few stray glasses and set them on one of the catering tables. "You know Dad hired a crew to do this?"

"I know, but they won't be here until tomorrow and—" Lane looked up. The storm clouds had cleared the way for an inky sky glittering with stars. The truth was, she wasn't ready for the night to end. So, she lingered, reliving her and Charlie's caught-in-the-rain moment. "I'm enjoying the night."

"Says the girl pretending she's not in love." Meagan winked. "What were you two doing out by your old fort?"

A commotion inside the house drew their attention, saving Lane from having to explain how she had run off into the woods like a lovesick teenager and indulged in a moment of weakness.

"Lane."

Whatever warmth she'd been reveling in was extinguished at the sound of her father's commanding tone. "Yes?"

"Sheriff Huggins and Deputy Lynch are here to speak with you."

Lane frowned. Charlie was back? With the sheriff? She followed her father into the house as Meagan trailed behind her. A tiny tremor of anxiety curled over her shoulders and clawed deeper when she found her mom, Wes, Sheriff Huggins, and Charlie waiting for her inside the living room.

She took a seat in the leather chair opposite her mom and next to Sheriff Huggins. Her eyes cut to Charlie. It was clear by his expression and rigid posture that this was a professional visit.

"Judge Sullivan, do you have a list of all the guests who were present tonight?" Charlie asked when her father took his place next to her mom.

Meagan was perched on the arm of the couch, near Wes—her worried gaze bouncing between each of them.

"I have the invitation list," her mother offered, rising. She went to the secretary desk and picked up a binder. "Not everyone on the list came, but Meagan has the names from the auction too, right, honey?"

"Yes." Meagan left the room and returned with a clipboard. She handed it to Charlie. "What's going on?"

Charlie looked over the pages. "What about the waitstaff? Valets?"

"There's a tab in the binder containing the contract from the caterer and valet service, along with the names." Her mother's voice held an anxiousness Lane didn't like. "Four servers. Three valets. And the bartender."

"Five servers," Lane's father said. "There were five servers tonight."

Lane's mother shook her head. "No, dear. Only four. You wanted us to get five so we'd have a backup in case one didn't show up, but—"

"Elise, there were five. I remember because one was wearing an earring and I asked him to remove it while he was working. I checked the other servers. Two women. Three men." Her father's eyes pinned Sheriff Huggins. "What does our guest list and the names of our waitstaff have to do with your visit, Sheriff?"

"There are only four signatures on the sheet," Charlie said. The slight to her father's question didn't go unnoticed. "Mrs. Sullivan, I need you to call the caterer and find out if they sent an extra waiter and get his name."

"Now? It's nearly midnight."

"Sheriff?" Judge Sullivan's tone was impatient.

"Judge Sullivan, we'd like to speak with Lane for a few minutes. Privately."

Charlie addressed her father, his voice strong and assertive, positioning himself as the officer in charge. Under any other circumstance, she might've appreciated the boldness. But tonight there was an intensity in his tone that wasn't sitting well with her or her father, judging by the deep furrow carved into his brow.

"Sir, I need you to verify the names of the staff the catering company sent." Charlie remained poised and unfazed by her father's challenging gaze. "When you return with those details and after I've had a chance to speak with Lane, Sheriff Huggins and I will discuss what we can with you."

"Dad." Meagan spoke up. "The caterers probably aren't going to respond to a call this late at night unless it comes from you."

The skin at her father's jawline flexed a few times until her mom reached for his hand and urged him in the direction of the door. He looked like he was going to say something but stopped himself. Instead, he took the binder Charlie was offering and stalked out of the room, with the rest of Lane's family following in his wake.

"What is it?" Lane fought against the tremor playing at her fingers. "Why are you here?"

"How's Noah?"

"Good." Lane didn't like the way her pulse skipped at his question. Her gaze jerked to the family room, where Noah, Paige, and Owen would be watching a movie if they weren't already asleep. The urge to go check on Noah pushed Lane to her feet.

"Lane." Charlie's tender grip at her elbow stopped her from rushing to Noah's side. Her eyes flashed to his deep blue ones, which looked apologetic. "I didn't mean to scare you. I only asked because I wanted to make sure we could talk with you for a few minutes."

"What is it?"

Charlie shifted a little, putting a professional distance between them. "When was the last time you saw Miguel?"

"Miguel?" She blinked, surprised to hear his name. "This morning."

"Before the incident on Old Ogeechee?"

"Yes." Lane searched Charlie's face for an explanation. "Why? Has something happened?"

"Honey"—Sheriff Huggins folded his hands, spotted with age, over his gun belt—"he's missing."

Lane dropped into a chair. "Missing?"

The sheriff gave a grim nod. "We just came from his house and he's not there."

Charlie moved to her side, but the calm his presence normally brought was overshadowed by the dread growing in her chest. He pulled a folded piece of paper from his front shirt pocket. Unfolding it revealed Noah's drawing. "We found this."

Lane took the coloring page. "Noah made it for Miguel. Why do you have it?"

"You know Miguel paints? Sculpts?"

"Yes." Her thoughts went to the barn behind Miguel's house. Canvases, paint, wood shavings, and stumps. She looked absently in the direction of the backyard, where the carved sculpture that she had no doubt Miguel's scarred hands had created claimed the highest bid of the night. And now the artist was missing? "But what does that have to do with him being missing?"

Charlie knelt in front of her. "We were called to Miguel's house for a reason. Sydney Donovan also painted."

There was a pause—she didn't know how long—before the meaning behind those words and their looks struck her like a bolt of lightning. "You don't think—no. You're wrong."

"Honey—"

"*You* think he's involved in Sydney's death?" Lane searched Sheriff Huggins's face. The two men were friends. Ms. Byrdie said they had served together in the war. "You know he can't be involved."

"The other night when he came in . . . when he hit you—"

"I told you it was an accident." Lane instinctively put her hand to her cheek.

Charlie nodded. "You said he's been different . . . PTSD can manifest in many ways."

"PTSD doesn't make him a killer," Lane snapped at Charlie. "You have no idea what it must be like for him."

"Lane, I'm not saying he's guilty of anything." Charlie's voice was soft. "But I've seen plenty of hurting people do terrible things they can't take back—"

"The catering company said they only sent four employees," her father said as he stepped into the living room. "They emailed the profiles of the servers, but the man I asked to remove his earring wasn't among them."

Charlie resumed his standing position, taking in the information even as his eyes remained on her. She looked away. How could Charlie even think Miguel was capable of killing Sydney? He didn't know Miguel like she did.

"Someone was in our home uninvited?" Wes walked in behind their father, his arms folded across his chest.

Lane's mother and sister hovered near the threshold, their faces a mixture of curiosity and concern—though Meagan's looked a little pale.

Charlie exchanged a look with Sheriff Huggins. He pulled out his phone, tapping something on it before turning it toward her father. "Sir, do you recognize this man?"

"No."

Sheriff Huggins sat forward. "Ray, you're sure you haven't see this man tonight?"

"Maybe one of the servers?" Charlie added.

"One of the waiters? No." Her father's lip curled. "That man would never have been permitted to serve my guests looking like that. Besides, the man with the earring was younger. They all were."

Lane couldn't see the image on the phone, but she could read the troubled expression on Charlie's face as he walked toward her mom. "Ma'am?"

Her mom shook her head. So did Meagan and Wes after they looked at whatever Charlie was showing them. He turned toward Lane next, but his eyes shifted to focus on something over her shoulder.

"Momma." The heavy energy in the room seemed to release at Noah's sudden presence. His sleepy eyes drifted around the room before finally catching on Charlie. "Hi, Charlie."

"Hey, buddy." Charlie held his palm flat for Noah and was rewarded with a palm slap.

Noah climbed into Lane's lap and she breathed in the sweet scent of his Rock-a-Saurus Blueberry Shampoo.

"Did you bring your dog?"

"Not this time."

"Oh." He leaned into her arms before perking up a bit. "Do you want to see my new toy?"

"Buddy, Charlie gave you that dinosaur, remember?" Charlie's gift remained Noah's most coveted toy. "I need to talk with Charlie and Sheriff Huggins for a few more minutes and then I can take you—"

"It's not a dinosaur." Noah wriggled out of her lap and reached into his pocket. "It's an alligator."

Lane's breath snagged at the sight of the small alligator resting in her son's hand. The smooth wood was carved into a scaly reptile like the ones they had seen at Miguel's house. "Where did you get that?"

Noah's eyes peeked up at her under long lashes. "I found it."

If Charlie and Sheriff Huggins had been at Miguel's house, would they recognize the similarities between the carved toy and the sculptures in Miguel's shop? She avoided their gazes and dropped to her knees, placing her hands on Noah's shoulders.

Her throat grew tight. "Noah, what have I told you about lying?"

"I'm not lying." His voice wobbled. "I did find it."

"Noah." Charlie dropped onto one knee. "That is a cool alligator. Can you tell me where you found it?"

"Well . . ." Noah drew out the word. "Aunt Meagan said we had to stay inside to watch the movie, but I wanted a chocolate donut—"

"Chocolate donut?" Lane looked up at her mom and then Meagan. They both shrugged their shoulders. "There weren't any chocolate donuts, Noah."

"Mm-hmm." Noah nodded. "Uncle Wes kept eating them."

"The éclairs," Wes said, as a tight grin lightened the worried features on his face. "I told him he could have one. I didn't know he was outside by himself."

Noah nodded as though verifying her brother's story. "Yep, so I asked a man with a tray and he said if I follow him, he'll get me one. Only—" Noah dropped his chin to his chest the way he did when he knew he'd done something wrong. "I didn't obey."

Lane lifted Noah's chin. "Who didn't you obey?"

"The man with the tray. I was supposed to follow him, only I heard a—" Noah puckered his lips together and blew out air. A squeaky noise came from his throat as he tried to whistle.

"You heard a whistle?" Charlie urged. "Then what?"

"I turned around and found this"—he lifted up the wood alligator— "on the steps. I can keep it, right, Momma?"

Lane's chest tightened. Miguel. The cuts on his hands. His erratic behavior. Could he have come to the house tonight? Why? He wouldn't hurt Noah, would he? Charlie's warning about Miguel's condition had planted seeds of doubt in her mind and it left her frustrated. Her heart longed to believe she deserved a second chance at love, but her responsibility was to keep Noah safe. She owed that to him, but especially to Mathias.

"I need to go home."

"It's late, honey." Lane's mom moved into the room. "You and Noah can sleep in your old room."

"I think that's a good idea," Charlie said, his voice dropping. "Until we get some things figured out."

He didn't need to say the words for Lane to understand the message. Charlie believed Miguel had been there tonight. Given Noah the toy. Was she wrong? Was Miguel capable of harming Noah? Killing Sydney? Lane wasn't stupid. Random attacks at schools, nightclubs, and shopping centers almost always centered on a person suffering from some kind of mental disorder. Did God predestine these individuals with a sickness that made them a danger to others?

Did that mean she was just as dangerous?

"We're going home." Lane stood, taking Noah's hand. "It's been a long day and night, and I'd really like it to be over."

She ignored the pain darkening Charlie's blue eyes. Regret ached deep in her chest. What had she been thinking? If something had happened to Noah while she was off skipping into the woods like an infatuated adolescent . . . her life would be over.

"It's probably good for everyone to be in their own beds to-night," Sheriff Huggins said. "I'll follow her home. Make sure she gets there safely."

It wasn't necessary, but she knew there was no arguing with the sheriff. And better his offer than her mother's. "I appreciate that."

She gathered their belongings while Noah said goodbye to his cousins and her parents. At the door, Meagan waited.

"I'm so sorry." Meagan's normally put-together façade crumbled. "I should've been watching him better."

"It's my fault." Lane swallowed against the fear of what could've been. She saw Charlie waiting on the porch. "I was distracted."

With the final goodbyes said, Lane brought Noah to her hip and walked out of the house and past Charlie toward her car.

"Can we talk?"

"Look, it's late. I'm tired." She willed herself to keep walking.

To not stop and look into his eyes because she knew it would make what she needed to do harder. "I'm sorry about what happened earlier in the woods."

"I'm not." Charlie's hand found her waist, and the warmth of his touch halted her steps. "I'm worried about you and Noah. I want to make sure you're safe."

She took a breath, refusing to meet his gaze. "We're fine."

"What about the toy? It's from Miguel, isn't it?"

"Charlie"—Lane closed her eyes for a moment, trying to calm the emotion rolling far too close to the surface—"even if it did come from Miguel, that doesn't make him who you think he is. I don't know why you and Sheriff Huggins think he's capable of killing Sydney, but you don't know him. Not like I do."

"Lane, he was here." Charlie ran his hand over Noah's head so tenderly that it nearly did her in. "If something had happened—"

"If something had happened, it would've been my fault. Miguel wouldn't hurt anyone." Lane's voice shook as hot tears began to fall on her still-bruised cheek, refuting her conviction. *It was an accident.* She shifted Noah to her other hip, giving herself a second to compose what she needed to say next. "If all you see when you look at Miguel is a man with a disease, someone capable of killing a teenager, then it's probably best if we go our separate ways."

"Is that what you want?"

No. She wanted nothing more than to fall into his arms. To make promises to be the woman worthy of his passionate whispers of love, but those were promises she had failed to keep once before and she wouldn't do it again.

"Lane?"

She backed away. Pushed through the splintering ache breaking her heart into two and left Charlie standing there. "I'm not worth the risk."

TWENTY-FOUR

LANE SCRUBBED THE OAK MANTEL with enough force that if she didn't stop, she'd rub straight through the polished stain. An entire day had passed and her thoughts were still stained with memories of Charlie. His words, their kiss, her dismissal. She threw the rag into the bucket and sucked in a sob. Putting her hand to her mouth, she peeked over at Noah. He was perched at one of the tables in the Way Station Café playing with the dinosaur Charlie had given him. It wasn't until the wee hours of the morning that the waves of tears soaking her pillow finally eased. Accepting the heartbreaking reality that she had pushed Charlie away wasn't going to be easy.

She grabbed a broom and started sweeping. It was Monday and they hadn't found Miguel, at least that was the rumor, and she still hadn't spoken to Charlie. Of course, if rumors were to be believed, he was probably busy trying to find the one person everyone in town could easily agree was capable of murder. So, early this morning she called Ms. Byrdie and told her the Way Station Café wouldn't be open today. It needed to be cleaned. And Lane wanted to avoid . . . everyone.

At least until her appointment with Dr. Wong. She'd been rescheduling for the last two weeks, but her bottle of pills was close to empty and the nightmares that began after losing Mathias had returned and meant she couldn't avoid the psych doctor any longer. He'd ask about her parents and she'd tell him they weren't interested. He'd ask about anything new in her life and . . . Lane swallowed against the lump thick in her throat.

Lane had been foolish to believe she could forget who she was. She didn't need to wear a scarlet letter to remind her of her guilt, but maybe if she had, Charlie would've known to avoid her and

Lane wouldn't be turning her café upside down in a cleaning frenzy to ease the pain.

Not worthy.

Flawed.

Mistake.

The words played in cadence with every sweep of the broom across the wood floor. Her phone buzzed and she saw Charlie's number. She ignored the call and continued to sweep. What if Charlie was right about Miguel? That thought haunted her. If she was wrong about Miguel she could be wrong about Charlie too.

Thunk!

The bristles of the broom hit something leaning against the wall and sent it crashing forward. A frame. Lane picked up the painting and recognized it as one of the auction items. A sunset—or maybe it was a sunrise—with gentle hues of peach and pink blossoming from the lavender and deep violet of night as the sun emerged.

Lane's fingers traced the colors. *"He makes all things new, every morning. Put your hope in him."* The saying was a favorite of Ms. Byrdie's, and she offered it freely and often to those who came into the café. How she knew when it was the right thing to say, Lane didn't know, but after a hug, a prayer, and maybe a tear or two, the customer would leave with a light in their eyes that hadn't been there when they came in.

Was it all a lie? Lane set the painting down and looked around her. Moving back to Walton and buying the Way Station Café were steps toward a *new* beginning—a fresh start. But no matter how many new mornings Lane was given, the truth woke up with her—she was responsible for Mathias's death and undeserving of knowing that kind of love ever again.

Sirens rang out. Lane and Noah both watched a Walton Sheriff's squad car race past the picture window. A blaring reminder of what was happening in the town. Where was Miguel? Was he the killer?

A knock on the back door rattled her. As she set the broom

against the wall, Lane saw Meagan peeking in through the open window.

"Hi." Meagan gave a timid smile. "Mom told me you weren't opening today and you haven't been answering your phone—"

"Cleaning." Lane's cutting tone sent Meagan's eyes downward. She hated that a part of her blamed Meagan for losing track of Noah. If Charlie was right . . . *no.* She wasn't going to go there. "Sorry. It's been . . . it's been a rough weekend and I just needed a day."

"I get that." Meagan tucked her lower lip between her teeth. "Can I come in?"

"Sure."

"Aunt Meagan!" Noah flung himself at Meagan's knees when she stepped inside. "Are Paige and Owen here too?"

"Hey, Noah." Her sister pressed Noah into a long hug. "They're at swim practice."

"I wanna go swimming. Momma, can I go to swim practice too?"

Lane considered her son's eager eyes. "Maybe, but not today."

Noah pinched his lips together and nodded. "Okay, maybe tomorrow?"

"Maybe. Now, go put your toys away so you can get ready for Pops."

Meagan watched Noah climb the stairs one at a time before she turned to Lane. A deep well of tears clouded her hazel eyes. "I'm so sorry, Lane. I should've checked on them. Stayed inside. I got carried away with the auction and—"

"It's not your fault." And it was true. Her sister was carrying more than her fair share of guilt. "I was . . . I wasn't where I needed to be either."

Lane blinked back the memory of Charlie kissing her. The way he smelled and the touch of his lips against hers. She said the moment was a mistake—wanted to believe it—but her heart wouldn't let her. Noah slipping out of the house unattended was a stark reminder that her purpose was making sure Noah was safe. Protected. It was the only reason she was still alive.

Meagan inhaled sharply and dabbed beneath her eyes with the tips of her fingers, trying to keep her eye makeup from running. "You know how much I love Noah. I just don't know what I would've done if something had happened to him—"

"But nothing happened to him." Lane squeezed Meagan's hand. "And I'd sorta like to forget the night ever happened."

"Ha. Me too." Meagan sniffled. "Well, not all of it. We did raise a lot of money at the auction. And I'm more than a little curious what you and Mr. Deputy were doing out in the woods—"

"Speaking of auction. Ian forgot a piece." Lane hurried to the table where the painting was. "I think this should've been in the auction."

"Oh, yeah." Meagan looked at it. "I think it's the one we didn't know where it came from or who donated it. Maybe we'll just donate it to the Benedict House. I can take it by there this afternoon when I get the measurements for the ribbon-cutting ceremony."

Lane's cell phone rang again. Probably Charlie. He'd been trying to call her since Saturday night, but she didn't answer—couldn't. She wasn't sure how much longer she'd be able to avoid him though. He did live in the house right behind her and it was a small town . . . but how could she face him when she couldn't trust her heart not to give her away? Lane wanted the hope back that he instilled. She wanted to be gathered in his embrace. She wanted to hear his voice speak life into her soul . . . but she also wanted him to be happy. He deserved a woman who could make him happy. What could Lane bring to him besides grief? It was better this way, and she'd just keep telling herself that until the lie became the truth.

Lane pulled the phone from her pocket and checked the ID. It wasn't Charlie. It was Dottie, Harley's wife. "Hello?"

"Honey, thank God you answered. I'm about fit to have my britches tied. Have you seen Miguel?"

Lane froze. "No. Why?"

"They think he killed that little girl. The deputy—the good-looking one—he came by this morning to talk to Harley." Dottie's voice was breathless, panicked. "Honey, they're getting a warrant out for his arrest."

Lane rubbed her forehead, catching her sister's concerned gaze. "I-I just can't believe it's Miguel."

"Me either, honey, and Harley tried his best to convince them, but they got something on him. Something bad."

When Charlie left the barbecue on Saturday night, he said it was because of work. When he returned, he told Lane they'd been at Miguel's. What had they found? Her heart thumped wildly in her chest. She peered out the window and could see the outline of the courthouse.

"They're wrong, Dottie. Whatever they've got . . . it can't be Miguel."

Lane ended the call just as Noah came traipsing down the stairs.

If Miguel had been at her parents' house on Saturday night—why? And why did she have such a strong feeling that he wasn't the killer? People hid the things that shamed them most. Maybe Miguel was a killer hiding out. Pretending to be normal . . . like her.

"Everything okay?" Meagan put a hand on Lane's shoulder. "You don't look well."

"I'm fine." Lane shook her head and shook off the dark thoughts pervading her mind. She really needed to see Dr. Wong, but first she needed to know if she was wrong and Charlie was right.

Noah peeked through the spindles of the stairs. "Can I take my train with me to Pops?"

Lane squeezed her eyes shut. She doubted she'd have enough time to drop off Noah with Pops before her father issued the warrant. "Change of plans, bud. You can't go to Pops's right now."

Noah's lips began to quiver and, like magic, crocodile-size tears filled his eyes. She definitely didn't have time for a breakdown.

"I can take him . . . or he can come with me." Meagan spoke

softly, her cheeks flushed. "I mean, if you need to be somewhere. Paige and Owen will be home soon and they can play in the sprinklers. I promise I won't let him out of my sight for even a second."

Lane knew what happened at the barbecue was an accident. Her sister really did love Noah and wouldn't let anything happen to him, but a tingle of fear kept Lane from answering her sister for a few seconds.

"Okay."

"Okay?" Meagan's eyes lit up. "Really?"

"I can play with Owen and Paige." Noah smiled. "Can I still bring my train?"

"Sure, but hurry."

Meagan smiled, but it was lacking something. "Thank you."

Lane studied Meagan. The last thing she wanted was for her sister to feel guilty about what happened, but Meagan's face held the same pale pallor it had the night of the barbecue. "Are you feeling okay?"

"Sure." Meagan ran a hand over the peach sheath dress that highlighted her perfectly tan skin. "You know, all the Junior League meetings leading up to the fund-raiser and the auction, added with the chaos of"—her eyes flashed to Lane's— "well, I think it's zapped my energy."

"I don't know about your kids, but Noah still takes a nap. Maybe that's what you need—a little nap."

"That sounds really good actually."

Noah came bounding down the stairs with his backpack on. Lane gave him extra kisses, which he quickly wiped away with the back of his hand, before she led him outside and buckled him in the back of Meagan's minivan. As soon as they pulled out of the drive, Lane locked up the café and started for the courthouse. How was she going to convince Sheriff Huggins and Charlie they were wrong about Miguel? And what evidence did they have that had Sheriff Huggins convinced Miguel could've killed Sydney? And what would she say if she ran into Charlie?

\\\\\\\\\\\\\\\\\\\

The steady cadence of determined purpose hummed from every desk inside the sheriff's station. The drone of reporters milling about outside had set Charlie's nerves on edge. They were waiting for a statement, but it wouldn't be issued until after Charlie and Sheriff Huggins spoke with Judge Sullivan.

Charlie looked at his phone. Lane hadn't answered any of his calls or text messages. And when he stopped by the Way Station Café, a simple sign in Lane's handwriting said the café was closed for cleaning. He tried knocking, but there was no answer.

Heaving a sigh, Charlie looked at the report he'd just finished. The evidence was strong and it pointed to Miguel. Deputy Wilson even found a chiseling tool in Miguel's workshop with traces of blood on it. It would take time to get the DNA results back, but the shape of the tool was unusual enough that a quick call to the medical examiner confirmed it could be the murder weapon.

"Deputy Lynch." Frost appeared at his side. "You need to see something. You too, Sheriff."

Sheriff Huggins had stepped out of his office and was now following Charlie and Frost as they headed to the back room. The bounce in Frost's steps, Charlie quickly learned, meant the young man had something important—and an endless supply of energy.

"Agent Padello sent these over a few minutes ago." Frost held up several still shots. "Recognize anyone?"

The two people in the photos clearly had no idea they were being photographed. The first photo was of a man and a woman sitting under an umbrella. They both wore sunglasses. She also had on an oversized sun hat. The next photo was a close-up of the same couple sitting at what looked like a beach or poolside bar. The woman was still wearing the hat, but her sunglasses were off.

Charlie's body went rigid. "That's Annika Benedict."

"And Deputy Lynch gets the point." Frost's lips curled into a goofy grin. "Don't feel left out, Sheriff. You get double points if you can guess who the man is with her."

There was only one logical guess, but Sheriff Huggins beat Charlie to it.

"Marco Solis."

"And the sheriff swoops in for the win." Frost held his hand up for a high five, but the sheriff left him hanging. "Okay . . . If you can't already tell, you'll notice that Ms. Benedict is a little less frigid in these photos—and I'm referring to more than the tropical location. Agent Padello said these photos were taken about three years ago on a lovely beach in the French Riviera."

"Why was the FBI taking photos of Annika Benedict and Marco Solis three years ago in France?"

"That is a good question, Deputy Lynch." Frost rubbed his hands together and then popped his knuckles before he started typing. "They weren't."

A second later, a picture of an Arab man flashed to the screen. With dark hair and a goatee, the man held a cigarette in his mouth as he looked off into the distance from the deck of a luxurious boat.

"Meet Abas Nawabi."

"Should we know this man?"

"Probably not." Frost lifted his shoulders. "But the FBI believes he's got connections with a terrorist organization inside Afghanistan."

"Frost, you have me completely lost." Sheriff Huggins exhaled. "What does this guy have to do with Annika and Marco Solis?"

Frost tapped the photos. "Sir, the real question is why is Annika hanging out with a drug dealer and a suspected terrorist?"

Charlie opened the desk drawer and pulled out a sketch. It was the face of the man Lane said was in her shop after hours asking questions about her dead husband and their little boy. The one who may or may not have been outside the café tampering with the alarm system. And possibly the one who ran Lane and Noah off Old Ogeechee Road. "Sir, this is Marco Solis."

Sheriff Huggins's face drew taut as his eyes passed between the sketch and the photo. "He's been here."

"And he may be the killer." As Charlie thought about how close Marco Solis had gotten to Lane and Noah, anger rose in his chest. But why was Solis going after her? His cell phone rang before he could voice his questions. "It's Agent Edmonds."

"Answer it," Sheriff Huggins said. "He might be interested in this."

"Agent Edmonds, I have you on speakerphone. Sheriff Huggins and Deputy Frost are here with me." He set his phone on the table between them. "We've got something here that might interest you."

"Hmm, looks like the stars are aligning in both our favors, because I've got some interesting news for you too."

Charlie looked to Sheriff Huggins for permission and received a quick nod. "You go first, Agent Edmonds."

"I have two pieces of information. Good and bad. Which do you prefer to hear first?"

"Good," Charlie said as his voice collided with that of Frost, who opted to hear the bad news first.

"We could use good," Sheriff Huggins said.

"We tracked that painting to Atlanta."

"The one that was in Miami on Saturday?" Charlie leaned forward. "How? There's no mail service on Sundays."

"The mailing labels they've been using are fake, or at least this one was. A man not wearing a uniform picked up the painting late Saturday night and delivered it yesterday afternoon to a house known for drug activity. Our team breached the location and found the painting being covered with a colored paste of methamphetamine."

Charlie frowned. "Say again."

"They melt the meth into a gelatin-type substance. They paint it onto the canvas and, once the gel dries, it can be scraped off, remelted, and then distributed."

"They're painting the drugs onto the canvas?" Sheriff Huggins seemed to be saying it aloud for his own benefit.

"We found several more paintings in various stages inside the home. They all had mailing labels with the address of the gallery in Savannah."

"Was the house occupied?"

"Just one man. One of the painters—we're assuming there are more than one by the number we found inside the house—but he hasn't been very cooperative. We believe he's the boyfriend of Marco Solis's sister, which brings me to the bad news. Marco Solis's body was discovered in a dumpster off River Street last night."

Stunned silence filled the room. If anyone other than Miguel was responsible for Sydney's murder, it was Marco—and now he was dead. Part of Charlie was relieved. If Marco was the one harassing Lane, then that meant she was safe now. But Miguel was still missing.

"Now, you tell me some good news." Agent Edmonds's deep voice cut into the silence. "Or is it bad news?"

"It's news. Good or bad might be up for interpretation after what you've just told us." Charlie was halfway through explaining about the photos when a thought occurred to him. "Agent Edmonds, do you know anything about Abas Nawabi?"

Silent seconds ticked by. "He's been on the DEA's watchlist for some time as one of the main contributors bringing meth into the Middle East and parts of Europe." Agent Edmonds's tone went flat. "I'm curious how you came up with that name."

Charlie studied the photos in his hand. "I'm looking at surveillance photos the FBI took of Abas Nawabi. They include Marco Solis and Annika Benedict together from three years ago. And I think I saw Abas Nawabi in Savannah the first time we questioned Annika."

"You saw Abas Nawabi in Savannah?" Agent Edmonds's question was leveled in disbelief.

"There was a man. That first day we were in the gallery. He had a smell about him I couldn't place at first, but it was strawberry tobacco. The kind they use in shisha pipes. The men in Afghanistan smoked it all the time. Add a couple of years and a few pounds. His beard is full now." Charlie looked at the picture. A lot of things could be changed about a person's appearance, but he learned eyes were the hardest feature to disguise. And they could almost always be read. "But those eyes are the same."

"If they're connected, then that would explain how El Chico's product has found its way into the Middle East." Agent Edmonds's cadence picked up. "They're using the art to smuggle the drugs."

Sheriff Huggins crossed his arms. "Is it possible Sydney knew about the drugs in the paintings?"

"Or Miguel?" Frost asked.

Charlie scratched his chin. "We've got pictures that prove Annika is connected to Marco Solis—a known drug dealer who's connected to the Mexican cartel run by El Chico."

"And the man whose sister is dating the guy painting drugs onto the canvases," Frost added.

"Which is where Floyd Hollins comes into play," Agent Edmonds said. "That punk is a lot of things, but a killer ain't one of them."

Charlie explained Marco Solis's questionable presence in Lane's life to Agent Edmonds.

"If Marco's connection is Annika, then why was he here in Walton? How does Lane fit into all of this?"

It was like they had the edges of a puzzle put together but didn't have enough middle pieces to decipher what the picture was—yet. "I think Annika is the connecting piece to this puzzle."

"With these shipping labels, her gallery's connection to the drugs was enough to get us a warrant to search her property. Lynch, you want in on it?"

His ears perked at the invitation. Of course he did. And he could see from Frost's tapping foot that he did too. "Yes, count two of us in."

Frost looked up, eyes round. "Me," he whispered, pointing to himself.

Charlie nodded.

"I'll give you a call as soon as I have details."

The call ended and Charlie ran both hands through his hair. This felt familiar. Painful weeks of routine waiting for intel to secure enough information on the enemy when—*bam!*—all at once data would come pouring in and the mission was a go.

"Charlie, it's time." Sheriff Huggins tapped Charlie's shoulder. "Judge Sullivan is ready with the warrant."

TWENTY-FIVE

CARS, TRUCKS, AND MEDIA VANS lined both sides of the street in front of the courthouse. The news of a possible suspect had drawn the attention of reporters and journalists from as far north as New York and all the way south to Miami. Camera operators jostled with one another for the best shot as their counterparts rehearsed their headline-grabbing hooks.

"He's a baby killer."

"Now her family can rest in peace."

"Hides in the woods."

Lane hurried up the steps of the courthouse, anxious to escape the scathing comments circling about Miguel, and pushed past the crowd hanging around the front door. Rumors were already starting and Miguel hadn't even been named as a suspect—at least not officially. What did they find at his house that would make them believe he killed Sydney? She didn't want to think about it. Whatever it was—there had to be an explanation.

The hallways of the courthouse were filled with people. Mondays were always busy arraignment days, but Lane guessed most of the people occupying floor space among the marble pillars were there because of Miguel. Lane paused outside her father's office. What was she going to say?

"Lane, what are you doing here?"

His voice had a way of turning her insides into mush, and today was no exception. Lane turned to face Charlie. Blue eyes crinkled with concern even though his lips held the hint of a smile like he was glad to see her.

"Finding out the truth." She hated the way seeing him made her heart race. How could she let herself fall for him so quickly? Believe there was a chance?

"The truth?"

"Yes." She licked her lips, avoiding the tender look in his eyes. "I want to make sure you aren't going after Miguel because of any medical conditions he might have."

He took a tentative step toward her. "Do you really believe we're going after him because of that?"

"I don't know." Lane's purpose began to waver in the wake of Charlie's gentle expression. "Why are you going after him then?"

"It's an active case." Charlie looked sorry. "I can't discuss details."

"Somebody's discussing something because there's a crowd outside that thinks Miguel's responsible for Sydney's murder," Lane said, her voice pitching defensively.

A few faces turned their way. A woman Lane recognized as an attorney's secretary stepped into the hallway and flashed a tight smile at her and Charlie. This conversation wasn't one Lane wanted to have in the middle of the courthouse. Charlie followed her into the corner of the hallway tucked behind one of the pillars. Her hand brushed against his, sending a longing to be wrapped in his arms again rolling through her body. She pushed away the desire.

Lane lowered her voice. "Please tell me you're not like them." Lane hitched her thumb in the direction of the courthouse's front doors. "Miguel has PTSD and lives in the woods and keeps to himself, but he is not what they're calling him. You have to believe me."

Charlie drew in close and looked like he wanted to pull her into his arms, but then he stopped. Pushing his fingers through his hair, his expression pained, he finally said, "People with PTSD have been known to act out in unexpected ways."

"He's never hurt anyone before."

"Maybe not, but people come home from war not right in the head—accident or not, they can be dangerous. I saw him the night when he hit you. I've seen too many buddies take the path of least resistance and try to numb their pain. It's never ended well."

Charlie's voice was soft, as though he was speaking from experience. His friend, Tate. The one he couldn't save. Her chest tightened. Charlie did understand—better than most—and yet it wasn't enough.

"Do you know that for as long as Miguel's come into my café, I've never even smelled a whiff of alcohol on him? Harley's known Miguel since they fought in the war and even he can't believe what you're doing—"

"The evidence is there, Lane." Charlie's jaw flexed. "I know he's your friend and you want to help, but it's my job to follow the evidence." Charlie closed the space between them by half. His fingers grazed hers. "Let me help Miguel by finding the truth. That's the only way we can help him."

"But have you heard what they're saying about him out there?" She lowered her voice. "Even if you prove Miguel's innocence, do you think the whole town will just forget he was once suspected of killing someone? It'll haunt him the rest of his life, and I don't know if he'll recover."

Suddenly, her father's insistence about keeping what happened two years ago quiet made perfect sense. If people found out what she did—the circumstances behind Mathias's death—her reputation would never recover. People would never let her forget. There'd be whispers. Questions. Assumptions.

This time Charlie took her hand in his, lacing their fingers together, and drew her close to him. "Then we'll make them see beyond their discrimination. We'll show them the beauty in his sculptures and art. And if after all of that"—he squeezed her hand—"they still don't see what you see, then it's their loss. Not his."

Whatever reasons Lane had built up to push Charlie away began to crumble. His confident voice of reason spoke louder than the whispers of doubt circling her mind. But what if Miguel wasn't innocent? What if he was capable of hurting someone . . . like she was? Lane pulled her hand away and took a step back. "It's more than that, Charlie. Miguel and I are the same."

"What do you mean?"

"The night my husband died. I—" She bit her lip. Was she really going to do this? Her stomach tightened with fear at what he would think of her when he knew the truth about what she had done. She licked her lips and started again. "I tried to kill myself. Swallowed a bottle of pills. But then Noah started to cry and I got scared. Mathias was on night duty. I called him and he was rushing home, but the roads were wet. His truck slid into an embankment and hit a tree.

"An ambulance and two state troopers showed up at my door, but it wasn't until I was in the hospital that they told me . . ." She swallowed against the painful lump in her throat, unsure if she could go on. The truth hurt just as much now as it did that night, but Charlie had to know the truth, so she pushed the words out as fast as she could. "Charlie, Mathias died because of me. I would've died that night, but Mathias had already called the ambulance on the way to the house and now I'm here and he's dead. It should've been me who died, but it was him. And I killed him."

Someone behind them let out a gasp. Lane looked over Charlie's shoulder and found a handful of people standing there, watching. Listening. Lane's heart plummeted at the sight of her father. His campaign advisor, Jeffrey Adams, stood next to him—his mouth agape.

A woman wearing a lot of makeup smirked, shaking her head at a man in a suit to her right. Lane didn't know who he was, but she thought she recognized the woman.

"So, this is how the justice system works?" The woman narrowed her eyes. "I should've known this small town was corrupt. Let me guess, as long as you're the judge's daughter or dating a deputy, you can kill someone and no one says anything. But if an innocent girl plays a joke on her friend, the whole town decides she's a monster."

"Ms. Carson, no matter what you think you heard, you don't

know what you're talking about." Charlie kept his voice low, but it held authority.

Lane's heart would've swelled with affection at Charlie's defense if it weren't pounding in fear. What had she done? She wanted to take it back. But it was too late.

"Don't pretend you didn't just hear her. She said she killed her husband," Ms. Carson rallied. "And yet Jolene can't even walk into school without someone whispering vile things about a silly little prank."

The woman's voice carried down the marbled corridor of the courthouse, drawing the attention of everyone nearby, including that of a very pretty woman hanging near the wall, her eyes fixed on the entire scene with insatiable interest. The reporter. Vivian DeMarco.

A loud commotion grabbed everyone's attention.

"Where's the sheriff?" a male voice boomed from across the hall. "I want to see the sheriff!"

Angry voices became amplified, causing the muscles in Charlie's face to become tense. He moved around Lane, his hand held steady on the gun at his hip. "Stay here."

The crowd parted and Lane's heart jumped into her throat. Sydney's father, face red and sweaty, stopped when he saw Charlie. Five more men stood behind him with something close to rage radiating from their faces. Near the back, Deputy Wilson, nostrils flaring, looked like a bull ready to charge.

"Sheriff Huggins isn't here," Charlie said calmly. "How can I help you gentlemen?"

"Where is the monster who killed my baby girl? I want to see him now!"

"Mr. Donovan, we're doing everything we can to find out who killed Sydney."

"You already know who killed her." Spittle flew from the enraged man's lips. "I want to know why you haven't found him yet. Brought him in."

Lane became nervous at the sight of the guns holstered on the sides of the men with Mr. Donovan. Probably why they had the attention of everyone in the room—including her father's, who moved in behind Charlie.

"Gentlemen, I know the great state of Georgia allows you to carry those firearms, but in my courthouse, they are not permitted. I'm going to have to ask you to leave—"

"I ain't leavin' till I get answers!" Mr. Donovan screamed, making people jump.

"I'd be happy to answer your questions, but this isn't the way it's going to happen." With slow, steady steps, Charlie moved forward. Lane held her breath. What would a hurting father do to bring his murdered daughter justice? "Judge Sullivan is right. Those guns don't belong in here, and you've got me and my fellow deputy feeling a little nervous. Let's do this the right way so justice can be served."

"Justice?" Mr. Donovan reared his head back and laughed. "My daughter didn't get any justice."

A man with a lip full of chewing tobacco stepped forward. "We can offer our own brand of justice."

"That's not something you want to do." Charlie set his jaw. "Any threat against another person is taken seriously. It's not a path you want to go down."

"But you got a name," a heavyset man said from behind Mr. Donovan. "That guy who lives in the woods out there on Coastal."

"They're sayin' you found something of hers in his house," Mr. Donovan said. "I want to know what and why."

"We can't discuss the details of the investigation, but we're getting closer to finding out who killed your daughter. Right now you and your friends are keeping us from doing our jobs."

Mr. Donovan scowled before taking a step back. "He's gonna pay for what he's done to my baby. I don't care if I go to jail. You better find him, Deputy."

Lane cringed at the implied threat left behind as the men left.

An old-fashioned lynch mob had formed with Sydney Donovan's father at the helm? *This* Mr. Donovan wasn't the same man who had stood next to his wife at the church's benefit for their daughter, docile but grief-stricken. This was a father who wanted to inflict his suffering on the one who caused it. And it was frightening as much as it was shocking to witness the man's transformation. Is that what Charlie meant earlier? People can do unexplainable things when they are suffering?

"Well, I tell you what"—her father's campaign manager used a handkerchief to wipe the sweat from his forehead—"the installation of metal detectors in every courthouse will be the first thing on your father's agenda."

"That ain't your only problem." Ms. Carson sneered. "Don't think that little fiasco erased my memory. I know what I heard—there are two killers living in this small town."

"Alright." Mr. Adams spread his hands out. "I think Judge Sullivan and his daughter need some privacy. Ms. Carson, I know your attorney charges by the minute, so I suggest you go on into his office, take care of whatever business you have, and make him earn his paycheck."

Ms. Carson looked ready to argue, but her lawyer took hold of her elbow and led her away.

Charlie returned to Lane's side. "Are you okay?"

"They're going to hunt him down," she said, her voice wavering. "They won't understand his condition. If they find him—"

"Lane, my office," her father said.

Charlie locked eyes with her and gave her a nod before she followed her father into the office, with Mr. Adams and Charlie following behind.

"Now, I have a signed warrant for Miguel Roa that explains why Deputy Lynch is here, but I want to know why you're here."

Lane's composure slipped under her father's penetrating stare, but having Charlie in the room made her feel less alone. "For Miguel."

The vein in her father's neck pulsed. "Why?"

"Did you not just see what happened out there?" She tried hard to keep the tremor shaking her hands from spreading throughout her body. "Those men are out there hunting him like an animal all because they think he did something he hasn't even been charged with. As a judge, you should be interested in making sure his rights are protected."

"His rights?" Her father's posture straightened, bringing him to his full height so she had to look up to him. "What about the rights of that young girl?"

"I'm not saying he's innocent," she said. "But doesn't he deserve not to be judged simply because his mind isn't like everyone else's? Or will he be forced to live a lie and take the fall for a crime he didn't commit so you can win your election?"

"Lane." A shade of red painted her father's face. He pressed his lips together. "You have no idea what you're doing or what you've done."

"Don't I? You think a second doesn't go by when I don't think about what I've done?"

"Well, this is great. Senate hopeful's daughter advocates for suspected murderer." Mr. Adams removed his glasses and slumped down into the couch, rubbing the bridge of his nose. "The press is going to eat this up."

"They can't access her medical files and Mathias's death was an accident," her father said, wiping a palm over his forehead.

Lane clenched her teeth. They were talking about her like she wasn't even standing there. "It's good they know the truth. I'm so sick of the lies. My whole life I've been pretending like I'm everyone else's version of normal. But how's anyone supposed to get help if they can't be honest about what they're facing?"

"You don't have to do this, Lane." A pained expression stretched across Charlie's face.

"No, I do." She looked at the disbelief in her father's face and felt her heart breaking. No matter what he believed, she knew that hiding in the shadows of lies to avoid the truth was hurting her more than the speculation of others. Fear of being defined by her depression and anxiety kept her from getting the help she needed. "I struggle every day, wondering if life's worth living. If I have a reason to keep breathing. Or if that night it should've been me. If everyone would've been better off if it had been me."

Lane couldn't be sure, but she thought her father flinched. The hard look in his eyes softened. He started to open his mouth to say something, but a knock at the door stopped him.

Sheriff Huggins stepped inside. "Everyone okay in here?"

"We're fine, Sheriff." Lane's father loosened the knot of his tie and picked up a piece of paper from his desk. "I was just about to give Deputy Lynch the arrest warrant."

"Thank you, Judge." Sheriff Huggins locked eyes with Lane before his attention went to Charlie. "Agent Edmonds is waiting for you."

Charlie acknowledged the sheriff before turning to Lane. His hand caressed her cheek. "We will get to the truth. Trust me, Lane."

TWENTY-SIX

ADRENALINE PULSED through Charlie's veins, forcing his mind to focus on the mission in front of him and not on the way he left Lane at the courthouse. He couldn't stop thinking about what she had said to her father about wondering if everyone would be better off without her—so desperate to break free of her illness that she swallowed a bottle of pills—and lost her husband. Charlie's heart ached for the guilt she bore on her shoulders.

"Hey, are we, like, supposed to wear masks too?"

Frost's question hauled Charlie's mind back to the present. He and Frost stood outside the circle of DEA agents with black knit caps pulled over their faces in the loading dock of an abandoned warehouse three blocks from the Bohemian Signature Gallery. Agent Edmonds was briefing them on their mission to infiltrate Annika's gallery in search for answers.

"Just them." Sweat gathered at his brow. Charlie's gut told him that uncovering the drug-smuggling ring would provide the answers to help them solve Sydney's murder. And to figure out Miguel's role. Charlie had already begun forming theories and the end result to all of them had Sydney as an innocent girl caught in something bigger than even he could imagine.

"This is my first sting operation," Frost whispered. "It's kinda cool."

"Listen and do whatever they tell you." The flak vest added bulk to Frost's small frame but didn't impair his nervous energy. "You'll do fine."

Agent Edmonds broke free of the group. "You ready?"

"Heck yeah." Frost slapped his vest.

"Good." Edmonds cast an amused look at Charlie. "We have

two unmarked vans. Both of you will be riding with me. We'll be breaching the front entrance. My boys will secure the rear."

"What about civilians—or, uh, customers? Pedestrians on the street?" Charlie asked. Summer was here and so were the tourists. He needed to assess such risks on every mission.

"Metro Police will be patrolling the blocks on either side of the gallery as well as the nearby parks. They'll be there to assist if necessary."

"I want first opportunity to question her." In the short time since Edmonds's call and his arrival in Savannah, they hadn't established who would get to question Annika first. Charlie wanted to make sure the steely DEA agent understood they both had vested stakes in the mission.

Edmonds took his time adjusting the Velcro straps on his vest—or was he using his silence to make a point? Finally, he said, "Your tip about Nawabi put me on the fast track for a promotion. You know what that means?"

"First in line for a desk job?"

"Got that right." Edmonds grunted. "I'm not a fan of sitting behind a desk . . . but my fiancée is. Got it in her mind that what we do can be dangerous."

"Reasonable concern."

"Yeah, well, I like making her happy, so I guess that gives you first rights to Annika." Edmonds dug in his pocket and pulled out two earpieces. His gaze held steady on Frost's edgy movements. "Here, you'll both need these. You'll hear a lot of voices, but the only one you need to listen to is mine."

The directive was aimed at Frost. There was nothing more unnerving than a jittery team member, whether the mission took place on a dusty road in an Afghani valley or on the suburban streets of Savannah. No one wanted an accident.

Charlie put in the earpiece and Frost did the same. Right away chatter filled his ear. A disgruntled voice argued with another.

"You ready to arrest the wicked witch of Savannah?" Frost smirked.

"I'm ready for some answers." Although Charlie wouldn't mind seeing a pair of silver handcuffs melt the icy glare off Annika's face.

"Load up. We roll in five." Agent Edmonds's voice spoke into their ears.

"You think Miguel Roa's the killer?" Frost asked as he climbed in one of the vans after Charlie.

"I believe Annika is the link that will connect all the pieces."

"You hear what they're saying about him?"

Charlie gave a tight nod. If Miguel was involved in Sydney's death, he'd never get a fair trial in Walton. Lane was right. The truth about Miguel's condition had colored him as crazy and capable of murder without anyone batting an eyelash that maybe there was more to the story. Maybe Lane and Miguel really were similar. Two people forced to suffer alone because people didn't understand them. They suffered in silence until it became unbearable. Like his friend Tate.

"I think it's pretty cool of Lane to stand up for him." Frost ran his hands down his pant legs. "There's an old bridge near Coastal Highway that crosses a narrow part of the Ogeechee River. They call it the jumping bridge because people go there to, you know, end it. Rode my bike there one day after school when the teasing was really bad."

Charlie's throat grew dry. He knew exactly what bridge Frost was talking about.

Frost tugged down on his vest. "I was ready to jump, but you know what stopped me?"

"What?"

"A girl on the trail below along the river waved at me. Smiled too." Frost blushed. "I guess it was enough that someone noticed me. Made me think maybe I'd be missed if I was gone. So, I turned around and went home."

Charlie swallowed as the memory of finding Lane on that same bridge pushed to the front of his mind. What would she have done if he hadn't shown up? He still didn't know if she had been planning to jump that day, but he couldn't imagine a single day without her in his life. She had to know—had to believe—that she'd be missed. And he was willing to do whatever it took to convince her.

The van brakes squeaked to a stop and a second later Edmonds slid the door open. "Let's move."

Frost pushed his glasses up his nose with a shaky hand.

"Stick by my side and you'll be fine." Charlie patted Frost's shoulder and slid the van door open. His phone vibrated. He didn't recognize the number and let it go to voice mail.

"Nice and easy." Edmonds's voice came through the ear mic. "Alpha team on approach."

Charlie and Frost fell into place behind Edmonds. Two other agents closed the ranks. The group was gathering curious looks from people on the streets, but a Metro cop was encouraging them to move along.

The inside of the gallery was dark. It was barely past six. The hours posted on the door said the gallery should be open for another two hours.

"Alpha team: we've got locked doors. What's your status, Bravo?"

"Why would the gallery door be locked?" Frost's whisper was strained.

An internal alarm rang inside Charlie's head. On the battlefield, when there was a variance in routine it was usually an indication that something was wrong. He flexed his hands a couple of times to release the adrenaline pounding in his ears.

"Bravo team: back door's been breached. Entering premises now. Stand by." Beams of light flashed through the gallery. "Lower level clear. Bravo team approaching front entrance."

An agent with a dark bandanna covering the lower half of his face opened the front door of the gallery. "My guys are heading upstairs."

Charlie's unease was confirmed when they entered the building. Paintings had been stripped from the walls. Frames were broken. Canvases were slashed. The computer at the front desk was smashed on the floor.

"What happened?" Frost looked around.

"Someone got here before us." Glass broke under Charlie's feet.

"Bravo team: building cleared and secured."

Someone found the light switch and illuminated the ransacked gallery in fluorescent lighting. Charlie followed Edmonds upstairs to an apartment. It was decorated in modern furnishings in shades of gray as cold as the woman who lived there. A single bedroom was off to the side. The drawers were opened, clothes scattered on the floor.

Charlie exhaled. "She's gone."

"Somebody was looking for something."

Edmonds led them back downstairs. Two DEA agents were collecting paintings while another had set up a table in the corner and was swabbing their edges.

"These paintings are, for lack of a better word, crap."

A petite redhead walked toward them. Frost nudged Charlie. He didn't recall seeing her at the briefing and he would've remembered, not because of her fire-engine red hair, but because she was the only one in a sea of DEA agents wearing a blue jacket with big yellow letters on it.

"Deputy Lynch, Deputy Frost, this is Agent Murphy. An art expert on loan to us courtesy of the FBI." Edmonds introduced them. "See, we can play nice with the fibbies."

Murphy rolled her eyes. "Most of that he got right, but no one said anything about playing nice."

Frost snickered and drew an amused look from the female agent, which colored his cheeks almost as red as her hair. Edmonds's cell phone rang and he excused himself.

Charlie gave Frost a pointed look before returning his attention back to the agent. "What were you saying about the art?"

"These paintings are amateurish at best. Most of the names I don't recognize. I'd say, based on my initial inspection of what's still intact"—Murphy looked around—"less than fifty grand worth of art and I'm being generous."

"Fifty thousand?" Charlie toed a piece of glass. "Sydney's single painting was listed at twelve hundred dollars."

"Some galleries overprice the art to make a profit, but usually it's on actual art." Murphy lifted a torn piece of canvas. "This is just above student level."

"Sydney's art fits right in then." Frost tried folding his arms across his bulky vest but after a few awkward seconds settled for sticking his hands in his pockets.

Charlie scratched at the stubble on his chin. "You don't recognize any of the names on these paintings?"

"Only a few," Murphy said. "Not enough to warrant this gallery's reputation."

"That first day we came by, two students from the art school were filling out applications to have their art displayed here. Said it was the first time the gallery's been open to students' work. What if Annika was exploiting unknown artists? You're the expert, but if you don't recognize the artists, then it's possible regular customers wouldn't either."

"Her computer might've been smashed, but it seems your gallery owner kept written records of her clients." Edmonds walked over. He held up a notebook. "Found this hidden behind a canvas propped up against a wall safe. Recognize any names?"

Charlie scanned the rows of names and landed on one. "Floyd Hollins."

"That book gives us the names of people she paid and used to ship her paintings." Edmonds lifted his eyebrows. "We've even got a couple of dealers listed on there."

"If Annika's involved in the drug smuggling, why would they do this to her gallery?" Frost asked. "Or kill Marco Solis? Wasn't he the kingpin's cousin or something?"

"Only by marriage, and maybe El Chico found out they had double-crossed him." Edmonds tapped the notebook. "Some of these names belong to members of a rival organization."

"Maybe it was a warning." Murphy looked around. "And they came back."

"You think that's why they killed Sydney?" Frost's glance moved between them. "She found out about the drugs and was going to rat on them?"

"You might be on to something." Edmonds raised his eyebrows. "If Annika and Miguel are connected, maybe she paid him to kill the girl."

That theory didn't make sense. Or maybe he was being blinded by his desire to prove Lane right. Prove Miguel wasn't the killer. "Jolene and Annabeth left Sydney at the gas station, but her body was discovered more than a mile away. Why would a teenage girl, alone and in the middle of the night, walk into the woods?"

"She wouldn't," Murphy said.

"Unless she knew where she was going." Frost's bounce returned. "Miguel's house was a few miles away, right? And remember the video—the one with Sydney leaving the studio the day before she was killed? She was carrying something."

"A painting." Charlie furrowed his brow. "What if Sydney was walking to Miguel's house? For help?"

"Maybe she gave him the painting?" Frost added.

"So, they know each other?" Edmonds shrugged. "He's your suspect."

"Maybe not. You said El Chico's cartel is responsible for the biggest drug distribution in Atlanta. Abas Nawabi's presence in Savannah proves El Chico's reach is crossing borders. I think it's safe to assume he'd probably do anything to keep that part of his business, well, in business."

"You think they're cleaning up?" Edmonds's forehead creased. "Came after Annika?"

Murphy spread her hands out at the mess around them. "If they are, it could mean they'll be going after Miguel next."

Charlie clenched his fist. "Or they've already found him."

~~~~~~~~~~~

Lane's hands shook. She looked at the bottle of pills and allowed herself to go back to that night. She knew growing up that she was different, and it wasn't just awkward adolescence. Her mood shifted so frequently that she was often punished for her insubordination, particularly when it happened in public. Lane's parents just didn't understand—and they never asked her about it.

In health class, Lane learned about depression and anxiety and all it took was a quick search on the computer for her to know she probably had both. She tried to talk to her school counselor, but the overworked woman handed Lane a couple brochures on the topic and gave her the number to a suicide hotline. What Lane needed was someone to listen. To hear her out and explain that she wasn't the same as those people on the news who went on killing sprees. She wasn't a killer . . . and yet it was because of her that Mathias was dead.

Lane dropped onto the sofa at the Way Station Café, thankful she'd thought to close it. After hearing what people were saying about Miguel—and now what they had heard about her—she didn't need the spectacle inside her home. It was bad enough to imagine what that reporter or Ms. Carson were going to say. This would affect her father's election. Mr. Adams made sure Lane was aware of that, but what about her father? He hadn't even mentioned the election after her little emotional blowup. *Give it time*, she thought.

A noise startled Lane. Had she forgotten to lock the door? "I'm sorry, we're closed—"

Ms. Byrdie stood there jingling her set of keys in the air. She set them on the counter and came to the couch. "Huggy called me."

Ms. Byrdie's concern was enough to cause the tears Lane had

been shoving down inside to burst forth like a geyser. Ms. Byrdie dropped next to Lane, wrapped her arms around her, and allowed her to cry.

Lane didn't know how many minutes passed, but when she pulled back she noticed that tears were streaming down Ms. Byrdie's face too.

"Are-are you okay?" Lane hiccupped.

Ms. Byrdie took Lane's face in her hands so that she was looking directly into Lane's eyes—into her soul. "Lane Kent, I love you. I do. I love you. There's nothing you have done or will ever do to make me stop loving you. From the moment you stepped into my library, the good Lord pressed a love for you so deeply on my heart that I couldn't ignore it. I love you. I love you."

Lane felt the wall of fear she'd built within her begin to crack. Those words were so simple, people tossed them around every day, but the power they held when said the way Ms. Byrdie was saying them . . . it ripped at the seams of doubt Lane had sewn so tightly around her heart.

Unlovable. That's what she felt like growing up with these thoughts. An unlovable mistake.

"I messed up." Lane took in a shaky breath. "I told Charlie about Mathias. I blurted it all out right there in the middle of the courthouse for everyone to hear." She cringed. "Including that reporter."

"Vivian?" Ms. Byrdie shook her head. "Honey, that young thing is in search of a story because she's desperate to forget her own. Don't you worry about her. Now, what did Charlie say?"

She had no reason to hide anything from Ms. Byrdie, but they weren't two girlfriends chatting about a crush. Charlie was her nephew. And this was more than just a crush. Her heart had begun to long for him in a way that Lane couldn't ignore any more than she could ignore her depression.

"He told me it wasn't my fault. That it was an accident."

"And you don't believe him."

Lane's breath caught in her chest. "It's my fault. If I hadn't called him—" She choked on the words. "He died because of me."

Ms. Byrdie wrapped her hand around Lane's and squeezed. "What happened to Mathias that night was an accident. Plain and simple. That boy loved you to the ends of the earth. Whatever God's reason was for taking him home that night does not rest on your shoulders."

A tear slipped down Lane's cheek. "What if God made a mistake by allowing me to live instead of Mathias?"

"Honey, God never makes mistakes. You are here on purpose, Lane. With purpose." Ms. Byrdie rose. "Come with me." She led Lane to the hallway where a large mirror hung on the wall. "Tell me what you see."

"I don't know. *Me?*"

"Come on, look harder. Tell me what you see."

Looking at her reflection, she didn't have to try harder. Her hair hung limply over her shoulders. The dark circles under her eyes had darkened, making her fair complexion appear washed out.

"I see someone who needs a haircut but doubts it'll make a difference. And it wouldn't hurt for me to spend a few hours in the sun or maybe get some sleep, but those seem to evade me as well." Exasperation edged her tone and she lacked the courage to look Ms. Byrdie in the eye.

"Here's what I see." Ms. Byrdie brushed a piece of Lane's hair from her forehead. "A woman who has faced tremendous obstacles and tragedy and still finds a way to persevere. Who, in the midst of too many sleepless nights, spends hours putting together ingredients so she can offer some home-baked love and kindness to those others overlook. Someone who looks past the flaws in others and sees their beauty and potential, even when she misses it in herself."

Tears stung Lane's eyes. She dropped her gaze at Ms. Byrdie's words. "I wish I could see those things, but all I see is a broken mess."

"Lane Kent, you listen to me. If all *you* see when you look in the mirror are your flaws, then you'll believe that's all anyone else will see. You are not broken. You are perfectly made. You have to stop punishing yourself for the way God made you—even for your depression. You need to forgive yourself and take captive those thoughts that you are anything but the woman our Creator designed you to be." Ms. Byrdie's soft words reached deep into her soul. "God used Mathias to save you that night for a purpose—his purpose—now fight for the life you deserve."

"But I don't deserve it."

"If that's true for you, then it's true for all of us." Ms. Byrdie brushed the tears from Lane's cheeks. "*He makes all things new.* Every morning you wake up is a day you can live in the freedom of knowing God has plans for you."

"And you believe those plans include Charlie?"

"Huggy and I aren't the only ones who see the beautiful, courageous woman you are. Charlie sees it too. He cares a great deal for you, and I think he imagines a future with you and Noah in it."

That light—the one Lane saw in the faces of the customers Ms. Byrdie spoke to—Lane thought she saw a glimmer of it in her own.

TWENTY-SEVEN

LANE'S KNUCKLES TURNED WHITE as she gripped the steering wheel. Ms. Byrdie's words had breathed new life into her, and the idea that God hadn't made a mistake . . . well, if that was true for Lane, then it had to be true for Miguel too.

Charlie's warning to stay away from Miguel lingered in the back of her mind, but she couldn't ignore the danger Miguel might be in if Sydney's father, or someone else bent on vigilante justice, found him before the deputies did. Lane's gut told her they were wrong about Miguel. He was hurting. Like her. And people like *them* didn't hurt others—they hurt themselves.

Lane pressed the accelerator and her Jeep sped closer to her destination—the jumping bridge. The place where not too long ago Lane allowed dark thoughts to overtake her, causing her to see suicide as an escape. Ms. Byrdie was right—Lane needed to take captive those thoughts. Focus on reasons to live and choose life. Fight for it.

The Coastal Highway stretched before her and Lane wondered if Miguel was in the dense woodland lining the Ogeechee River. Or would he be on the bridge? Would the deputies know to look there for him—a man on the brink of giving up on life?

POP!

Lane didn't have time to react to the noise or where it came from before her world rolled in front of her eyes. The sound of shattering glass and screeching metal filled her ears, muffled only slightly by her own screams until it all stopped and everything went black.

———

The crunch of dry leaves and twigs reverberated in her throbbing head. Lane fought to remember where she was . . . what happened?

299

She'd been driving on Coastal Highway. An explosion—had it been her tire? More crunching.

Lane licked her lips and tasted blood. Her blood. She squeezed her fingers and toes to assess the damage. Sore spots screamed their protest, but she didn't think anything was broken. Taking a deep breath, Lane opened her eyes.

Carefully, Lane rolled to her back. She blinked several times trying to get her eyes to focus on the deep violet hues of the sky. The sun was setting and soon it would be too dark to see. She forced herself into a sitting position and regretted it instantly. Nausea accompanied the killer headache that felt like nails were being driven into the back of her skull. Where was she? The smell of wet earth answered her. She was in the woods.

And she wasn't alone.

"Why are you here?"

Miguel stared at her from the trunk of a fallen tree. "Miguel?" Her heart thumped at his messy appearance. He wore a T-shirt and jeans covered in dirt. His hair was matted with sweat. "What happened? Where are we?"

Miguel looked around. "Your little boy wasn't in the car."

"No. H-he"—Lane pushed herself off the ground and felt the world tilt around her—"he's with my sister."

"You have a cut. On your head." Miguel fidgeted with a tool in his hand. "You shouldn't be here."

Lane looked around at her surroundings. They were definitely in the woods. "Miguel, how did I get here?"

"I pulled you out." An owl hooted and Miguel's eyes flashed in its direction. "But you need to go."

"Miguel, I came out here to find you. Sheriff Huggins wants to ask you some questions."

"I didn't do it. I didn't kill Sydney." He lowered his head. "I taught her how to paint."

Lane watched Miguel shift the tool back and forth in his hands. Her stomach knotted when she recognized it. Noah had picked up one like it in Miguel's workshop—but they were nowhere near his workshop. At least she didn't think so. Nothing around her looked familiar.

"You need to tell the sheriff that."

"No." Agitation rose in Miguel's gruff voice.

"Okay." Lane held up her hand. "Did you see her that night?"

"She was scared. I should've protected her."

"From who?" Lane's hands grew clammy. Asking the question scared her almost as much as finding out the answers. "Do you know what happened to Sydney?"

"She died. Just like the rest of them."

Lane swallowed. "What do you mean 'the rest of them'?"

"Sydney didn't want to paint anymore. She was scared." His grip tightened over the tool in his hand. "I didn't protect her."

"Miguel, do you know what happened to Sydney?"

"It was—" His eyes grew round. He slipped his hands along with the tool into his pockets. "You need to leave. Now."

Lane shifted, grimacing. Miguel looked rough and fidgety. She had to convince him to come with her, but unless he came willingly, her body was in no condition to force him. Would he trust her? "Okay, but I need your help. I don't think I can make it by myself. We'll go see the sheriff and you can tell him—"

A dark silhouette appeared out of the shadows, making the hairs on the back of Lane's neck rise. Annika's sudden presence chilled the summer heat and drained the color from Miguel's face. "You know, you really should listen when people try to warn you about something."

Lane scooted back. "What are you doing here?"

Annika's eyes narrowed as she looked down at her. "I guess I could ask you the same thing. Unless what they're saying is true. Did you kill your husband?"

Heat climbed its way up Lane's neck. "No."

Annika crossed in front of them. She paused next to Miguel, who shifted from side to side and rubbed his arm. "I knew I'd find him out here, but I didn't think I'd find you too." Her gaze snapped to Lane. "Walton's two killers hiding here in the woods—"

"That's not true. You have no idea what you're talking about."

"Oh, but I do, my dear. I mean, your situation is slightly different since you didn't actually drive your husband's truck off the road and into the tree, but he'd still be here if you hadn't swallowed a bottle of pills and called him." Annika's accusation swam around Lane's head, making her dizzy. "And now, here you are hiding out with the man who killed Sydney."

"What is she talking about, Miguel?"

Miguel swayed.

"Don't tell me that handsome deputy boyfriend of yours didn't tell you? They found Sydney's phone in Miguel's house."

Lane's heart stopped. That was the evidence Charlie had been talking about. The evidence that made Miguel a suspect. She was wrong. Lane looked at Miguel. How could she have been wrong? "Miguel?" Lane's voice cracked. "Did you—"

"No. I didn't kill her." Miguel shook his head and then clarity reached his eyes as he focused on Annika. "It . . . it was you. You did it. She was scared of you. She didn't want to paint anymore, but you . . . you killed her."

Annika's cackle echoed. "You think they're going to believe you? An alcoholic veteran with mental health issues? It was only a matter of time before you snapped. Besides, Sydney's phone wasn't the only thing they found. The tool used to kill Sydney was found at your house too."

The tool? Like the one in Miguel's pocket? But how did Annika know? Unless . . . "He's telling the truth. It was you."

Annika clapped her hands together mockingly. "At least I know your mental deficiencies don't make you stupid like him."

Anger bubbled inside of Lane. "He's not stupid. And the sheriff will believe me. I'll tell them the truth."

"Actually, you won't." Annika raised a gun. "I warned you, Miguel, that others would get hurt."

The despondent look on Miguel's face morphed into an angry one as he lunged at Annika, knocking her to the ground. He wrapped his hands around her throat. Lane needed to run. To get help. But her legs felt like rubber and she couldn't leave Miguel.

"Miguel, stop!"

A gunshot pierced the air. Miguel crumpled to the ground.

"Wha—" Lane crawled to Miguel's side. Blood began to spread from a hole in his arm. She turned to Annika. "What did you do?"

Annika pushed herself up from the ground. She kept the gun aimed at Miguel. "Get up. Both of you."

"He's bleeding." Lane pressed her hand to the gunshot wound on his arm. He needed an ambulance.

"He's lucky that's all he's doing and that I didn't kill him right away." Annika plucked a dead leaf from her hair. "Now, get up."

"Why?"

"We're going to take a little trip."

Lane helped Miguel to his feet. His face was pale. "I didn't kill her. Tried to protect her."

"I believe you," Lane said.

"Try something like that again, Miguel, and I'll kill her." Annika jabbed the gun into Lane's temple. "Now, tell me where the painting is."

Miguel's eyelids fluttered open. He looked at Lane and moved his lips, but no sound escaped.

The cold metal of the gun dug into Lane's temple. "Where's the painting?"

Tears slid down Lane's cheeks. "I don't know what you're talking about."

The gun made a noise that sounded like Annika was about to pull the trigger again and Lane's stomach lurched. "The painting your friend Miguel gave to you. I know you have it, so tell me where it is."

"I really don't—" And then it hit Lane. The painting with no name. No label indicating where it had come from. Lane looked at Miguel. He brought her the painting? Why? *Because he trusts you.*

"Five seconds and your little boy will be an orphan."

"N-no! I know where it is. It's at the Benedict House."

Annika snorted. "How poetic."

"You have what you want. Let us go." Miguel slumped against Lane's shoulder. Salty tears blurred her vision. "He needs to go to the hospital."

"In a few minutes, it won't matter."

TWENTY-EIGHT

"YOU THINK THEY KILLED MIGUEL? That's why we can't find him?"

"I don't know." Charlie clenched his jaw, his hand gripping the steering wheel. "But I think it's safe to assume anyone connected with Annika Benedict is in danger."

Charlie's cell phone rang. It was Sheriff Huggins.

"Frost and I were just about to call you with an update."

"Are you still in Savannah?"

"About ten minutes outside."

"Charlie, we can't get ahold of Lane." The sheriff's serious tone sent Charlie's heart plummeting to his stomach. "I sent Byrdie to check on her after what happened at the courthouse and she said Lane seemed good. But Charlie . . . I've answered a suicide call or two and it almost always happened when the family thought the person was good."

"Do you think she'll try—" Charlie couldn't finish the thought. His mind went to the week before Tate ended his life when, just like the sheriff said, everyone believed he'd gotten over the hump and was on his way to recovery. The temporary lucidness in his friend's eyes was just enough for him to plan everything, down to the note he left behind.

Sheriff Huggins exhaled. "I just don't know."

Charlie didn't want to believe what the sheriff was suggesting. Not Lane. Not this time. "Has anyone tried calling her?"

"There's no answer. Her father went to her house and found her phone there."

Charlie's heart wrenched inside his chest. He looked over at Frost—the jumping bridge. "Sir, Frost and I are going to search the area along Coastal Highway. I'll call you if we find anything."

"What's wrong?" Frost asked as soon as Charlie ended the call. "Where are we going?"

"The jumping bridge." Charlie accelerated, unwilling to let his thoughts dwell on the possibility of what Lane might be doing there. He hoped his uncle's fears were wrong. "Nobody can find Lane."

Frost gripped his seat belt with one hand and used the other to grab the overhead handle as Charlie flew down the interstate at speeds that scared other drivers out of his way. The inky black night was illuminated only by the headlights of the patrol car, which turned the draping Spanish moss that Charlie once thought was beautiful into menacing tendrils with every tense minute that passed. He finally slowed when they got to the narrow stretch of road a mile or so away from the bridge.

"What's that?" Frost pointed at something shining a few yards in from the trees that lined the road.

Charlie swung the spotlight in the direction of the trees. The light illuminated the silver bumper of a small SUV. He slammed on the brakes, causing the seat belt to squeeze his chest. It was Lane's Jeep.

"Radio dispatch and tell them we've found Lane's car." Charlie got out of the vehicle and hurried toward the Jeep, afraid of what he was going to find. His steps slowed as he inched toward the driver's side. A breath escaped his lips. It was empty.

"They're on their way." Frost jogged up behind him carrying a first aid kit. "Where is she?"

"I don't know." Charlie looked around. "Maybe someone found her? Took her to the hospital?"

"Or she walked?"

"To the hospital?"

"No." Frost shook his head. "Into the woods."

Charlie's gaze went to where Frost was looking. A set of footprints crossed the tread left behind by the Jeep's tires, indicating that whoever made the impression did so after the Jeep skidded to a stop. The prints led into the woods. "You got your flashlight?"

"Yes, but shouldn't we wait?"

"There's no time." Based on the condition of her Jeep, there was no way Lane had walked away. But if she had, they needed to find her before shock set in and killed her.

With Frost close behind, the two of them started for the woods. The underbrush scraped his pant legs with each hurried stride toward the river and the bridge. Charlie swung the beam of his flashlight back and forth looking for any sign of Lane.

"Ouch!"

Charlie pivoted to his right. Frost was on the ground. "What happened? You alright?"

"Yeah. I tripped on a stump." Frost pushed himself up. "Dropped my glasses—ew. It's wet."

"Stop."

Frost froze. "What?"

With his flashlight trained on Frost's legs, Charlie looked closer. He ran his hand over the wet spot and turned his fingers over. Red. Blood. A chill ran down his spine.

"Is that blood?" Frost's voice sounded weak.

The sound of sirens broke in the distance.

"Lynch?"

"We need to call Search and Rescue." Charlie swallowed against the dryness in his throat. "Water rescue too."

"Lynch."

The sky shrouded them in a blanket of stars as the moon cowered behind a copse of trees. The darkness mocked Charlie. He had to find her. He wouldn't stop until he did. He couldn't let her down. Not like he did Tate.

"Lynch!"

"What?" Charlie spun around to face Frost, who was still on the ground. "What is it?"

Frost stood up and lifted his hand. He held something. "These aren't mine."

Charlie took a step toward him, staring at the glasses. "Those are red."

"Only one person I've ever seen who wears red glasses."

Footsteps and voices echoed behind them.

"Did you find her?" Sheriff Huggins carried a floodlight and lit up the area around them. Deputy Benningfield wasn't far behind him.

"She's not here, but I think she's in trouble," Charlie said.

"What?"

"We found these glasses." Frost handed the glasses over to the sheriff. "We think they're Annika's."

"And there's fresh blood."

"I thought Annika was supposed to be in Savannah?"

"She wasn't there, sir." Charlie briefed the sheriff on what happened in the ransacked gallery, including their conclusion that someone might be after Annika and anyone associated with her.

"We think Miguel's disappearance might have something to do with her too," Frost added.

Charlie squeezed his eyes shut. He had to think. Had to stop looking at the blood on Frost's knee. Whose was it? Lane's? Annika's? Why would they have been together? His eyes shot open. "Miguel didn't kill Sydney."

Sheriff Huggins's forehead creased. "How you figure that?"

"It was Frost's idea, actually. That video of Sydney leaving the gallery with what we believe is a painting. If Annika is connected to the drug smuggling, it's safe to assume she'd want that painting back. What if the reason she was looking for Sydney was because of what she was carrying?"

"Bad enough to kill?"

Charlie nodded at the sheriff. "The gas station where Jolene left Sydney was about a mile away from where her body was recovered, which means Sydney began walking, but not in the direction of town—"

"In the direction of Miguel's home." Sheriff Huggins's eyes rounded. "She knew where she was going."

"Right. If Sydney was afraid of Miguel, chances are she wouldn't go to his house." The adrenaline in Charlie's body surged. "The

ME said the fractures in Sydney's legs were most likely the result of being hit by a car."

"Miguel doesn't own a car," Frost said.

Another thought occurred to Charlie. "The numbers Lane got from the car that ran her and Noah off the road. What do you want to bet they belong to Marco Solis's car?"

"I'm not a betting man, Charlie." Sheriff Huggins reached for his radio. "But I've heard enough to know we need to be looking for Annika."

"Wasn't Annika at the fund-raiser?" Frost asked.

Heat filled Charlie's cheeks. "What's the number for Lane's sister?" Sheriff Huggins gave it to him and after several minutes on the phone with Meagan, Charlie had the information he needed. "I think I know where they are."

"Where?" the sheriff asked.

"Benedict House."

"The veterans' home?"

"Yes," Charlie answered. "Meagan said that Lane gave her a painting this morning that should've been in the auction, but Ian—Meagan's husband—forgot to get it. Meagan dropped the painting off at the Benedict House this afternoon."

"Go." Sheriff Huggins reached for his radio again. "I'll get backup on the way."

Charlie had only one prayer as he and Frost sped down the highway. *God, please let me get there in time.*

***

"Y-you don't have to do this."

Lane cast a sideways glance at the woman holding a gun to her head. The car bumped along the dirt road and Miguel groaned from the back seat. The Benedict House came into view. The empty plantation mansion would soon be the home to recovering veterans, but tonight, with its dark windows and their lives in Annika's hands, it held an ominous threat.

"Park the car around the back."

Lane obeyed, her palms sweaty and her head woozy from her own accident. Fear for her life was the only thing that kept her from giving in to the temptation to black out. "Please, I have a little boy."

"Funny. He wasn't a good enough reason to stop you from trying to kill yourself before."

Lane hated the truth in Annika's words. Right now, she'd give anything to see Noah again.

"Let's go." Annika kept the gun pointed at Lane as she and Miguel climbed from the car. "Around the front."

Lane's body trembled next to Miguel's as they made their way to the front of the house and up the steps to the porch. His blood was thick and stained her hands as she tried to stem the flow.

"He's bleeding too much."

"That's the least of my problems. Or yours." Annika held the gun to her back and shoved them both inside. Only the moonlight shone to guide them into the dark house as Annika slammed the door shut behind them. A second later, illumination from a spotlight mounted on scaffolding filled the house.

The odor of fresh paint filled the newly renovated space. The first floor of the mansion had been remodeled into one large open area separated only by a semi-circle desk that butted against the back side of a large brick fireplace. Coiled electrical wires hung from holes in the ceiling where light fixtures would be installed. In the corner were boxes. Some marked with pictures of the decorative items within. Others plain. Lane saw the painting she gave Meagan sitting behind them.

"Move him here."

Lane helped lean Miguel against the stone hearth of the fireplace. His body slid to the floor. Sweat coated his forehead. There was a rag on the floor. She used her toe to drag it over and wrapped it tightly around his arm, causing him to wince. "Sorry."

"She was just a girl." His fist tightened. "You didn't have to kill her."

"She was a pawn." Annika bent over Miguel and tapped the barrel of the gun against his forehead. "Just like you. And from the lucidity in your eyes, I see you've stopped appreciating my gifts. Those pills weren't cheap, ya know."

"You drugged him?" Lane shot a look at Annika. That explained his erratic behavior. "You won't get away with it. I'll tell them the truth. That he's innocent."

"My dear, do you really think you'll get the chance? And why would you defend this baby killer?" She paused in front of them. "Went to Nam and shot up an entire village of innocent women and children. Didn't you, Miguel? You were a killer then and everyone will believe you're a killer now."

Miguel turned to Lane. His eyes searched her face. "I tried to save them. Protect her." He repeated it again. And again. As though if he said it enough Lane would believe him.

"It's going to be okay, Miguel." There wasn't time to figure out what Annika was talking about or to convince Miguel she believed him. Lane's eyes flicked to the door only a couple yards away. Could she risk making a run for it?

"You're wasting your breath." Annika went to the corner of the room and picked up a loose floorboard. She pulled out a black duffel bag and dropped it at Lane's feet. "Here."

"Wh-what do you want me to do?"

"Help me." Annika's lip curled into a sneer. "Open up the bag and get the crowbar. And just in case you think bravery will win you or your *friend* any chance at escape, please understand that your fates have already been sealed. Death can come in one of two ways. Quick. Or painful."

Lane unzipped the bag and found the crowbar. The thought of using it to smash the gun out of Annika's hand crossed her mind but quickly passed. If she missed, she wasn't going to be faster than the bullet Annika had promised.

"Why are you doing this?"

"Because if I'd done this right the first time, I wouldn't be standing here." Annika shot a scathing look in Miguel's direction. "Take that crowbar and reach it up into the chimney."

"What am I supposed to be doing?"

"Just keep poking around. You'll feel it."

The crowbar hit something. Not hard like stone but something pliable. She pushed a little harder and something dropped, bringing a cloud of ash with it.

"Very good." Annika wrenched the crowbar from Lane's hand and tossed it across the room. "Get back."

Lane stepped back and knelt at Miguel's side. Annika reached into the fireplace and took hold of another black duffel bag. She opened it to reveal stacks of money, along with passports. How? Then it struck Lane that this old mansion had belonged to Annika's father before it was offered up as the new veterans' home. That explained why Annika knew about the loose floorboard, but how long had that money been there?

"And here I thought the renovations had been put on hold because of permit issues," Lane mumbled. "You got what you came for. You should let us go."

"Make a deal with the devil and you never know when you'll have to cash in your chips." Annika smirked. "It would've been nice to secure a little more, but I've got enough for a nice bungalow on the beach. And in less than thirty-six hours, I'll be sipping a fruity beverage with my toes in the sand."

"You're running?"

"Yes. But not before you give me my painting."

Lane forced herself not to look at the painting. It was the only piece of leverage she had to get her and Miguel out of this mess. "When I give it to you, you'll leave. You'll have everything you want. You won't need to hurt us."

"Oh, I wish it were that simple. Now, get up." Annika motioned with the tip of the gun for Lane to move and she rose to her feet. "It's sad you didn't find out the truth about Miguel's instability until it was too late. Only seconds before Miguel killed you."

"What?" The pounding in Lane's ears turned to ringing. "No one will believe he killed me. People know we're friends."

"That'll make it all the more disturbing when they discover that the friend you've been defending snapped and killed you. Just like he did with Sydney. Only this time, in his total despair, he turned the gun on himself. Murder-suicide."

"You won't get away with it," Lane said through gritted teeth. "How are you going to explain the gunshot wound in his arm?"

"Trying to earn my father's respect by attending law school might've been a waste of time, but it enlightened me to the advantage of reasonable doubt. And I'm sure you were wily enough to try and stop him but only succeeded in a single misaimed shot to his arm. Pity, really."

Lane kept her eyes on the gun. She was going to die. This was her last day in this world, and the whole town would believe Miguel killed her and Sydney. The urge to live crashed over her like a wave. She needed to fight the current. *"Fight for it."* Ms. Byrdie's words echoed in her mind.

Lane looked down at Miguel. His head hung limply to one side while blood pooled next to him. His stare vacant. "It'll be okay, Miguel. You tried to protect me. Protect Sydney. The truth will come out." Their eyes met. "I believe you."

Annika clicked her tongue against her teeth. "Well, it's a shame neither of you will live long enough to prove it. You have a minute to tell me where the painting is before I kill you both."

"You are a good man. Don't listen to anything she says. She's the killer. Not you."

"Shut up." Annika's hand connected with Lane's face, sending a shooting pain into her jaw. "You think anything you say matters?"

A coppery taste filled her mouth. "Annika's right about us. You and I, we're the same. We've both been hiding who we are because we're afraid something's wrong with us. That we have no purpose and we don't deserve to live—"

Metal connected with her skull and she crumpled to the

ground. Her face smacked the hardwood floor, blurring her vision. Her head throbbed. She tried pushing herself off the ground, but the room swam around her and forced her back down. She grazed the side of her head with her fingertips until she found the lump. She looked at her hand and it was wet with blood. *Fight. For Noah. For Mathias's sacrifice. For the promise of a future with Charlie.*

"We're not broken, Miguel. We have to fight."

His body stiffened. She was baiting him with the words of truth he needed to hear. Words she needed to hear and believe about herself. They both had a reason to live—they just needed to fight for it.

"Time's up." Annika bent down and pressed the gun against Lane's head.

Miguel lunged from the floor and dove into Annika, sending her crashing against the wall. She screamed as he wrestled her to the ground. The gun slid across the room and Lane dove for it. Annika released another blood-curdling scream and Lane turned to see Miguel straddling her, the wood tool from earlier bloody and pressed against Annika's side.

"Miguel, no!" Lane scrambled for the gun and pointed it at Annika. "Stop. It's over."

With his eyes still focused on Annika, he crawled off her and back to the fireplace. He threw the bloodied tool across the room. "I should've protected her."

Annika rolled over and cursed as she clutched her side. A bloody stain was smeared across her blouse. A creaking noise drew their attention to a dark corner of the old mansion.

A lone figure emerged. When he came into the light, the only thing Lane could do was stare at the jagged scar stretching from the top of his left eyebrow to his eye and then continuing down his cheek. She didn't see the gun in his hand until a psychotic laugh escaped Annika's lips.

"I guess I got here just in time." The man pointed the gun at Lane. "You can give me that, *mi amor*."

Lane wanted to challenge him, but fear loosened her grip on the gun trembling in her hand and the man snatched it from her.

"Just kill them, Benito," Annika snapped. She slowly got to her feet and removed her hand from her waist. The blood was spreading. She moaned. "Kill them."

The gunshot exploded and Miguel slumped to the floor.

"Miguel!" Lane screamed. She rushed to his side. "Miguel!"

"Well, now." Annika walked over to them and winced as she knelt down to look in Lane's eyes. "It appears you're responsible for the deaths of two men who tried to save you. Quite a reputation."

A soft groan slid from Miguel's lips. Lane's throat tightened as tears spilled over her cheeks. "I'm right here, Miguel."

"What are you waiting for?" Annika barked at Benito. "Kill her."

Benito strolled over to the duffel bag with the money and passports inside. "Are you planning a trip?"

Annika's face paled. "Just tying up loose ends."

"I stopped by the gallery today. I was curious why Mr. Nawabi has not yet received his product. Curious why your gallery has piqued the interest of the DEA. Curious to find you here with bags of money asking about a painting that doesn't belong to you."

"The painting was stolen and I was going to use this money to pay for more product. For Mr. Nawabi," Annika spoke quickly. "You have no reason not to trust me, Benito."

"I have every reason not to trust you. Your loose ends have been bad for business."

"Benito—"

Gunshots echoed and Lane screamed. The murderous look in Annika's eyes was replaced with a blank expression as her body dropped.

"It has been my experience that rats caught in the corner tend to bite the hand that feeds them."

Lane choked on a sob. Miguel didn't move. A puddle of Annika's blood stretched across the floor. Lane closed her eyes and brought to mind the images of everyone she loved. If this was going to be her last moment on earth, then she wanted her last thoughts to be filled with all the reasons she had to live. *God, forgive me for waiting so long to find my purpose.*

~~~~~~~~~~~

Charlie's body went rigid at the sound of gunshots. *Oh, God, I'm too late.* "Call in Code 25. Shots fired."

"Wait," Frost whispered. "We need backup."

There was no time to wait. Charlie drew his gun and sprinted toward the Benedict House. The moon slipped behind some clouds and shrouded the landscape in darkness. A dim light shone from the windows.

A twig snapped behind him and Charlie swung his aim around.

"Whoa." Frost held his hands up. "Backup's coming."

"I almost shot you," he hissed. "What're you doing?"

"I came to help." Frost went to push up his glasses when he realized they weren't there. "I have an astigmatism. I can still see without my glasses."

"Watch the house. Make sure no one leaves." They were losing seconds they didn't have. He saw the disappointment in Frost's face, but the decision was made. He wasn't going to lose a man in the field. Especially a man who might not be able to see without his glasses. "I'm going in through the back. Keep an eye on the front. And Frost, keep your head down. Chicks prefer heroes who are alive and can buy them dinner."

"Yes, sir." Frost smiled before he removed his gun from the holster and moved toward the front of the house.

Charlie crept around the back. Thorns tore at his skin as he climbed through a thicket of tall weeds to get to the back door. He drew in a breath and held it as he pressed his ear to the wall. Two voices. A man and woman. Their voices were too muted to tell if the woman talking was Lane.

With his gun in one hand, Charlie tried the door handle and said a prayer of gratitude when it turned. Slowly, he inched it open and saw Lane moving on the floor next to two bodies. He struggled to hold in his emotion. Thank God, she was alive.

Charlie took in a slow breath and looked at the man standing over her, pointing a gun at her head. The man matched the photo Agent Edmonds showed them of Benito Rodriguez or *El Chico*. Lane wasn't out of danger yet.

A loud crash seized Benito's attention and he turned his aim toward the front door. Then he turned back and pulled Lane up by her hair and held the gun to her head. *No.* Charlie's fears were realized when Benito stalked over to the door and Frost stepped into the house. With the gun still pressed into Lane's temple, Charlie couldn't risk the shot. *What was Frost thinking?*

"I didn't think they would send *Mighty Mouse* to the rescue." Benito laughed and cracked Frost across the side of the head with the butt of the gun. Frost dropped to the ground.

"Leave him alone!" Lane cried.

Benito shoved Lane to the ground before he planted a solid kick into Frost's ribs. "Are you here by yourself, Mighty Mouse?"

Another kick landed against Frost's side, pushing a fiery rage into every fiber of Charlie's being.

Frost looked in Charlie's direction and gave a subtle nod before pushing himself upright. He looked up at Benito and smiled. "Anyone ever tell you that you have hands like a girl?"

Two shots rang out before Benito could take aim at Frost's head. The man collapsed forward onto the ground. Charlie kept his gun aimed at Benito until Frost confirmed the man was dead and then he hurried to Lane's side.

"Lane, are you okay?" She grabbed his shirt and buried her face into his chest. "Shh, it's okay. I've got you," he whispered in her ear. "You're safe."

TWENTY-NINE

CHARLIE FORCED himself to breathe. Annika Benedict and Benito Rodriguez were dead. Miguel was in the hospital. And Lane was right where he wanted her. Next to him. In the hours since they had left the Benedict House, they hadn't had a moment alone together to discuss his feelings, or hers. It made him nervous. What if she still didn't believe him? Given the chance, he'd gladly spend the rest of his days proving his love and commitment to her. For as long as it took.

Deputy Benningfield brought in two cups of coffee and a cup of tea as Sheriff Huggins went through another round of questions. Charlie was ready to argue, but Lane refused to go to the hospital for treatment until she had recounted what Annika had said about killing Sydney—proof of Miguel's innocence.

The dark circles under her eyes, bruised face, and bloodied gash were heart-wrenching reminders of the trauma Lane had just been through and how close he'd come to losing her. He could wait a little longer to take her to the hospital.

"The DEA's using Annika's records to track smugglers and dealers across the country and several in the Middle East and Europe." Sheriff Huggins hitched his thumbs into his gun belt. "Agent Edmonds said this bust is going take millions of dollars of drugs off the streets."

"Sydney's death wasn't for nothing." Lane's voice trembled. "What about Miguel? Will he be in trouble?"

Charlie's desire to wrap his arms around her made it difficult for him to keep his composure. Lane had a beautiful heart for the suffering, even at the cost of her own comfort and life. And Charlie was falling in love with her. But did she feel the same way?

"Annika owned two vehicles. One was a black Lexus with damage on the front passenger side. Forensics was able to pull a sample of Sydney's blood from the bumper, along with a strand of her hair. As soon as Miguel's released from the hospital, he'll be free to return home."

Charlie shifted. "Actually, after Mr. Benedict's lawyers arrived at the scene, they mentioned they'd already been considering renaming the Benedict House. It will be called Home for Heroes, and when Miguel's ready and if he wants it, they've promised him a room. Said Noble Benedict would've insisted on it for the suffering Annika caused."

"Thank you." Tears rimmed her eyes, making them appear even greener than they already were. She sniffed. "I still don't understand why she had to kill Sydney."

Sheriff Huggins sighed. "We won't know the answer for sure until Miguel comes out of surgery, but if what you say is true, we think Sydney learned about Annika's drug business and stole a painting to prove it. We think she tried to tell Miguel because she trusted him. Mrs. Donovan remembered that Sydney volunteered at the community center and helped with the veterans' art program. It's probably where they met."

"And Annika exploited that relationship," Charlie added.

"Annika called him a baby killer. Said he killed innocent women and children in Vietnam."

"Vietnam was a different war. Miguel's Army unit was involved in a horrific act of violence against a small village. However, Miguel and two other servicemen tried to halt the violence and protect the hiding villagers." Sheriff Huggins let out a long sigh. "Soldiers come home as heroes nowadays, but not back then. We returned home to humiliation. Were spit on. Called names. Came home as scapegoats for a war no one understood. For Miguel, it was much, much worse. When it was reported what took place in that village, he and the two other soldiers were called traitors. They were shunned and humiliated by the country they swore to protect. After a long investigation into the massacre and a trial, it was determined Miguel acted heroically. Ten or so years ago, they issued him a medal, but it was too late. The damage to his reputation and his mind had already been done."

"That's why he kept saying he was protecting her." Tears streaked down Lane's face and fell into her lap. "Protecting them."

Raw emotion choked Charlie. He doubted anyone in Walton knew about the hero who kept himself hidden in the woods. How many others were like Miguel—like Lane—hiding in the shadows of lies, believing they didn't deserve to live?

"One of the symptoms of PTSD is flashbacks or memory confusion. It's likely Miguel was confusing Sydney's death with the deaths of the villagers," Sheriff Huggins explained.

There was a knock at the door. Deputy Wilson stepped inside Sheriff Huggins's office. "Sir, Miguel Roa is out of surgery."

"I'd like to see him." Lane wiped her face. "I want to be there when he wakes up. Make sure he knows he saved my life."

"Are you sure you're up to it?" Sheriff Huggins's fatherly concern returned. "You've been through a lot."

"Not as much as Miguel has." Her gaze moved from the sheriff to Charlie. "I just want him to have a friend there."

"I'll go with you." Charlie held his breath. "If that's okay?"

"I'd like that."

Lane's smile reached her eyes and he breathed deeply.

"I can't tell you how happy Byrdie and I are that you're okay." The sheriff came around his desk. He pulled Lane into his arms and hugged her. "I want you to know you saved Miguel's life too. In more ways than one. Your kindness . . . your ability to see beyond what's on the outside. I wish there were more of you in this town."

Lane cleared her throat. "Thanks. Can I have a few minutes with Charlie?"

"Sure." Sheriff Huggins kissed her forehead and stepped out of his office, closing the door behind him.

Lane's cheeks turned pink. "I owe you an apology—"

"No you don't."

"I do. I owe an apology to a lot of people. I took my life for granted. I saw myself as someone living life without purpose. I felt like a burden to those around me and believed it was better if I wasn't around." She slipped her hand into his. "I'm not saying my life won't be messy, but I've decided to live my life on purpose. And I'm hoping you will give me a chance to prove I'm worth the trouble."

He rubbed his fingers over her hand and up her arm until he tilted her chin. She closed her eyes and he leaned in—

His cell phone rang. He groaned and opened his eyes to find Lane smiling. A quick look revealed the caller's identity. His father. What was he calling for?

"I'll wait in the hall."

"Five minutes." He lifted her hand to his lips and kissed it. "Then we go." He watched her leave and then answered the call.

"Charlie, it's Dad. Your mother told me they found the Walton killer."

"Yes, sir." He denied himself the satisfaction of revealing his role in closing the case.

A few beats of silence passed between them. Did his father hang up?

"Did I ever tell you what made me join the Marines?"

Charlie glanced at Lane waiting. He knew she was anxious to get to the hospital, but a trip down memory lane with his father was rare. "No, sir."

"Your grandfather, my father, was an alcoholic. Moved from job to job, leaving your grandmother and me to fend for ourselves most days." Charlie's father let out a ragged sigh—an emotional sound that brought wetness to Charlie's eyes, forcing him to turn away from Lane as he continued to listen to his father's story. "I was so terrified I'd follow in his footsteps that I chose the only path I knew wouldn't allow me to mess up. The Marines told me what to do, when to do it, and how to do it. Signing up back then

322

was a lifetime commitment, but it was the only way I knew how to not be like him."

"Dad—"

"I'm sorry I missed out on so much, Charlie, but I want you to know I'm proud of you. I'm proud of you for choosing your own way."

Charlie took a few calming breaths before responding. "Thank you for telling me that."

His father cleared his throat. "Now, your aunt tells me there's a girl."

Lane stood outside Sheriff Huggins's office, her green eyes beckoning him.

"Lane's more than a girl. She's an amazing woman who inspires me to believe I have a purpose here."

"You believe you made the right decision?"

Charlie went to Lane and wrapped his arm around her shoulder. She rested her head on his shoulder. "I believe it's the best decision I've ever made."

THIRTY

"MOMMA!" NOAH RACED DOWN the tiled hallway of the hospital and jumped into her arms.

Lane couldn't stop the flow of tears. Happy tears of relief. She kissed Noah's neck and his ears and his cheeks until he squealed. She breathed him in.

"Momma, what happened?" Noah's eyes turned serious. "You got hurt?"

"Your mommy is a hero." Charlie ran his hand down the small of her back, sending a charge of anticipation through her chest. "She helped us catch two bad guys."

"A hero like my daddy?"

"Yep, just like your daddy." Charlie leaned in. "I hope you don't mind me having your sister bring him here. I missed him."

Lane squeezed Charlie's hand, unable to voice the love growing for him.

"Lane!" Meagan's voice echoed down the hall. Her eyes grew round. "Oh my goodness, are you alright?"

"Do I look like a mess?" She touched the bandage on her head. There was a tender spot on her cheek where Annika had hit her with the gun and her lip was swollen. The paramedics said nothing was broken, but there'd be bruising for a couple of weeks.

"You look beautiful." Charlie winked at her.

"You do," Meagan agreed.

"You're both terrible liars." She smiled. "But I don't mind."

"Can I . . . can I hug you?"

"Yes." She'd barely put Noah down when Meagan grabbed her into a tight hug. Her ribs cried out, but she ignored it and embraced her sister . . . who was sobbing. "Meagan, what's wrong?"

"I'm sorry." Meagan released her before pulling a tissue from her purse and wiping her eyes. "I've never been so scared in my life."

Lane bit her lip. "I'm sorry—"

"No, I'm sorry, Lane. I should've been there for you . . . when we were younger. *Now*. I was just caught up . . . in my own life. I was selfish."

Charlie walked Noah to the nurse's station to give them privacy.

"You weren't selfish. You were a teenager. How could you know?"

"No. I knew. I mean . . . not when we were little, but a few years ago. After I had Paige." Meagan sniffled and looked down at the wadded piece of tissue in her hand. "I struggled. She was my first baby and I was supposed to be excited, but I wasn't. I was angry. And sad. I thought I had done something wrong. Ate the wrong things. Didn't exercise."

Lane lowered her gaze to the white tiled floor. If she had spoken up about her own depression, maybe Meagan wouldn't have suffered alone. Like Miguel. How many others kept their illness quiet out of fear or embarrassment?

"When I became pregnant with Owen, I tried to do things differently, but when he was born the same things happened. I shut down. Didn't want to leave the house. I hid in my bedroom. That's when Ian hired the nanny. He made me go to the doctor. They said I had postpartum depression. I never told anyone. Made Ian promise not to tell. I was ashamed." A tear slipped down Meagan's cheek. "I'm sorry, Lane."

"It's okay." Lane hugged Meagan. "I'm okay."

A female nurse passed them, pushing a patient in a wheelchair. She gave Lane a small nod. After a few more seconds, Lane disentangled herself from Meagan's grip.

"I feel like people are staring at me."

"People are talking about you." Meagan dabbed at her eyes and waved her hand. "About Mathias. Your suicide attempt."

Lane cringed. The reporter. She was worried people were staring at her because of her injuries, but maybe it was because of what they knew about her. About how Mathias died. At that moment, Lane's mother and father rounded the corner into the hall. They paused at the nurse's station when they saw Charlie and Noah.

"I'm sorry." Lane swallowed. "I didn't mean to embarrass you or the family."

"Lane, you're not embarrassing me." Meagan took hold of her shoulders. "Honey, I'm proud of you. You were brave enough to speak out about your condition. Do you know what you've done? You've forced people to have a conversation."

"I don't understand." She squished her eyebrows together. "Who's having a conversation?"

"Everyone. Ms. Byrdie invited that reporter from the courthouse over and talked with her. Told her she suffered from depression after she and the sheriff found out they couldn't have kids."

"She did?"

"Ms. Byrdie said the biggest regret she had was not being brave"—Meagan squeezed her shoulders—"like you."

"I wasn't trying to be brave. I was trying to help Miguel."

"It sounds like you did. And that's not all. Daddy called that reporter and threatened to sue her and the paper she works for if they reported any false information regarding your medical history or Mathias's accident. He told her if she wanted a story, it should be on the stigma society has placed on those with behavioral and mental health issues. That, as a country, we should be ashamed that so many people are forced to suffer in silence because they are afraid of being ostracized if they ask for help."

Movement at the nurse's station caught Lane's attention. Her gaze found her father's. Even from a distance, Lane could see the emotion warring over his features. "He did that?"

Meagan nodded.

It took Lane several heartbeats before she could meet her father's eyes again. Her mother looped her arm through his and they stood back as though waiting for permission to approach her. Lane's lips trembled into a small smile. At this her parents charged forward and embraced her in a hug that seemed to say everything all at once.

Charlie returned with Noah holding a rubber glove blown up to look like a turkey. "Visiting hours will be over soon. If you want to see Miguel, we should go now."

Lane hugged her parents one more time before they left. Tears had ruined her mother's makeup and her father tried for nonchalance as he wiped a hand to his cheek. They had a lot of healing to do, but this was a start—an emotional one that needed to happen.

Meagan wiped the remnants of her tears from her face. "You're sure you're okay?"

"I promise I look worse than I feel."

Meagan looked up at Charlie like she was trying to confirm Lane's answer.

He tucked a loose strand of her hair behind her ear before running the back of his knuckles over her cheek. His eyes trailed to her lips. "She's been checked out."

Lane's heart soared within her chest. Would she ever get used to his touch or the way a simple look could melt her insides into mush? She hoped not.

"Okay. Please tell Miguel thank you. Your newest nephew or niece needs their auntie."

"What?" Lane's attention was pulled back to her sister. She saw a twinkle in Meagan's eyes. "Are you? You're pregnant?"

"Mm-hmm." Meagan placed a hand on her belly. "I don't need a special diet or extra exercise. I need you, sis. To help me through it."

Lane hugged her sister as tears stung her eyes. "I promise I'll be here for you. Whatever you need. Even if it's locking ourselves in a room full of chocolate."

"Sounds perfect." Meagan giggled. She kissed Lane's cheek. "Now, go see your friend."

Meagan walked down the hall and stepped into the hospital elevator, taking Noah with her. They waved as the doors closed.

"I'm going to be an auntie again." She smiled up at Charlie. "Congratulations."

"Thank you for coming here with me." She slipped her hand into his. "And in case I didn't tell you before. Thank you for saving my life."

Charlie lifted her hand to his lips. He kissed each finger until his lips rested on the gold wedding band Mathias had given her.

"You're a woman worth saving, Lane Kent."

Acknowledgments

I CAN'T EVEN BELIEVE I get to do this! As a reader, one of my favorite things to do is read the acknowledgments page. I love seeing authors reflect on their journey and thank the ones who helped them get there. As a writer, I now realize that behind every book is a village of professionals, mentors, friends, family, and supporters who, whether they know it or not, have made a writer's dream come true. How unbelievably cool is it that I get the chance to acknowledge them now?

Lane and Charlie's story would not be in your hands right now without the hardworking and diligent team at Revell. My editor, Andrea Doering, saw this story in its infancy and believed, even back then, it was worth telling. Amy Ballor, Hannah Brinks, and Gayle Raymer, y'all are amazing!

Tamela Hancock Murray, agent extraordinaire—I'll never forget telling you I had an appointment to pitch this story to Steve and you told me no. I'm so grateful I've been listening to you ever since. You champion not only the words of my heart but also my spirit when doubt begins to cloud my vision. Thank you for everything!

Tom R. and familia—talking drugs, cartel, and international trafficking wouldn't have happened without you. Let's do it again!

Aaron F. and Tim F. Thank you for your assistance on police procedure. Any errors are my fault alone.

To my BWF, Emilie Hendryx—girl. Where would I be on this journey without you? Your friendship extends beyond the giddy brainstorming sessions, the extremely long voxes, the equally long video chats, and the invaluable story edits that have made this moment possible. Your words of encouragement and prayers have carried me through some of my darkest moments and there aren't enough words to express how grateful I am for you. Love you, friend. You're next!

One of the best things about this writing journey has been the amazing friendships that have come through it. Jaime Jo Wright— you keep sending me Poe-ish snippets of your work so I have to sleep with the light on and I'll keep sending you cute GIFs of you-know-who! Christen Krumm, I couldn't imagine living the #bookballer life without you! I wouldn't be the writer I am today without the guidance I've received from DiAnn Mills and Ronie Kendig—thank you! There are so many more who've gathered me into the folds and encouraged, prayed, and cheered me on. I wish I could name you all, but apparently these pages have to be shorter than the actual novel . . . who knew? Please know that even if your names are not here, they are never far from my grateful heart.

To my Newsies, street team, and readers—*thank you*. What's the point in writing if no one reads your story? I appreciate every one of you and the sweet notes of love and encouragement you send me. Some days those very things keep me going. I hope you enjoyed my debut novel and I can't wait for you to see what's coming next!

I wouldn't be able to thank any of the above mentioned individuals if it weren't for the greatest blessings of my life. To my G.I. JOE—you won my heart with a single look and have been winning my heart every day since. Thank you for being the hero of our family and of my life. I love you oodles to the oodle power. To my three precious treasures—out of all the stories in the world, being part of yours is my favorite. More than anything else, I hope my stories make you proud.

Finally, Lane's story came to life through the heartache and devastation our family experienced with depression. Topics such as depression, anxiety, suicide, and mental health facilities had never even crossed our minds when suddenly they became reality. I didn't realize how traumatizing the stigma surrounding mental health was until we were drowning in it. My hope is that *Living Lies* will open up a conversation surrounding the disease and offer the kind of hope we need to be speaking daily to those fighting to live.

You are loved.

You are wonderfully made.

You have purpose.

Dear Lord—thank you for the gift of writing this story. I pray that through these words your gifts of love, hope, and mercy reach those who desperately need them.

Natalie Walters is a proud Army wife and mother of three adult children. She grew up tucked between the pages of a good book and spent many hot summer days in New Mexico at the Erna Fergusson library. Reading had been her greatest adventure until she met her husband. They've moved more than fifteen times, lived in seven states, and served overseas in Egypt. Natalie began her writing journey in 2010 when she started the Christian Writer's Guild Craftsman program. Her nonfiction pieces have appeared in *Proverbs 31* magazine and *Guideposts* online. In addition to balancing life as a military spouse, mom, and writer, she loves traveling, cooking, watching movies, and playing games so long as her family surrounds her. Natalie and G.I. JOE are currently stationed in Hawaii with their kids.

www.NatalieWaltersWriter.com

f Natalie Walters, Writer

🐦 @NatWaltersWrite

📷 @nataliewalters_writer

Author Photo Credit: © Emilie Hendryx